WINGS OF FIRE

BOOK ONE
THE DRAGONET PROPHECY

BOOK TWO
THE LOST HEIR

BOOK THREE
THE HIDDEN KINGDOM

BOOK FOUR
THE DARK SECRET

BOOK FIVE
THE BRIGHTEST NIGHT

BOOK SIX
MOON RISING

BOOK SEVEN
WINTER TURNING

BOOK EIGHT
ESCAPING PERIL

BOOK NINE
TALONS OF POWER

BOOK TEN
DARKNESS OF DRAGONS

LEGENDS
DARKSTALKER

WINGS OF FIRE

LEGENDS: DARKSTALKER

by
TUI T. SUTHERLAND

SCHOLASTIC INC.

Text copyright © 2016 by Tui T. Sutherland
Map and border design © 2016 by Mike Schley
Dragon illustrations © 2016 by Joy Ang

This book was originally published in hardcover by Scholastic Press in 2016.

ISBN 978-1-338-05362-3

12 11 10   20 21

Printed in the U.S.A.   40
First printing 2017
Book design by Phil Falco

For Amanda, who is always wonderful, patient, funny, and brilliant — thank you, thank you, thank you for EVERYTHING.

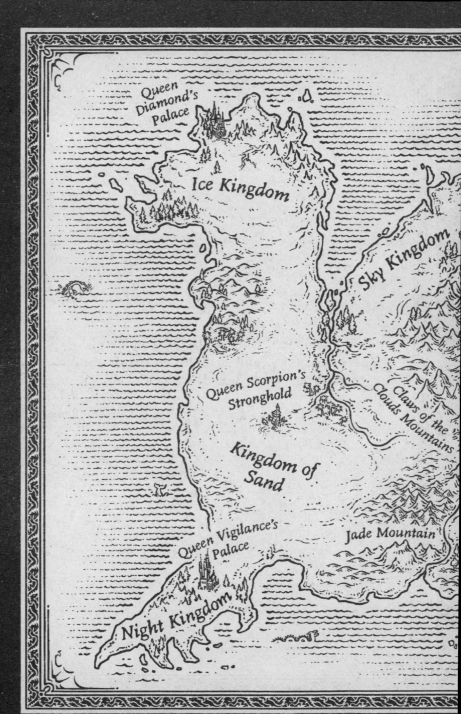

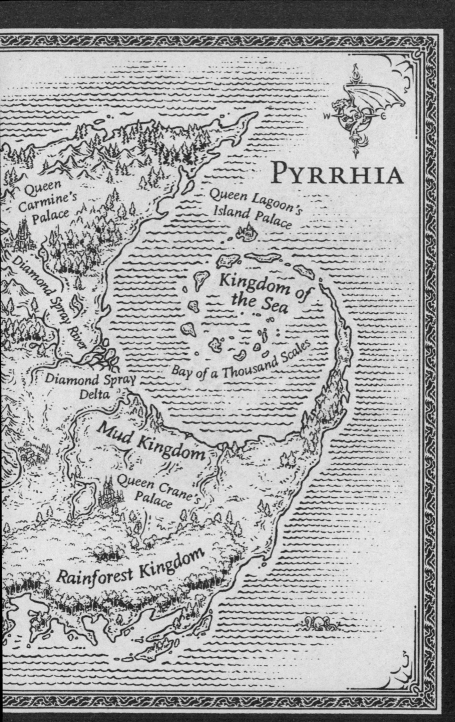

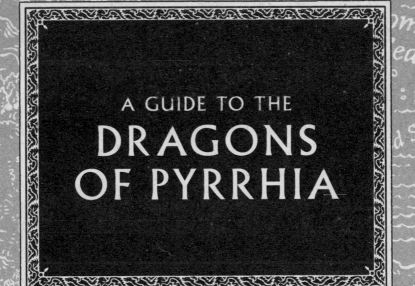

A GUIDE TO THE
DRAGONS
OF PYRRHIA

Queen
Carmine's
Palace

Queen Lagoon's
Island Palace

Queen Crane's
Palace

Rainforest Kingdom

NIGHTWINGS

Description: Purplish-black scales and scattered silver scales on the underside of their wings, like a night sky full of stars; forked black tongues

Abilities: Can breathe fire and disappear into dark shadows; some hatch with the power to read minds or see the future (or, very rarely, both)

Queen: Queen Vigilance

Known Animus Dragons: None

SANDWINGS

Description: Pale gold or white scales the color of desert sand; poisonous barbed tail, forked black tongues

Abilities: Can survive a long time without water, poison enemies with the tips of their tails like scorpions, bury themselves for camouflage in the desert sand, breathe fire

Queen: Queen Scorpion

Known Animus Dragons: Jerboa (whereabouts unknown)

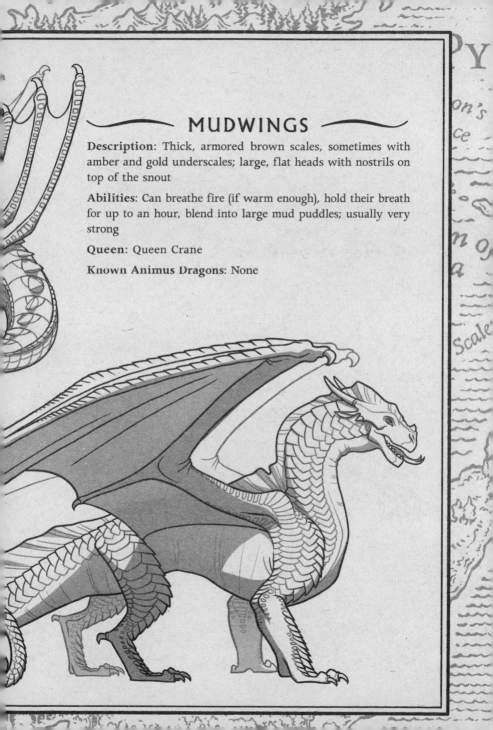

MUDWINGS

Description: Thick, armored brown scales, sometimes with amber and gold underscales; large, flat heads with nostrils on top of the snout

Abilities: Can breathe fire (if warm enough), hold their breath for up to an hour, blend into large mud puddles; usually very strong

Queen: Queen Crane

Known Animus Dragons: None

SKYWINGS

Description: Red-gold or orange scales, enormous wings

Abilities: Powerful fighters and fliers; can breathe fire

Queen: Queen Carmine

Known Animus Dragons: None

SEAWINGS

Description: Blue or green or aquamarine scales; webs between their claws; gills on their necks; glow-in-the-dark stripes on their tails/snouts/underbellies

Abilities: Can breathe underwater, see in the dark, create huge waves with one splash of their powerful tails; excellent swimmers

Queen: Queen Lagoon

Known Animus Dragons: Albatross, brother to the queen

ICEWINGS

Description: Silvery scales like the moon or pale blue like ice; ridged claws to grip the ice, forked blue tongues; tails narrow to a whip-thin end

Abilities: Can withstand subzero temperatures and bright light; exhale a deadly freezing frostbreath

Queen: Queen Diamond

Known Animus Dragons: Queen Diamond and her son, Prince Arctic

RAINWINGS

Description: Scales constantly shift colors, usually bright like birds of paradise; prehensile tails

Abilities: Can camouflage their scales to blend into their surroundings; shoot a deadly venom from their fangs

Queen: Queen Anaconda

Known Animus Dragons: None

The events of this book take place in Pyrrhia's shrouded past, more than two thousand years before the War of SandWing Succession and the events of *The Dragonet Prophecy*.

— PROLOGUE —

ARCTIC

"Prince Arctic?"

A silvery white dragon poked her head around the door, tapping three times lightly on the ice wall. Arctic couldn't remember her name, which was the kind of faux pas his mother was always yelling at him about. He was a *prince*; it was his *duty* to have all the noble dragons *memorized* along with their *ranks* so he could treat them according to exactly where they fit in the hierarchy.

It was *stupid* and *frustrating* and if his mother yelled at him about it *one more time*, he would seriously enchant something to freeze her mouth shut forever.

Oooo. What a beautiful image. Queen Diamond with a chain of silver circles wound around her snout and frozen to her scales. He closed his eyes and imagined the blissful quiet.

The dragon at his door shifted slightly, her claws making little scraping sounds to remind him she was there. What was she waiting for? Permission to give him a message? Or was she waiting for him to say her name — and if he didn't, would she go scurrying back to the queen to report that he had failed again?

Perhaps he should enchant a talisman to whisper in his ear whenever he needed to know something. Another tempting idea, but strictly against the rules of IceWing animus magic.

Animus dragons are so rare; appreciate your gift and respect the limits the tribe has set. Never use your power frivolously. Never use it for yourself. This power is extremely dangerous. The tribe's rules are there to protect you. Only the IceWings have figured out how to use animus magic safely.

Save it all for your gifting ceremony. Use it only once in your life, to create a glorious gift to benefit the whole tribe, and then never again; that is the only way to be safe.

Arctic shifted his shoulders, feeling stuck inside his scales. Rules, rules, and more rules: that was the IceWing way of life. Every direction he turned, every thought he had, was restricted by rules and limits and judgmental faces, particularly his mother's. The rules about animus magic were just one more way to keep him trapped under her claws.

"What is it?" he barked at the strange dragon. Annoyed face, try that. As if he were very busy and she'd interrupted him and that was why he was skipping the usual politic rituals. He *was* very busy, actually. The gifting ceremony was only three weeks away. It was bad enough that his mother had dragged him here, to their southernmost palace, near the ocean and the border with the Kingdom of Sand. She'd promised to leave him alone to work while she conducted whatever vital royal business required her presence. Everyone should know better than to disturb him right now.

The messenger looked disappointed. Maybe he really was supposed to know who she was. "Your mother sent me to tell you that the NightWing delegation has arrived."

Aaarrrrgh. Not another boring diplomatic meeting.

"I can't possibly be expected to attend them," he said, waving his claws at the translucent walls of his room. "I only have three more weeks to prepare."

"Well," said the other IceWing, "she did mention that . . ."

"But she doesn't care," he finished when she trailed off.

The poor dragon looked profoundly uncomfortable, caught between a prince who outranked her and a queen who outranked everyone. Arctic sighed.

"Very well," he said, sweeping shards of ice aside with his tail. "I'm coming."

She stepped back with relief, and he realized that

the silver chain around her neck had only one circle on it. Uh-oh. That meant she was ranked in the First Circle — how could he have forgotten a First Circle IceWing? First and Second Circle dragons usually lived in the queen's ice palace alongside the royal family, and he was sure he'd memorized them all.

Except for the nobles who lived in the outer three palaces . . .

"Snowflake," he blurted. He really was an idiot. This was the one his mother had chosen for him to marry. Respectable family, loyal, likely to have a daughter who could replace Queen Diamond one day, since he had no sisters or aunts who might try for the throne. Snowflake was probably the real reason he'd been dragged on this trip.

"Yes," she said, dipping her head. She was pretty in that boring, glassy way his mother liked, but he had gotten absolutely no sense of her personality at their one prior meeting. He was a little afraid she might not have one.

"Uh," he said, following her down the frozen hall. *There must be something we can talk about.* "Have you ever seen a NightWing before?"

"Only the one who came to the wall a few months ago to request this meeting."

"Do you know what they're here for?"

She shook her head. So. That was apparently the end of that conversation.

Ooo, how about an animus-touched object that can make any dragon interesting. Skies above, now that would be useful.

Don't waste your gift! his mother's voice echoed in his head. *Blah blah blah! Careful consideration! Months of planning!*

Sometimes he got a strong feeling that she regretted her own animus gift to the tribe: the gift of healing, which was a set of narwhal horns that could heal frostbreath injuries. It helped when young IceWings played too roughly or when fights broke out within the tribe . . . but it certainly would be a much more useful gift if the horns could heal *any* injuries. He bet Queen Diamond wished she could reach back through time and fix *that* mistake.

"What would you give the tribe?" he asked Snowflake. "If you were an animus, I mean, and had to come up with a gift?"

"Oh," she said, fidgeting her wings in little flippy waves. "I don't know."

"Well, think about it," he said. "I'd really like to know."

"All right," she said. They kept walking through the halls of the palace, which were smaller and more cramped than the ones at home, with odd little mismatched ice carvings everywhere — here a polar bear, there a wolf, there a screaming scavenger, here a lumpy owl. There was no consistency, no sense of an artistic vision, and everything was too close to him. It made Arctic want to smash through the walls just so he could see the sky.

About a minute later, Snowflake said, "Sorry, I can't think of anything."

Arctic couldn't hide the irritation that flashed across his face. "*Really* think about it," he said. "Tell me tomorrow, or whenever you come up with something."

She gave him a look that, to his surprise, was nearly as irritated as his own. "Seems like kind of a waste of my time," she said. "Unless you're having trouble coming up with an idea for yours."

"No, no," he said quickly. "Of course I already have a plan." *Well, Mother has a plan. Which is why I am trying to come up with a better one.*

She didn't ask what it was. Instead she stopped at one of the flight ledges and nodded down at the dome below them. In the gathering dusk, it glowed from within like firelit marble, covering most of the plain between the palace and the ocean. Snow dusted the outside and the ground all around it; more crystalline flakes were falling softly from the sky.

The ocean itself was gouged with streaks of orange and gold as the sun set on the distant western horizon. Dragon wings sliced the air like darting bats as hunters dove to catch dinner in the sea for the welcome banquet tonight.

Arctic and Snowflake flew down to the entrance of the guest dome. Inside, he knew, it would be warmer than he liked, heated by the bodies of the fire-breathing NightWings and also by the gift of diplomacy. (*Created by an animus named Penguin about fifty years ago,* chatted his overstuffed brain. He had studied every animus gift in careful detail, trying to come up with something new and original for his own. Which was perhaps why he didn't have room in his brain for the faces of dragons he barely knew.)

The dome itself was not an animus gift, though; these blocks of ice had been carved by ordinary IceWing talons. It must have taken ages, and he wasn't entirely convinced that it wouldn't all melt on top of some fire-breathing guests one day.

Maybe I could improve the dome as my gift, he thought. *An indestructible welcome dome for any allies or guests from other tribes.* He dismissed the thought almost as soon as he had it. It was derivative and not nearly as impressive as he wanted it to be. He wanted his gift to be one that IceWings would marvel about for centuries after he was gone — something like Frostbite's gift of light.

They landed with a crunch on the snow, but just as they were about to enter the tunnel into the dome, a dragon came charging out.

"Sorry!" she cried breathlessly as she narrowly avoided knocking them over. "I just needed to be outside for a moment. *Look* at that sunset! Great king-doms, it is freezing out here! I might literally die! But obviously I can't go back inside and miss this sunset. I can handle a little cold, right? If I just . . . keep . . . moving . . ." She began stamping furiously in a circle around them, whacking herself with her wings.

She was a NightWing — the first NightWing Arctic had ever seen. He'd known she would be black, but he hadn't expected the underscales of dark green on her chest or the silver scales that glittered here and there across the underside of her wings. Her eyes, too, seemed a little closer to dark green than to black, and they caught his without any fear. Her wings snapped with energy and he felt his own wings responding, lifting as though he might suddenly take off and touch the moons.

"I'll meet you inside," he said to Snowflake.

She paused, giving the NightWing a disapprov-ing look.

"You can tell my mother I'm coming," he suggested. "Better hurry. She doesn't like to wait."

Snowflake's forehead wrinkled into that irritated expression again, and she turned to whisk down the tunnel without even a bow or ritual farewell.

I suppose that's what I deserve, he thought, *since I didn't give her the greeting her rank requires.* He stared after her for a moment, trying to imagine what it would be like to be married to Snowflake. *Maybe she does have a personality: repressed fury. Or maybe she's as unexcited about this match as I am. I'm not sure how to improve that situation. I mean, I am a prince; if she marries me, she could hatch the next queen. What more could she want?*

"Who stuck an icicle up *her* snout?" asked the NightWing. She started jumping up and down in place, grinning at him.

"I'm afraid that was me, probably," he said. "It took me far too long to remember her name."

"So?" said the black dragon. "I forget names all the time."

"Well, I'm not supposed to forget anyone's," he said. "Also, we're kind of engaged to be married."

The NightWing started laughing so hard she had to sit down, which immediately made her leap up again with a yelp, shaking snow off her tail.

"Are you all right?" he asked.

"Just c-c-cold," she said, stamping her feet again. "All right, I'm on her side. That's pretty terrible. You're the worst."

"I'm not the worst!" he protested. "We've only met once! I barely know her! Also, she is extremely unmemorable!"

"Seriously the worst!" she cried, laughing again. "That poor dragon! I am completely telling her not to marry you. I pity whoever gets tricked into that. You'll be like, 'Happy fortieth anniversary . . . what's your name again?' and she'll be all, 'It's our FIFTIETH, you slime weasel, and my name is you're sleeping on an iceberg tonight.'"

"I promise I would remember that name," he said. "Sticks in the brain a bit better than Snowflake."

"And what's your name?" she asked. "Or I can keep calling you slime weasel, although I suspect that might get me kicked off the peacekeeping committee."

"My name is Arctic. Prince Arctic."

"Oh, *fancy*," she said. "I guess I shouldn't bother telling you mine, since you'll forget it in the next five minutes anyway."

"I promise I won't," he protested.

"Oh, you only forget your girlfriends' names?" she joked. "Or future family members?"

"I remember any dragon who seems likely to change my life," he said.

"That's not me!" she cried, looking genuinely startled. "I'm under strict orders not to do any damage or break any ice palaces or corrupt any IceWings or change any lives. Then again, I'm pretty sure I've never followed an order in my life, so . . . you know, watch your back, ice palaces."

Never followed an order in her life! Arctic blinked at her, enchanted and mystified. How was that possible? Life was nothing but a series of orders; if you didn't follow them, wouldn't you get lost or drop to the bottom of the rankings or be thrown out of your tribe? *Imagine disobeying an order — any order. Where would I even start?*

"AAAAAAAH, why is it SO COLD?" The NightWing leaped into the air and started doing vigorous somersaults.

"Because this is the Ice Kingdom," he said, standing back out of her way. "It's true, though, our climate is one of our best-guarded secrets."

"Oh, he's a wise guy, too," she said, righting herself and landing again. "Do you have any *useful* skills, or maybe an extra one of those magic bracelets that keeps your guests from freezing?"

"That's the gift of diplomacy," he said. "It keeps our guests warm and helps them travel safely over the Great Ice Cliff. The tribe only has three bracelets — are there more than three of you?" he asked, surprised.

"I'm the fourth," she said. "My mother and I are sharing her bracelet; there was some back and forth silliness to get over your cliff. I *probably* should have asked for it before I came outside."

"We could go inside," he said reluctantly. Inside there would be other dragons, infinitely more boring dragons, not to mention his mother, and probably a new set of rules about appeasing Snowflake, staying away from NightWings, and generally acting more like an obedient puddle. "Or we could stay to watch the rest of the sunset . . ."

"The sunset is great," she said, "but honestly I had to come out here because my mother is driving me *crazy*."

He couldn't control the smile that split his face like ice cracking. It seemed possible that he would never be able to stop smiling at her. He'd never heard an IceWing say anything like that about his or her parents; it was beyond forbidden to complain or talk back or criticize your elders in any fashion.

"Please tell me *all* about it," he said.

"Oh, she's always lecturing me about how I ruin everything. Foeslayer, why are the scrolls shelved in the wrong places again? Foeslayer, you smiled at the wrong dragons this morning! Foeslayer, the queen will never want you on her council if you insist on having opinions all the time. Foeslayer, I'm bringing you on this mission because I don't trust you if I leave you behind, but if you say *one word to any IceWing*, I will mount your head on a spike in the throne room." She snapped her mouth shut as if she'd just understood that last instruction, then gave Arctic a rueful look. "Um . . . oops."

"Aha," he said, with a thrill like the first time he'd touched fire. "I have cleverly deduced that your name is Foeslayer."

"Oh no," she said. "That's just how my mother starts all her sentences."

He laughed and she smiled and he thought that perhaps nothing would ever be boring or frustrating again as long as he was near her.

"So really," she said, "no secret extra magic bracelets? Or a blanket or anything?"

"Sorry," Arctic said, wishing he could offer his own wings for warmth — but his scales were as cold as the snow underfoot and would only make things worse.

She sighed. "Then I guess I do have to go back inside."

"Wait," he said. He didn't stop to think about it. It was wrong, worse than wrong: a broken rule, a betrayal of his entire tribe, but next to this shining dragon he didn't care. He'd do anything for another few minutes with her.

He unclipped the diamond earring from his ear, held it between his talons, and said softly, "I enchant this earring to keep the dragon wearing it warm no matter the temperature . . . and to keep her safe no matter the danger."

Her dark green eyes were wide with disbelief as he leaned over and gently curled the earring around her ear. His talons lingered there for a moment, brushing against the smooth warmth of her long, dark neck. The shivering in her scales slowed to a stop, and she cautiously held out her wings to the cold air.

"Whoa. That — that *worked*," she said. "So the rumors are true — your tribe *does* have magic."

"Only a few of us," he said. "And so does yours, doesn't it?"

"Only a few of us," she echoed, "and not like that. I don't have anything, for instance. You just — can you enchant anything? To do anything?"

"Animus power," he said, taking a step closer to her. "That's how it works."

"Then why don't the IceWings rule the entire continent?" she asked, her tail skipping nervously over the snowy ground. "You don't even need this alliance. You could destroy the SkyWings easily, couldn't you?"

He shook his head. "The tribe has strict rules. We're only allowed to use our power once in a lifetime."

Foeslayer's talon flew to the earring and she stared at him, shocked into stillness for the first time.

"Well," he said with a shrug, "perhaps I'm not much of a rule follower either." He felt another thrill at the idea of being that dragon, of being seen that way by *this* dragon. He reached out tentatively and brushed her wing with his. She didn't pull away.

"Why?" Foeslayer whispered.

"It's these old legends we have," Arctic said, "warning us of the dangers of animus magic — use it too much, you lose your soul, some mystical mumbo jumbo like that, which probably isn't even true. But once there's a law set down in the Ice Kingdom, every-one better follow it with no questions asked." He decided not to mention the ancient stories of animus dragons gone mad.

"No," Foeslayer said, touching the earring again. "Why did you do this — for me?" She wrinkled her snout, half teasing, half serious. "Aren't you worried about your soul?"

"Not anymore," he said. "It's yours now . . . if you want it."

Glittering petals of snow fell softly on her black wings, melting into her heat. Foeslayer hesitated, then reached out and took one of Arctic's talons in hers.

This is a bad idea, whispered Arctic's conscience. *The very worst. Neither of our tribes would forgive us. Mother will never allow it.*

All the more reason. I won't let the queen crush my entire life between her claws.

It's my life, my magic, and my heart.

"I'm going to say something really sappy," Foeslayer warned him.

"More sappy than what I just said?" he asked. "I'd like to see you try."

"I just — I have this strange feeling," Foeslayer said, looking into his eyes, "that the world is about to change forever."

Ice Kingdom

Sky Kingdom

Queen Scorpion's
Stronghold

Claws of the
Clouds Mountains

Kingdom of
Sand

Queen Vigilance's
Palace

Jade Mountain

PART ONE

CHAPTER 1

FATHOM

Fathom had never thought of himself as anyone special, and he certainly wasn't expecting that to change the day of the animus test.

Eight SeaWing dragonets were lined up on the beach that morning, their blue and green scales wet from the hissing waves of the ocean behind them. All of them had turned two years old within the last few months. The sun was beating on Fathom's snout and his eyes felt prickly and sore from the brightness. He couldn't wait to get back to the underwater palace, where it was cool and dark.

But he sat quietly, patiently, waiting without moving (even though they'd been sitting there for ages), like they had been told to do. Unlike *some* dragonets.

Swish. Sand pattered across his back talons, just enough for him to be sure it wasn't the wind that had done it.

"Shhh," he said out of the corner of his mouth.

"Who, me?" said the dragonet next to him. "What did I say? Nothing, that's what. *You're* the one being noisy. I'm just sitting here. Perfectly still. A model dragonet, me." She lifted her chin and put on an angelic expression.

A large, sleek seagull landed up the beach from the dragons, near the tree line, and eyed them suspiciously. It had the face of a bird who knew things — a shrewd bird who had managed to survive this long in a dragon world. It was clearly trying to figure out why a bunch of dragons had popped out of the water and then decided to sit quietly in a row on the sand. Were they about to drop bits of food for a crafty seagull? Or were they all conspiring to eat him?

The bird pivoted its head to study them with its other eye.

"I dare you to grab it and eat it," Indigo whispered.

"Quit talking to me," Fathom growled.

"You know you want to." Her voice was as light as feathers, barely stirring the air.

He *did* want to. He was *very hungry*. But the queen had told them not to move, and he was not going to be the dragonet who failed. Being the queen's great-nephew would not save him from whatever trouble that would cause.

Swish. This time a hermit crab got caught in the sweep of Indigo's tail and bonked against his side as the sand sprayed over his feet. Fathom felt the crab stagger dazedly across his claws, trying to figure out what had just happened to it.

"Stop. That," he growled, keeping his face as still as he could. On his other side, he heard his sister, Pearl, let out a small, exasperated sigh.

"I think *you're* the one who should stop *distracting*

everybody with all your *chitchat*, Highness," said Indigo with mock primness.

"Indigo." Queen Lagoon materialized suddenly behind them, rising out of the ocean like a sinister iceberg. She stalked slowly up the beach between Fathom and his troublemaking friend.

"Your Majesty," Indigo said, her dark blue-purple claws gripping the sand. She managed to keep her anxiety out of her voice, but Fathom knew that the queen terrified her. Given how openly Queen Lagoon disliked her, in fact, Indigo would be quite justified if she tried to bury herself in kelp whenever the queen appeared.

"I hope you are taking this test seriously," said the queen. She turned her gaze to scrutinize Fathom, and he felt as though eels were wriggling under his scales. He liked it much better when the queen ignored him, as she did most of the time. He was only a minor prince in the palace, nobody important.

"Of course, Your Majesty." Indigo widened her eyes as if she'd never done anything wrong in her entire life.

There was another splash behind them, and Fathom found himself holding his breath as a new dragon stalked up the beach to join the queen.

It was *him*.

The most respected dragon in the SeaWing tribe, second in power only to the queen: Fathom's grandfather, Albatross.

Albatross was from the same hatching as his sister, Queen Lagoon, but he was nearly a neck length taller than her, with long wings that swept majestically across the sand. His scales were bluish gray but so pale that in places they looked almost white, while his eyes were a blue so dark they were nearly black. In fact, his coloring was somewhat similar to the seagull, which had now retreated to the safer vantage point of a palm tree.

His expression, too, was as suspicious as the seagull's. He looked down his long, hooked snout at the dragonets.

"This is a waste of time, Lagoon," he said. "Nobody ever tested me, but we figured out quickly enough what I could do. If any of them have a shred of power, surely they would know by now. Or it will become obvious, sooner or later."

"I'd prefer sooner," the queen said silkily. "If we find another animus in the tribe, that would make us twice as powerful, which would be quite useful given how the MudWings and RainWings have been behaving lately. And the earlier we find her, the sooner you can start to train her, and the sooner I can start to use her.

"Besides," she added in a lower voice, so Fathom had to strain to hear her, "I think we would all prefer to discover our next animus in a less . . . dramatic fashion than you were discovered. Don't you?"

Albatross flinched, just slightly. He cast a skeptical eye across the young dragons. "My power is more than enough for whatever you need. I've given you everything you've asked for, haven't I? And I don't *want* an apprentice."

Lagoon coiled her tail and bared her fangs. Suddenly she

did not seem smaller than Albatross at all. Fathom dug his talons into the warm sand, trying not to shiver.

"You are done complaining about this," she hissed. "The animus tests will continue. You will administer them whenever I tell you to. You will train any dragonet we find with powers like yours. And you will never question my decisions again."

There was a long pause, and then Albatross bowed his head. "Yes, Your Majesty." He folded his wings and paced down the line of dragonets, avoiding everyone's gaze. "Some of you may have heard of animus magic. It is a rare kind of immense power, and a dragon is either born with it or he isn't. What we are doing today is a simple test to see if you have that power. Almost certainly you do not," he added.

Albatross flicked his tail at the trees. The seagull let out an alarmed screech as eight coconuts suddenly wrestled themselves loose and came flying down to the beach, rolling to a stop on the sand, one in front of each dragonet.

"Pick up your coconut," Albatross said.

Fathom hesitated. There was something a little terrifying about this order. Albatross sounded bored, and yet a coconut that flew through the air by itself might do anything when you touched it. Would it explode in their claws? Turn into a sea urchin and stab them? Was this the kind of test that might hurt?

Pearl was the first to lift her coconut into her talons, with Indigo a moment behind her. Neither of them started screaming, so Fathom reached out and picked his up as well.

It seemed like an ordinary coconut — hairy, a little heavy, warm from the sun.

"Now," said Albatross, "tell your coconut to fly over here and hit me."

The dragonets glanced at one another in confusion, shuffling their feet. Fathom felt the ocean lapping at his tail as the tide started to come in.

"Um," said Indigo — of course it was Indigo, the only dragonet who ever spoke up about anything. "Sorry. How do we do that?"

Queen Lagoon glared at her, but Albatross looked obscurely pleased. "You use your power, if you have any," he said. "An animus dragon can enchant any object to do what he wants it to do. I can do it now without even speaking, but saying it out loud is the way to start. Simply whisper to your coconut that you want it to fly over here and hit me." He smiled.

"Huh," said Indigo. "Wouldn't it be easier to just throw it at you?"

Albatross barked a laugh. "But then you might miss. An enchanted coconut will never miss, no matter how I dodge or try to block it. Go ahead and try."

Small voices began to murmur on either side of Fathom. He glanced over at Pearl, who was frowning hard at her coconut, and then at Indigo, who met his eyes, grinned, and gave a "well, *this* is the dumbest thing we've done all day" shrug.

Fathom curled his claws around the brown sphere and brought his snout close to it, feeling quite silly indeed.

"Coconut," he whispered. "Um. Would you please go hit my grandfather?"

The coconut didn't move. It wasn't a magical ball of danger. It was just a coconut.

Fathom exhaled. He didn't know *what* he felt. A part of him had hoped . . . well, it was ridiculous to hope. Albatross was the only animus in the tribe — the only animus any SeaWing had ever known. There were rumors that other tribes had them, but who could tell if that was true. Maybe Albatross was the only one ever. The chances of finding another SeaWing animus just a generation or two after Albatross, when there had never been one before . . . and the chances of it being him, Fathom, of all dragons . . .

"Fathom, you jellyfish," Indigo whispered, giggling. "I don't think you're supposed to ask politely. He said *tell* it what to do."

"How would you know?" Fathom whispered back. "*You* don't know how effective politeness can be because *you* have atrocious manners."

The other dragonets were starting to whisper to one another as well. Nobody's coconut had done anything interesting. Albatross turned to the queen with an "I told you so" smirk.

"It's a coconut." Indigo rolled her eyes. "I think you're allowed to boss it around."

"Fine." Fathom held the coconut a bit higher and gave it a

stern royal stare as imposing as his great-aunt's, trying to make Indigo laugh. "Coconut, listen up. I *command* you to fly across this beach and strike my grandfather."

The coconut shot out of his talons so fast that Fathom stumbled forward, thinking he'd dropped it. He let out a yelp of surprise, but it was not enough warning for Albatross, whose eyes were on the queen. Fathom's coconut smashed into his grandfather's chest hard enough to knock him backward, his wings flying out, sand blasting in all directions like waves.

Silence dropped over the beach.

Fathom had never known it was possible to feel this elated and this terrified at the same time. He wished he could dive into the ocean and scream at the top of his lungs, but he couldn't move a single muscle.

"Whoa," Indigo breathed.

Albatross slowly rolled to his feet, struggling against the sucking, shifting white sand. He shook out his wings and stood up, wincing. He looked suddenly a lot older than he had before. Without looking at the dragonets or the queen, he carefully picked up the coconut that had attacked him, stared at it for a moment, and then held it to his chest. Fathom thought he could hear tiny crunching sounds. Had he cracked his grandfather's ribs? Was Albatross using the coconut to heal himself?

Was he in the very worst trouble he'd ever been in?

Finally Albatross looked up.

"Who did that?" he asked. Queen Lagoon swiveled her

head, staring down the line of dragonets until she came to Fathom's empty claws.

Fathom hunched his shoulders and saw that Pearl was pointing at him.

"It was my brother," she said. "Fathom's an animus!"

"Leaping barracudas," Indigo said to him. "I can't believe you never told me!"

"I didn't know!" he protested. "I had no idea!" Frankly it had never occurred to him to give orders to inanimate objects before.

"Prince Fathom," said the queen, stepping toward him with a glittering smile. "How perfectly wonderful. You are going to do such wonderful, important things for m — for your tribe."

Fathom held out his talons and stared at them. *I'm an animus. The rarest of all dragons. ME. I am special after all. I have magic like no other dragon in the Kingdom of the Sea.*

Except one.

He looked up and met his grandfather's eyes.

"Yes," said Albatross, smiling. "What happy news."

Behind him, out of view of the other dragons, a vine curled slowly out of the jungle and wrapped itself around the seagull's throat. Fathom watched, transfixed, as the bird was strangled to death without a sound.

Albatross patted Fathom on the shoulder, his face calm and friendly. "Another animus in the tribe," he said. "I'm so very, very pleased."

CHAPTER 2

DARKSTALKER

His earliest memory was the voices that came from outside the darkness.

"Are you sure it's time? Now? Tonight?"

"Yes. NightWing mothers always know. And it's the brightest night, like Foreseer said it would be. Three full moons . . . we haven't had a thrice-moonborn dragonet in over a century! Snakes and centipedes, *quit pacing*. It makes me want to bite your ear off."

"Try anything like that and I'll enchant all your teeth to fall out."

A slight pause. "Arctic. *I* was just kidding."

"Right. Me too."

He couldn't understand the words yet, but he was flooded with the emotions that poured from both minds. One (*Mother*, he knew without knowing) was absorbed with worry, protective, ready to love and defend and rage at a moment's turn. The other radiated resentment and cold anger, rotten around the edges.

A scratching noise, and he felt the world tilting. Suddenly

there was light, dim and soft but there, beyond the wall he had only just discovered around him. The light was calling him: *Come out, come out. Come out* now.

"Why are you moving them?" the angry voice demanded. "We leave ours buried in the snow."

"Ours have to hatch in the moonlight," Mother answered. "Stop scowling at me. It's completely safe. NightWings have been doing this for hundreds of years."

There was a sharp, loud tap near his ear.

"Don't touch them!"

A dizzying rush of motion, followed by warmth and stillness.

"Why are they two different colors?" asked the voice he didn't like, as loud and splintery and jagged as the tap had been. "Is it because of us? Maybe that one's more of an IceWing?"

"No," she said. "Most NightWing eggs are black, but the ones that hatch under full moons turn silver like this. I don't know why that one's still black. They should hatch at the same time."

"Something is wrong with it," he muttered.

"Nothing," said Mother, "is *wrong* with *my dragonets.*"

The world tilted again, and he felt himself settling into a place that wouldn't roll or shift so easily when he moved.

Now he could sense something else — another heartbeat, slow and steady and very close by. He reached for her mind, but there was only peace and quiet there. None of the urgency to escape that he felt. He knew he didn't have forever. *Now,* that's what he had, *only now.*

"We're up too high," grumbled the angry voice. "They could fall. This is a stupid tradition. We should have taken them back to the Ice Kingdom to hatch."

"So they could freeze the moment they came out?" Mother said acerbically.

"They wouldn't," he growled. "They *are* half IceWing, remember."

"And your mother would have been *so* pleased to meet them," she snapped. "At least my family won't kill our dragonets on sight. They'll help us protect them."

"Your family has nothing to complain about. I brought royal IceWing blood to their line."

Mother hissed dangerously. "I see. I'm so sorry about mixing it with my peasant NightWing blood."

A burst of violence, of bloody scales and frozen claws, flashed through the dragonet's mind. His mother was in danger. Bad things were about to happen. But he could stop it. He just had to come out *now*.

He pressed his talons hard against the walls around him, shoving and kicking and straining. A satisfying *crack*, and the sensation of something giving way beneath his back claws.

"He's coming, look." It worked. They were both distracted from their anger, especially Mother, all her thoughts now on her dragonet, her mind shimmering with excitement.

He tried to reach the quiet heartbeat again. If he'd had the words, he would have thought *Come out with me! Just try! You have to fight!*

your moon ...

"I don't think s...
gets here. Look how stron...
almost shared the same emotion,...
not *superstitions*, by the way. You do...
eros nostril just because you don't understan...

The danger flashed before him again. Time to ti...
He dug in his claws and squirmed, pushing in every direction at once.

The light, the light, the light wanted him out, wanted to run
its talons over his wings, drip through his scales, fill him with
silver power. He wanted that power, too, all of it, all of it.

CRACK-CRACK-CRACK.

The walls fell away.

The moons poured in.

Three silver eyes in the sky, huge and perfectly round,
with darkness all around them. It felt as if they were sinking
into his chest, melting into his eyes. He wanted to scoop
them into his talons and swallow them whole.

He was in a carved stone nest lined with black fur, at the
peak of a sharp promontory. Another egg sat quietly in
the nest, nearly camouflaged against the fur and the shadows.

Below him stretched a vast landscape of caverns and
ravines, glowing with firelight and echoing with the flutter
of wings. It looked as though a giant dragon had raked the

ons and caves

n, some of them stretching

a in the distance.

er several heartbeats he realized there were two large dragons behind him, their wings drawn tight against the wind that buffeted them all. One was black as the night, one pale as the moons. He glanced down at his scales, but he didn't have to see their color to know he belonged with the dark one. That was Mother. She sparked with anger from snout to tail, but there was immense room inside her for love, and she adored him already, heart and soul. He could feel it. It filled him like the moonlight did, setting the world quickly into understandable shapes in his head. He loved her, too, immediately and forever.

The danger came from the white dragon. This was Father, some kind of partner to the dragon who cared. The newly hatched dragonet could hardly look at him without seeing a spiral of confusing flashes: pain, fury, screaming dragons, and blood, everywhere, blood. This white dragon had done something terrible that haunted him, and he might do worse someday. Father's mind had patches of damp, rotten vileness all over it.

The dragonet immediately wanted to turn him into a fireball and blow his ashes away. But inside Father, hidden under layers of ice, pulsed a small, warm ember of love for Mother. That was the thing that saved him.

Wait and see, thought the dragonet. He did not understand yet that he could see the future. He had no idea what the flashes meant. He couldn't follow the paths that were unfolding in his brain; cause and effect and consequences were all still beyond him. But in his mother's mind he found the idea of hope, and in his father's mind he traced the outline of something called patience.

He could wait. There was much still to come between him and this father-shaped dragon.

"Darkstalker," said Mother. "Hello, darling." She held out her talons and he climbed into them willingly, content to be closer to that warmth.

"Darkstalker?" Father snorted. "You must be joking. That's the creepiest name I've ever heard."

"It is *not*," she snapped, and the dragonet bared his teeth in sympathy, but neither of them noticed. "The darkness is his prey. He chases back the dark, like a hero."

"Sounds more like he creeps *through* the dark. Like a *stalker*."

"Stop being horrible. It's not up to you. In my kingdom, mothers choose their dragonets' names."

"In *my* kingdom, the dragon with the highest rank in the family chooses the dragonets' names and the queen must approve them."

"And of course you think your 'rank' is higher than mine," she snarled. "But we're not in your kingdom. My dragonets will never set foot in your frozen wasteland. We are here, whether you like it or not, and he is my son, and his name is Darkstalker."

Father's eyes, like fragments of ice, studied Darkstalker's every scale, and Darkstalker could feel the cold, congealing weight of Father's resentment.

"He looks every inch a NightWing," Father growled. "Not a shred of me in him at all."

Suspicion, hatred, outrage flashing on both sides, but none of it spoken.

"Fine," said Father at last. "You can have your sinister little Darkstalker. But I want to name the other one."

Mother hesitated, glancing at the unhatched egg, which was still black. Darkstalker listened as her mind turned it over, already half detached. She wasn't sure anyone would ever come out of that egg. She was ready to give all her love to Darkstalker, her perfect thrice-moonborn dragonet. All of it, and he was ready to take it.

But Darkstalker knew his sister was in that egg. Alive, but not restless. Quiet. She didn't care for the moons that had called him forth. She couldn't hear them.

Something tingled in his claws.

He could change that.

He could touch her egg and summon her. He knew it, somehow; he could see in his mind how her egg would turn silver under his talons, how it would splinter and crack open as she scrambled out. He could see the beautiful, odd-looking dragonet that would come out, and he could see the moons sharing their power with her, too.

Then they would be the same. She would be born under three moons as well. She would have the same power as him . . . and the same love from Mother.

Which he already had to share with the undeserving ice monster across from him.

No. This was his. All he had to do was nothing. His sister would come out in her own time, tomorrow when the moons were no longer full. Then he would be the only special one.

"All right," said Mother. "If that egg hatches, you can name the dragonet inside. Only . . . remember she has to grow up in the NightWing tribe. It'll be hard enough —just, try to be kind, is all. Think of her future and how she'll need to fit in."

Father nodded, seething internally at being instructed like a low-ranked dragonet in training.

She'll be all right, Darkstalker thought. A thousand futures dropped away before him as he made his first choice. Futures where his sister joined his quest for power; futures where she fought him and stopped him; futures where they were best friends; futures where one of them killed the other, or vice versa. As Darkstalker folded his talons together, choosing to keep them still for tonight, every possible future with a thrice-moonborn sister disappeared.

He saw them blink out, and although he didn't know exactly what it meant, he felt somehow a tiny bit safer, a tiny bit bigger and stronger.

Sorry, little sister, he thought, not in so many words, but with visions of his future cascading through his mind. *This is my mother. Those are my full moons.*

This is my world now.

CHAPTER 3

FATHOM

A few days after the animus test, Albatross summoned Fathom for the first time. It was right in the middle of their geography lesson, and Fathom felt his stomach lift and drop and zigzag just like the lines of the canyons around the Deep Palace.

Grandfather wants to see me? he echoed. *Right now?*

He said to meet him at the sunset beach of the Island Palace, the messenger reported. *Alone.* The phosphorescent scales under his wings flashed, transmitting the words in the SeaWing underwater language, Aquatic. An eel swam by the window, peered in at the dragons, and then wriggled quickly away.

Can't Indigo come? Fathom asked, glancing at his friend. She was perched beside him on the pink coral ledge around the interior of the room, their talons anchoring them down while their wings drifted in the water. On her other side, Pearl was giving her tail a bored inspection.

His sister glittered with coils of gemstones, long twisted ropes of pearls and opals and sapphires circling her torso and ankles. Indigo's only adornment was a necklace woven from dark purple seaweed, which Fathom had made for her last week. He liked it because the color matched her eyes. He liked *her* because she wore it with delight even when she was surrounded by the sharp-eyed, bejeweled dragons of the Deep Palace.

He didn't want to leave the Deep Palace without Indigo. He rarely went anywhere without her; they'd been together almost since hatching. Her mother had been in Queen Lagoon's army, where she'd become close friends with Fathom's mother before she died. Indigo's father curated the museum at the Island Palace and was quite happy to leave his only dragonet's upbringing to the caretakers who'd been assigned to Fathom and Pearl. Indigo was the only dragon invited to every royal family gathering despite having not a drop of royal blood in her.

Hang on, does Indigo want to come? Indigo said, poking his wing with hers. *Perhaps someone with manners should try asking her. She might be extremely busy, you know.* She reached out to tap the large terrain model of the kingdom that filled most of the room, and the tip of an underwater mountain broke off in her claws. *Oops,* she said with a guilty look at their frowning tutor. *Never mind, I'm totally free.*

He specifically said "alone," the messenger flashed with a shrug.

I think you two can survive an afternoon's separation, Pearl chimed in, rolling her eyes.

Fathom knew that, but it felt so weird to have something he couldn't share with his best friend. And he kept thinking of that seagull . . . although he knew it didn't mean any-thing, and possibly he'd seen the whole thing wrong and maybe the bird had accidentally strangled itself. Right? It was possible. Wasn't it?

I agree with Pearl, said their tutor. *Perhaps with you gone, Indigo will miraculously be able to focus on the geography of the Kingdom of the Sea.*

Indigo sighed a little whoosh of water around her snout. *Not likely,* she said sadly.

Why are you acting like an indecisive jellyfish right now? Pearl demanded, glaring at Fathom. The scales flashing along her wings were brighter than they needed to be, and he blinked several times, trying to avoid a headache. *You're the chosen one or whatever. Go have special chosen-one bonding time with Grandfather.*

Yeah. Indigo nudged his wing again. *Get excited! You've been waiting for this!*

She was right. Albatross had forbidden him to try any magic until their first session, and it felt as though Fathom's claws had been trapped in sand the last few days. He knew they could do marvelous things and he wanted to set them free. He wanted to start playing with his power; he wanted to find out everything he could do. And for that he needed his grandfather, the only one in the tribe who understood how animus magic worked.

All right — I'll be back soon, he said. *I think.*

Sure, if you're not too special and magical to hang out with us anymore, Pearl said.

Fathom gave her a sideways look, trying to figure out if she was mad at him. For what? Being an animus? There wasn't much he could do about that.

And he wasn't sorry. Their whole life, his sister was always "the one who might be queen someday." She had special diplomacy classes, extra policy sessions with the queen, private lessons to improve her handwriting (which was terrible), even advanced etiquette courses (those he was fine with missing). Wasn't that enough specialness for her?

Whereas he could never rule the tribe . . . but now he had *magic*.

His wings felt as if they had an extra current underneath them, shooting him along as he flew through the water to the Island Palace. He took all his strange little whispery feelings of dread and squashed them flat. He *was* special. He wasn't just another SeaWing prince, destined to lead a wing of the queen's army, sitting through normal lessons, on track for an ordinary dragon's life.

He had power, and he could use it to do something amazing.

Exactly what that would be, he wasn't sure yet. He'd been trying to think of some good ideas so he could show Albatross what a smart, thoughtful dragon he was.

The Island Palace was an elegant, sprawling complex of pavilions and courtyards, rooms and terraces, gardens and walkways that covered an entire island at the heart of the Kingdom of the Sea. Several of the walkways led to pavilions over the water, with glass floors so the dragons could have the sea at their talons at all times. Carvings of pale pink sea horses and bone-white dolphins dotted the gardens. Iridescent-blue paua shells gleamed in wave patterns, with white foam made from inlaid pearl, all along the polished wooden walls.

This was where Queen Lagoon entertained visitors from other tribes with elaborate feasts and entertainments that went on for days. This was also where the regular royal family gathering happened once a month, so Fathom had his own bungalow there, which he shared with Indigo and Pearl.

There were two main beaches used for palace events. The sunrise beach was the one dragons went to for tranquility or quiet conversation, for peace and quiet and solitude. So Fathom was surprised that Albatross had summoned him to the sunset beach instead, where parties often began that could last all night long. Royal weddings usually took place on this beach, including the one five years ago between his own parents, Manta and Reef.

But in the middle of the day, with the sun high above them, it was deserted. Albatross stood alone on the white sand, watching with his odd dark eyes as Fathom swam up to the beach. Waves clawed and pounced at his feet, eating away the sand below him, but Albatross didn't seem to notice he was sinking.

"Hello, Grandson," he said, spreading his wings as wide as his smile. "Do you feel powerful today? Ready to do some magic?"

"Yes!" Fathom said.

"Let's see those claws," said Albatross. Fathom held out his front talons and Albatross inspected them, one side and then the other, as though he were selecting a pair of precisely matched emeralds.

"Hmmm, yes, very interesting," Albatross said. "This talon definitely has more power than that one."

"It *does*?" Fathom said with awe, stretching it out so the sunlight shone through the webs between his claws.

"Oh, clearly," said Albatross. "Can't you tell?"

Fathom nodded thoughtfully. "I — yes — of course, it's more — more tingly, like —" He caught the mischievous expression on his grandfather's face. "Wait a minute. You're messing with me!"

Albatross laughed a warm, fish-smelling laugh. "I couldn't resist. I've never had a fellow animus to tease before. This is going to be fun, isn't it? Finding out what your magic can do?"

Fathom nodded, beaming. His grandfather had never been so jovial with him before. Albatross was always too busy, too untouchable, spending all his time on Queen Lagoon's projects. He'd been a kind but distant presence all of Fathom's life.

"All right, then," said Albatross, splashing into the sea. "Let's go."

"Go where?" Fathom asked. He'd been picturing a training session on the beach, maybe with more coconuts, or in one of the shaded courtyards while servants brought them mango drinks and platters of shrimp.

"My sister wants me to show you my most top secret project," said Albatross. He tossed his head carelessly and winked at Fathom. "In case I die and you need to finish it, I suppose."

"Oh *no*," Fathom protested. "Never do that! I could never make something as amazing as what you've made." But as he said it, he wondered if it was true. Would his creations be as brilliant as his grandfather's one day? Would he eventually be as beloved and respected and important as Albatross?

Fathom had only seen a few animus-touched objects in action. The most striking was a conch shell that pulsed with light whenever someone lied. It was intended for the queen to use in interrogations and negotiations, but Lagoon let her family use it whenever they asked. That was how Manta had forced Indigo and Fathom to confess that they were the ones who put squid ink in everyone's toothpaste (Indigo's idea, of course, but Fathom accepted half the blame rather than run the risk of being separated from her).

"You might be surprised," Albatross said. "But as for me never dying, I am also in favor of that plan." He smiled and dove into the ocean, and Fathom had to scramble to catch up to his grandfather's powerful wing strokes.

They swam for what seemed like a long time, and not in the direction of the Deep Palace. *Where are we going?* The islands in this direction were more scattered, with strong currents in between them. Golden sunlight filtered down through the water, illuminating the schools of brightly colored fish that darted by.

Up ahead, Fathom saw the foundation of a large island rising from the ocean floor; all around it, gray boulders and tall spires of rock jutted out of the water. Albatross led the way to a wavering forest of orange-yellow kelp and swam straight into it. Fathom followed him through the sticky fronds to a tunnel in the cliff ahead of them.

They swam into the tunnel, from light into darkness, and Fathom's night vision kicked in so he could see every bend and twist in the rock as they went deeper. He was beginning to wonder if they were going to swim right through the island when, all of a sudden, they emerged into a wide open lake.

Fathom popped his head out of the water beside his grandfather. They were in the heart of the island, surrounded on all sides by craggy, soaring cliffs. Up above them, cormorants wheeled about in a bright blue sky.

In the center of the lake, a vast, strange shape was growing out of the water. It looked at first glance like a gigantic narwhal tusk, as if someone had taken four towering pillars of white stone and braided them together. Huge flat bubbles of stone grew out of the pillars at regular intervals. Fathom realized with a start that they were literally growing — expanding, inch by inch, as slow as a sea slug inching across the ocean floor.

The whole thing was an amorphous, misshapen blob, a weird growth on the insides of the beautiful island.

"Oh no," he blurted. "What went wrong?"

Albatross paused for a long moment, studying the shape,

before answering. "What makes you think something is wrong?"

"Um . . . I'm sorry," Fathom stammered. "It's — is it — supposed to look like that?"

Albatross ducked his head under the water and came up with a smile on his face. "It's not finished," he said lightly. "It's still growing into its final shape. I must admit, I didn't think it would take so long. But when it's done, trust me, it will be the pride of the Kingdom of the Sea."

"Oh, I'm sure it will!" Fathom's mouth tumbled on ahead of him. "Everyone will love it! Because it's a . . . the best possible . . . such a cool . . ." He trailed off, feeling like a sinking snail.

"It's a new palace, grandson," said Albatross. He turned to swim to the nearest beach. "Entirely grown by animus power. I call it the Summer Palace — a place where royalty can escape to enjoy the warmest weather of the year."

Fathom blinked at the twisting, growing pavilion. He had a million questions, like *Does Queen Lagoon know about this?* and *Would anyone really want to live here?* and *How will it know when to stop growing?* and *Doesn't it feel kind of . . . creepy?*

But he didn't want his grandfather to see him as unimaginative or full of doubts. He wanted to be an *ideas* kind of dragon, all energy and enthusiasm.

He scrambled out of the lake beside his grandfather, feeling rough pebbles scrape his underbelly and tail. They both regarded the enchanted pavilion for a moment.

"Here's what it will look like when it's finished," Albatross said, opening a box on the beach beside him and pulling out a scroll. Fathom unrolled the drawing and let out a gasp.

"This *is* beautiful," he said. "It's going to grow into this?"

"That's the plan," said Albatross. "I check on it regularly, making adjustments and adding features. It's been growing for more than seven years, so it shouldn't be much longer."

"Seven *years*?" Fathom said, startled. His voice echoed too loudly around the cavern.

"I enchanted it to grow carefully and precisely, like a tree," said his grandfather proudly. "Anything faster and wilder could have damaged the ecosystem of the whole island."

Is that true? Fathom wondered. *Or did he make a mistake with the original enchantment? Maybe he just told it to grow and didn't specify how fast. I bet that would be really frustrating.*

"I have an idea," he blurted.

"Already?" said Albatross. "How . . . impressive."

"I mean," Fathom said, "I don't know if it's a *good* idea. Or if it would work. Can you use animus magic on plants?"

"Oh, yes," said Albatross. "I've done that several times."

"Well," Fathom said, getting excited, "I was thinking this Summer Palace would be more secure if it was hidden from above. Don't you think? Because right now, any dragon flying overhead can see it. But you could enchant the greenery up there to grow together and create a canopy, couldn't you?

Shielding the palace from the sky? But still letting in sunlight through the leaves?"

His grandfather tilted his head back to study the roof of the cavern. "Yes," he said slowly. "Yes, that could definitely work. What a clever idea, grandson."

Fathom's wings felt as if they might float off into the sky. "Can I do it?" he asked excitedly. "Can I do it right now?"

"Hold on," said Albatross, taking the scroll of detailed palace sketches. He set it carefully back in the box and cleared his throat. "I — I have to warn you about something."

Fathom shifted impatiently on his talons. His life was full of lectures and warnings. *Don't offend the elders of the royal family. Don't eat until everyone else has been served. Be careful of sharks until you're full-grown and can eat them. Never explore the deepest trenches alone.* The lecture he got the most often but still didn't understand was from the queen, who seemed compelled to inform him at every family gathering that he shouldn't get "too attached" to Indigo, whatever that meant.

"The first lesson of being an animus," said Albatross, looking into Fathom's eyes, "is that you must always be careful. Remember this is powerful, powerful magic. It can go wrong very easily. It's so powerful that you can do almost anything, except bring a dragon back from the dead."

Fathom managed not to look at the weird shape growing in slow motion behind him. "I'll be careful," he promised quickly. "I won't do anything wrong."

"I know," Albatross said, patting Fathom's shoulder. "You're very fortunate. I didn't have anyone to guide me." He hesitated again. "Do you know the story of my first animus spell?"

Fathom shook his head, shivering with excitement. He'd always wondered how Albatross discovered his power. "Was it amazing?" he asked. "Do you still have the first object you enchanted? Can I see it? Did you feel like the biggest, most incredible dragon in the whole ocean? Did you want to enchant absolutely everything else around you right away?"

Albatross sighed and swept his tail in an arc across the sand until it drifted into the water. "Maybe you're too young to hear this."

"I'm not!" Fathom protested. "I really want to know. Please tell me."

"It was an accident," his grandfather said. "Remember that. I had no idea it would work. I didn't know I had this power — I barely knew such power existed, and we all thought it was only in stories. Also, I was very young. Younger than you are now."

There was a long pause. *I'm not* that *young,* Fathom thought. *I already know lots of things.*

"It was an empty clamshell," Albatross said in a rush. "You know — the kind where the two halves are still connected, but hollow inside. A big one, but nothing extraordinary. I was playing with it on the sunrise beach, pretending it was a dragon mouth that was chasing the crabs and seagulls."

This was beyond Fathom's imaginative skills. He couldn't

begin to picture his stately, intimidating grandfather scampering around with a toy.

"And then my sisters came down to see what I was doing." Albatross's voice kept getting quieter, and his eyes turned to the water as if the scene in his mind were reflected there. "Lagoon and Sapphire. Our mother was still queen back then — it was years before either of them would be old enough to challenge her. But they were both bigger than me, and they started to tease me. They said my scales were a weird color, that my tail was a funny shape, that my teeth were too small, and I swam like a feeble old duck. Normal brother-sister teasing, but it made me so angry. So very, very angry."

Normal teasing? Fathom wondered. *Is that what other brothers and sisters are like?* He didn't always get along with Pearl, but she never followed him around just to be mean for no reason. And his older cousins simply ignored him, politely uninterested in his stories or Indigo's games.

No one in his family had ever made him really angry, that he could remember. Wait — Queen Lagoon, once, when she ordered Indigo to go deep-sea fishing at night because the palace had run out of her favorite snack. Fathom's mother had stopped Indigo and gone herself, and Lagoon had rolled her eyes and muttered something about coddling the lower class. Fathom didn't know what it meant, but he knew he didn't like the way the queen looked down her snout at Indigo. It made him feel all roary and snarly inside.

Angry like that? Was that what Albatross had felt?

"Sapphire tried to grab the clamshell out of my talons.

'What have you got here?'" Grandfather's voice went high and mocking, imitating his sister. Great-Aunt Sapphire — Fathom had heard her name before, but he'd never met her. She'd never attended a royal family dinner. He didn't actually know if she was dead or alive or where she lived.

A sinking feeling swept through his stomach. He suddenly didn't want to hear the rest of this story at all. But there was no stopping his grandfather now.

Albatross's claws curled into the sand, his gaze anchored on a spot over Fathom's shoulder. "'That's mine!' I yelled. 'Oh, is this your precious treasure?' Sapphire cooed, peeling my talons off it easily. 'Everything you have will be mine when I'm queen, you know. Even stupid beach trash like this.'" Albatross took a deep breath.

"I don't know why I spoke to the shell next instead of her — maybe because I'd been pretending it was real, or maybe because of some animus instinct curled up inside me. But I did. I squeezed the edge of it that I still held and I shouted, 'Bite her! Bite all her claws off!' and then I let go."

Fathom's jaw fell open in shock. Albatross finally looked at him again and winced.

"I know. You are lucky that your talent was discovered in a much less gruesome way," he said, touching his chest absently, as if remembering the pain. "It took several days for all the blood to wash away from the beach. Sapphire, of course, could never be queen after that — a dragon with no claws cannot hunt or fight, and as for swimming . . . well, who looks like a feeble old duck *now*." He barked a dry laugh.

"She went a little mad, I'm afraid. Now she is kept on an island far away from everyone else, tended by two very well-paid servants. Lagoon visits her occasionally, but I never have. I assume Sapphire would prefer never to see me again."

He sighed.

Fathom looked down at his own talons, subdued. He'd been thinking of all the bright, shiny, amazing things he could do now. But what if one of his great ideas turned out all horrible and dark? What if he made a mistake and hurt someone?

I won't, a voice whispered inside him. *I'll be careful and smart. Smarter than Grandfather.*

"I'm not telling you this to scare you," said Albatross. "But you needed to know so that you'll understand my rules — mine and the queen's. You must listen to me. You must never use your magic unless I am there to supervise you. You must consider every spell carefully for weeks before you cast it, and you must run them all by me first. I know you feel powerful now — I understand that better than anyone. But you are also dangerous."

"All right," Fathom said. "I know. I understand. I promise to be careful and all of that stuff. Can we try some magic now?" He twitched his wings hopefully.

Albatross rubbed his forehead. "I suppose enchanting a few plants wouldn't hurt."

"YES!" Fathom shouted. "Thank you, thank you!" He shot into the air, arrowing toward the sky above them.

A few moments later, he burst into the open sky, soaring over the circle made by the top of the cliffs, with the lake and the Summer Palace far below him. The heat of the sun was startling after the cool temperature inside the island — but even more startling than that was the yelp that came from a patch of foliage near the edge of the cliff top. He twisted in the air to squint at the shrubbery as his grandfather appeared beside him.

"A spy?" Albatross said, his brow darkening. He flicked one claw sharply, and the entire bush tore free from the dirt and hurled itself into the sea.

Exposed underneath it was a small, very anxious-looking purplish-blue dragonet.

"Indigo!" Fathom cried. "What are you doing here?"

"Making sure you're all right," she said. She sat up, squaring her shoulders. "Sorry, Albatross, sir. I didn't mean to spy on you. I only followed Fathom to watch out for him."

"That's perfectly silly," Fathom said. He swept down to land beside her. "You don't need to keep an eye on me. What do you think you're going to stop me from doing? You cause a lot more trouble than I do."

"Do not!" Indigo protested. "When have I ever caused trouble?"

"Well, you're certainly *in* trouble," Albatross interjected. "The queen won't be pleased that you've seen her most secret project."

Indigo raised her chin defiantly.

"But since you're here anyway," Fathom said, "you can watch me do my first real spell! With plants! I have this great idea about plants and things!"

"Actually," Albatross said. "I'm getting tired. I think we should swim back to the Island Palace now."

"What?" Fathom cried, his wings drooping. "Just one vine? Please?"

"There will be plenty of time for you to practice magic, youngster," Albatross said firmly. "But I am a wizened old dragon and you've surely been taught something about respecting your elders. It's time to go."

Fathom didn't dare argue with him, although his scales felt as if they were seething with frustration. Nobody spoke, not even Indigo, all the way back to the Island Palace. Albatross landed on the beach in the orange light of the sunset.

"Good session today, grandson," he said to Fathom, tapping his wing lightly with his own. "I can see that you are full of promise. We'll make an excellent team, you and I." He glanced briefly at Indigo, who was dripping quietly onto the sand beside Fathom, close enough that Fathom could feel the heat of her body all along his scales. "Just remember what I told you about being careful. Now good night, both of you. I'll see you soon, Fathom."

He slipped away in the direction of the frangipane garden. As soon as he was gone, Fathom stamped his foot in the sand and blew all the air out of his lungs.

"Good *session*?" he cried. "We didn't even do anything! He just talked and talked!"

"Yeah, but has he ever talked to you that much before?" Indigo asked. "Wasn't that still pretty great?"

"No," Fathom grumbled. "I wanted to enchant something. I thought he was going to let me practice."

"Maybe it was my fault," Indigo suggested, her face falling. "Maybe he didn't want you to practice in front of me."

"I don't think that's it." Fathom sat down and started sweeping sand into a castle mound with his tail. "He was acting weird about it even before you got there. Doesn't he remember what it's like to be excited about something?"

"Old dragons," Indigo said, shaking her head as though they were just too hopeless. She added a few rose-colored seashells to his castle. "Do you — um, do you think the queen is going to yell at me? Or . . . or make me stop being friends with you?"

"She could never do that," Fathom said firmly. "I'd enchant her face to shut up first."

Indigo giggled, but he could see that she was still worried. Maybe Queen Lagoon had been saying mean, divisive things to her, too, behind his back.

Fathom twisted around and found a piece of bleached-white driftwood on the beach behind him. He held it up, grinning at Indigo.

"Don't you dare," Indigo said, guessing what he was about to do, as she often did. "He told you not to use your power without his approval! You have no idea what you're doing!"

"I do, too," he said. "One tiny spell won't hurt anything. I just have to make sure I don't say something stupid." He clasped his talons around the driftwood. "I enchant this wood to carve itself into the shape of a gentle little octopus."

He set it down on the sand between them and watched with amazed elation as small curls began peeling off the edges of the wood, and then bigger wedges, and then slowly a perfect head emerged, followed by eight sculpted tentacles.

Several minutes later, it was done. The little white octopus was about the size of a full-grown dragon's foot, with cheerfully flippy tentacles and a mischievous expression. Fathom picked it up and dusted off the sand.

It was the most perfect carving Fathom had ever seen; it matched exactly the vision he'd had in his head. That never happened when he tried to carve things with his claws.

"For you," he said, handing it to Indigo.

"Wow." She took it carefully. He could tell she was trying not to smile too much at it; that she loved it, but was still trying to look disapproving, which didn't work at all on her.

"You could have just carved this yourself," she pointed out.

"I know," he said, "but then it wouldn't have turned out so well."

"I think your carvings are perfect. I still have the beluga."

Fathom laughed, remembering his first gift to her. "Hello, that was *supposed* to be a graceful dolphin."

She snorted. "Well, I like belugas better anyway. The point is, you didn't need magic to make this."

"Maybe not," said Fathom, "but without magic, I couldn't do this." He rested one claw on the octopus's head and whispered, "Now come to life, with the sweetest, most loyal, most agreeable personality of any pet in Pyrrhia."

The octopus blinked its large, dark eyes at him, and then up at Indigo. She gasped softly, and the octopus wrapped its tentacles around her wrist as if it were hugging her.

"How are you going to hide this from your grandfather?" Indigo demanded.

"Let me worry about that," Fathom said. "Isn't it adorable?"

The octopus snuggled in closer, and now Indigo really couldn't stop herself from smiling. "I can't believe you magicked me a pet," she said. "You're such an idiot."

Fathom stroked one of the tentacles, which still felt oddly like wood, but malleable and warm. The octopus reached up and poked Fathom's snout curiously. "What are you going to call it?"

"Obviously Blob," Indigo said immediately. "He's clearly a Blob. Aren't you, Blob?" The octopus moseyed in a dignified curling way up Indigo's arm to her shoulder, proceeded to climb up her neck, and settled contentedly on top of Indigo's head, tentacles flopping over her ears on each side.

"Oh dear," said Indigo. "Please tell me octopus hats are in this year."

Fathom fell over laughing and got sand up his nose. As he tried to sneeze it out again, he caught a glimpse of Indigo's delighted face trying to look up at the octopus on her head.

See, Grandfather? Our power can be used for good things. It can make dragons happy.

I won't make mistakes like you. I can be trusted.

Everything's going to be just fine.

CHAPTER 4

CLEARSIGHT

Clearsight was in the library.

She was always in the library. Her parents often joked that they should have let her egg hatch there instead of on the lunar hatching peak. Of course, if they had, she wouldn't have been born under a full moon, so she wouldn't have gotten the gift of prophecy, and then she wouldn't have needed to spend so much time in the library in the first place. But whenever she pointed this out, her parents always shook their heads and sighed as if she just didn't understand their spectacular sense of humor.

The librarian had given Clearsight a study room of her own, although she suspected that was because he thought she was insane and he wanted the option to lock her in if necessary.

Partially blank scrolls were unrolled all the way across the five tables around her, and she hurried from one to another, scratching quick notes and trailing ink splatters from her claws.

Would it change anything if she did pretend to be insane?

She closed her eyes and tried to see if a future unfolded around that idea. Would she end up in the asylum? Would it save the tribe? Would that life be better than the other options?

It was too unlikely; no one would believe her even if she tried it. There was no path there.

No escape.

Keep searching. She went to the next table and tried to follow the timeline she'd started on that scroll. But it was so muddled. Step one: meet *him*, step two: chaos along every potential timeline.

A heavy sigh came from the doorway.

"Hello, Father," she said without looking up. This note — when did she write this? *The SeaWing brings death. The SeaWing brings salvation. Don't let him come. He must come, or all is lost.*

Aaaaaargh. Clearsight put her head down on the desk and thumped her tail on the stone floor.

"Clearsight," her father said. "You are too young to worry this much."

"I should worry *more*," she said, lifting her head and squinting at the SeaWing note again. Something really terrible was going to happen in the Kingdom of the Sea not long from now — something involving a lot of death. The kingdom was so far away, it was hard to be sure of the details. Should she try to warn someone? She wanted to, but she couldn't see any paths where anyone would believe her. Poor SeaWings. "I mean, what is the point of seeing the future if you can't fix it? If I just concentrate harder, I can follow all the paths. I can figure this out."

"All the paths?" her father echoed. "Every future that spirals out of every choice you and every other dragon make for the rest of your life? Can't you hear yourself? It's impossible, dearest. That way lies madness."

"No," she said absently. "I just checked. No madness in my future, not a viable option."

"This gift is not supposed to consume your entire life," he said. He stepped over the scrolls on the floor, narrowly avoided a blue ink puddle, and stretched one of his wings between her and the table. She looked up at him, rubbing her forehead.

"Listen," he said with infinite gentleness. "I know your power is stronger than any future-teller the NightWings have had in generations. I know it feels like you can see everything ahead of you."

"It's not that simple," she said. "It's not, 'here's your life, that's the way it will be.' It's every possible life, all the things that *could* happen to me and the tribe, and it all depends on what I do next. But there are so many — I can't keep track — and the further I look into the future, the more confusing and random it gets . . ."

"I understand." He wrapped his wings around her and she leaned into his chest, listening to his steady heartbeat. She knew he was trying, but he actually didn't understand at all. He didn't have either this power or mind reading. He was sweet and ordinary and not tortured, and his choices made almost no difference to the future. "But Clearsight, even if you could see everything, that doesn't mean you can control everything. Or anything. Things will happen. Other dragons will change your path and you won't be able to stop them."

That is far more true than you know, Father.

Darkstalker's face flashed in her mind again: the face of a dragon she had yet to meet, but who came with a torrent of visions — joy and love and pain and horror, so mixed-up she couldn't untangle it, couldn't even breathe whenever she thought about it.

"I should go away," she blurted. "Far away. Maybe the rainforest. Maybe the Mud Kingdom. Maybe the lost continent. Oh, *that* would change everything — it would have to!" She leaned back to look up at his face. His eyes were sad, but she knew they would get much sadder in many, many of her futures.

"I could have a whole different life, Father. I could be an explorer; I could chart the rest of the world. I could be alone, and then I'd be the only dragon who could change my destiny, right?"

If I never meet him . . . is the darkness lighter? Is everyone safer?

She closed her eyes, trying to follow that path — that weak, trembling thread of a future where she flew off across the ocean tomorrow, all by herself. It wasn't impossible. It was only nearly impossible. But she didn't see any success that way . . . that fog at the end of the path probably meant she died somewhere over the sea. And there was still blood and darkness for the tribe, even with her gone. Maybe worse.

That was the worst part; most of the futures where she avoided him were even more scary. As if knowing her made a difference to his path, but only maybe.

A flash of a silver-and-gold crown, twisted into sharp thorny points, tumbled through her head.

Which timeline was that — oh, table three. She untangled herself from her father, leaned over, and made a note.

"What are you so afraid of, dearest?" her father asked, taking her claws gently to keep them still. The blue ink smudged his talons like IceWing bloodstains.

Why do I even know that IceWing blood is blue?

Because I've seen it, way too much of it, down hundreds of paths.

"I can't tell you," she said. "I'm sorry, Father." *In the futures where I tell you his name too early, you end up dead. I can't see how or exactly why, but that's where they all go, and that is one thing I can prevent. One choice that will keep someone I love safe.*

He sighed again. "Clearsight, your mother and I have been discussing this. We think it's time for you to go to school. Every other NightWing dragonet started when they were one, and you're nearly two and a half."

"No," Clearsight said, panic rising in her chest. "I can't. I told you. That's when everything speeds up — that's when I lose control. I need more time to plan." She turned frantically to point at the scroll on table two, which was covered in desperate spiky handwriting. "That's what happens after I go to school. Look at all the timelines! They just explode! I have to chart them all before I get there. If the teacher puts me in that art group instead of this one, things change. If I sit with these dragons at lunch instead of those dragons, futures ripple in new directions. If I miss a day here or give the wrong answer here or share my scroll with this hapless dragon here, *the entire tribe might die*." She stabbed at the scroll, leaving little rips all the way across it, and burst into tears.

"Oh, Clearsight," her father said with hopeless distress. "It can't be that bad. One two-year-old dragonet isn't going to doom the entire tribe to destruction. The worst that can happen is you don't get into the astronomy program, and maybe your mother will be disappointed, but no one will die. Trust me." He patted her back sympathetically.

He had no idea, NO IDEA. Maybe most two-year-old dragonets couldn't affect the future of the whole tribe, *but she could*.

"Besides," he said, "we don't think this is healthy, what you're doing in here. School might be a good distraction — give you something else to work on, friends to keep your mind off things. Maybe it'll help you see that we're not all so doomed after all." He laughed a little, and she wondered what a mind reader would find in his thoughts. Was he really not worried about her visions of war and bloodshed? She hadn't told her parents everything she'd seen, but she'd woken up screaming enough nights for them to get the general idea of what the future held.

Probably. Maybe. Unless she could fix it.

She *had* to fix it. No one else could.

"Please don't make me go yet," she said, battling down a sob.

A long, horrible moment passed; futures hung trembling in the balance.

He sighed. "All right, dearest. We'll wait until you're three." He tipped her chin up to look at him. "But then there's no more delay. The queen wants her seers properly trained, and we're pushing her patience already with our special requests. So. When you turn three, you're going to school. Are we in agreement?"

Not a lot of viable paths where she could change *this* fate. Her mind flicked through them, then gave in.

"Yes, Father. I'd better get back to work, then." Maybe she should start over with the school scroll. If this was inevitable, maybe she needed to fill all the tables with what-happens-when-I-go-to-school scrolls — yes, with more room for all the possibilities. She'd bought herself some time. She could hide in here for a few more months and figure this out.

"Don't hurt yourself, Clearsight," he said, sweeping to the door. "It's not the end of the world if you let yourself sleep, you know."

That's what you *think.*

She dipped her claws in the inkwell again and missed the moment when her father left.

So I will have to meet him before too long. My Darkstalker, my fate. I always knew the other timelines were unlikely. He has this power, too; he would find me.

It was almost calming, accepting that. She didn't have to worry now about the futures where he was alone and it made him angry and callous. She didn't have to worry about the flimsy paths where he found someone else (*with no powers and no backbone,* she thought with a really annoying flare of jealousy). As those timelines dropped away, she saw how bad they would have been — for both of them.

But what was left was such a daunting tangle. Two dragons who could see the future, each trying to stay on a particular path.

Start at the beginning. Follow one thread at a time.

Her claws scratched across the paper, spilling her visions into cluttered mountains of words that she'd have to puzzle out later.

Just keep trying. It's for the sake of the tribe.

I must have this gift for a reason.

If I can see all our possible destinies — surely I can make sure we get the right one.

CHAPTER 5

DARKSTALKER

He could hear his parents' voices echoing off the cliffs as he swooped down to the landing outside their home. They were arguing again, and as usual, he could see their neighbors peeking avidly out of their own windows, ears pricked. Everyone in the tribe was interested in every detail of the disintegration of the Night Kingdom's most famous couple.

At least a few of them had the decency to duck back inside when they saw him coming. He shot a cold look at the two across the ravine. One didn't even notice him; the other was only pretending not to as she fussed unnecessarily with her doorway vines. Stupid — everyone knew he could read minds. Maybe she thought a three-year-old's skills wouldn't be that advanced yet.

She doesn't believe the rumors about me. He chuckled softly, but the smile dropped off his face as he touched down into the wave of fury and bitterness that was rolling out of his home.

"I'm not going to help her fight my own tribe, Foeslayer! *I would never do that!*"

"They're not your tribe anymore — we are! And you could work for her some other way!" Foeslayer shouted back. "You don't have to join the army, but you can't keep saying no to the queen! She's offering you a position at the castle! You *love* stupid castles and hanging out with royalty and all of that! You could stick your nose in the air all day long and fit in just fine!"

"She's not doing me an honor," Arctic growled. "You know what she wants. She wants my power. The gift I should have given the IceWings — she wants it for *your* tribe."

"This is your tribe now, too," Foeslayer insisted again. "No one is trying to use you. We're just trying to give you something to *do* so you'll stop *slithering* around the house *complaining* and *moping* and *getting on my nerves* all the time."

Darkstalker stepped through the archway into their small, cramped living room and dropped the three hawks he'd caught by the door. His parents were in one of the back rooms — maybe his mother had been listening the last time he'd asked her to make their discord more private, although they were so loud it didn't really help.

But his sister was huddled on the floor by the fireplace, wings over her head.

Don't they know she's here? he thought with a flash of anger. *How dare they fight like this in front of her?*

His father always behaved as though Whiteout was his only dragonet, his precious snowflake of a daughter, but he was completely careless of her feelings. He brought her special fish and paraded her around the tribe, and then they got home and he acted like she was a necklace he could hang in the corner until he needed her again.

"Hey," Darkstalker said softly, crouching beside his sister. He spread one of his wings over her. "How long have they been doing this?"

"I don't know," she whispered.

"Well, if you're SO MISERABLE HERE," Foeslayer yelled, "why don't you go BACK TO THE STUPID ICE KINGDOM ALREADY?"

"Oh, there it is," Darkstalker said. Their mother's favorite line, and the one that usually signaled they'd run out of breath for the moment. "That means it'll be over soon."

Whiteout nodded, but kept her talons over her ears.

Darkstalker had heard the whispers (and the thoughts — all the millions of thoughts) about his sister, so he knew he wasn't the only one who thought she was the most beautiful dragon in Pyrrhia. Her scales along her body were black with hints of dark sapphire blue, but her wings were an icy bluish-white, as were the spikes all along her back and her sharp, curving claws. Instead of silver starlike scales under her wings, she had a scattering of black scales that gleamed like jet against the snowy white. Her head was narrow and elegant like an IceWing's, and she had their father's startling blue eyes.

It was easy to tell with just one look at her that she was an IceWing-NightWing hybrid. The other things that were different about her were harder to see, unless you were a mind reader.

Darkstalker had been in Whiteout's mind often, but he still couldn't figure it out. It was different from other brains, as if she thought in colors and waves instead of in words. He could sometimes guess what she was feeling, but he almost never knew what she was thinking. He'd assume it was so quiet in there that she must not be paying attention, and then she'd make an observation that he never would have thought of. She was the only dragon he knew who could surprise him.

Would that be different if she'd been moonborn? he wondered. *If I had helped her out of her egg sooner, would she be more like other dragons?*

He shook off the guilt. It didn't matter. He wouldn't want her to be like other dragons. She was perfect the way she was.

Whiteout leaned into his shoulder and he twined his tail around hers.

"Maybe I *should* go home," Arctic spat, his words crawling like frost centipedes across the walls and into their ears. "I've been offered amnesty. My mother says she'll end the war and take me back — on one condition."

There was a clattering sound, like a metal tablet being tossed onto the table.

"How did you get a message from Queen Diamond?" Foeslayer asked sharply. "This could be considered treason, Arctic."

"Just read it," he said.

A long pause followed. Darkstalker closed his eyes, tracking the thoughts of both his parents.

"What is it?" Whiteout whispered to him.

"Nothing," he whispered back.

"It's something," she said. "You got colder and harder all along here." She pointed to the line from his jaw to his heart.

"I'll tell you later," he said. *When I come up with a lie that you'll believe.*

"Arctic," Foeslayer said in a tight, shaking voice. "If I thought for one minute that you'd consider this —"

"You should stop making threats," he said, "when you know you can't do anything to me. But don't worry. I'm not planning to accept. I just want you to know exactly what's on the table, so you can think about that the next time you tell me to leave."

It's time to stop this, Darkstalker thought. He tightened his wing around his sister for a moment, then stood up and went to the hall that led back into the other rooms.

"We're here," he called. "*Both* of us."

Guilt from his mother, anger from his father — well, that was normal. At least they fell silent. He picked up the hawks and began tearing them into pieces to split among the four places at the table.

Foeslayer appeared first, taking deep breaths. *How much did they hear?* flashed through her mind.

"Everything," Darkstalker answered her. "Especially Whiteout. She was here when I got here." He didn't hide his anger.

Even . . . she thought.

"No," he said, glancing at his sister. "Only I know that."

Foeslayer came to the table and moved a piece of hawk from her plate onto Darkstalker's, then another piece onto Arctic's. Darkstalker wordlessly moved the gift from Arctic's plate to Whiteout's.

I'm sorry, she thought at him.

"Say it to her," he said.

Foeslayer went over to Whitcout and hugged her, just as Arctic came stamping out of the back rooms.

"Oh, hawks again," he said bitterly. He didn't look Darkstalker in the eye. He never did.

"I thought they reminded you of the Ice Kingdom," Darkstalker said. In fact, he knew they did, because he'd seen that in his father's mind every time he brought hawks home to eat. That's why he looked for them particularly — because he knew they brought his father a little bit of happiness and a little bit of despair at the same time.

Stay out of my mind, moon-eyes, his father thought, glaring at him.

"Wish I could," Darkstalker answered briskly. "Whiteout, time to eat."

As the family moved to the table, he swept past his father into the back hall, acting as though he was going to wash his talons. But he had another mission in mind. He needed to see the message for himself.

There it was, tucked under a corner of the blankets on his mother's side of their sleeping room. A hammered piece of silvery metal with words carved into it.

He'd read their minds correctly. Here it was, clear as starlight.

Dearest Arctic,

We want you to come home.

You must have realized your mistake by now. You must be growing to hate that insidious NightWing, the source of all your misery. You know she was only sent here to tempt you away. But now you have seen through her, haven't you? You're starting to realize that your mother was right all along.

So I'm giving you one chance to take it all back.

Come home.

We'll call a truce with the NightWings. The war can be over. You can return to my palace, rejoin your tribe, and all will be forgiven.

And we have only one condition. One small, easy request that can save so many lives — and give you back your destiny.

It is this: Kill your dragonets.

Kill them, bring us proof, and you can come home.

A small price to pay for your life back, isn't it?

I love you, Arctic. Despite your poor choices and terrible mistakes.

I hope to see you soon, back in the tribe where you belong.

Queen Diamond

Darkstalker slid the tablet back into its hiding place, thinking.

He knew from his father's mind that Arctic wasn't seriously considering this possibility — yet. True, Arctic was miserable in the Night Kingdom, where he had no friends and no status and the climate was all wrong for him, but he could also remember all the things he hated about the Ice Kingdom: the rules, the expectations, the way his life was completely planned out without any regard for his feelings.

Moreover, Queen Diamond had clawed too many of Arctic's nerve endings with her comments about how she was right and he was so foolish. Arctic was too proud to go back with his head hanging, and most important, there was still a kernel of him that didn't want to leave Foeslayer or Whiteout.

Darkstalker never worried about how his father hated him. It was mutual and instantaneous upon his hatching, so it didn't particularly affect his life. Besides, he knew his father couldn't do anything to him, considering Darkstalker's powers.

But visions were flashing in his head where Whiteout was in danger. Unclear, muddled paths; he couldn't trace them exactly, but he knew that something led from this tablet to a scene of pain and violence and his own helpless fury.

I need a better future-seer to help me figure it out.
I need Clearsight.

Darkstalker smiled, trailing his claws along the wall as he went to wash in the stream at the back of their cave. He hadn't met her yet, but he knew it would be soon, and once he did his whole life would change for the better. It was almost impossible to wait this long, knowing his soulmate was so close by. But he'd managed it, for her. He saw that their relationship would eventually be stronger if he did. He was a master of patience.

When it came to his father, though, his patience was starting to wear thin.

Nobody threatens Whiteout, Darkstalker thought. *Not the IceWing queen, not my father. I won't let anyone hurt her.*

No matter what I have to do to stop them.

CHAPTER 6

FATHOM

"Maybe I shouldn't come tonight," Indigo said, flopping across Fathom's sleeping couch. Blob expertly held on to her ear with one tentacle to stay in place and looked very pleased with himself.

"Oh no. No way," Fathom said. "I don't want to make boring conversation with all my ancient aunts and uncles either, but we're in this together. That's the deal. How am I supposed to survive without you?"

"They're *your* family," Indigo protested. "Why do *I* have to be tortured, too? Besides, the queen doesn't even want me there."

Fathom winced. She was probably right about that. Queen Lagoon's comments had been getting meaner and more pointed lately. Now that she knew Fathom was her second animus, she unfortunately seemed to care a lot more about which dragons he spent time with. Albatross and Pearl: acceptable. Indigo and anyone visiting from other tribes: decidedly not.

Which reminded him. "Don't you want to see the SkyWings up close?" he asked. "This could be your last chance, if we end up going to war with them over the new shore villages." It was unlikely — Queen Lagoon was skilled at negotiating peace, especially with the threat of an animus in her back talons; they hadn't heard a peep out of the RainWings or MudWings in years. And the three new SeaWing villages didn't encroach very *far* into SkyWing territory, after all. No SeaWing would want to live any distance from the ocean.

"I saw them across the gardens when they arrived two days ago," Indigo said. "They looked pretty displeased."

"I thought SkyWings were supposed to be the friendly tribe," Fathom mused.

"You're distracting me," Indigo said. "The point is, the queen would be much happier if I stayed here, *especially* when she has the SkyWings to impress. I'd be the only one at the gathering who wasn't dripping with jewels." She arched her eyebrows at the new gold armbands Fathom wore — carved with royal symbols, they matched his grandfather's — and the emeralds that glittered in his ears.

"You're perfectly impressive," Fathom said, hauling her up onto her feet again. "You don't need jewelry; you have the best smile in all the kingdoms."

Their wings brushed, light as ripples on a pond, and Indigo pulled her talons away quickly.

"*Smile* in front of the *queen*?" she said with a feigned gasp of disapproval. "Surely that's not allowed!"

"Here," Fathom said. He bounded into the next room, where Pearl was pivoting slowly in front of a series of mirrors to examine herself on all sides. "You can wear those pink pearls Mother bought for Pearl."

"I do hate those," Pearl said in the new, exceedingly bored voice she'd been trying out lately. Even now, more than three years since the test, she still acted irrationally jealous whenever Fathom went off to train with Albatross. But most of the time she was back to normal, which involved a lot of sighing at how loud and immature Fathom and Indigo were.

"And they'll look really cool on you, Indigo," Fathom said. He crossed to the far wall, where all of Pearl's jewels were displayed on a tall tree of dark brown mahogany with many branches, which he had carved for her for their birthday last year. (*Without* magic, since Indigo insisted.)

"Are you sure?" Indigo asked Pearl. "Won't Manta be upset if she sees me wearing them instead of you?"

"She'll be thrilled," Pearl said. "Mother thinks you're very entertaining."

Indigo wilted a little and Fathom flashed Pearl a glare. "Mother loves you," he said to Indigo. "She wants you at the party, and she won't mind what you have to wear to fit in." He unhooked the string of pearls and the bracelet. Each of the pearls was slightly irregular instead of perfectly round, and they were all different shades of pink from almost white to deep rose. He could see why Pearl didn't like it — she preferred everything perfectly symmetrical — but he thought it was really cool.

He clasped the bracelet around one of Indigo's wrists and then helped her drape the long cord of pearls around her neck and wings. They glowed against the deep purplish-blue of her scales. Fathom could feel her heart beating as he leaned over her back to adjust the length. His talon rested on her neck for a moment and she curved her head toward him.

Why does everything feel different lately?

It wasn't weird that he wanted to spend time with her more than anyone else. That had always been true. It wasn't weird that she was the first dragon he thought of whenever he had something to share. It wasn't weird that she could make him laugh when no one else could.

It was a *little* weird that his own heart sped up when she stood this close to him.

"You two are HOPELESS," Pearl barked, bundling Fathom aside, and for a moment he was startled into thinking she'd guessed his thoughts. "Have you never seen a dragon wear pearls before? They can't hang this way or they'll make it impossible to swim, and besides, everyone knows a double wind around the neck is most flattering. You have to tighten the slack here and drape it like *this* . . ."

She busied herself adjusting Indigo's adornments while Indigo stood still, looking uncomfortable.

"There," Pearl said at last, standing back with a nod of triumph.

"That looks exactly the same," Fathom said.

"*Thank* you," Indigo said to Pearl before she could snap at her brother. "I really appreciate it."

Pearl waved her tail dismissively. "You can thank me by distracting Great-Uncle Humpback if he tries to corner me again with stories about the grand old days. 'You know, when I was a young whippersnapper, we had scavenger sashimi every afternoon. But where have they all gone, can you tell me that, eh? They can't have gotten smarter! Someone's been interfering with my scavenger supply! Some toothy little blowfishes, I'll show them.'" Her imitation of Humpback's creaky old voice was pitch-perfect.

Indigo giggled. "Someone should eventually tell him that *he* probably ate them all."

"It's not going to be me!" Pearl said.

"Me neither," Fathom chimed in with a laugh.

"You know you have to leave your weird little thing behind," Pearl said, flicking her tail at Blob. Indigo wrinkled her snout with disappointment, but she lifted down the tiny octopus and tucked him onto his perch on her side of the room.

"Stay," she told him sternly.

Blob blinked at her with an innocent face. It was very unclear whether he understood any of her instructions. Sometimes he was dutiful, obedient, and perfect, and sometimes he immediately did exactly the opposite of whatever she'd asked him to do. Fathom occasionally worried this might be because he'd forgotten to give the octopus ears.

Pearl studied herself in the mirror for another long moment. Fathom realized that Indigo hadn't even gone over to check what she looked like.

With a sigh, Pearl said, "Well, this will have to do. Let's go."

As they swept out the door of the bungalow into the garden, Fathom turned to Indigo and whispered, "You look great."

"I look like a squid pretending to be a sea horse," she said with a laugh. She winked at him and hurried after Pearl through a shower of white jasmine petals.

Fathom smiled as he followed her. Another boring royal gathering, another yawn-inducing feast. Thank goodness he'd convinced Indigo to go with him.

He couldn't imagine what he would ever do without her.

Fathom's parents, Manta and Reef, were already on the terrace when he arrived, hovering by the buffet table and laughing. His cousins Scallop and Current were there, too, with their father, his uncle Eel. The murmur of their voices mingled with the ebb and flow of the waves and the music from a trio of SeaWings playing the queen's favorite instruments.

Most of the family dinners were at night, without much lighting because SeaWings could see in the dark. But in honor of the SkyWing guests, this gathering was being held shortly before sunset, with the golden western horizon as their backdrop, and lanterns had been lit around the gardens (by the SkyWings themselves, since SeaWings had no fire and no need for it). Fathom liked the unusual warm glow this gave to the Island Palace, as though little suns had snuck in and hidden in some of the trees.

Giant aquariums around the terrace were full of luminous blue jellyfish, some of them trailing tangles of slender tentacles longer than a dragon. The scents of vanilla, ginger, and basil came from the long tables of food. Hibiscus flowers as brightly colored as gemstones dotted the bushes and were scattered across the conversation couches, ruby and topaz and pink against the dark green backdrops.

Manta came over to greet them, smiling and tipping her wings down to avoid the string of hanging lanterns.

"You look lovely, Indigo," she said without batting an eyelash at the borrowed pearls. "And you, as always, are the picture of majestic splendor," she added to Pearl.

There was always a weird vibe between Pearl and Manta, which Fathom couldn't entirely figure out. Indigo said it was because the only way Pearl could become queen was if Manta first challenged Lagoon and won, and then Pearl would have to challenge her own mother. Fathom wasn't quite sure that was right — because Lagoon had a daughter, Splash, who had no dragonets of her own. If she became queen, couldn't Pearl challenge her? Indigo said no, because Pearl was technically Splash's first cousin once removed, not her niece, and then Fathom had to yell "LA LA LA" and stick his claws in his ears because complicated family trees and succession laws were not only boring and impossible, but frankly irrelevant to his life anyway.

"Is there coconut rice tonight?" he asked his mother. "And tuna rolls? And that mango-lime drink from last time?"

"There's everything," she said with a laugh. "We should

invite dragons from other tribes to our gatherings all the time — the chefs really went overboard."

"I'm going to get one of those macadamia things before Current eats them all," Pearl declared, gliding away.

Before Fathom could dare Indigo to race him to the tuna rolls, a conch shell fanfare sounded from the top of the palace wall. Queen Lagoon and her husband, Humpback, came parading down to the terrace with their daughter, Splash, and the two visiting SkyWings.

"Whoa," Indigo whispered, sidling a step closer to Fathom.

It wasn't that the SkyWings were bigger, exactly — well, their legs were longer, so they did seem taller than the queen. And their wings were definitely bigger than a SeaWing's. And their horns were straighter and sharper, and their talons were not webbed . . . but most of what was startling about them was the color of their scales. They were such a shiny, polished red, like hibiscus petals or drops of blood or giant walking rubies.

As they all reached the terrace, Fathom saw the queen's eyes dart around quickly, and a shiver ran down his spine. By now a few other distant cousins (twice removed? eighteenthish removed? Fathom had no idea) and some of the queen's elderly aunts and uncles had arrived, so the terrace seemed full in an intimate way.

But Fathom knew who she was looking for, and he was not there.

"Where is Albatross?" his mother whispered to him, apparently noticing the same look on Lagoon's face.

"I don't know," he whispered back. "I haven't seen him since training this morning."

I hope he's not mad at me. Fathom was trying hard to convince Albatross that he was ready for more challenging animus work — like enchanting objects from afar without touching them, or casting spells without speaking, the way Albatross could. But Albatross was convinced that Fathom wasn't ready for any of that yet.

"When you're seven. That's how old I was when I first cast a spell like that," he had said. "Until then, don't we have quite enough to do?"

Albatross had been letting Fathom design small corners of the Summer Palace, and now that it was essentially complete, the only thing left was the spectacular throne on the top level of the pavilion. Fathom had spent months drawing it, down to the smallest detail, and then his grandfather had changed so much about it that Fathom could barely recognize it as his own.

But today they had set the enchantment together, and by next week the throne should have grown into its final shape, and then they'd be able to present the whole thing to Queen Lagoon.

Fathom wasn't sure why Albatross wasn't more excited. His grandfather had been so quiet all morning, his eyes more hooded than usual.

And now he was missing the family gathering.

Where could he be?

Queen Lagoon was taking the SkyWings around, introducing them to each family member. Indigo saw her coming and stepped on Fathom's tail trying to sidle away, but it was too late.

"My niece, Manta," Lagoon said to the SkyWings. "And her son, Fathom." She glanced at Indigo for the briefest moment, then tipped her snout upward and adjusted her crown. "I'm delighted to introduce the SkyWing envoys, Eagle and Princess Sunset."

"Welcome to the Island Palace," said Manta.

"Hmm," said Eagle.

"It's hotter than I expected," said Sunset, fanning herself with her wings.

"This is my friend, Indigo," Fathom interjected, tugging Indigo a step closer.

Eagle and Sunset looked supremely uninterested. Queen Lagoon managed to keep her frown small and refined.

"Have you tried the shrimp?" Manta said quickly.

Eagle sniffed. "Everything is so . . . raw," he said.

"I guess we could set it on fire." Sunset sighed. "Then perhaps it would be palatable."

They moved toward the buffet table with Manta, but Queen Lagoon lingered for a moment, twitching her nose as if her own dinner had been unfortunately scorched.

"You," she said to Indigo. "Go find me a drink. Something with pineapple in it."

"Yes, Your Majesty." Indigo bobbed her head and whisked away.

Fathom tried not to look irritated. Lagoon always spoke to Indigo exactly the way she spoke to the servants. But she was the queen; she could order around anyone she liked. There was nothing he could do about it.

Something snapped in the garden beyond the terrace — someone stepping on a branch, perhaps, out in the growing shadows beyond the lanterns. Fathom twisted to look around, but couldn't see anyone out there.

"Fathom," said the queen. "I'm going to be blunt with you."

That'll be different how? he thought, steeling himself.

"I thought I had dropped enough hints, but they don't seem to be registering. Perhaps subtlety is not the best approach in a case like this." She spread her wings, cornering him. "You need to stop wasting your time with that . . . that low-born purple dragonet."

Fathom actually had to think for a moment to figure out what she meant. "Stop being friends with Indigo?" he blurted. "Why would I do that?"

"I cannot allow your affection to grow any stronger," she said, emphasizing *affection* as though it were a rotten oyster. "I don't know why your mother hasn't intervened. Obviously you cannot marry her, so it would be best to get rid of her before other prospects hear any rumors and get scared off. Of course, as an animus dragon you'll be in high demand. It was such a chore to choose a match for Albatross back in his day. Such a shame she died and he was too stubborn to marry again."

"Wait," said Fathom, his head reeling. "I — who said anything about getting married? I'm only five!"

"Please," the queen scoffed. "I see the way you look at her. I see how she brings you what you need before you ask for it. I see how you create treasures for her out of your claws."

Another twig snapped behind them. Fathom still couldn't see anything out there — the sun was going down, and the lanterns were messing with his night sight. But he suddenly had a crawling feeling down his spine, as if the jellyfish tentacles had slithered out of the aquariums to ensnare him.

Someone was out there, staring at them. Staring at *him*.

"What is this?" Eagle called to the queen. He was standing by the decorative pond in the center of the terrace.

"Get rid of her yourself," Lagoon hissed to Fathom, "or I'll find a place for her that suits her station, as far away from you as possible." She turned with a swirl of blue wings and went over to the SkyWings, her poised public face back in place again.

She couldn't be serious. Indigo wasn't — she wasn't a danger to Queen Lagoon's plans.

Although I'm not exactly thrilled about being the subject of those plans, I have to say.

But Lagoon didn't have to make threats and order him around. He wasn't in love with Indigo or anything.

Am I?

Across the floor, he caught sight of Indigo at the drinks table, bobbing slightly to the rhythm of the music. She touched her head unconsciously for a moment, and he realized she was reaching to make sure Blob was safe before remembering the octopus wasn't there.

Unless that's what this happy feeling is, the one I get every time I see her.

Uh-oh.

"That is a statue of me, of course," the queen said to Eagle, smiling. Inlaid with sapphires that matched her scales, the marble statue coiled over the fountain with her wings spread, water spraying from her mouth.

"How does it work?" Sunset asked, circling the fountain. "Where does the water come from?"

"Oh, it's enchanted," Lagoon said, with barely suppressed glee. "By one of my animus dragons."

If she'd been hoping this news would hit the SkyWings like lightning, she couldn't have been more successful. Eagle and Sunset both froze and stared at her as if she'd cut off her own head in front of them.

"Didn't I mention I have those?" she said. "Well, I do. That's probably an important point to remember during negotiations tomorrow."

"You have animus dragons," Sunset cried, "and you let them *live*?"

"Whatever do you mean?" Queen Lagoon asked. "Of course I do. They're extremely valuable."

The SkyWings glanced at one another. "We do not tolerate dangerous differences in the Sky Kingdom," Eagle said firmly.

Sunset leaned toward Lagoon, her amber eyes fierce. "Doesn't your tribe know the legends? How using their magic eats away at their soul?"

"Well, in order for that to work," said a voice from behind her, "you'd probably have to have a soul of your own to begin with."

Albatross stepped out of the shadows, or melted out of them, was how it seemed to Fathom. One of the lanterns cast a halo around his head, making his eyes seem even darker than usual, as he stepped across the terrace toward his sister and the SkyWings.

"*There* you are," said the queen. "It's about time."

Indigo appeared beside Fathom again, holding two coconut bowls and looking nervous. She handed one of them to Fathom, and he realized it was full of the mango-lime drink he loved. *She brings you what you need before you ask for it.*

"I don't want to interrupt the queen," Indigo whispered to him, "but do you think she'll be mad if I don't bring her drink to her? Or more mad if I do?" She fidgeted with the other coconut shell, picking off shreds of brown fibers.

"I think she's forgotten she asked for it," Fathom said honestly. "She was just trying to get you out of the way so she could lecture me. Again."

"Oh." Indigo gave him a curious sideways glance, but didn't say any more, because now most of the terrace had fallen silent. Only some of the more elderly cousins kept talking, a murmur over by the musicians. Albatross was still pacing slowly toward the queen.

"Here is our first animus," Queen Lagoon said to the SkyWings, who seemed to have figured that out themselves, judging by the looks of terror on their faces. "My brother, Albatross. We were just talking this morning about what his next project should be. I'm thinking big this time. Something that makes me invulnerable, perhaps. Or something that kills any dragon who might be a threat to me."

Beyond Albatross, over by the couches, Splash stiffened, and Fathom saw her crush one of the hibiscus blossoms between her claws. He glanced around and saw his father put a wing around Manta, who had gone pale.

"Yes," Albatross said. "Although you might recall I wasn't exactly enthused about any of those ideas."

"Then it's lucky you're not my only animus dragon," Queen Lagoon said coldly. Fathom felt a shiver all the way down to the tip of his tail. If she asked him to do a spell like that, would he? Would he obey his queen and put his own mother in danger? Or disobey her, and perhaps put everyone he cared about in even worse danger?

What would she do to Indigo if I ever said no to her?

Albatross stopped right in front of the queen, snout-to-snout with her. Fathom couldn't read his face. He looked as though he'd been carved from stone, any emotions chipped away.

"Do you think you're done?" Queen Lagoon said to him softly. "Do you think you'll ever be done atoning for what you did to Sapphire? It's not going to end, Albatross. You'll always be mine."

Something clinked in the background, and Fathom turned, thinking he'd seen a flash of silver in the air, and then a line of red sliced slowly, darkly, murderously across Queen Lagoon's throat like the widest smile in the world.

She blinked at her brother in surprise and lifted one talon to her neck. Her last words were, "But I'm *the queen*," and then her body fell in slow motion, legs crumpling, wings crashing down, head landing with a splash in the fountain. Clouds of blood spilled out, turning the water red and black.

The queen of the SeaWings was dead.

And her animus, Fathom's grandfather, was holding the knife.

CHAPTER 7

CLEARSIGHT

Clearsight had been awake all day, fidgeting scrolls into tiny shredded pieces and knocking over inkwells with her tail as she paced around her room.

"Time to wake up!" her mother called cheerily, poking her head into the room. "Oh dear."

"I know, look at this mess," Clearsight said, her wings twitching jumpily. "Maybe I should stay home for one more night to clean it up."

"The real mess in this room is you, sweetheart," said her mother. "It's time to go and you know it. Come eat a nice rattlesnake for breakfast, and you'll feel all energized and ready for school."

"No, rattlesnake will make me hiccup during the introduction circle," Clearsight said. "Fish could make my talons slippery so I land awkwardly. I'll have a squirrel; I can see that that has no unfortunate consequences."

Swiftwings rolled her eyes and retreated.

Breathe, Clearsight told herself. *Tonight. You'll meet him tonight. You know it, and he almost certainly knows it, too.*

It was strange to feel so excited and so terrified at the same time.

This doesn't have to change everything. I'm still holding the threads. I can control what happens next.

For instance, she knew Darkstalker was going to be waiting for her right outside the school. He wanted to meet her as soon as she landed. He might try to pretend for a moment that it was all a coincidence — Who are you? Have we met? What do you mean, what destiny? But she wasn't going to play those games. He surely had her face in his head as clearly as she knew his.

She could trick him, but only by being early. He could linger if she tried to arrive late, but he wouldn't be able to get there with his sister as early as she could. And he wouldn't expect it; her foresight was stronger than his.

Clearsight hesitated for a moment over one of her scrolls. The branching timelines for today — should she bring it for reference?

No, stopping in the hall to consult a scroll every time she had to make a decision was bound to get her some weird looks. And if anyone took it and read it, they'd think she was crazy.

It's all in my head anyway.

She bolted through the other rooms, scooped up the squirrel, knocked over a bookshelf by accident with her tail, called "Sorry! Sorry sorry! I have to fly!" to her parents, and made it to the front entrance before they intercepted her.

"What's the rush?" her father asked. "Suddenly you're desperate to get to school, after dragging your wings about it for years? What's going on?"

"Don't you want us to come with you?" her mother chimed in.

"No — no, no," Clearsight said as brightly as she could manage. She had to delay the meeting between them and Darkstalker for as long as she could, mostly to avoid a lot of awkward arguments she could see lurking in the immediate future, but also partly for their own safety, for complicated reasons. "I'm fine! I know where I'm going. I'll see you in the morning!" She tapped her snout against each of theirs and they reluctantly moved aside.

Outside, the night was just starting to spill into the ravines, reaching its long dark claws down to the rivers and less desirable homes at the bottoms of the cliffs. Clearsight's wasn't quite at the bottom, but it was more than halfway down.

One day, if she could use her power to do something valuable for the queen — a vision that helped defeat the IceWings in the war, for instance — her family would be able to move to somewhere higher and more skylit, closer to the stars. That was something else she had to think about when she studied the futures.

She spread her wings and soared up the rocky cliff face into the sky. From up here, it was easy to navigate the Night Kingdom; all the canyons and outcroppings were spread out below her like a scroll.

The school was to the north, not far from the palace, each of them forming one side of the Great Diamond with the museum and the library on the other two sides. The palace was the biggest of the four buildings and wrapped around Borderland Mountain, but the school was designed to look very similar: lots of black and gray marble terraces, hanging gardens, and long glittering waterfalls. And at this hour, as night fell for the nocturnal tribe, both the school and the palace were mobbed by hundreds of beating black wings.

Clearsight had flown all the possible routes to the school six times in the last two days. She was prepared; she knew exactly where to land. Of the three entrances to the school, the quietest and least crowded was on the side facing away from the palace.

She spiraled overhead for a moment, checking the dragons below her — no sign of Darkstalker — and then swooped down. Her talons landed neatly on the marble tiles and she folded in her wings.

Several other dragons were arriving and hurrying into the school, but no one even looked at her.

Right, she remembered. *They don't know yet that I'm important. They don't realize that soon everyone will know my name, or that I can save them from so many horrible things.*

A shiver ran down her spine. She spent so much time thinking about the future, but this was now, actually now. Now was when the future would be shaped.

She stepped into the arboretum entrance, a damp, leafy

space where the last rays of sunshine poured through the skylights and plants lined the room. A colonnade led from here past the library to a vast hexagonal courtyard, with classrooms lining the six sides. The courtyard was designed as an obstacle course for flying practice, full of trees, twisting vines, loops, mazes, and tricks.

Clearsight followed the sound of the longest waterfall to a pavilion on an upper level, to the main office, where a tired-looking dragon crouched behind a desk, moving piles of paper around.

"Hello, Professor Truthfinder," she said. "I've come for my placement."

"Oh," said the dragon, pressing her talons to her temples. "Where did I put that?"

Oh, please don't make me take all those tests again, Clearsight thought. She'd spent an entire day filling out scroll after scroll to demonstrate that she was ready for class with the other three-year-olds, instead of having to start at the beginning with the one-year-olds. She was sure she'd done well.

"Yes, yes, you did," said Truthfinder absently. "Well enough that we could put you with the four-year-olds instead, we were thinking."

That's HIS class. "No, thank you, that's all right," Clearsight said quickly. "With the other three-year-olds would be fine."

Truthfinder tilted her snout suspiciously. "Something you need to tell me? Are we going to have a problem?" The silver scales glittering from the corners of her eyes declared *Don't lie — I can hear everything you think.*

"I would like to be with dragonets my own age," Clearsight said as winningly as she could, clearing all other thoughts from her mind. "My parents think it would be best for my social development." Maybe she should have brought them with her after all; maybe the clutter of their thoughts could have obscured hers.

Not that there's anything to worry about. I am SO excited to be starting school at last! Hooray for wonderful school!

Truthfinder stared her down for a long moment. Clearsight was pretty sure the smile on her face was getting a little manic, but she couldn't get rid of it now.

"Very well," Truthfinder said slowly. "Three-year-olds, advanced reading group, special seer training elective. I'm including a note that your maneuvers could use extra work in flight class, with an eye to possible remedial lessons. Any extracurriculars?"

"Not right now," Clearsight said. "Thank you." *Extra work? Flight class? Remedial lessons!* She tried to squash down her indignant feelings. *It's true, I've spent more time in the library than flying. But for good reason!*

Truthfinder gave her a stern look and made another note on the scroll in front of her. "Give this to your teacher — room 3A." She rolled it up and passed it to Clearsight.

"But when is my seer training class?" Clearsight asked, glancing at the scroll. "I don't see any information about it in here."

Truthfinder raised her eyebrows at her. "When you are ready for it, you will know."

Oh dear. It's a test, Clearsight realized. But kind of a backward one, surely. If you were good enough at reading the future to figure out where and when your class would be, then did you really need any training?

I shouldn't think that way. I'm sure I need training. A really skilled seer will help me figure out how to read the timelines better and how to steer other dragons along the best paths.

So she would find the class on her own; she could do that.

"Thank you," Clearsight said again, backing out of the room. She started down the hall and paused at one of the windows that overlooked the school's main entrance.

There was one dragon in the milling crowd down there who stood out from all the others — one with white wings and white claws. Clearsight knew who that was — which meant the dragon standing next to her, scanning the crowd with a puzzled expression, must be *him*.

Darkstalker.

He's looking for me. He thought I'd be down there, arriving just about now.

She felt a small tingle of glee in her talons. *So he doesn't know everything after all.*

As if he'd heard her thoughts, Darkstalker suddenly raised his head and looked up at her window. Their eyes met, and as Clearsight ducked away she saw him start to smile and wave.

Ack! He did *hear my thoughts.*

Of course he did, Clearsight, you idiot.

She had only one advantage over him: her visions of the future and how carefully she studied them, whereas he barely bothered to glance ahead. But to use it, she needed help. She needed to learn to control her power better.

I need to get to that seer training class as soon as I can.

But on my first day? Will that throw off all my visions?

She closed her eyes, trying to see ahead. She saw herself in partial sunlight — so it was an early class, before night completely fell — in a circular room with no windows or doors. A tall NightWing paced the circumference, frowning at her and the other three dragonets in there.

Mostly frowning at her, actually.

How am I supposed to find a room with no windows or doors to give me a clue about where it is?

But wait — there was sunlight all through the room, so where was that coming from? She squinted into the vision, furrowing her brow. The walls were impenetrable black marble, sparkling with flecks of silver and copper, and hung with mirrors that caught the light. The light from . . .

She looked up. The room had no roof. Far above their heads, it was completely open to the sky, with only the tip of a mountain peak poking into view.

So it must be up reasonably high. At the top of a tower? Maybe that's also why the walls are curved.

Clearsight crossed the corridor to a window that looked inward, toward the courtyard and the other levels of the school. There were five towers, but she couldn't tell from here which ones had windows and which didn't.

With a glance around at the bustling halls, she carefully climbed onto the sill and launched herself into the sky. There were dragons flying every which way, and she had to dodge and weave to avoid colliding with anyone.

But once she got close enough to fly around the towers, there was only one possible choice. Four of the towers were regular dragon towers, with multiple levels open to the air and pavilions on top. But the central tower was different. At first glance, it didn't even seem to have an interior; it was hung all about with ivy and vines that cascaded down through levels of gardens where dragons were gathered, socializing before school started. The top of it was so shrouded in greenery that it was hard to tell there might be a room inside there.

Clearsight spread her wings to hover in the air and checked her school map again. This tower was marked "Tower of Knowledge," which sounded promising. She looked up at the setting sun again and guessed that this class was happening right now — first class on the schedule.

She hesitated. Did it make sense to start here, before checking in with her regular teacher? This wasn't what she'd done in most of the timelines she'd examined for today, but maybe it was the best choice — maybe it would speed up her ability to control the future.

Also, she didn't want to miss any seer training, especially since she'd already missed two years of school. And according to her parents, this was the most important part of her education, from the queen's point of view.

But she had such a careful plan for today . . . this could tip everything out of balance. She hadn't studied this alternative enough. Besides, the scene she'd glimpsed felt awash in dread and awkwardness and confusion. She got a big "you're going to regret this" vibe from the whole picture.

Maybe I should wait until I know the school better. Or, really, until I can study what happens when I drop into the class — so I can find the best way to introduce myself to the other seers.

Suddenly something rippled, hard and fierce, through all of Clearsight's visions at once.

Something terrible was happening.

Something terrible that would affect her future. It was happening a world away, but it was happening *now* and *now* and *forward* and *forward,* and it would rip apart a lot of dragons' lives.

She staggered sideways in the air, losing the updraft for a moment before catching herself.

The green SeaWing . . .

Fathom.

The tragedy in the Kingdom of the Sea was happening now — the one she'd foreseen.

Oh no. Clearsight pressed her talons to her head. *His poor, sad futures.*

If he even survives tonight.

This, *this* was really why she needed training. Not to outwit Darkstalker, but to save lives. To make dragons in power *listen* to her, so she could make the changes she needed to make and help dragons like Fathom.

She twisted in the air and arrowed to the very top of the central tower. Yes — it was open to the sky — and below her was the room she'd seen, full of light and mirrors, with four dragons clustered in the center of the floor.

Here goes nothing.

Clearsight swooped down, dropping dizzily between the walls and landing with more of a thump than she'd intended. The marble was startlingly cold under her claws and she resisted an urge to hop back up into the air.

The other dragons all jumped and turned, blinking at her. Three of them were students, but older than her — perhaps five or six years old — and the fourth was the large, scowling teacher she'd seen in her visions.

"H-hello," Clearsight stammered nervously. "I'm sorry — I'm looking for seer training — this is it, isn't it? I'm —"

"Don't bother," said one of the other students. He flicked his tail at the teacher. "She already knows who you are and everything about you. She's the queen's own seer!"

The other two students turned eagerly toward the teacher, who narrowed her eyes at Clearsight. "You claim to be a seer?" she barked. "How do you know? What have you seen? We don't tolerate play-acting in here."

"I — I've seen lots of things," Clearsight said, faltering. What did she mean? Major events, like the next NightWing queen challenge? But which ones, along which timelines?

"How do you know they weren't ordinary dreams? Or products of your imagination?" the teacher pressed. She took a looming step toward Clearsight.

"Because they came true," Clearsight said. "Or will come true." What an odd question. She'd never doubted her power for a moment. It was always there, spinning out possibilities in her head, throwing up pictures and flashes of scenes and dragons she would know.

"Ha!" The teacher lashed her tail, looking wickedly amused. "How old are you — three? Your powers have barely begun to evolve yet, even if they are real. Whatever lucky guess brought you here, you should go away again until you are truly ready. Talk to me when you've had a few more visions than *oh no, my mommy is going to yell at me for splattering rabbit bits all over the floor*."

The other students giggled, and Clearsight felt a flare of temper. "I've had more than a few visions," she said. "And I can prove how real they are!" She pointed to her teacher. "I know that your name, for instance, is Allknowing." She whirled toward the other dragonets. "And you three are Jewel-eyes, Morrowwatcher, and Vision. I know a huge storm is going to roll in three days from now and class will have to be cancelled for a week of rain. I know the queen is planning to evaluate all her potential seers in a month and she won't be pleased. How's that for knowing things?"

There was a long pause. Allknowing seemed to be swelling up like a poisonous viper.

"*Dragon of chaos, tangling the webs,*" she said suddenly. "*Too many eyes and too many threads.*"

Jewel-eyes let out a small gasp.

"That's *her*?" whispered Vision.

"You must be Clearsight," said Allknowing, her voice dripping with icicles.

"That's right," Clearsight said, feeling a bit smaller suddenly. Had she really been in one of Allknowing's prophecies? *Dragon of chaos* — how could that be her? She wanted to create order out of the chaos, not cause more. And surely she didn't have more eyes or threads than anyone else.

"Obviously I knew you were coming." The teacher stalked around her, studying every inch of her scales. "But you seem to be early."

"I wasn't sure," Clearsight said. "I mean, it's my first day, so I didn't know —"

"Your first day?" Morrowwatcher interrupted. "At the school? How did you find us so fast?"

"I . . . looked?" Clearsight answered. "Into the future?"

The three students stared at her with wide eyes, and then turned as one to Allknowing.

"Can she really do that?" Jewel-eyes demanded.

"Will *we* be able to do that?" asked Vision.

"Why haven't you taught us that?" Morrowwatcher chimed in.

"Isn't that what you do?" Clearsight asked, bewildered. "Aren't we all seers?"

"Yes, but we can't just *look* at whatever we want to," said Vision. "We have to wait for visions to come to us. Here we mostly practice writing them down, making them sound like real prophecies, and interpreting them."

"Also figuring out what's a dream and what's a vision,"

Jewel-eyes said ruefully. "Like, we're pretty sure I'm not actually going to lose all my teeth all of a sudden one day. Or forget to study for my final exams."

Clearsight's wings were sinking slowly to the floor. That did not sound like the kind of seer training she needed at all. Turning her visions into cryptic prophecies? How would that help anyone? Did these dragons even realize that there were multiple possible futures?

"Well," Allknowing said in a clipped, unfriendly way. "Obviously Clearsight's gift is a little different from everyone else's. I'm sure we'll all learn *so* much from listening to her tell us about it. But for now, I suggest we get back to our curriculum."

The other dragons shuffled obediently back into a semicircle around her, although they kept stealing sideways looks at Clearsight. She crouched on the end beside Vision, wishing her scales were thicker.

"As I was saying," Allknowing hissed, "here is the first verse of one of my earlier prophecies." She flicked her tail at the large slate board mounted on the wall, which had something like a poem scrawled on it in chalk.

"From far to the north, a prince will arrive,
Seething with darkness and sparkling with ice,
In his blood runs a gift for the whole NightWing tribe,
But it comes with a terrible price."

Clearsight felt sudden uncontrollable giggles bubbling up inside her. She dug her claws into her other arm, trying desperately not to laugh. It mostly worked, but Allknowing glared at her anyway.

"Any theories what this was about?" Allknowing demanded. "Clearsight, you seem tremendously amused by something."

"No, no," Clearsight said quickly. "It's very impressive. I like how it, um . . . scans? And is so . . . mysterious?"

"Certainly it was *more* mysterious before it was fulfilled," Allknowing spat. "Care to analyze it for us?"

"Well, it's about Prince Arctic," Clearsight said. "And his animus powers, which have made him darker on the inside each time he's used them. The terrible price is the interesting part, because it could mean the current war with the IceWings, or the consequences of having animus power in the NightWing tribe. Or is it the price for him, meaning how his soul is affected? Or the price for the dragons who love him? It could refer to what his descendants will do if they inherit his power, which, obviously, there are a lot of . . . possible terrible things . . ." She trailed off under Allknowing's withering scowl.

"The terrible price is the war," Allknowing snapped. "There's no need to show off by concocting wild fantasies. We already know that neither of Arctic's offspring inherited his animus power. Vision, did you have something to add?"

Clearsight hoped her face didn't give away how confused she felt. She knew it was still a secret to most dragons, but was it possible Allknowing hadn't had any visions about

Darkstalker's animus power? That seemed like a fairly huge future development for a seer to overlook.

I'm not going to learn anything from her at all, Clearsight realized with despair. She should have listened to the little warning bells in her visions. Allknowing was dangerous — dangerously ignorant, and dangerously resentful of Clearsight's power.

Whatever lay ahead between them . . . Clearsight had a feeling it would not end well.

CHAPTER 8

FATHOM

Fathom stared at the dripping red knife in Albatross's claws. Drops of blood spattered the floor, his grandfather's talons, his tail.

Fathom couldn't move. Part of his brain was still thinking, *Did he slip? Did someone throw that knife by accident? Why isn't the queen getting up? Albatross can fix it; he fixes everything.*

And the other part of his brain was sending panicked alerts to every part of his body at once. *Swim! Fly! Run! Fight!*

Albatross looked at the knife curiously, as if he'd just found a charming new pet. Over by the bar, the dragon who'd been slicing coconuts was still looking around in confusion, wondering where it had gone.

The SkyWings reacted first, taking to the air with shrieks of fear. Albatross glanced up at them, turned the knife over for a moment, and then let it go. The knife flew through the air and stabbed Sunset in the spot where her jaw met her neck. A moment later, it yanked itself free and spun to catch Eagle in the heart.

He's killing them, Fathom thought, his mind trapped in quicksand. *He could kill all of us.*

The red dragons thudded down to the terrace, knocking over one of the jellyfish aquariums as they landed. Glass shattered and water cascaded out over the dance floor, where the jellyfish flopped and squelched under the talons of screaming, fleeing dragons.

"Can you stop him?" Indigo asked, grabbing Fathom's arm.

"Me?" he yelped. "No! I'm not strong enough! And he's my grandfather — I can't —"

"He just killed your queen and two SkyWings!" Indigo said.

"But he was angry at them." Fathom felt as though words were just cascading out of his mouth without checking through any higher brain functions first. "He won't hurt anyone else, will he? If I try anything, it could just make everything worse."

"I'm not taking any chances," Indigo said. "We have to hide you." She dragged him out of the circle of lanterns to the path between the gardenia bushes.

"What about my parents?" he said frantically. He tried to pull back and his wings caught on a trailing vine. "What about Pearl?" He couldn't see his sister, but through the melee he spotted Manta struggling to get closer to Albatross. *What are you doing, Mother?* he thought in a panic. *Run away! The opposite way!* She was going to try to calm Albatross down, he was sure. That was her way of handling everything.

"We can't get to them," Indigo said, "and if Albatross kills anyone else, it'll be you, sure as sunshine."

"Me?" Fathom said. "But —"

Fathom looked over his shoulder and saw his grandfather scanning the terrace with his strange, fierce eyes. He did look like he was looking for something — someone . . . could it be Fathom?

Behind Albatross, Splash suddenly lunged around the fountain, pointing a spear at his heart.

Albatross didn't even look at her. The spear twisted in her talons, yanked itself free, and plunged into her chest, pinning her to the ground.

He's not finished, Fathom thought with horror.

"*Come on,*" Indigo cried, pulling Fathom free of the vegetation. They ran full-tilt along the winding paths, leaving clouds of scattered petals in their wake. Away from the lanterns, the island was full of long shadows, waiting for their moment to pounce. One of the moons was rising, enormous and low on the horizon, a strange orange-red color, as though it had been stained by the pool around Lagoon's body.

"Should we fly?" he said to Indigo, panting.

She tilted her head up just as a scream of agony came from the sky. "Easy targets," she panted back.

Everyone's an easy target to him, Fathom thought with another stab of fear. *He can send a knife after me no matter where I run to.*

I may already be dead.

The gravel under their talons suddenly changed to wood and they found themselves pounding along one of the walkways that led to an overwater pavilion. The sea rushed madly below them, chasing itself up the sand and down without getting anywhere. The sun was almost gone, barely flicking its tail over the far edge of the ocean. Stars glittered in the deepening purple sky and the dark water below them.

The pavilion was deserted, lit only by moonlight through the windows overhead and bioluminescent plankton shimmering under the glass floor. A dead orca and a pair of fishing spears were mounted on the sky-high ceiling. A balcony looked out on the dying sunset and a pair of strange shapes hulked against the side wall.

It took Fathom a moment to remember what they were. Queen Lagoon had called them "boats" — Humpback had found mentions of them in some old scrolls. They were for riding on the water instead of swimming in it, which was a weird concept. But Lagoon had ordered them built so she could take the SkyWings out on the ocean tomorrow.

That's never going to happen, Fathom realized as the shock washed over him again, *because they're all dead.*

"Let's swim," Indigo said, hurrying to the balcony. "He'll have to search the whole ocean for us."

"No," Fathom said. "I can't leave — my family — I need to stay close so I know when — when it's safe."

"Then we hide." Indigo circled the boats for a moment. She finally seized one in her talons and tilted it back far enough from the wall that Fathom could crawl under it. He held it up so she could join him, and then let it fall quietly back against the wood.

They huddled in the darkness.

Fathom could feel Indigo's breath on his face, his neck. He wasn't sure if he was imagining it, but it seemed as though he could feel her heart racing as fast as his was. He knew he wasn't imagining the trembling in her wings.

Now that they'd stopped moving, they could hear the far-away screams.

Indigo wrapped her front talons around Fathom's and bowed her head.

"Do you really think he would hurt me?" Fathom whispered. "We're partners. He's my grandfather."

"He had no problem killing his sister," Indigo pointed out. "And you're the only one he has any reason to be afraid of."

Because I'm special. Because of my magic, which I thought was so wonderful.

"If we die —" he whispered.

"Shhh. You're not allowed to die," she whispered back without looking up.

"Do you think it's true that animus dragons lose their souls?" Fathom said softly. "Is that why he's doing this?"

Her shoulders lifted and fell, and he could hear her unspoken thought: *The question isn't why . . . it's how do we survive this?*

But he thought *why?* was kind of important, too.

"Maybe I shouldn't have run away," he whispered.

"Shhh," she said again, clutching his talons tighter.

He fell silent, listening.

The screams had stopped.

Somehow, that was worse.

They waited for an eternity, frozen in the gathering dark.

What is happening?

A small bar of moonlight tipped in the window and inched across the floor toward them.

Is everyone dead?

Or did they stop him? Maybe Mother managed to talk to him. Maybe she calmed him down. Maybe everything's all right now.

Apart from the dead queen and murderous grandfather, that is.

Fathom took shallow, quiet breaths, trying unsuccessfully to slow down his heart. He couldn't put them together — the grandfather who'd joked with him about the throne design this morning and the dragon who'd held the bloody knife over his sister's body.

Creeeak.

The softest of noises. It could be the wind shifting the walkway. It could be a turtle bumping into one of the columns below them.

Or it could be talonsteps on the planks outside.

Maybe it's Mother, to tell us it's safe to come out, Fathom thought desperately.

But she wouldn't approach so quietly, so carefully.

Like a dragon hunting for his prey.

Closer.

And closer.

One deliberate step at a time.

I'm about to die, Fathom thought. His heart was trying to swim out of his body, thumping in his ears far louder than the steps on the boards outside.

Please don't kill Indigo, too.

Maybe there's still time for her to escape if I distract him. He has no reason to go after her. She means nothing to him.

But he couldn't get a message to his petrified muscles. He couldn't move, could hardly even think as the talons stepped lightly into the pavilion.

"Grandson." The hiss slithered around the room like smoke. "Hiding like a nervous hermit crab. Interesting choice. One I should have expected, though, from such a little dragonet with such a limited imagination."

Albatross paced slowly closer. Indigo's trembling stilled and she took a deep breath.

"You may be wondering why you're still alive," Albatross said. "Especially when your entire family is dead."

No, Fathom thought, drums beating misery through his head. *No. They can't be. No.*

"You know I could easily kill you from a distance. It would barely take a thought. But you've been such a thorn in my side the last few years. Every chance she got — 'I don't really need you anymore. Perhaps Fathom will be better at this than you are. You're so expendable now that I have a replacement. What a pathetic creature you are, little brother, with your tiny teeth and oddly colored scales. Fathom is so much more presentable than you are.'" Albatross growled in the back of his throat.

"So, no, I couldn't dispose of you from afar. That wouldn't be satisfying at all. I want to see your *face* as you die."

The boat flew away from them as Albatross ripped it off the wall and flung it across the room. It landed with a crash that shook the whole pavilion.

At the same moment, Indigo uncoiled and sprang at Albatross. Her front claws sank into his neck and her back claws dug at his chest, while her wings flared up to blind him.

"Fathom, get out of here!" she screamed.

She's going to die for me.

Albatross roared, a sound of pure rage and hatred.

She's going to die.

Fathom would never, never let that happen.

He was on his feet suddenly, stretching one talon toward the ceiling. He couldn't touch them, but he felt power surging through his claws and he leaned into it.

"Spears!" he shouted. "Kill my grandfather!"

The fishing spears wrenched themselves off the wall and shot toward Albatross.

"No!" Albatross yelled. "Spears —"

Indigo seized his snout, smothering his words, and bit down hard on his ear.

A spear smashed into Albatross's back. He grabbed the pearls around Indigo's neck and twisted as she let go of him with a strangled yelp of pain. One of his claws sliced across her neck as the second spear slammed into his side.

Both dragons collapsed to the floor.

Blood seeped over gray scales, pale blue scales, indigo scales, all across their wings, all over everything.

Fathom's talons were deep in blood.

"Indigo," he cried. Sobs rose from his chest, threatening to tear out his ribs. "Indigo." He slipped and slid through the blood over to her body and pulled her free from the weight of Albatross. His grandfather's dark eyes glared sightlessly up at the moons. The spears had done their work well. He was gone.

But Indigo was not. There were bruises all along her throat and a gash that bubbled horribly below her jaw, but her eyes were open, and they saw him. He cradled her head gently, taking her talon when she reached for him.

"Such an idiot," she whispered, wincing as the effort made the gash bleed harder.

"Yes, you are," he said through his tears, and she managed a smile.

"Told you you weren't allowed to die," she said. Her eyes drifted shut.

"Yeah," he said, "well, neither are you."

He wrapped his claws around the pearls and whispered, "Heal this dragon and save her life. Please. Please. Please save her life."

He could feel the struggling, slow flutter of her pulse under his claws; he felt it jump, pause, and then start to beat stronger and steadier.

The pearls glowed warmly for a moment, like little fire-breathing roses.

And then the bruises faded away. The gash in her neck closed up, scales knitting back together. So did the deep lacerations along her side, which he hadn't even been paying attention to.

Time passed, and then Indigo took a long, shuddering breath and opened her eyes.

He helped her sit up and threw his wings around her.

She didn't say anything. She didn't have to. They were both crying too hard to talk at this point anyway.

Fathom knew he would have paid any price to save her life.

But he also knew she must be wondering the same thing he was.

Was the price a piece of his soul?

Would his power slowly turn him evil?

Was every spell he cast bringing him a step closer . . . to becoming like Albatross?

CHAPTER 9

CLEARSIGHT

Clearsight was relieved when Allknowing finally released them and she was able to find her way to Room 3A. It turned out to be a beautiful classroom — airy and full of light, with plants and little water features everywhere. The teacher showed her around and Clearsight's anxiety gradually began to fade.

"These are our pet scavengers," said the teacher, beaming as she patted the top of a large glass cage. "Two females. They're quite fierce, so don't stick your talons in the cage, just to be safe. We rotate whose turn it is to feed them, and we're doing a yearlong study of their behavior. They're not just adorable; they're also quite fascinating."

The two little creatures in the piles of grass inside didn't look fascinating; they looked asleep. Clearsight wondered what they ate.

"A lot of fruit," said a dragon hovering nearby, "nuts, seeds, and sometimes bits of meat if we roast it for them."

"Oh, Listener," the teacher said. "Would you take care of our new student for the rest of the day?"

"Sure," Listener said, brightening. She was large for three years old, with curves that suggested she was a very successful hunter. And she had the mind reading silver scales beside her eyes.

Uh-oh, Clearsight thought. *A mind reader. That's just what I need.*

The other dragon glanced down at her claws, her wings drooping slightly.

"I'm sorry," Clearsight said quickly. "I'm just not used to mind readers. I don't know how to shield my thoughts or only think nice things or anything. I'll probably think lots of horrible stuff and you'll end up hating me really fast. Or lots of crazy things and then you'll think I'm crazy."

"I already know you're crazy," Listener said with a small laugh. "When you walked in, you looked around the classroom and immediately categorized every student into 'safe to be friends with' and 'doomed if I talk to them.' What is that about? And just checking — I'm not in the doomed camp, am I?"

"Not as far as I can see," Clearsight said. In fact, most of the paths involving Listener were a lot warmer than the paths without her, with more laughing. This friendship would definitely be a turn toward the right future. As long as they avoided that fight about Clearsight's timeline scrolls, and that other fight about Darkstalker, and, oh dear, all the fights about Listener's crushes on various —

"By the Scorching, all right, all right!" Listener cried,

flinging up her wings. "You're one of those! I'll stay as far out of your brain as I can, I promise. I don't want to know *anything* about my future."

"Nothing?" Clearsight asked curiously. "Even if it meant I could stop you from —"

"Nothing!" Listener yelped. She pressed her front talons to her ears. "Don't you dare!"

How completely strange, Clearsight thought, blinking at her new friend. "But why?" she asked. "I could change your future and make it better."

"My family is superstitious about seers," Listener said, cautiously lowering her talons. "We'd rather be surprised by life than know too much."

This was such a bewildering and unfamiliar concept that Clearsight fell silent, staring at the scavengers. One of them was waking up, yawning and stretching and rubbing the cloud of dark hair on its little head.

"I have a secret plan," Listener whispered. "Maybe you know that already."

Clearsight shook her head. That is, she knew of a few crazy Listener plans that might lie ahead, but she wasn't sure which specific one might be bubbling up right now.

"I'm going to free the scavengers one day." Listener glanced furtively over her shoulder, but the teacher was busy reviewing another student's journal on the far side of the room. "As soon as I figure out the best way to do it."

"Why?" Clearsight asked.

"Because they're sad," Listener said simply. "I can feel it. They don't like being trapped in here. They like being together, but they would rather be free."

"You can feel it?" Clearsight echoed, tipping her head. "Like — real emotions?"

Listener nodded. "Small and muddled but very powerful. I feel it all the time when I'm in here. Poor little things."

The awake scavenger tripped over the sleeping scavenger on the way to the water dish, and the sleeping one woke up with a lot of loud squeaking noises. Clearsight watched them stomp around squeaking back and forth, just as if they were having an actual conversation. Then there was a pause, and after a moment the first scavenger brought over a piece of apple to share.

"That looked like a peace offering," Clearsight said.

"Exactly! That was exactly her feeling," Listener said. "Their feelings are *crazy* similar to ours. I need to ask some other mind readers if they've noticed it, too. Or maybe there are scrolls about it in the library. I don't think we've had many captive ones before, so maybe I'm making an awesome new discovery."

"I'll help you," Clearsight said impulsively. "Free them, I mean. Whenever you're ready, I'll help." This was something completely separate from her confusing, tangled-up future. This was something she could do just for herself. Because she'd made a friend, and nobody was going to die as a result.

Hopefully. Not along most of the paths anyway. Maybe

she should study those two vague dark possibilities a little more carefully . . .

She was about to ask for a scroll to take notes on when Listener grinned sideways at her and flicked her tail. Clearsight felt a burst of weird bubbles in her chest. What was that?

Happiness?

Maybe her dad was right. Maybe they weren't all completely doomed after all.

"Uh-oh," said Listener. "Here comes Weirdout."

Clearsight turned, trying to imagine who would give their dragonet such a strange name, and saw Darkstalker's sister walking toward them. Her startling pale blue eyes were fixed on Clearsight.

"She's four," Listener whispered, "but she's with us because whenever someone asks her what two plus two is, she says something like 'Archaeology?' or 'Lavender?' and no one knows what to do with her."

"I thought her name was Whiteout," Clearsight stammered.

"Yes," whispered Listener, "but she's *super weird*."

"Hi," Whiteout said to Clearsight. She stopped in front of her and stood very still, and Clearsight got the strange feeling that Whiteout was already gathering more information about her than Listener had been able to, even after reading her mind.

"Hello," Clearsight answered.

"Are you the dragon my brother's been waiting for?"

The question hung in the air for a moment as Clearsight debated all the possible answers to it. Lying, she could see, would set them off on a bad path. Whiteout trusted either completely or not at all. And it might be very important — life or death important, although Clearsight wasn't sure exactly why yet — for Whiteout to trust her. Claws of prophecy squeezed her heart, and she could give only one possible answer.

"Yes," she admitted.

"Good," said Whiteout. "I'm glad you're finally here." She dipped her snout toward Clearsight and moved off to work on a puzzle that was spread across a long table in the corner.

"See?" Listener said when she was out of earshot. "Weird."

"I think she's . . ." Clearsight hesitated, not sure how to sum up Whiteout, especially when almost everything she knew about her hadn't actually happened yet. "Interesting," she finished.

"It's possible to be both," Listener said with a shrug. "So what was that about? Darkstalker? You *know* him?"

"No — not yet," Clearsight admitted.

"He's intense," Listener offered. "Maybe the smartest dragon in the history of the NightWings. You know he hatched under three full moons? He can read minds *and* see the future. It's a little unsettling. He has a total vibe of knowing way too much about everyone."

It suddenly occurred to Clearsight to wonder why Darkstalker hadn't been in the seer training class. *Maybe he was smarter than me, and met Allknowing first, and realized that she's terrible, so he's still pretending he hasn't found the class yet. Or he doesn't want anyone to know that he's a good enough seer to have found it already.*

He's been keeping all his powers pretty quiet so far. I wish I couldn't see so many good AND bad reasons for that.

Listener was peering at her curiously. Clearsight had to shut down this line of thought before she revealed too much by accident. She glanced around the classroom. "When do we sit down and start learning?"

Her new friend laughed. "That's not how it works. There are stations all around the classroom and you're allowed to work on whatever interests you. Then we come together for a group discussion before free outdoor time. There's a schedule on the wall over there."

Huh, Clearsight thought. *If I can work on anything I want — that means I could keep doing my timeline scrolls.*

Wait — nope. There was a very uncomfortable trip to Truthfinder's office with her parents in that future. Better stick to what the other dragons were doing.

She did her best to act normal, but as the school night went on, Clearsight found it harder and harder to breathe through the pounding of her heart.

I can't put it off any longer.

I'm meeting him soon. Very soon.

But I'm doing it on my terms.

The teacher released them into the courtyard when the moons were high in the sky, giving them two hours to hunt, play, or practice flying, whatever they chose to do.

Clearsight stopped in the shadow of a tall pine tree, watching the wings that swirled around her. Dragons called out greetings to one another, tossed pinecones, checked their reflections in puddles. A few settled at outdoor tables to study together; others launched races around the upper branches. One dragonet was trying to convince his friend to try something called a pomegranate.

Everyone seemed happy. No one seemed to know that a very momentous thing was about to happen.

But where was Darkstalker?

Maybe he was angry that she'd avoided him that morning; maybe he'd gone off hunting and decided he didn't want to meet her after all.

There was one future where that happened. It wasn't a good one.

"Hey!" a voice shouted from one of the clusters of dragonets. "Watch where you're walking!"

Clearsight saw Whiteout emerge from the group serenely, looking as though she didn't realize someone was yelling at her. Behind her, three frustrated NightWings were scrambling to recover the marbles she'd scattered with her tail.

"Can't you *use* those weird eyes of yours?" one of them barked.

"Or are IceWings blind as well as arrogant and vicious?" another snarled.

And then Darkstalker was there, materializing beside his sister as though the shadows had unfolded him.

"That was a little rude, don't you think?" he said to the three marble players.

They shuffled their feet nervously. "She ruined our game!" the biggest one blurted.

"What a disaster," Darkstalker said. "No wonder you had to resort to name-calling and bigotry."

Bewildered silence. Blinking.

Darkstalker put one wing around his sister's shoulders. "Whiteout, these dragons are upset because you knocked over their marbles when you walked through here."

"Oh," she said. "I thought the marbles represented chaos theory and I was just another unpredictable whim of the universe." Darkstalker gave her a look and she smiled sweetly at the three dragons. "I did not intend to disrupt your faith in controllable outcomes."

"That's all right," said the biggest one gruffly. "Sorry we yelled at you."

"Yeah," said the other two. "Sorry."

"Did you?" said Whiteout. "Yell at me?"

"Don't worry about it," said Darkstalker with a smile. He pointed to each of the players in turn. "*She* was cheating anyway, all *he* can think about is his crush on her sister, and *he* is thoroughly sick of both of them and wishes he knew anyone interesting. Have fun with your marbles, friends."

He turned and escorted Whiteout away, leaving the three dragons glaring at one another.

Clearsight waited until they were passing her tree, then stepped into his path with her eyebrows raised. Whiteout went around her and kept going, but Darkstalker stopped with the most wonderful expression of delight, anxiety, and triumph she'd ever seen.

"Very impressive," she said.

"What?" He gave her a charming grin. "What'd I do?"

"I don't know how you engineered it," she said, "but, wow, you covered everything, didn't you? Courage, check. Cares about his sister, check. Defending the vulnerable, standing up to bullies, making sure everyone apologizes neatly. With a little demonstration of power to show off your intelligence at the end, too. Did you pay those guys? Because that was just perfect."

"Do I know you?" he asked.

She laughed despite herself, although she was fiercely trying not to. He just looked so *wounded* and so *mischievous* at the same time.

"Oh, wait," he said. "Did we meet on that fishing trip last month? No, hang on, I'll remember. Aha! You're on the queen's Council of Ancient Elders, is that it?"

"You goober," she said, wrinkling her snout at him.

"*You're* the one taking all the romance out of this," he said. "It's *supposed* to go, 'that was so brave, how you stood up for your sister like that!' 'Oh, that, what, no, it's what any dragon would do.' 'No, no — you're special. I can tell.' 'Not as special as *you*. There's a magic about you that I've never found in any other dragon!' 'Why — why do I feel as though

I've known you forever?' 'Because you have . . . and you will.' Fireworks! True love and happiness for the rest of our lives!"

"You didn't prepare actual fireworks, did you?" she asked.

"N-nooooo," he said. "Not if you . . . hate fireworks?"

"Hmm," she said, squinting. "I see a terrible fire ravaging the school gardens . . ."

"You do?" he said, sounding a little panicked. "When? Now? I — wait a second, you're making that up."

She giggled. "Has anyone ever told you that you are a *terrible* seer?" she asked. "That whole fluttery drippy conversation sounded nothing like me."

"That's a relief," he said with an even bigger grin. "But couldn't we let this be a *tiny* bit more romantic? I mean, it's not every day that I meet my soulmate. Just this once, in fact. Right now."

Now, Clearsight thought. *It's true. It's happening right now, the beginning of everything.*

What was this pounding in her chest? Joy, love, terror? She wanted to wrap her wings around him and never let go, and she also kind of wanted to set him on fire. She definitely wanted to fly away as fast as her wings would carry her, but she also wanted to keep having this conversation as long as dragonly possible; for the rest of eternity would be fine.

She'd seen *what* might happen, but she'd never realized what it would *feel* like.

Darkstalker suddenly leaned forward and took her front talons in his.

"Don't worry about the future," he whispered intently. "Just be here, with me, in this moment, when we are both as happy as we've ever been in our whole lives so far."

She wanted to, she would have, but as their claws touched, she was suddenly spun into a hurricane of visions so brutal she thought her head would split open.

Darkstalker, older, in the twisted crown, killing dragons from across the room with a flick of his claw.

Darkstalker, close to the age he was now, holding out a scroll to her with a hopeful smile.

A SeaWing screaming in pain.

Her and Darkstalker, older again, wrestling with their six little dragonets in a noisy sprawling cliff house of their own.

Darkstalker, collapsing in front of her as thunder rumbled.

IceWing blood everywhere.

A gift of sapphires.

Sunset over a valley as she walked creakily on her ancient talons to rest beside him, on their porch, at peace.

Opening the royal treasure room to bestow gifts on their grandchildren.

Five NightWings writhing before the throne, screaming as they clawed out their own eyes.

Betrayal woven into copper wires.

A trip to the sea.

A green dragon in tears.

She spiraled finally back into herself and blinked, there

again, back in the present. Where none of the terrible or wonderful things had happened yet.

"Are you all right?" he asked.

"You didn't see all that?" She gently pulled her talons out of his grasp.

"I will never invade your thoughts," he said. "I promise. I'll stay out of your mind, always."

That's true . . . in some futures. Not all of them.

"Thank you," she said.

"It's not that bad, is it?" he asked, tilting his head. "Our future? I've seen mostly good things."

"No, it's great," she said, "depending on how much you like the average apocalypse."

He laughed, which confirmed that at least for now he was staying out of her head — because she hadn't been joking.

With another charming grin, he said, "I'm Darkstalker, by the way."

"Oh, I'm Tailbite," she said. "You weren't expecting someone else, were you?"

He laughed and laughed and laughed, and in the sunlight of that laugh, she could almost stay in the present — in the moment of soulmates meeting, in the moment of falling in love.

She could almost forget the violence, the lies, the danger . . . the blood and betrayal yet to come.

CHAPTER 10

DARKSTALKER

The weather was perfect: rain poured from a grumbling, fire-breathing sky. The rivers at the bottom of the canyons swelled and roared and ate the walls, sending all the dragons who lived down there scrambling for higher ground. The wind was so fierce that it seemed to have been sent by vengeful IceWings to rip every NightWing out of the sky. It was veering quickly from a storm into a baby hurricane.

Darkstalker had been waiting for a day like this. Surely even Clearsight wouldn't expect him *today*.

But as he swooped down to the ledge in front of her house, there she was, sitting out in the rain, waiting for him. He hadn't quite figured out all her expressions yet, but he thought this one might be her trying-not-to-laugh-at-him face.

"Surprise!" he shouted, thumping down beside her.

"Why are you crazy?" she said, raising her voice over the thunder. "Go home!"

"And be trapped indoors with my squabbling parents all day?" he said. "No thanks! Let's go to the sea!"

"The sea will eat us alive if we go there today," she protested.

"I didn't say *in* the sea." He shook his wings, accomplishing nothing because he was still getting drenched. "I said *to* the sea."

"I'm not a dragon who goes flying in hurricanes!" she said. "Do you know how unpredictable they are? The smallest wind shift or one piece of debris spinning in the wrong direction, and suddenly you're in a whole other timeline — or everyone else is, because you're dead."

"It is *virtually impossible* for us to die today," said Darkstalker. "It would be a waste of lots of very melodramatic prophecies if we did. Why are you even arguing about this? You know that we go and it's wonderful."

"On the contrary," she said. "I see this really awesome future where I go back inside and drink tea by the fire and read a scroll about funny scavenger antics for the rest of the day and also, by the way, stay completely dry. That one is definitely winning right now." She saw the expression on his face and relented a little. "We could go tomorrow, when the sun will be shining."

"But then there will be dragons everywhere," he said. "Today the beach is all ours!"

Clearsight gave a little shiver, and although he was trying not to listen, something fluttered through her mind: a whisper, an echo, his own voice shouting, *"It's all ours! The whole kingdom is ours!"*

He rested his wing against hers, dripping scales sliding across one another. "Come back," he said softly. "Be here now."

She took a deep breath and looked into his eyes. "I am," she said. "I'm here. All right, fine, let's go drown there before we drown here." She glanced back at the door and he wondered if she was trying to get out of there so he wouldn't meet her parents. He was occasionally hurt by that idea, but then, he didn't want her to meet his parents either. He didn't want his father's scornful eyes anywhere near this one happy thing in his life.

They dove into the storm, battered by raindrops as big as oranges and wind that howled as though kingdoms were falling under its claws. Clearsight was not the best flier, which perhaps he should have thought about, but she didn't complain, even in her mind. He let himself sneak into her thoughts a little bit while they flew, since they couldn't keep up a conversation through the rain anyway.

Tick tick tick tick flip flip flip flip. Her brain never stopped. She was constantly running scenarios, tracing paths forward into different futures. Darkstalker had thought he was pretty good at this himself — he could see not just the most plausible future, but a few alternates where things were different. But she had thousands of strands gathered in her mind, weaving and interweaving and knotting and tangling.

He regretted promising to stay out; it was fascinating in there.

It also meant she could easily skip him onto a timeline he hadn't seen coming. She changed one small thing, and their entire meeting was different. She twitched the future like a long tail, keeping him off balance. It was fun. Maybe it wouldn't always be fun, but it was for now.

More than all that: she *knew* him. She knew he wasn't just a hybrid mistake with loud, fighting parents and a strange sister. She knew he was hers; she knew he was gifted beyond any other dragon in the world; and she knew he was going to do such amazing things that he changed the face of Pyrrhia forever.

Not that she was impressed by any of that. But he kind of liked that about her, too. He'd have enough worshippers, one day.

They reached the edge of the cliffs and suddenly soared into empty space; the land dropped away sharply below them, veering down to a long rocky beach. Which, at present, was being pounded by waves taller than they were.

"Looks fun down there!" Clearsight shouted to Darkstalker.

"All right, yes," he shouted back. "This isn't quite what I was picturing."

She smiled and flickered away, soaring south along the coastline. He followed her, battling to keep his wings straight as the wind kept trying to knock him into the cliffs on his right.

Just as he was starting to wonder if she was punishing him by keeping them out in this weather, she dipped one of her wings and soared down toward the beach. He realized she was aiming for an enormous cave mouth that faced the ocean. Normally it might have had several feet of beach between the opening and the sea, but today it was flooded up to the front door.

They swooped inside, into a world of emerald green and vaulted ceilings. Phosphorescent moss clung to the rocks and walls and stalactites, giving the cave an eerie glow that was matched by the chandeliers of glowworms up above. Water dripped softly here and there, and a rivulet ran through the cave, connecting some of the tide pools and circumventing others.

The wind shrieked outside, but it could only reach its thin tendrils in to try and grab at them. The farther back they went in the cave, the warmer and quieter it was.

Clearsight landed on a tilted ledge of rock above a tide pool full of elongated starfish and anemones the color of sunrise.

"How did you know about this place?" Darkstalker asked, settling beside her.

She looked at him in confusion, and he saw the shift happening behind her eyes as she overlaid the present and the future and tried to make them fit.

"From the visions," she said. "We came — come — we *will* come here a lot. Maybe." She shook her head. "I thought you brought me here on our first trip to the sea — I mean, today — but if you didn't know about it, then I can't explain it. It's like a loop in the timelines that can't be pulled free." She worried at a piece of algae that was coming off the boulder underneath her.

"Hey," he said, brushing her wing. "It doesn't matter. We're here now, and it's great, that's all that counts."

What if I messed something up? she thought. *What if I jumped ahead and skipped over something important? What if we're not supposed to be here yet, and this changes something?*

Darkstalker came within a heartbeat of answering her before he remembered he wasn't supposed to be reading her mind. He snapped his jaw shut, trying to pull back. It was hard not to just leave his mind open, listening to everything both spoken and unspoken. But he'd practiced blocking out his father enough; he should be able to do the same for the dragon he loved. Was going to love, eventually. Was starting to love, he was pretty sure.

"Can I ask you something nosy?" she said after a moment.

"Ominous," he said with a grin.

"Well, you and Whiteout are the only hybrids I've ever met," she said, "so I have no idea if this is a rude question. Tell me if it is and I'll shut up, all right?"

"You can ask me anything," he said.

"It's just . . . you don't seem like a hybrid," she said. "You look like all the other NightWings. Is any part of you IceWing?"

"Oh," he said. "*That* question. My father asks me that every day, but much less politely, don't worry." He extended his wings fully and pointed. On the inside, along the edge where his wing membranes met his back, a long row of silver-white scales marked the seam on either side of his body. "Ironically," he said, "these are a lot easier to hide from other dragons than the identity of my father."

Clearsight reached out and ran one claw lightly along the ridge of IceWing scales. It tickled, and he bit his tongue trying not to laugh.

"Whoa," she said. "They even feel cold."

"I know," he said. "It's weird." He hesitated. "There's . . . one other thing I inherited from my father. I'm an animus."

"Right," she said. "I know that. Obviously."

Of course she did. "No one else knows that yet," he said.

"No one? You haven't cast any spells?" she said, her eyes wide. "In four years?"

He peeked again and saw a ripple of hope jump across her mind. She was impressed; she trusted him a little more.

"Just one, to make sure I could," he said. "I suspected I was an animus, from my visions of the future and this *sense* I had, but I needed to know. The Ice Kingdom has a test for anyone who might have inherited animus powers — I gave myself sort of a modified version."

"Didn't your father test you?" Clearsight asked.

"He did, but I deliberately failed it," Darkstalker explained. "I didn't want him getting any ideas about controlling me while I was still too young to defend myself. He's suspicious, though. The incessant drumbeat in my house is all about being careful with animus magic." Darkstalker hunched his shoulders and folded his wings back in. "Basically from the moment we could hear, my father has lectured my sister and me about what the magic means, what it can do to us, how we have to be SO careful or absolutely TERRIBLE things will happen." He rolled his eyes.

"But he's right," Clearsight said earnestly. "Can't you —"

"No, *no*," Darkstalker snapped. He knew she didn't like the way he was frowning, but he couldn't stop himself. "Never, never tell me that my father is right about anything. Not if you care about me."

"I do," Clearsight said. "I just . . . I've *seen* those absolutely terrible things, you know."

"In *my* future?" he asked, startled.

"In ours," she answered. "Haven't you?"

"I didn't look carefully much further than meeting you," he confessed. "I knew that now was when everything would start to get better. That I'd be . . . well, I'd be happy, finally." He grinned sheepishly at her.

Clearsight twined her tail with his and leaned into his shoulder. "This version of you is the sweetest," she said.

"I think it's worth noting," he said, "that this is actually the *only* existing version of me."

She was quiet, but the *tick tick tick* of her brain was almost too loud for him to avoid hearing.

"I'm not reading your mind," he said, "but I can tell that you're thinking I'll only stay this way if I don't use my animus magic."

"I don't want to scare you," she said. "If you haven't seen those futures — the ones where you use it too much, where you start killing other dragons, where you steal the throne to become king . . . well, that's probably better. If you haven't seen them, then they mustn't be very likely, right?"

It was his turn to be quiet.

He had maybe, sort of, kind of maybe glimpsed a future where he was king of the NightWings.

But it was an *awesome* future. He was a *great* king. He would make the NightWings the most powerful tribe in Pyrrhia, and all his decisions would make them stronger and safer. Even if the path to get there was a little dark . . . once they *were* there even Clearsight would have to admit it was totally worth it. Better for everyone. The best possible future.

It wasn't the most likely future, not yet. But he sometimes thought it should be.

She wouldn't love hearing that, though. She had to be steered carefully into that timeline, until she could see how perfect it was.

"I've had visions here and there of the distant future," he said with a shrug. "But you of all dragons must know that it's nearly impossible to predict events that are too far in the future. Little changes now can cause such big changes later that it's almost not even worth it to look that far ahead, right?"

From the tension in her wings, he guessed this wasn't the answer she was looking for.

"Hey," he said, ducking his head to meet her eyes. "Don't be mad at me for things I *might* do one day, all right? I'm not evil now. I haven't done any of that. And I probably won't. Will you focus on that, please? Stay in the present with me?"

"Yes," she said, dropping her wings. She stepped away from him and shook them out, as if her visions were clumps of mud stuck between her scales. "I know. I'll try." She gave him a wry smile. "Sorry. We're going to have this argument a lot."

Well, that sounds fun. If you know that already, he thought, *then can't we* not?

"So what was it?" she asked. "The one spell you've cast?"

With an effort, he made himself grin at her again. "If I tell you, you're going to make fun of me."

"Ooo, even better," she said, perking up. "Tell me!" She poked his chest with her tail. "Tell me!"

"It was just — this toy of Whiteout's," he said. "It's a little carved scavenger. She loves it in kind of an obsessive way. Once it got lost and she cried for a whole day, until we finally found it again. So after that, I enchanted it to always return to her. No matter where I hide it, or where she loses it, it always turns up on her pillow by that night." He shrugged. "It's just a little thing."

"Awwwwwwwwww," she said. "You are working the sympathy vote so hard right now."

"I am what I am," he said, spreading his wings again. "I can't help my noble heart and generous nature."

"We might be able to do something about the size of that head, though," she said, laughing.

"What, this perfect specimen?" he asked with mock incredulity.

Her ears flicked up suddenly. "Shh," she whispered. "Did you hear that?"

They both fell silent, and against the backdrop of water dripping and the distant roar of the storm, Darkstalker heard a strange, muffled sound. He swiveled his head around. Toward the back of the cave, toward the long shadows.

Clearsight twined her tail around his again and he felt the tension prickling through both of them.

*Is someone in here? Or . . . some*thing?

The sound came again — a low moan just weak enough to perhaps be the wind, but with something unmistakably dragon about it.

Darkstalker hopped off the ledge and stepped cautiously into the dark. Clearsight was close behind him, which was reassuring, because presumably if they were going to be mauled by something in this cave, she would have seen that coming.

With their night vision, they could see that something large and lumpy was lying in the last tide pool, where the rivulet ended. Darkstalker glanced at Clearsight, then let out a small burst of flame to give them more light.

It was a dragon, but in that moment of brightness they could see it was not a NightWing. Its scales were blue.

The dragon made another mournful noise and slowly, painfully, flopped its head around to look at them.

"NightWings," it hissed softly.

"Are you hurt?" Clearsight asked. She circled the blue dragon cautiously. "Oh, there's a gash on this side . . . but it doesn't look too awful."

"It's something else," Darkstalker said, scanning the SeaWing's mind. "He's exhausted. He's been swimming for days. I see blood and screaming and — tentacles?"

The SeaWing shuddered and tried to sit up.

"Don't make it worse," Clearsight said, nudging him back into the water. "Just rest. Can you tell us what happened?"

"Albatross," the dragon whispered.

Darkstalker froze. He'd heard that name before. In his father's mind, in a secret compartment where Arctic sometimes turned over the names of the other known animus dragons in Pyrrhia. Queen Diamond, Arctic's mother. Jerboa, a SandWing who had vanished from the SandWing court years ago and was now either a fugitive or dead. And Albatross, brother to the queen of the SeaWings.

If there were any others, they were just rumors. Those three were the ones Arctic worried about.

"You were attacked by an albatross?" Clearsight said skeptically. "With . . . tentacles?"

"Albatross is Queen Lagoon's brother," Darkstalker told her.

"Oh," Clearsight said. Her eyes clouded over, and he saw her knitting together all the things she knew and would know about the SeaWings. "Oh no . . ."

"He went mad," the SeaWing whispered hoarsely. "He attacked us. He killed . . . everyone. My brother, my father. I barely escaped with my life. I swam and kept swimming . . ."

"Everyone?" Clearsight echoed. Her thoughts were so loud and tangled with grief that Darkstalker couldn't avoid hearing them (or so he told himself). *The whole tribe? Or the whole royal family? What about Fathom? Is he dead, is everything wrong now?* She shook her head, brushing away tears. *No, I see the timelines still; he can't be dead. He* can't *be.*

Darkstalker felt a rush of jealousy. He had seen the SeaWing in their future, too: a timid, jittery green dragon, sad and lonely. A friend one day, perhaps, but certainly no one to be so devastated about if he didn't make it. A peripheral character in their great love story. So why was Clearsight so upset? Was this someone he had to worry about?

"I don't know if anyone is left alive." The SeaWing stared at Clearsight with haunted blue eyes. "Albatross killed the queen. I saw it. He killed two SkyWings and the princess and the king and my —" He choked on the words, letting out a sob. "He was still killing when I fled into the ocean. But I don't know *why*. He was our prince. We loved him. He was loyal to the queen. He made such beautiful magic for her. Why would he do this?"

Clearsight lifted her eyes to meet Darkstalker's.

"He was an animus," Darkstalker whispered. She nodded, knowing that already.

"I think I know why he did it," she said softly to the SeaWing. "He did a lot of magic for the queen, didn't he? He wasn't careful with his soul at all."

She shot Darkstalker a "what did I tell you?" look. He didn't love it.

"Weren't you listening to me?" Darkstalker said, lashing his tail. "Look at *me*, Clearsight, the way I am *now*. I'm not whoever you're seeing in your visions. I *am* careful."

The SeaWing lunged out of the water and seized Clearsight's talons. "Maybe it was another tribe. Maybe they put a spell on Albatross — that could happen, couldn't it?

The IceWings have magic, too; maybe they were trying to wipe us out. Or maybe the RainWings drugged him. They have all kinds of plants that do weird things in the jungle, that's what I've heard. That makes sense, doesn't it? It must have been someone else using him. It wasn't Albatross at all."

Clearsight guided him back into the pool. "We're going to get you help," she said. "Queen Vigilance will want to hear about this. She'll make sure you're taken care of in exchange for your story. Just . . . wait here."

The SeaWing slumped forward, letting the water cover his snout. He took a deep breath, gills fluttering, and closed his eyes again.

"How are we going to get a message to the queen?" Clearsight whispered to Darkstalker, edging around the tide pool and back toward the cave entrance.

He growled under his breath. "We'll have to tell my father. He has her ear — he can tell her about this dragon and what's happened in the Kingdom of the Sea."

She hesitated in front of a wall of glowing moss, her wings spread so she looked silhouetted. "Is this a good idea?" she said. "Queen Vigilance wouldn't attack the SeaWings while they're in trouble, would she?" She wrinkled her forehead, not waiting for his answer; she was already a hundred days away, a thousand, studying all the possible outcomes.

"She'll start with a messenger or a spy," Darkstalker said. He could at least pretend that Clearsight really wanted to know what he thought. "To find out for sure what happened. It wouldn't make sense for her to attack, though. The

Kingdom of the Sea isn't geographically useful for us to invade."

He couldn't imagine the trip the surviving SeaWing had made — all the way around the bottom of the continent, past the rainforest? Or through the middle of the continent, along the rivers?

"Besides," he added, "she's busy enough with the IceWing war. She'll know we don't need another front or another enemy to deal with."

Clearsight looked at him as if she were slowly returning to earth. "I don't see any NightWing-SeaWing battles ahead," she said. "I think it's safe to tell her."

"That's what I said," he pointed out.

"And we should find out what really happened," she said. "The more we know about animus magic . . . the safer we'll all be, right?"

"I know a lot about it," he said. "IceWings have had it longer than any other tribe. Trust me, I hear about it every day."

"So why aren't you scared?" she asked. "Wasn't it his animus power that drove Albatross insane? Isn't that why he killed all those dragons? Aren't you afraid that — that —"

"That that could be me one day?" he said. "No, Clearsight, I'm *not* worried that that will happen to me. If there's any animus you should be worried about, it's my father."

Could Arctic lose his mind the way Albatross had? Those rotten patches inside him — those came from using his magic, didn't they? Darkstalker didn't know the whole story, but he did know that Arctic had done *something* with his animus power to escape the Ice Kingdom safely with Foeslayer. How many times had he used it? How big were his spells?

How much of his soul did he have left to lose?

Darkstalker was not the dangerous dragon in this tribe. It was Arctic; he had no doubt.

But how was he going to convince Clearsight? He needed a way to make her believe in him — to stop being so afraid of what he *might* be one day. He needed her to see that he was different from all the other animus dragons . . . that he was *nothing* like his father.

Something chimed in his mind, like the bell that rang quietly to signal the end of library time at school.

He *was* different. He was smarter. And he could prove it.

He knew what he had to do.

CHAPTER 11

FATHOM

The Kingdom of the Sea was in shock.

Queen Lagoon and her husband, Humpback, were dead, as was their daughter, Splash. Current was missing — one of the dozens who had escaped into the sea — but his brother, Scallop, and his father, Fathom's uncle Eel, were not so lucky. One of the musicians had tried to fight Albatross when everyone fled; she was dead, too. Fathom would have to find out her name later.

Fathom's parents were both dead. Manta had followed her father into the gardens, pleading for Fathom's life, and he had killed her and Reef together. Not even Fathom's magic could bring them back from death.

But as he'd stood with Indigo in the wreckage of the party, heartbroken, a dragon had crawled out from under one of the tipped-over couches.

It was Pearl, bleeding from a thousand cuts, but alive.

"I sliced myself up with the glass from the aquarium," she told Fathom, her voice shaking, her injured wings hanging awkwardly. "I covered myself in blood and pretended to be dead. He walked right past me."

She was the only dragon left to rule the kingdom, other than their mad aunt, Sapphire. Five years old and the new queen.

Of the two SkyWings, Princess Sunset had died, but Eagle, miraculously, had survived. He survived to berate them all about the dangers of animus dragons. He survived to threaten revenge and war and the extermination of the SeaWing tribe. And he survived to take a message back to the SkyWing queen that the disputed shore villages would be abandoned immediately.

Queen Pearl promised that SeaWings would never encroach into Sky territory again, in exchange for amnesty for Sunset's death. She also promised them tributes of gems and seafood for the next five years, in exchange for keeping the massacre a secret. The last thing the SeaWings needed right now was for anyone to find out how vulnerable they were.

On her first day as queen, Pearl issued one edict. It outlawed animus magic anywhere in the Kingdom of the Sea.

Fathom stood beside her in the throne room as she signed the proclamation, and he thought perhaps he was the only one who noticed how wobbly her handwriting still was.

After the messenger left to announce the edict, Pearl sent away everyone but Fathom.

"How did you kill him?" she asked when they were alone.

"It was Indigo," he said. "She got him with a spear. She saved me. Us." He looked away. "Some of us."

He'd have to get Indigo to match his story later. He knew she would do that for him, even if she didn't understand why.

He didn't want anyone to know he'd killed his grandfather. He didn't want to be seen as a hero — especially not for that. He wasn't a hero at all, not even close.

"I know the edict is about me," he said. "You don't have to worry. I'm not like him."

"You think that now," Pearl said sadly. "But maybe the SkyWings are right about what to do with animus dragons."

Fathom felt a shiver through his bones. Had he survived his grandfather's massacre only to have his own sister put him to death?

"I mean, how am I supposed to trust you, Fathom?" Pearl asked. "Whenever I look at you, I see everything he did. Won't you always be tempted to use your magic? What would stop you? What could ever stop you?"

"*I* will," he promised, bowing his head. "The soul that I still have, and wish to keep. Queen Pearl of the SeaWings, I pledge you this oath, on my life and sealed with my blood: I will never use my animus magic again, not for the rest of my days."

He took a sword from the wall and drew an *X* in blood across his palm. It hurt so much, a bright sharp pain that was easier to bear than the hollow one inside him. He looked at the cuts all over Pearl and was tempted to do the same to himself.

"All right," Pearl said. "I accept your oath. But there's one other thing."

"Anything," said Fathom.

"You can never have dragonets," she said. "If this power runs in your veins, you could pass it down. But if you have no dragonets, it may die with you, and all of Pyrrhia will be safer for it."

Fathom was quiet for a moment. Was she picturing animus nieces challenging her for the throne? He wanted to tell her that if he could pass it down, he thought perhaps so could she. But it wasn't an option for her to avoid having dragonets; the kingdom needed heirs, especially now, with most of the royal family dead.

"I agree," he said. He never wanted dragonets anyway. What kind of father could he ever be?

"Fathom," Pearl warned. "That means you have to stay away from Indigo."

"What?" he cried, his heart twisting painfully. "But why?"

"Because you're in love with her," Pearl said bluntly, "and you'll do anything, break any rule for her. Maybe even your oath to me."

"I . . . no, I . . ." Fathom trailed off. Pearl was worried about the wrong oath, but she was right about one thing: if Indigo were ever hurt like that again, he knew he would still use his magic to save her, no matter what he had promised.

"Besides, it's not fair to her," Pearl said, uncoiling from the throne. "She's my friend, too, and I want her to have a happy life. Don't you? Think about it. What could she ever have with you? No dragonets, no future, nothing but constant danger. Do you want that for her?"

Fathom shrank into his wings. Was it selfish of him to want to keep Indigo's friendship? And how could he make a decision like this without talking to her? It was *her* life. She'd be furious if she found out he was choosing her future without telling her.

But maybe furious was good. Maybe furious would keep her away from him.

"Shouldn't I ask her what she wants?" he tried. "Or at least explain —"

"I'll do it," Pearl said, cutting him off. "She'll tell you anything you want to hear, but she'll tell me the truth. Don't worry, Fathom, I'll take care of her. I'll make her part of my honor guard, promote her up the ranks quickly. In a few years, I'll find her a minor noble she can have a family with. She'll have a safe, normal life."

Far away from me, Fathom thought miserably. *With someone else.*

But Pearl was right: that was how it had to be.

He knew the truth about himself now. He was not special. He was someone who ran and hid while his whole family was massacred, when he was the only one who could have stopped it.

He should have stopped it sooner. He might have been able to save his parents if he'd been faster, braver, more sure of his power. More sure that his grandfather needed to die.

Losing his magic and his chance to have dragonets . . . and worst of all, Indigo, the love of his life . . . that was exactly what he deserved.

CHAPTER 12

CLEARSIGHT

"Here comes your stalker," said Listener with a sniff.

"Don't be mean," Clearsight said. She could see Darkstalker, too, winding his way across the atrium toward them, and her heart gave a little happy jump. It was the end of the school night, the sun was coming up, and the grounds were busy with dragons coming and going. A few of them stopped Darkstalker, joking and exchanging stories, but his eyes kept stealing back to hers, and in his smile she saw that he was as thrilled to see her as she was to see him.

"I'm just saying." Listener tossed her head. "You could do better. There are at least two dragons in our classroom who think about you all the time."

"Stop," Clearsight said, bumping her side. "If you won't let me use my power to help you find someone, then you can't use yours for me, either."

"That's different," Listener argued. "And I think it's weird that I can't read Darkstalker's mind. How is he blocking me? I thought that was a skill nobody learned until they were at least seven."

"If he doesn't want you to read his mind, you should probably respect that," Clearsight observed. "He stays out of *my* head."

"No, he *tells* you he's staying out of your head," Listener said. "You have no way to know whether he really is."

That was true. Clearsight had to admit — to herself, not to her friend — that she'd worried about this. Sometimes he really seemed to know what she was thinking . . . but wasn't that because he understood her so well? If he were reading her thoughts, he'd know how afraid she was all the time . . . and then how could he still love her?

She knew what her line here should be; Listener was waiting for Clearsight to say, "I trust him," like any dragon would. But Clearsight couldn't quite say that yet, not even to reassure her friend.

"What about you?" she asked instead. "Where's the new dragon you're stalking?"

"Shh!" Listener cried, whacking Clearsight with her tail. "He's over there," she added in a stage whisper.

The dragon she flicked her tail at was half a courtyard away, joking with a pair of friends. He was tall and elegantly handsome, with the aloof expression that Listener always seemed to fall for.

"Don't tell me anything!" Listener said quickly. "Don't even look ahead! We're totally destined for each other, so don't you dare tell me we're not!"

"Really?" Clearsight said, trying not to see the futures

where this dragon cheated on Listener and then dumped her. Oooh, she hated him already. "But — what if —"

"No!" Listener covered her ears and closed her eyes. "I want to live my life like a normal dragon! LA LA LA LA LA."

"Oh, Listener," Clearsight said with a sigh. "All right."

"I'm leaving now," Listener said without opening her eyes. "Before you make a face I don't want to see and I have to get super mad at you. Don't talk to me until you get your face under control!" She leaped into the sky, bumped into a tree, got tangled in the branches for a minute, and finally flew away, trying to look dignified.

"What was that about?" Darkstalker asked, materializing at her side. He often managed to time his arrival to Listener's departure, but Clearsight tried not to worry about why they didn't like each other. He tucked one wing around her and she leaned into him with a sigh. A green vine with heart-shaped leaves trailed over their shoulders.

"She's falling for the wrong guy again," she said. "But she won't let me stop her."

"Ah," he said. "Listener's weird insistence on a prophecy-free life."

"Right," she said. He smelled like cinnamon and roasted sugar cane, remnants of his after-school cooking class.

He made a "hmmm" noise, and she glanced up at his face. Darkstalker was trying to look serious, but his eyes were sparkling.

"What?" she said. "Wow, you are dying to tell me something."

"I am," he burst out. "I have something to show you. Can you come over? Right now?"

"But — your parents . . ." she said. Everything she knew about Foeslayer and Arctic made her fairly completely terrified of them. Both from her visions and from the rumors that blew around the tribe.

"Mother is on guard duty at the border, and Father is at the palace," he said. "Helping interrogate the SeaWing we found yesterday, probably. They won't be home for ages. Please? It's pretty genius. You'll love it. Don't look ahead!" He poked her snout. "Let it be a surprise."

She already had half a guess what the surprise might be. Still, she could avoid peering at the nearest branching paths for now, for him.

"Sure," she said. "As long as there are also snacks."

Clearsight wondered if she was just imagining the murmurs behind them as she left with Darkstalker. Nobody at school knew quite yet how important the two of them were — how could they, unless they could see all the futures like she did? But it still felt as if they got more looks than other couples, and more whispers followed them when they walked the halls together.

Maybe the extra attention was because of Darkstalker's notorious parents. Most dragons wouldn't say out loud that the war with the IceWings was Foeslayer and Arctic's fault, but everyone pretty much believed that it was.

Beside her in the sky, Darkstalker made an odd dismissive gesture with one of his wings.

"What was that?" she asked.

"Oh, nothing," he said. "Just a thought."

My thought? she wondered. *Was he listening to me?*

"Look," he said, pointing at the palace. "Queen Vigilance has a new prisoner on display."

Is he trying to distract me?

She twisted to look at the top spire of the palace, where the queen had set up a cage for special prisoners. Someone with glittering white scales hunched behind the bars, curled away from the heat of the sun.

"That must be awful," said Darkstalker. "Being that miserable with all your enemies staring at you."

"Maybe they'll do another exchange," Clearsight said. She was so glad her mild-mannered parents weren't part of the queen's army. They were safe in their quiet, low-level jobs.

Darkstalker's home was closer to the school than hers was, and much higher up the side of the canyon. He looked a little embarrassed as they swooped down toward it.

"We moved up here when my father accepted his position at the palace," he explained. "On the plus side, it's bigger with nicer views; on the minus side, we're closer to my grandmother, who hates all of us. But at least we have a brand-new set of nosy neighbors."

He waved pointedly at the snout poking out of a window below his and whoever it was withdrew in a hurry.

"Our last neighbors had terrible luck with their window boxes," he said with a little too much glee. "Turnips kept growing in them instead of chrysanthemums or tomatoes or pear trees. It was SO mysterious."

"You didn't!" she said.

"They deserved it," he said as they landed outside his front door. "I haven't decided what I'm going to do to these ones yet."

She shot a worried look at his back, but his excitement had taken over again and he didn't notice. His claws unlocked the pale blue door and they slipped inside, into a sunlit room decorated with white rugs and glittering crystals. Clearsight wondered if Arctic had chosen the décor, or if Foeslayer had been trying to evoke the Ice Kingdom for him.

It was a lot bigger than her home; she'd never been in a place this big before apart from school and the library. One entire wall was lined with scrolls tucked into little niches, and the impossibly clean kitchen had contraptions in it that she'd never seen and couldn't imagine how to use. Her father's idea of cooking was to set a fish on fire and then swallow a whole lemon with it.

There was a painting over the fireplace of the family together: Darkstalker on one side, Arctic on the other, with Foeslayer and Whiteout between them. The whole painting was done in shades of blue, from a dark midnight blue for Darkstalker's scales to an iridescently pale blue for Arctic's. It was an interesting effect that made them all look more related than they did in real life. They also all looked peculiarly kind around the eyes and mouth, more than most dragons ever did — and, Clearsight was fairly certain, more than Arctic could possibly really look.

"Whiteout painted that," Darkstalker said, noticing the direction of her gaze. "It's from what I call her *Wishful Thinking* series." He pointed to a room down a short hallway, and when Clearsight peeked into it she saw that it contained several paintings of IceWings and NightWings flying together, all in the same shades of blue as the portrait. Whiteout's bedroom was like a miniature alternate universe of peaceful interaction between two tribes who in reality hated each other.

There were also a few paintings of the three moons and different starscapes behind them, different constellations scattered across the skies. Clearsight wanted to go in and study them more closely, but Darkstalker was dancing around behind her, grinning his head off and nearly stepping on her tail.

"Great kingdoms, calm down," Clearsight said, nudging him sideways. "Did you eat a kangaroo for breakfast or what?"

"Come see, come see." Darkstalker darted down the hall to the room at the end and unlocked it. Clearsight glanced at the lock as she followed him in. She had never once thought of trying to put a lock on her bedroom door. She could just imagine how startled her parents would be at the idea. They never snooped in her scrolls, and she wouldn't expect them to understand her notes about the future even if they did see them.

On the surface, Darkstalker's room didn't look like a place

full of secrets. His sleeping corner was marked by a pile of neatly folded blankets, purple and white. The desk held nothing but three little inkwells (black, royal blue, emerald green) and a cloth for wiping the ink off his claws. A rack of scrolls beside it was neatly labeled, and each scroll was either a school-approved text or the kind of scroll every young NightWing owned — *Geography of Pyrrhia; Myths of the Lost Continent; Ten Little Scavengers (Recipes Included!); Goodnight, Moons.*

There was a locked trunk at the foot of the blankets, but instead of opening it, Darkstalker went straight to his scroll rack and slid it to the side. He stuck his claws into the gap around one of the wall stones and slowly worked it out, revealing a hidden hole containing a square of paper and a black leather case.

"This," he said, taking a scroll out of the black case. He turned to her, his face aglow with hope, and one of her visions clicked gently into place.

"What's the other piece of paper?" she asked.

"Oh — that's a drawing of you," he said shyly. "I drew it before we met, from my visions, so it's not very good. I didn't want my father to see it or know about you . . . but I needed to have it, to look at. You know, to remind myself that things were going to get better."

She felt a twist of guilt in her chest. She'd put off their meeting for years, afraid of what it would mean, while he had waited patiently for her. He'd always had faith that one day they would be happy together.

Why can't I just be happy like he is? Why can't I trust this?

"So," she said lightly, taking the scroll from him and unrolling it. She could see right away that it was blank. "Hmmm. You've decided to become a writer?"

"Can you sense it?" he asked. He touched the edge of the scroll. "Can you guess what it is?"

It was so light in her talons. It didn't feel like anything much. Not like something that could change the whole future.

She could guess, but she knew he didn't really want her to. "Tell me," she said.

"I took all my animus power," he said, "and I put it in here."

She blinked at him. "All — all of it?"

"It's not in me anymore," he said. "Now it's like I'm not an animus at all, so my soul is safe. Everyone's safe. Watch." He picked up one of his inkwells. "Inkwell, I command you to fly up and touch the ceiling."

A little shiver of fear ran through Clearsight's wings — but the inkwell didn't move. It sat innocently on Darkstalker's palm, thoroughly uninterested in flying anywhere.

"You gave away your power?" she said, genuinely astonished.

"But we can still use it — it's just somewhere else, instead of in me." He took the scroll from her talons and unrolled the beginning of it, setting the inkwell down gently to hold it in place. He dipped the tip of his claw into the green ink and wrote on the scroll, *Enchant this inkwell to fly up, touch the ceiling once, and fly back into my talons without spilling a drop, then return to normal.*

As he reached the end of the sentence, the inkwell floated up into the air, rising all the way to the stones overhead. It tapped against them once, lightly, and then drifted back down to land between Darkstalker's claws.

"By all the stars," Clearsight whispered.

"Do you see what this means?" he asked, a little anxiously. "I've found a way to use my animus power without losing my soul or turning evil or anything terrible happening. We can cast as many spells as we want with this scroll. But because it's all separate from me now, it won't affect my soul. I'll always be me." He touched the scroll with one claw and studied her face. "Do you like it?"

"Can I look?" Clearsight asked him.

He nodded, understanding what she meant. She closed her eyes and saw the spiraling paths. Yes, she'd seen visions of this scroll before. In some futures, he'd come up with it himself. Sometimes she'd suggested it and he'd agreed, with varying degrees of defensiveness. But in more than half those paths, the scroll had been made to imitate his power, not contain it.

Although she knew it was possible, that it happened in some timelines, she had never expected Darkstalker to completely remove his animus power from his own talons.

And it *did* change the future — so many futures. The paths to happiness and peace were suddenly brighter, shining with possibility. The darkest paths faded back. The timelines where his power consumed him were almost gone.

He might still launch a coup to steal the throne; he might still be a danger to dragons she cared about.

But right now, the Darkstalker in front of her had made an enormous sacrifice to make everyone safer. And to make her *feel* safer.

He must have looked at the futures, too. He must have seen that the other versions of the scroll wouldn't be enough — that this was the right thing to do.

That this was the only thing he could have done to make her fully trust him.

She opened her eyes and looked at him. His hopeful face, his emerald-ink-stained claws, his midnight-black wings that were shaking just a little bit.

This is Darkstalker before he's done anything terrible. This is the best version of him. The one who is safe to love.

He gave up all his power for me.

She threw her wings around him and hugged him so fiercely they both fell back onto his blankets.

"I guess that means it works," he said with a laugh, hugging her back.

"I can't believe you really did this," she said, sitting up and picking up the scroll again. "What happens if the scroll gets destroyed? Is your magic gone forever?"

"No, then it comes back to me," he said. "But then I'd make another scroll, don't worry."

"What if someone steals it?" she asked.

He frowned. "Then they can use it the same way I could." He sat up, too, wrinkling his snout at the scroll. "I should have enchanted it so only I can use it. That was stupid of me.

If anyone else gets their claws on it — that would be pretty terrible. Maybe I should destroy it and start again."

"No," she said, intercepting his reaching talon. "Then you'd have to use your magic again, and that's more damage to your soul. We'll just be really, really careful with it. Don't let anyone else know you have it, and I promise I'll keep it a secret, too."

"That was my plan anyway," he said. He still looked worried.

"This is a good thing," she said. "The best thing. Believe me."

He thought for a moment, then smiled again. "Let's enchant something! What should we make? Anything at all, whatever you want."

"Really?" she said. "Even . . ." She hesitated. It was kind of awful to admit that she already had something in mind; that she'd considered what she would ask for, if she ever had a chance.

"Anything," he said again, more firmly.

"Could you make me something that hides my thoughts from any mind readers?" she asked.

That was a mistake. His expression — he was so hurt, it nearly convinced her that he'd been keeping his promise all along.

"It's not about you," she said quickly, and not entirely truthfully. "You know my best friend — Listener — she's a mind reader, and so is the principal of the school. I can't shield my mind the way you can. I'm always worried about what they might hear about the future. And now they might see something about your scroll, too. Wouldn't it be safer if no one could listen to me?" She hesitated again. "If you want to make it about any mind readers except you, you can do that. I trust you, Darkstalker."

She did now, she thought so . . . but it was still kind of a test.

"No, no," he said. "I understand. You're right, it will keep the scroll safe — and us. I can see that, too." He took the inkwell and weighted down the scroll on his desk. "Here, I've been meaning to give this to you anyway." Darkstalker pulled open one of his drawers and withdrew a bracelet made of woven copper wires, with three milky white moonstones caught in the middle.

She shivered. *I've seen that bracelet somewhere up ahead.*

Darkstalker rested the bracelet on the scroll, thought for a moment, and then wrote, *Enchant this bracelet to shield the wearer's thoughts from any mind readers.*

"The wearer?" Clearsight echoed, reading over his shoulder.

"That way you can pass it down to one of our dragonets," he said, smiling at her. "I mean, if I'm going to make a powerful animus-touched object like this, shouldn't it be something that can be used forever?"

"Very smart," she said. He clasped the bracelet around her wrist and she held it up to watch the moonstones glow in the torchlight. She smiled at him. "I think Eclipse will love it, and she'll need it the most."

He let out a little gasp of surprise. She'd never talked about their dragonets before — certainly never admitted that she knew what their names might be.

"Are we definite on that name?" he said after a moment. "I was thinking Shadowhunter."

"That's one of her big sisters," Clearsight said, and laughed again at the look on his face. "Didn't you know that already?"

"Of course I did," he said. "Eclipse, Shadowhunter, and Fierceclaws."

"No, no, no," she said, laughing harder. "Fierceclaws? You definitely don't win *that* argument." She'd obviously spent a *lot* more time studying the timelines than he had.

"We could name one after my mother," Darkstalker suggested, a little shyly. "She's pretty awesome. And Foeslayer's a good name, isn't it?"

"It is," Clearsight said with a smile. She had a weird feeling they *did* name a dragonet Foeslayer in some future timeline, but there were layers of reasons for it that felt sad and complicated to wrangle out.

"Let's make something else," Darkstalker said, flicking his tail happily. He seized one of the blankets from his bed and wrote, *Enchant this blanket to keep any dragon it covers at the exact perfect temperature.* Grinning, he flung it over Clearsight's shoulders.

"Ooooo," she said. She hadn't even realized she was cold until the blanket's magical warmth swept through her. "I have one! Can you enchant our boring history scroll to read to us?"

"Of course!" he said. He dug his *Ancient Wars of Pyrrhia* scroll out of his pack and set it on the desk. Carefully he dipped a claw in the blue ink this time and wrote, *Enchant this history scroll to read itself aloud whenever a dragon says, "Bore me to sleep!" and stop reading whenever someone says, "Spare me!"*

"You lunatic," she said affectionately.

"Ready?" He stole a corner of the blanket and curled up beside her with the history scroll in front of them. "Bore me to sleep!"

"*Ancient Wars of Pyrrhia*," the scroll droned. "Introduction. Every dragon knows the history of the Scorching and the tribal shifts and alignments that followed, but many may not realize that five hundred years later, the continent of Pyrrhia was in a state of constant warfare."

"Screaming scavengers," Clearsight said. "It sounds just like Professor Truthfinder!"

"So bored, but also very suspicious of all of us!" Darkstalker agreed.

They were laughing so hard, they didn't hear the front door open.

They didn't hear the clawsteps approaching.

They didn't notice the dragon in the doorway, staring at them and the speaking scroll, until he spoke in a thunderous, glacier-cracking voice.

"What is going on in here?" snarled Prince Arctic.

CHAPTER 13

CLEARSIGHT

Darkstalker leaped to his feet and faced his father, lashing his tail. Clearsight grabbed the history scroll and whispered, "Spare me" at it. The droning voice stopped.

A cold, menacing silence filled the entire house.

"This is my room," Darkstalker snapped. "You're not welcome in here."

Arctic stepped inside. He seemed to be growing bigger as Clearsight stared at him. She'd never seen an IceWing up close before. She hadn't realized that they actually radiated a chill from their scales, like a hissing, fanged glacier. His scales were polished white with hints of pale blue, but not as shiny as she'd expected. He looked sort of . . . scuffed, as though he needed to go roll in some snow to clean off.

His eyes were the color of a cloudless sky; they were piercing but tired at the same time. She wondered if he had trouble sleeping this far away from his own kingdom, and on a schedule where everyone stayed awake all night and slept all day. He must miss the ice and snow. He must miss his family, his tribe, everything he'd grown up with. She couldn't imagine being so far from home, surrounded by dragons who looked nothing like her.

As she stared at him, a vision stabbed into her brain: Arctic holding one of Whiteout's drawings of Foeslayer, half-frozen tears dripping from his eyes. She blinked, trying not to fall into the visions. This sometimes happened when she met a new dragon — especially a significant one with alarming futures. But here, in this room with these dragons, she wanted to draw as little attention to herself as possible.

"Did you enchant that scroll to speak?" Arctic asked, staring down at his son.

"Yes," Darkstalker answered. He lifted his chin defiantly.

"So." Arctic exhaled a hint of frostbreath. "You're an animus after all."

"I guess I am," said Darkstalker.

Clearsight could not imagine having a conversation with her parents that had so few words and so many giant unspoken feelings. She was very glad not to be a mind reader at this moment. She could just imagine the furious thoughts that were shoving and clawing up against one another in the air right now.

The scroll! she remembered suddenly. Not the history scroll — the animus-touched one. The one with all of Darkstalker's power in it. The one Arctic should definitely never, ever find out about.

It was lying open on the desk, displaying Darkstalker's enchantments in his jagged, messy handwriting.

Arctic hadn't noticed it yet. Clearsight took a sidling step toward the desk, then another when nobody even looked at her. The two male dragons seemed to be testing whether it was possible to freeze someone with just your eyeballs.

"Have you not heard a word I've said," growled Arctic, "about the dangers of using animus magic frivolously?"

"I didn't need to hear it," said Darkstalker. "I can see it in every rotting spot on your soul. But you don't have to worry about me; I'll *never* be anything like you."

Clearsight winced. That seemed crueler than necessary.

Another vision flashed through her mind: Arctic slashing the throat of a NightWing she didn't know, with two IceWings lurking in the shadows behind him.

That was . . . worrying.

"I used my magic to keep your mother alive," Arctic hissed. "I used it to help her escape the IceWings who wanted her dead. I have only ever used it out of necessity — never to make *playthings* to impress little girl dragons." He shot a glare at Clearsight and she froze in front of the desk, hoping her wings were hiding the scroll well enough.

"That's not even true," Darkstalker said heatedly. "I know what you made for Mother when you first met. She still wears that earring all the time."

Arctic hissed. "That's different."

"Why?" said Darkstalker. "Because you and Mother have such a great love? One worth starting a war over?" He paused. "Wow, that *is* what you think."

A war, a war, a war, chimed inside Clearsight's head, and she felt the spinning rush of visions descending on her. *Not right now!* she tried to command her power, but on they came.

Foeslayer wielding a long spear, in the middle of a battle, IceWings and NightWings clashing over a desert sunrise.

Arctic dying in a pool of royal-blue IceWing blood.

Arctic leading Whiteout through a palace of ice, her wings shivering.

Darkstalker with a spear through his chest, his eyes going blank.

Arctic in Queen Vigilance's display prison, screaming furiously through the bars.

A squadron of NightWings following Arctic into battle against a sea of white dragons.

Darkstalker writing in his scroll by firelight, writing as if his life depended on it.

There was so much, so many paths ahead, and most of them tending toward terrible violence. This lost IceWing had almost no chance at a peaceful future. Betrayed, betrayer, murdered, murderer; death and treason surrounded him with their vast wings, no matter what he did.

Was that the price of his animus magic? Had he already lost too much of his soul to his power?

Can I save him? Can anyone?

"What's wrong with her?" Arctic's voice was not as harsh as she'd expected. He sounded actually concerned.

Clearsight's eyes opened, and she realized she was crouching with her talons pressed to her head and her wings folded around herself. Darkstalker was beside her, gently touching her back.

"Are you all right?" he said. "What did you see?"

"I'm . . . not sure," she said. He looked disappointed, but it was true. *All* those visions couldn't come true; she needed to study them to figure out what order they happened in, which ones were most likely, what were the turning points that led to each one. And how to stop them, or which timeline was the least awful. Whether there was any way to bring this IceWing back from the abyss that lay ahead of him.

And save Darkstalker, her inner voice whispered, remembering the worst of the visions. She was quite sure she shouldn't tell Darkstalker about that one. She wondered if he'd seen it himself — if he'd followed the path that led from his father to his own death, and whether that was part of why they hated each other so much.

"You're a seer?" Arctic said, squinting at her. "That looked like quite a vision. Got any prophecies to share?"

She shook her head, but words were bubbling up from inside her, the kind she normally only wrote down. *"Beware your two queens,"* she whispered. Arctic jerked back, eyes wide. *"Beware your own power. Your claws will betray you in your final hour."*

She clamped her mouth shut. She hated prophecies like that — the kind that possessed you and confused everyone. The kind that Allknowing taught her students to imitate. If you asked Clearsight, no good could come of telling dragons vague cryptic things about the future, which they then tried to interpret and second-guess and fulfill and avoid.

No. Without the portentous fancy talk, she could give everyone real information: details, an action plan, knowledge to steer them along the right path. She just needed to concentrate and figure it out.

But Arctic's mind was clearly already spinning through the possibilities, trying to guess what her words meant.

"I need to write that down," he said, starting toward the desk and Darkstalker's scroll.

"Not in here, that's my homework," Clearsight said in a rush. She swept the inkwell off the scroll and rolled it up, sliding it quickly into its case. "I should go. I'll see you at school tomorrow, Darkstalker. Thanks for — thanks for studying with me." She'd nearly said "thanks for the bracelet," but she was sure he didn't want his father to know about any other animus spells he'd cast.

"Wait," Darkstalker said as she slid his scroll into her bag. "I —"

"Don't worry," she said, brushing his wing lightly with hers. "I'll take care of our project." She'd bring it back tomorrow, when it was safe.

She backed hurriedly out the door, but Arctic didn't seem to notice her nervousness, or anything suspicious about the scroll. He still looked dazed by the prophecy, muttering it over to himself and studying his claws with concern.

As she flew away, Clearsight wondered if there was anything to her prophecy — anything she should worry about.

"Beware your two queens; beware your own power.
Your claws will betray you in your final hour."

At least it didn't say anything about Darkstalker, she realized. *But Arctic's bound to be more worried about him now that he knows Darkstalker's an animus.*

How had she been careless enough to let them be caught by Arctic?

She should have known he'd come home early.

She should have protected Darkstalker better.

Except . . . now she could feel something in the shifting timelines. Something about today's events would have ripple effects far into the future.

Some of them terrible . . . but some of them good.

Someone will be coming, whispered her seer voice.

Was that one of the good things, or one of the terrible things?

There's only one way to find out, she thought. *Well, two ways: I could wait and see what happens. Or I can go home and try to study them all.*

She caught an air current and dove into it, swooping home to her scrolls and her notes as fast as her wings could carry her.

CHAPTER 14

FATHOM

Fathom dragged his tail as he made his way through the halls to his sister's throne room. A summons from the queen: this couldn't be good.

Over a year had passed since the massacre. A long, lonely year.

He'd kept his promise; he'd stayed away from Indigo, although it made him feel like his wings had been cut off.

It was hard to divide up his grief, when he had so many dragons to mourn — his cousins, his uncle, his queen, his parents most of all, but even his grandfather, or at least the grandfather he thought he knew.

Losing Indigo, though . . . most days, that was the worst of all.

As the dragon who stopped the massacre, Indigo was the hero of the Kingdom of the Sea. Pearl had kept her word: Indigo had been promoted to the queen's honor guard immediately and assigned to the squadron that protected the queen herself, night and day. Pearl rarely let Indigo leave her side . . . which certainly made it easier for Fathom to avoid her.

He hadn't seen either of them in months, not even from a distance. He spent most of his time studying quietly in a back room of the Deep Palace, alone.

He didn't know what he was going to do with his life anymore.

The three guards at the throne room door saw him coming and bristled dangerously, their spears at the ready, their teeth bared. That was pretty much the way most SeaWings reacted to him these days. He understood it. He couldn't exactly produce his soul as evidence that he still had one.

Fathom stopped several steps away from the guards and bowed his head. "Queen Pearl sent a message asking me to attend her in the throne room."

The guards conferred in suspicious murmurs, and then one of them whisked inside. A few minutes later, she came out again and beckoned to him.

"All right," she said. "Go on in. But we're watching you, animus."

He nodded and slipped past the barricade of sharp points and unfriendly eyes.

Pearl was on her throne, with another row of guards assembled across the room between him and her. Surely she knew that would do no good. If he went evil, he could kill her no matter what the guards did. He wouldn't even have to be here, standing in front of her.

But it was all part of the performance — reassuring the court that she was strong and safe and invulnerable. A show of force was what they needed to see.

He had promised himself he wouldn't do this, but his eyes darted around the room against his will, looking for deep purple-blue scales.

And there she was, standing just behind his sister. Staring down at the spear in her talons. Ready to die for her queen.

A tidal wave crashed over him, memories and longing and despair crushing the air out of his chest. He remembered claw painting with Indigo when they were tiny dragonets, dipping their talons in blue and gold paint and stomping on each other's scrolls until she knocked him over and he ended up rolling gold scale patterns across their paintings, sticky and delighted with himself.

He remembered the hours he'd spent carving that first dolphin for her, trying to get it just right. He remembered swimming and diving with her, filling out their fish journals until they'd seen every variety in the sea. He remembered how she teased him for taking their tutors so seriously.

He remembered adjusting the pearls around her neck, the beat of her heart so close to his. He remembered holding her as he willed life back into her body, his tears falling like rain on her battered scales.

I'd do it again, he thought. *Again and again, anything to save her. I'd give up my whole soul, let it crumble into darkness, if that's what it took.*

Pearl was still right about him and Indigo, even after all this time apart.

"Hello, brother," Queen Pearl said, and he forced his eyes back to her. Her face was knowing, wary, as if putting him in the same room with Indigo was a test, and she was watching him fail it.

"Your Majesty," he said with a bow.

"Look who's come home to us," she said, flicking her tail at a SeaWing coiled a few steps below the throne.

It took Fathom a long moment to recognize him. The last time he'd seen his cousin Current, he'd been laughing and joking with the rest of the family. When he never reappeared after the massacre, everyone assumed he had been wounded and died somewhere out in the ocean.

But here he was, alive — and yet this dragon was not the confident, easy-to-smile cousin Fathom remembered. This dragon was thin and shivered constantly, and he couldn't look at Fathom without flinching away.

"Current?" Fathom said.

"I d-d-don't — I don't —" Current stammered.

"Where have you been?" Fathom asked, worried. He took a step closer. The guards raised their spears and Current flinched so hard he nearly knocked himself over.

"You'll never guess," said Pearl, and for a moment he heard his sister under the regal voice, excited to know a secret he didn't.

"Another kingdom?" he said.

"The *Night* Kingdom," she said.

Fathom raised his eyebrows. That was about as far away as anyone could get from the Island Palace without turning into an icicle.

But why had Current been gone for so long? He must have heard the news about the new queen of the SeaWings, even across the continent.

"I d-don't want to see him," Current whispered, covering his eyes. "P-please don't make me."

Pearl sighed. "All right. Take him away," she said to one of the guards, and for an awful moment Fathom thought that was it — less than a minute of being in the same room with Indigo, as if to torment him before ripping her away again.

But the guard went to Current instead, taking the SeaWing gently by the wing and steering him out of the throne room.

"Current has been a . . . guest . . . of the NightWing queen all this time," Pearl said, watching him go. "And now she's finally sent him back with a message, and an offer."

Uh-oh. His pulse throbbed ominously in his skull. *Here it comes. The reason I was summoned.*

Pearl picked up a tablet and glanced down at the words as though she found it hard to meet Fathom's eyes. "Apparently the NightWings suddenly have an animus of their own. Their very first."

"But —" Fathom started.

"How?" she cut him off. "Remember the rumors about that IceWing prince who ran away with a NightWing? They must have been true. This animus is his son, a dragon named Darkstalker."

Another animus out there.

Is he going to kill his entire family, too?

"Apparently Current told Queen Vigilance all about Albatross and the massacre," Pearl said. She frowned slightly. Fathom knew she'd been hoping to keep that a secret from the other tribes for a lot longer. "Queen Vigilance is, naturally, worried about whether her animus might go all homicidally crazy, too. She says he is apparently quite careless with his magic, no matter how often his father, the IceWing, warns him about the effects."

A twist of guilt and fear stabbed through Fathom's chest.

"We have to do something," he cried. "Someone has to stop him!"

"Agreed," said Pearl, looking slightly taken aback at the urgency in his voice. "Someone is going to stop him. You."

Fathom glanced around at all the blue and green eyes that pinned him to the floor. "Me?"

"We're sending you to the Night Kingdom." Pearl tapped the tablet neatly against the arm of her throne. "Queen Vigilance will shelter you and introduce you to this animus. You will tell him your sad story and teach him the error of his ways."

But nobody listens to me. Why would anyone listen to me?

"And then the NightWings will be our new allies," Pearl said, examining her claws. "Everyone wins."

Beside the queen, Indigo finally looked up and met

Fathom's eyes. "But," she blurted, and Pearl shot a dangerous look at her.

Indigo plowed on bravely. "But is it safe for — is it safe?" she asked the queen. "What if this is a NightWing trap to steal our animus, the way they stole the IceWing one?"

"That story is nonsense," Pearl said, already standing to leave the room. She paused to look down at Fathom. "Who would *want* an animus?"

The cold, hard truth of that sank in for a moment.

"Your Majesty," Indigo said abruptly. Her claws dug into the wood of her spear. "I ask permission to accompany Prince Fathom to the Night Kingdom. As — as the head of his personal guard."

Fathom's heart leaped and then immediately sank. *With me? Indigo and me, together?* It was what he wanted, desperately, but it was also too dangerous, and Pearl would never allow it.

Pearl narrowed her eyes at Indigo. "Who says I'm sending any guards with him?"

"Very amusing, my queen. I know you are too wise to send a powerful, magic member of the royal family to a faraway kingdom unguarded," Indigo said. "All kinds of terrible things could happen to him. That other animus could kill him."

Fathom thought perhaps Pearl wouldn't mind that at all. This was a convenient way to get rid of a dragon who made everyone uncomfortable . . . and if he never came back, well, problem solved forever.

"Please, Your Majesty." Indigo folded her wings and bowed respectfully. "It sounds like the NightWing animus could be a threat. I could assess the situation and report back to you. I am not afraid of his magic."

"She can save everyone from him!" called one of the queen's advisors.

"That's true!" called another. "Send the Animus Slayer!"

"She should be wherever there is danger from an animus dragon! She can stop him before he threatens our kingdom!"

"Yeah! She can kill them both if she has to!"

There was an awkward pause after that last shout. Fathom deliberately did not look around to see who'd said it. He knew enough of them were thinking it.

Is that what Indigo's thinking? That she might have to protect the world from me?

From the look on Pearl's face, he guessed the queen highly doubted Indigo would be able to pull that off. But she was also stuck. She couldn't deny the Hero of the Massacre, the Animus Slayer, the one thing Indigo had cvcr asked for, not in front of her court.

"I don't need guards," he forced himself to say. "I can go by myself."

Indigo gave him a wounded look and he felt like the lowest sea slug in the ocean.

She drew herself up taller, tearing her eyes away from him. "With respect, Your Majesty," she said. "Your animus should not be allowed to leave the kingdom unsupervised."

"Very well," Pearl said, with an expression as though she'd just swallowed a spoiled oyster. "I will assign you two other guards, and you may accompany my brother to the Night Kingdom."

She turned with a flourish of her wings and swept out of the throne room, lashing her tail furiously. Perhaps it was a good time to travel halfway around the world from her, after all.

And I'll be with Indigo, he thought. *I know I shouldn't be happy about that. I should be terrified.*

Guards were moving forward to usher him out, but across the room he was able to catch and hold her gaze for a moment.

He couldn't read her face. Was she angry with him? Was she really going with him because she didn't trust him?

Or is she worried about this other animus?

He realized with a surge of guilt that he was flying straight toward a new, unknown, potentially enormous danger . . . and he was dragging Indigo right along with him.

Ice Kingdom
Sky Kingdom
Queen Scorpion's Stronghold
Claws of the Clouds Mountains
Kingdom of Sand
Queen Vigilance's Palace
Jade Mountain

PART TWO

CHAPTER 15

DARKSTALKER

The first invitation to the palace came two months after Arctic discovered Darkstalker was an animus.

Darkstalker knew it was coming, and not because of any prophetic vision. He'd expected it ever since the night Arctic told Foeslayer everything, at dinner after Clearsight was gone. He'd been listening to Arctic wrestle with whether to tell anyone all evening. It actually made him like his father a tiny bit when Arctic finally decided he couldn't bear to keep it from Foeslayer.

"Did you know," Arctic had said, stabbing his claws into the rabbit on the table, "that our son has been keeping a secret from us?"

"I know he had a girl here today," Foeslayer had responded. She smiled at Darkstalker. "What's her name?"

"Clearsight," Darkstalker said, smiling back. "You'll like her, Mother." There was no need to hide her anymore. Arctic was too unnerved by her prophecy to bother her or try to ruin their relationship.

"She's exactly right," Whiteout offered. "Definitely azure on the inside. I like the way she knits."

Darkstalker had no idea what that meant. He'd never once seen Clearsight knit. But the fact that his sister liked her was really all he needed to know.

"So when do we get to meet her?" Foeslayer had asked, her eyes sparkling.

"That is *not* the secret," Arctic barked. "Pay attention. Darkstalker is an *animus*. He's probably known for years without telling us. And he's *using his magic*."

Foeslayer dropped her rabbit and stared at Darkstalker.

"Magic brother," Whiteout said thoughtfully. She reached across the table, lifted one of Darkstalker's talons, and flipped it over, tracing the lines of the scales. "That's all right; he's not going to snow for a while."

"Thanks," Darkstalker said with a grin, resisting the urge to hug her. He sensed new fear from both his parents, but nothing different in the starscape of Whiteout's mind. He didn't know what she was thinking, but he knew she loved him with all his weirdness, the same way he loved her.

He shrugged at Foeslayer. "It's not that big a deal."

"It rather is, actually," she said. She rubbed her snout between her eyes. "Oh, Mother is going to be horribly pleased."

Darkstalker and Whiteout rarely saw their grandmother, who used to be one of Queen Vigilance's closest advisors. She'd been demoted after the fiasco with Foeslayer and their diplomatic visit to the Ice Kingdom, even though the queen had officially pardoned Foeslayer. Grandmother had always looked down her snout at Foeslayer's hybrid offspring, muttering about how the only way this mess could have been worth it was if one of them had at least turned out to be an animus.

It's going to be sort of beautiful, Darkstalker thought. Grandmother would have to admit that perhaps Foeslayer's forbidden love wasn't the biggest mistake any NightWing had ever made. Because if it brought animus blood to the NightWing tribe . . . surely that was worth a mere little war with the IceWings?

And then perhaps she'd even have to be nice to her daughter once in a while. Darkstalker would enjoy watching that.

"She's going to eat her tongue," Whiteout agreed.

"Gross," Darkstalker said, making a face at her. She giggled.

"How do you propose we leash him?" Arctic asked Foeslayer. Darkstalker saw bubbling flashes of ideas in his mind — things he could enchant to keep his son under control.

"Stop thinking what you're thinking," Darkstalker said quietly, dangerously.

Arctic gave him a sharp look. "Stop *listening* to what I'm thinking."

"You can't afford to use your magic again," Darkstalker said. "It will destroy you. You'll end up like that SeaWing. I know; I can see the holes in your soul."

There was a twist of genuine fear inside Arctic, which

sort of surprised Darkstalker. Not only was Arctic more worried about his soul than Darkstalker had expected, but he also apparently believed that Darkstalker could see how close he was to turning evil.

Across the table, Whiteout nodded. "I had an apple like that once," she said ruefully.

Foeslayer leaned toward Darkstalker. "If you can see the damage it's done to your father," she said, "doesn't that frighten you? Doesn't it make you want to be careful?"

"I'm not damaged," Arctic snarled, but internally he was counting all the times he'd used his magic. *It must be the magic I used for our escape from the Ice Kingdom. Or the spell that keeps Mother's magic from working on me. But those enchantments were necessary . . . Will I really go mad if I use my power again? I should do something to contain my son . . . but what if I turn evil and hurt Foeslayer?*

"Yes," Darkstalker answered his mother. "Don't worry, Mother. I am being careful." He held out his talons. "There are no spots on *my* soul."

"Only stripes," Whiteout said, and burst out laughing.

Oh dear, Foeslayer thought, regarding her daughter with a puzzled expression. *Why couldn't either of my dragonets be the slightest bit ordinary?*

"Life's more interesting this way, right?" said Darkstalker, and she smiled at him.

On his other side, he could hear his father thinking venomous thoughts. Even after all these years among the NightWings, and despite his own son's power, Arctic couldn't seem to hide what he was thinking and didn't even bother to try. *I hate when they communicate like that,* he thought in a dark grumble. *I don't get to know what she's thinking, but he does? And she doesn't care that he just invades her mind like that. NightWings and their horrible powers.*

"We should tell Queen Vigilance," said Foeslayer. "Shouldn't we?" She worried at the corner of the table. *It's the right thing to do, as a loyal NightWing (and to prove that I am a loyal NightWing, despite everyone's suspicions) . . . but what will the queen do about it? Will she try to use my son? What might she ask him to do?*

"Let's talk about that in private," said Arctic.

"Oh, good," said Darkstalker. "No reason to involve *me* in that decision."

But he had dropped it, knowing they would decide to tell the queen. He didn't mind if they did. He was ready for the whole tribe to know.

Which didn't take long, because Whiteout started mentioning it at school. Keeping secrets was not something she ever did. Darkstalker got the impression sometimes that she thought if she knew something, everybody must know it, like they all shared one mind.

So she'd slide comments about his animus power into ordinary conversations, without seeming to notice how it blew up everybody's brains. It was sort of fun to watch.

Suddenly Darkstalker had throngs of new friends to choose from. Everyone treated Clearsight like she was royalty, or at least royalty-adjacent. His teachers were more cautious with their criticism, more likely to love his ideas. Nobody made fun of his sister anymore. And all the oldest dragons around him seemed to feel entitled to ask him thousands of nosy questions a day about his new power.

He rather liked being the NightWing tribe's first animus.

Then the first invitation to the palace came, and Darkstalker met the queen in an awkward private meeting, where she assured him she was looking forward to hearing any ideas he had about how best to use his power. Perhaps against the IceWings. Hint, hint. He promised he would put a lot of thought into it, to make sure anything he made for her was worth the risk to his soul, and then they both thought about the SeaWing massacre for a minute, and then she quickly excused him.

But more invitations followed, one after another. Dinner parties, tea with the queen, hunting weekends, races and tournaments and games — everything he and Foeslayer had been carefully excluded from for years, even after Arctic became a fixture of court life. Queen Vigilance was more interested in what his power could give her than frightened of what might happen to him. She wanted him close to her, dependent on her, and Darkstalker liked going so he could study her and see how palace life worked.

The only problem was that Clearsight refused to go with him to any of the royal gatherings. He kept telling her that other dragons brought guests. He could certainly bring his soulmate with him. But she wanted to be invited to the palace on her own merits — by doing something to help the tribe and catch the queen's attention herself, not by slipping in on another dragon's arm.

There wasn't much he could do to change her mind. But his foresight said it wouldn't be much longer; he'd had a vision of the two of them at the palace that he was sure would happen soon. And in the meanwhile, he just had to put up with a LOT of boring court conversations.

There was something different about this latest invitation, though. As he moved around his room, getting ready, he felt a weird spark of anticipation zapping through him.

A welcoming party. That's all it had said. Welcoming who?

Darkstalker had looked into the immediate future and seen a cluster of SeaWings, which was surprising. But he didn't linger on it. Studying the future was Clearsight's obsession, not his. He knew how quickly and easily the future could change, so trying to keep track of all the possibilities was a waste of his time. He accepted the visions that burst into his head, since those were usually warnings. And sometimes he looked ahead to the futures where he and Clearsight were married with their own dragonets. A future without Arctic — that was the promise his gift of foresight gave him.

He took an earring out of his jewelry chest — silver, designed to look like a snake twining down his ear. This one was enchanted to make everyone who met him think he was exceptionally handsome and charming. Clearsight had made him promise to never wear it around her.

"I like seeing you the way you really are," she'd said.

"Which is *not* exceptionally handsome and charming?" he asked, half joking, half offended.

"Just handsome enough," she had said, "with a head that still fits through doors. Also, I don't like watching other dragons fawn over you."

"Jealous?" he'd asked with a grin.

"No, it's just . . . creepy," she'd answered, not joking at all.

Well, she wouldn't be there tonight, and he should try to make a good impression on whoever was being welcomed, surely.

The other accessory he chose for the evening was a tail band, the latest fashion trend. His wound around his tail five times and was also silver, like his earring, and carved to look like dragon scales. It was a bit heavier than he liked and he also thought tail bands looked sort of ridiculous. But this one had a particularly useful enchantment on it, so, although it was unwieldy, it was nonetheless a good idea to wear it.

"Are you still primping?" Arctic demanded, shoving his head into Darkstalker's room. "The queen will not be pleased if we're late." He was one to talk about primping: his moon-white scales were set off by necklaces of black jet and bright green emeralds, and matching rings glittered on a few of his claws.

"You can go ahead without me," Darkstalker said, trying not to show how much that would please him. They rarely attended the same court events if they could avoid it. But in this case they had both been expressly commanded to attend.

"I'll wait," Arctic said with a heavy sigh. *Need to make sure he gets there,* his brain muttered. *Important night. Can't be late. One of the conditions was that we must not embarrass her in front of the SeaWings. Or else she'll send them back, or kill them, or whatever she plans to do.*

Hmm, Darkstalker thought to himself. That was mysterious. But if the fate of the SeaWings might depend on his punctuality, he supposed he could hurry himself up.

Foeslayer was waiting for them by the door, wearing emeralds and white moonstones that complemented his father's black gemstones — a trick they often played with their jewelry. It gave them the illusion of matching, of fitting perfectly together. Foeslayer reached out and adjusted one of Arctic's chains, her talons drifting lightly down his neck.

It'll be all right, she thought. *Arctic's idea is clever. It's just what Darkstalker needs.*

"Me?" Darkstalker said to her, suddenly suspicious. "What do I need?"

"Nosy mind-snooper," Arctic growled at him.

"You'll see," Foeslayer said patiently, brushing her wing against Darkstalker's. "Whiteout, be good while we're gone."

"No wild parties," Darkstalker joked.

"You're the one going into the wild," Whiteout answered from her spot by the fireplace without looking up from her scroll.

"Oh," said Foeslayer. "All right, then."

Whiteout generally was not included in the invitations.

Various excuses had been given, but the truth was, the queen still wasn't entirely comfortable with such an obvious hybrid roaming around her court. She never said so out loud, but Darkstalker could see it in the thoughts Queen Vigilance tried to shield from him. He'd be more offended on his sister's behalf, but he knew she would hate the stilted formality of palace functions anyway.

"Let's go," snapped Arctic impatiently. "Come on, come on."

It was a short flight to the palace, which was lit up from end to end, firelight blazing in nearly every window. There was no prisoner in the display cage, perhaps so it wouldn't scare their visitors. A light drizzle had started to fall, misting them each with wet sparkles and steam as they proceeded from the landing ledge into the grand ballroom.

"Prince Arctic, Foeslayer, and their son, Darkstalker," announced the dragon at the head of the staircase. Darkstalker always enjoyed hearing his father's inner turmoil that he was no longer proclaimed as "Prince Arctic of the IceWings" — although really, he should be grateful to still have any royal title at all.

Heads turned in their direction all across the room, which was decorated for the evening in swathes of blue and green fabric. Small rock pools had been set into the floor and tiny waterfalls cascaded in the corners. The banquet table smelled more like fish and shrimp and seaweed than normal.

There were special lessons at school for mind readers, teaching them how to survive in crowds without getting overwhelmed. Darkstalker, fortunately, had learned quickly how to melt everyone's voices into the background. He knew most of these dragons were too boring to listen to anyway.

"Hello, dear," said Queen Vigilance, sweeping up to capture Darkstalker's attention as soon as he reached the bottom of the stairs. She wore an ostentatious crown and her wings were loaded with an unnecessary amount of diamonds. She was considered to be one of the shrewdest queens in recent NightWing history, and she certainly did a superb job of intimidating her daughters, such that none of them had mustered the courage to challenge her yet.

But Darkstalker had been inside her mind. He knew that a lot of her apparent menace came from one trick: the fact that she spoke very little, allowing the dragons around her to fill in all the gaps with their own nervous chatter. She was also deeply paranoid, often killing off perceived threats long before they were actually dangerous. That might seem shrewd to outside observers, but Darkstalker thought it was a sign of her own anxiety and shortsightedness.

"Your Majesty," Arctic interjected before Darkstalker could speak. "You look radiant and regal, as always."

"Hmm," said the queen, touching her crown. Darkstalker wondered how his father had never noticed that she wasn't susceptible to flattery. Vigilance found compliments highly suspicious. Arctic's remark just made her think: *What does this slippery IceWing want now?*

"Is this the new Tunesmith composition?" Darkstalker

asked, deflecting her attention. He tipped his head toward the musicians playing on a stage at the end of the room.

"It is," said Vigilance, pleased.

"She's so talented," Foeslayer said.

Our composer laureate could sneeze out a better song than this, Arctic thought bitterly. "Any news of the war?" he said to the queen.

She narrowed her eyes at him, just a tiny bit. In her mind: *It could be over by now if you would be the slightest bit helpful.* Her gaze stopped briefly on Darkstalker and he heard her wonder if he'd be of more use than his father.

"Nothing new," she said aloud.

Queen Vigilance left one of her usual momentary silences after this remark, and Foeslayer was the first to rush in and fill it. *Poor Mother,* thought Darkstalker, *exactly the kind of nervous dragon the queen loves to trifle with.* He'd have to find a subtle way to make Vigilance pay for making his mother so uncomfortable.

"A very successful battle last week, though," Foeslayer said. "We drove the IceWings back and took a lot of desert territory, with very few casualties. And our air defense team is unbeatable. It's such an honor to be working with them. No IceWings will ever get into the Night Kingdom with them on watch."

Well, thought several minds at once, *except for the one who's already here.*

Arctic allowed himself a small, grim smile as Foeslayer fidgeted with her claws.

"Hmm," said the queen again. She turned to Darkstalker. "Come meet someone." His parents started to follow them and she gestured to stop them in their tracks. "Not you."

Foeslayer was all relief and eagerness to get to the food, but small geysers of resentment were going off inside Arctic as Darkstalker walked away with the queen.

You won't look so smug when the IceWings do get into your kingdom.

Darkstalker turned to look back, wondering if he'd heard his father's last thought correctly. But Arctic had vanished into the crowd, his mind just another part of the commotion coming from all the other dragons in the room.

It didn't matter. Arctic had bitter thoughts about the downfall of the NightWing tribe all the time, but none of those thoughts had ever led to action. Darkstalker was confident he didn't need to worry about his father's treacherous fantasies — not for a while, at least, according to Clearsight.

The queen led him to a roped-off area with low purple couches and tables of sparkling drinks. Four SeaWings stood awkwardly inside, looking more trapped than honored. Two of the queen's sons were making small talk with them, and one of her councilors had taken over a couch as though she'd given up.

"Prince Fathom of the SeaWings," said the queen, indicating a green dragon only about a year older than Darkstalker. He had an oddly anxious aura, as if he were gripping the floor with his claws in order to avoid being blown away. "This is Darkstalker."

The other animus, Fathom thought with a jolt of fear. He took an unconscious step closer to the dragon beside him, whose scales were a deep blue that was almost purple. She looked outwardly calmer than he did, but her heart was racing as fast as his and terrifying images were flashing through her head. Neither of them even seemed affected by the spell his earring cast; they were too busy being scared to find him handsome.

Darkstalker realized several things at once.

Fathom was an animus as well.

Fathom had been in many of Darkstalker's visions of the future.

Fathom was here for him.

And: both of these dragons had witnessed the massacre when the SeaWing animus turned violent . . . at a party very much like this one.

No wonder they were terrified — a party plus an unfamiliar animus, where they were the guests, much like those SkyWings who'd been attacked.

Darkstalker checked Queen Vigilance's brain, but he didn't find any intentional malice there. She wasn't trying to traumatize the SeaWings. She just hadn't thought about the effect this particular welcome might have.

"Hello," Fathom said, trying to summon years of etiquette lessons. "V-very pleased to meet you. This is — these are my guards, Wharf and Lionfish . . . and Indigo."

She's not just a guard, Darkstalker guessed, but she held

herself like one, strong and serious-looking. The other two were background noise, irrelevant to Darkstalker's future.

"I'm honored to meet you, too," he said. *I have to get this poor SeaWing out of here.* "Has anyone shown you the view from the Royal Tower yet? May I?" He turned to the queen. "I know you have many duties with your guests, Your Majesty." He would have preferred to separate Fathom from the others, but he could sense that Indigo would never let that happen. "I'll take Fathom and Indigo for a short flight and we'll be back soon."

The queen, unsurprisingly, found this highly suspicious, but she couldn't think of any way to stop it without offending the SeaWings. "Of course," she said. She pointed one claw at Darkstalker. "Soon, though."

"Yes, Your Majesty." He bowed and spread one wing to point the way out of the ballroom, ignoring the tumult of worries inside both SeaWings. *Should we insist on bringing the other two guards?* Indigo wondered, while Fathom thought, *Is he taking us away to kill us?*

Calm DOWN, jittery SeaWings, Darkstalker thought with an internal eye roll. *I'm trying to help you.*

The closest exit led from the ballroom down to one of the hanging gardens. The noise of the party faded behind them as the three dragons flew through the ancient trees, where moss and vines hung down from the branches like shrouded wings. Mirrors set up throughout the gardens captured and reflected the silvery light of the three moons. The rain had stopped, but everything still glistened and wet leaves fluttered damply at their scales.

Darkstalker landed on a small island in one of the dragon-made lakes. The moonlight was bright here, pouring down over the columns of a temple that had been built to honor the first librarians of the Night Kingdom. *We give thanks to those who gathered the scrolls, who preserved the knowledge of previous generations,* and so on and so on.

"This doesn't look like a tower," Fathom said, landing but keeping his wings spread. Indigo swooped around the island once and then started pacing out every inch of it, checking all the dark corners. Keeping up her conscientious bodyguard act, when Darkstalker could see that what she really wanted to do was put her wings around Fathom and take him far, far away from here.

"I'm giving you the grand tour," Darkstalker said to Fathom. "Well, actually, I'm just trying to save you from that awful party."

"Oh," Fathom said, flustered. "It's not — I mean, it's very nice of the queen to — I just —"

"It's torture," said Darkstalker wryly. "I mean, it's torture for *me*, and I've never had my whole family killed in front of me at a party like that."

Indigo stopped and stared at him. Fathom's gaze dropped to his talons.

"Oh, nobody talks about it in the Kingdom of the Sea?" Darkstalker guessed. "All right, I won't if you don't want to. But if you were sent here to be *my* friend, then you

don't have to suffer through all that diplomatic tedium —
especially with the bonus post-traumatic stress."

"You know why I'm here?" Fathom said.

"Because we're both animuses," Darkstalker answered.
"Animi? Huh, I'm not sure. That one doesn't come up very
often."

There was a soft *click*, and Darkstalker realized that
Indigo suddenly held two dangerously sharp throwing stars
in her talons.

"Indigo —" Fathom said anxiously.

"He's here," Indigo said to Darkstalker, "to make sure *you*
don't turn out like his grandfather."

"That'll be an easy mission," Darkstalker said charm-
ingly. "I'm not murderous at all. I'm entirely delightful."

So was Albatross, they both thought.

Indigo and her throwing stars were not the real threat
here. The danger was that these dragons might never see him
for himself. If they only ever saw Albatross when they
looked at him, they'd always fear him, and that might make
one of them do something stupid.

Darkstalker decided to turn the full blaze of his attention
on Fathom. "Listen, if you're worried," he said, "why don't
you make something? A — a soul reader, you could call it. It
could reassure you about who's harmless and full of soul,
like me, or who's teetering on the edge of soulless killing
rage. Liiiiiiike *not* me." That was a pretty good idea, if
Darkstalker said so himself. He could use one of those to
keep track of Arctic's soul, perhaps.

But Fathom was shaking his head furiously. *I can't I can't I can't,* his mind cried.

"All right, settle down," Darkstalker said, surprised. "I can make it for you."

"No!" Fathom yelped. "You mustn't. You *have* to stop using your magic. That's why I'm here, to help you stop."

Darkstalker eyed him for a moment, listening to the tornado of grief and guilt and worry that had apparently taken the place of logical thought in this dragon's head. Should he tell Fathom about his scroll? Surely he would find it reassuring. Maybe Fathom could even make one for himself and stop worrying so much.

On the other hand, he didn't know Fathom at all yet. Could he be trusted with a secret that big?

Completely, and not at all, whispered a half-formed vision of the future, which was rather unhelpful.

Not yet, Darkstalker decided. *Get to know him first.*

How am I going to do this? Fathom was thinking. *I failed so badly before. How can I possibly save him, and everyone?*

"You don't have to be this miserable," Darkstalker said softly.

Fathom lifted his chin, and Indigo thought sadly, *I wish I could help him.*

"You went through something awful." Darkstalker held out one talon as though he could crush the memories in his claws. "All you need to do is enchant something to make the pain bearable. Just — an earring that helps you stop thinking about it so much. An armband that lifts all the grief or stops the flashbacks."

Indigo's eyes flicked to Darkstalker's jewelry, and he heard her wonder what magic he might already be using on them. *Clever dragon,* he thought. *I should be careful of her.*

"I have to remember," Fathom said, looking straight into Darkstalker's eyes. His were gray green, like miniature oceans after a storm. "I can never stop thinking about it." *Or else it could happen to me. The memories make sure I keep my vow to Pearl.*

His vow formed, word for word, in his mind, and Darkstalker repressed a sigh. What kind of animus gave up all his power forever? What kind of life could he have, always haunted by the past and ruled by fear?

"Don't you want to be *happy*?" Darkstalker asked. "I can help you with that."

All at once he felt cold steel pressed against his neck. Indigo was suddenly behind him, her wings pinning his, his throat on the knife's edge. She'd moved with astonishing quickness, and Darkstalker caught a glimpse in her mind of the hours she'd spent training in the year since the massacre, making herself stronger and faster so no dragon could ever hurt her or Fathom ever again.

"Indigo, don't!" Fathom froze, his eyes fixed on the blade at Darkstalker's neck.

"He's too dangerous," Indigo cried. "He's already trying to mess with your head, can't you tell? This isn't safe, Fathom.

I should kill him right now, to protect everyone." *To protect you,* her mind confessed.

Darkstalker raised his tail quietly. One touch from his silver tail band, and she would be dead. It wasn't quite as secure as having all his animus power in his talons, at his disposal whenever he needed it. But he was sure he could kill her before she killed him.

First, though, he wanted to see Fathom's reaction.

"*No,* Indigo, we can't," Fathom said. "He's not Albatross — he hasn't hurt anyone." *Yet,* chimed in their minds. "And killing him could start a war with the NightWings."

"Or maybe save them," she pointed out. "Maybe save all of Pyrrhia."

"But I want to know him," Fathom said. "He doesn't seem dangerous." *He seems like . . . he seems like he could be a friend,* the SeaWing thought wistfully. The earring must be working on him — along with Darkstalker's natural charm, of course.

"That could be a trick — he could be using a spell on us right now," said Indigo. "Maybe he's planning to kill us later."

No, just you, Darkstalker thought pleasantly.

"And I bet he's a mind reader," she added, pressing the blade a little harder against his throat. "Are you a mind reader? Don't lie to us!"

Darkstalker flicked his tail a hair closer to her. "I am," he said. "That's not a secret. Any NightWing with silver teardrop scales by their eyes is a mind reader — I'm certainly not the only one in the tribe."

"An animus who can read our minds!" Indigo said to Fathom, her thoughts flaring with alarm. *If Albatross had been able to do that, we'd both be dead.* "Fathom, this could be our only chance to take out the most dangerous dragon in Pyrrhia."

"Indigo," Fathom said sadly. "Think for a moment. Isn't this what our tribe wants to do to me?"

Hmmm. Interesting. Fathom was smarter than he looked — or he knew exactly what to say to this dragon, at least. Indigo's thoughts hit a wall of sympathy and she hesitated, struggling against it.

Darkstalker took the moment to check the immediate possible futures. Indigo killing him — pretty unlikely. Him killing her — easy enough. But, wow, it would destroy Fathom. Oooh, all kinds of terrible things might come from that decision. A heartbroken animus with nothing left to lose would be pretty hazardous company.

I have to let her live — for now — and let her think she could have killed me, he realized. *That will make Fathom trust me even more.*

But if I want him to really trust me, for the sake of our future friendship, I'll have to get rid of her somehow. Some clever way that he won't suspect.

Otherwise he'll always be worrying about what she thinks of him. It's her eyes on him that make him so afraid of his magic. He'd be much happier and less worried without her around.

As would I, frankly. I don't particularly like dragons who point sharp things at me.

"All right," Indigo said finally. She stepped back, still

holding the stars poised in her talons. "I hope you're right about this, Fathom."

"Please don't be mad," Fathom said to Darkstalker. "She's trying to protect me. It's her job."

A small flicker of pain from Indigo. It was so much, much more than her job.

"I completely understand," Darkstalker said, rubbing his neck. "I'm not mad at all."

If he was, Fathom thought, *he could use his power on us right now. He could have used it to escape from her. Maybe he really can be trusted, after all.*

I hope I didn't just make a really terrible enemy, Indigo was thinking.

Ha ha, Darkstalker thought. *Oh, you certainly did.*

"Hey, I promised you a view from the Royal Tower," he said, nudging Fathom with one of his wings. "You can see almost the whole Night Kingdom from up there. Come on, we'll have plenty of time for serious talk later."

He lifted into the sky, stretching his wings wide and letting the moonlight cascade over him. *Nothing to be mad about,* he thought to himself. *In fact, I learned quite a lot here tonight.*

Poor Fathom, with all his anxiety and self-loathing. I can make it better. I'm going to show him what a gift animus power is. I'll give him a reason to be happy he's alive. I'm going to take away all his fear and guilt and replace it with joy.

And then, once he has something else to live for . . . that's when I'll take care of his Indigo problem.

CHAPTER 16

CLEARSIGHT

"This is such a terrible idea," Clearsight whispered, tipping her wings to catch the wind. Below them, the school was dark and still, as if all the light and noise had been sucked into the party at the palace next door. Darkstalker was there tonight, again, but that was for the best, since it meant he couldn't stop her from doing this, or even notice she was doing it.

"It's not a terrible idea," Listener shot back, "or you wouldn't be letting me do it, because you'd have seen it go wrong and you'd know we were going to be caught. Ipso facto, clearly we'll be fine, because you're just grumbling and not actually trying to stop me."

"Maybe I see that you'll learn a valuable lesson from your criminal mistakes," Clearsight said airily. "Maybe you need to be caught in order for that to happen."

Listener shot her a suspicious look. "You wouldn't do that to me."

"Maybe this is the only way to save you from spiraling into a life of crime and infamy." Clearsight put on her most pious face.

"Quit freaking me out!" Listener whacked Clearsight with her tail and Clearsight started giggling so hard she nearly lost the air current holding her up.

"Besides," Listener said, angling toward the school's upper entrance, "we're not criminals, we're heroes! We're liberating the oppressed! Righting all wrongs! Saving the day!"

"Somehow I don't think that's how the teachers are going to see it," Clearsight pointed out. They landed and stepped carefully into the dark spiraling hall that led down to the classrooms. Student projects and artwork lined the walls, sharpening into focus as her night vision adjusted. Here was one student's research study on RainWing camouflage; over there was a diagram comparing MudWing and SeaWing physiognomy.

A little farther down was the portrait of her that Darkstalker had painted, with what looked like a spiderweb of fireworks behind her. Only the two of them knew that was supposed to represent the intersecting timelines of the future. Unfortunately his skill at painting was nowhere close to Whiteout's, and Clearsight looked a *bit* more like a horse with a hippo butt than she would have liked. She had politely refrained from telling him that.

Listener sighed. "I *tried* to do this through official channels, you know. I talked to Truthfinder — I mean, if *I* can feel what the scavengers are feeling, surely she can, too. But she totally didn't care! She said it made them fascinating subjects for study, but that we shouldn't overidentify with them, because 'they're not dragons, after all.' No matter how sad or scared or lonely they get, they're still just animals, according to her. 'Big, hairless squirrels who can do a few more tricks than your average monkey.' Isn't that crazy?"

"Darkstalker agrees with you," Clearsight offered. She didn't add that he thought Listener's scavenger obsession was a little kooky. "He says the new one they got for his class is severely depressed. He is all in favor of Operation Scavenger Rescue."

"Did you tell him we're doing this tonight?" Listener asked, stopping abruptly so Clearsight bumped into her.

"No," Clearsight said. "He's at some party at the palace and I didn't want him to worry. I'll tell him about it tomorrow when we're done and the scavengers are all free."

"Was there some reason it has to be tonight?" Listener asked, scrutinizing her in the dark. "We've been talking about this since the first day I met you, and suddenly you tell me it's go time. Because tonight is the safest time to do it? Is that why?"

"That's right," Clearsight reassured her. "And it's the best time for the scavengers, too — not too cold outside, a bright night so they can see their way."

It was more than that. Clearsight knew tonight's party at the palace wasn't just any regular gathering. New dragons were coming into their lives and soon everything would be different. She wasn't sure exactly how things were going to change — more dragons meant more variables, which was harder to predict — but she wanted to make sure she did this one awesome thing with her best friend while she still could.

"Here's the first classroom," Listener whispered. They crept into the room, a science lab for the seven-year-old senior class. Aquariums and terrariums covered the tables and walls, some of them glowing with little phosphorescent rocks or glow-in-the-dark plankton. Long-finned fighting fish drifted in their separate bowls, dark purple-and-red. A tortoise snoozed under a trailing fern in a glass cage that smelled of bananas and old lettuce.

A flutter of wings by the window made Clearsight jump, but it was just the two owls, wide-awake and hopping around their cage impatiently. She was sure they would rather be out prowling the night sky, but this was not a mission to rescue all the animals. The scavengers were the ones Listener worried about all the time. The ones with intense, dragonlike emotions, apparently.

"They're asleep," Listener whispered, crouching beside the little warren someone had built for the senior study scavengers. "Should we take the whole cage?"

"No." Clearsight shook her head. "We have to make it look like the scavengers escaped on their own."

Listener gave her a skeptical look. "All six of them? From four different classrooms?"

"You're the one who thinks they're just like dragons," Clearsight argued. "If a dragon had to escape a place like this, wouldn't she rescue the other dragons trapped here along with her, even if she didn't know them?"

"*You* would," Listener said. "I'm not sure most dragons

would risk it. But do you really think scavengers have that much . . . I don't know, empathy?"

"Well, hopefully that'll be the most plausible explanation tomorrow," Clearsight said. "Although I should warn you that if you've talked to Truthfinder about this, that will probably make you her number one suspect."

"I don't care!" Listener bristled, her neck spikes flaring. "She can expel me if she wants! I don't need school to become an animal rights activist!"

"Every NightWing needs school," Clearsight said, digging in her pack. "Here, I thought we could carry them in these."

Listener took one of the burlap sacks between two claws and held it away from her, frowning. "We're going to toss the scavengers in a *sack*?"

"Were you hoping to stick them on your shoulders like baby lemurs?" Clearsight shot back. "They'll be fine; we won't leave them in there for long." She carefully unlatched the cage, moving the levers as quietly as she could, then sliding open the door.

One scavenger was sleeping under a scrap of blanket; the other was sprawled on a pile of shredded paper. Clearsight grabbed the one with the blanket first, scooping up the fabric along with it.

The scavenger woke up immediately and started screaming as though its fur was on fire. Clearsight was so startled she nearly dropped it.

"You're scaring it!" Listener cried.

"It's scaring *me*!" Clearsight shouted back. She wrestled her thrashing bundle into her sack. "Grab the other one!"

The second scavenger was awake now and darting around the cage, perhaps looking for a place to hide. As Listener reached in, it dodged around her claws and began scrambling up the wire side toward the open door at the top.

"Stop being annoying!" Listener snapped at it. "We're *rescuing* you! If you escape inside the school, you'll just end up getting eaten tomorrow!"

The scavenger swung itself onto the inside of the cage roof and kicked at Listener's talons. She yanked it loose and shoved it quickly into her own sack.

"They're more ferocious than I expected," Clearsight said. Her heart was thumping, and every animal in the lab was awake now. The tamarin monkeys rattled their cage, letting out indignant shrieks. In the biggest terrarium, a crocodile was glaring at her with unpleasant yellow eyes.

"Let's hurry up before someone hears us." Listener ran out of the room and Clearsight followed her. Down to Darkstalker's classroom, where they scooped up the depressed lone scavenger without any trouble. It flopped sadly in Clearsight's talons, looking entirely resigned to being eaten.

Then to their old third-year classroom, to the two scavengers Clearsight had admired on her first day. These two were awake — perhaps awakened by the noise coming from other parts of the school — and it took several minutes to capture them. By the end of it, Clearsight was almost willing to wager that Listener was right about them being like dragons. These two seemed to work together, collaborating to trick or distract the dragons. It was kind of adorable and kind of unsettling at the same time.

The last scavenger had recently been acquired by a first-year teacher as a class pet to entertain the youngest dragonets. Listener took one of the naptime blankets and carefully wrapped the scavenger, who watched her with bright, curious eyes instead of fighting back.

"This one still has hope," Listener explained to Clearsight. "I think she kind of gets the idea that we're rescuing her."

"These others don't," Clearsight said, lifting her wriggling sack. "I'm not a mind reader, but I'm getting a definite 'we're about to be eaten' vibe over here."

"I think it's your creepy sacks," Listener said. "They look like something Darkstalker's scary father might drown tigers in."

"Just because Darkstalker's father is an IceWing doesn't mean he's scary," Clearsight argued. "Besides, I'm sure whoever's in charge of acquiring tiger skins has a better method than drowning them in sacks."

"Darkstalker's dad is *absolutely* scary," Listener said, shaking her head. "I ran into him at school once and he demanded directions to the principal's office. His entire head was, like, vibrating with all his thoughts about hating everything and everyone here."

She froze suddenly, pricking up her ears. Clearsight's heart sped up. She put one talon on her sack, trying to muffle its squeaking.

"Someone's here," Listener whispered. "He just landed at the upper entrance. He's wondering what all the noise in the animal lab is about."

"Let's go, quick," Clearsight whispered back.

They fled swiftly through the courtyard, along the hall, and out to the atrium entrance. Clearsight checked the sky — clear as far as she could see — while Listener pressed her talons to her head.

"He's just getting to the lab now," she said.

Together they spread their wings and flung themselves aloft, clutching the sacks of scavengers in their claws. Their weight made Clearsight's flying a little lopsided, especially when the little creatures kept thrashing around. But exhilaration swept through her whole body as she soared away from the school with Listener. They'd done it! They'd freed the scavengers!

"Where are we taking them?" she called to her friend.

"I thought you had a plan!" Listener called back.

"Me? This was *your* crazy idea! In all your years of planning, you never figured out where to let them go?"

"All right, all right." Listener swerved to head north. "It's not safe for them in the Night Kingdom. We'll have to hope they can find a scavenger den in the desert somewhere."

"Wait." Clearsight beat her wings to catch up. "We can't cross the border. It's a battlefield out there." So far the war with the IceWings had stayed outside the walls, consisting mostly of skirmishes in the skies over the Kingdom of Sand. The NightWings couldn't get past the Great Ice Cliff that guarded the Ice Kingdom, and the IceWings couldn't break through the NightWings' air defense. Every few months there was a cease-fire while Queen Diamond and Queen Vigilance "negotiated." According to Darkstalker, that meant they exchanged increasingly furious letters accusing each other of treachery, until one of them snapped and sent her troops to attack again.

So, inside the Night Kingdom: safe. Across the border: war zone. Not exactly something Clearsight wanted to risk to help out a few scavengers.

"No way," Listener agreed. "We drop them as far north as we can, that's all."

"North Beach," Clearsight suggested. "That's not too far from here, and maybe they can swim across to the Kingdom of Sand. Can scavengers swim?"

"I doubt it," said Listener. "Their paws would make useless flippers, and they have barely any blubber to keep them afloat. But yeah, let's take them to North Beach and they can fend for themselves from there."

The expanse of beach at the north end of the Night Kingdom peninsula was rocky and pebbled, unlike the smooth sandy beaches of the southern shores. It faced a bay with the Kingdom of Sand on the far side, just out of dragon eyesight but close enough that most NightWings avoided the area. Clearsight was afraid there might be a few intrepid swimmers practicing at midnight, but when they got there, the moonlit beach was deserted.

They landed among the giant boulders that were strewn

across the beach. Clearsight carefully set down her back talons first, holding the sack up so the scavengers wouldn't get smashed.

"This is so exciting," Listener said, her eyes shining. "We're really doing it! Clearsight! You're my best friend ever!"

Clearsight smiled back at her, wondering how long that would last this time. She could see at least three possible arguments that might explode in the next few months, sending Listener into a rage where she wouldn't talk to Clearsight for a while.

Stop living in the future, Darkstalker's voice echoed in her mind. *Be here now.*

He was right. Because now, here, she had a best friend, and they were doing something wild and wonderful together.

"Ready?" she said. Listener nodded, grinning.

Clearsight set down her sack and held open the mouth of it. There was a surprisingly long pause, as if the scavengers inside had to first figure out how to stand up, and then decide whether this was a trick.

Finally one of them crept to the opening and peeked out. Seeing the two dragons staring down at it, it let out a little yelp, and then bolted toward the ocean. After a moment, another scavenger burst out of the sack and went racing after the first one.

Clearsight waited a moment, then shook the burlap until the third scavenger — the sad one from Darkstalker's classroom — came tumbling out. It curled up on the sand, covering its shaggy head with its paws. She lowered her snout and nudged it gently, but it only whimpered. Finally she used her talons to slide it into the lee of a boulder, where at least hopefully it wouldn't get too wet when the tide came in. Maybe it would feel better in the morning, when the dragons were gone.

She glanced over at Listener, who was arranging her sack the same way, open side toward the ocean. Suddenly all three of Listener's scavengers shot out of the sack at the same time, grabbed the nearest pebbles they could lift, and started flinging them at the two NightWings.

"Hey!" Listener yelped, jumping back. "Ouch! Rude! We're your saviors, you stunted gorillas!"

Two of the scavengers took off running, zigzagging along the beach and waving their paws at the two scavengers from Clearsight's sack. The scavenger with the bright eyes started to follow them, then noticed the one that was curled up on the sand. She ran over to it, poked it, grabbed it, and hauled it up until it was running with her, leaning across her back.

"Did you see that?" Clearsight said excitedly. She jabbed Listener's side. "Your scavenger took my scavenger with her! Come on, didn't that look like empathy to you?"

"It did," Listener said, rubbing her neck where a rock had gotten her. "Although, sheesh, a little gratitude would have been nice, too. Where's the empathy for their heroic dragon rescuers? I ask you."

Clearsight folded her wings, watching the scavengers run away with a pleased sense of accomplishment.

But then . . .

Something tugging at the threads . . . a knot in the timelines . . .

Danger was coming. Danger that could end her life and Listener's right now, here, tonight.

"Get down!" she cried, throwing herself at Listener. She knocked her friend to the ground and spread her wings over her, melting them both into the lumps and shadows of the boulders.

"What the — ?" Listener started.

"Shhhh," Clearsight whispered. "Don't move."

Her friend lay still, although Clearsight could feel her heart pounding through their scales. Sand tickled her snout. Cautiously she peeked out with one eye. Where was the danger coming from?

The ocean.

An unnatural ripple moved across the waves, sliding in toward the sand.

And then, all at once, a pale white head lunged out of the water and snapped its jaws shut around one of the fleeing scavengers.

Clearsight bit her tongue trying not to hiss. The remaining five scavengers screamed and changed course. She saw the sad one let go of the bright-eyed one and run on its own, jolted into action by new terror.

We should save them, she thought. But it was too late for the one in the IceWing's jaws. And the dragon seemed uninterested in chasing the others. He settled into the rushing waves with his catch.

Moreover, it was worth noting that the IceWing was much, much bigger than her or Listener.

That's an IceWing, she finally registered with a rush of panic. *Here. On the shores of the Night Kingdom.*

Another blue-white dragon surfaced beside the first one. "What are you doing?" she snarled.

"Having a snack," he growled back.

She glanced up and down the beach, her gaze lingering suspiciously on the dark lump of Listener and Clearsight. "Back in the water," she snapped. "Now."

Grumbling under his breath, the IceWing dragged his prey into the water with him. The second IceWing scanned the beach again, then dove after him. There were a few more splashes, and then silence.

Clearsight's head was starting to spin. Visions crowded in, piling up on one another. She saw this same beach, but on a different night, with the moons in different positions in the sky and huddled clouds hiding most of their light. She saw a wave of pale silver IceWings slithering ashore, with more behind them, and more, and more. An entire army of IceWings, slipping into the Night Kingdom under the water and far below the noses of the NightWing sky protectors.

They were planning an invasion. The two dragons tonight were advance scouts on a test run. The IceWings had found a way into their territory, and someday soon, the war would be here, inside the walls.

Except it won't, Clearsight thought. *I'll stop them.*

This is why my instincts brought me here tonight. So I could see the IceWings, have this vision, and warn the queen.

This was it, the turning point she'd been waiting for. Her moment to serve the queen, save the tribe, and advance her family's standing. She'd known there would be a way eventually, but she hadn't been sure which timeline would unfold it for her first.

And now that it had happened — now that she had to face the queen — she was terrified all the way down to her bones.

"Are they gone?" she whispered to Listener.

"Yes," Listener whispered back. "I could hear them thinking grumpy thoughts about each other as they swam away."

Clearsight stood up gingerly. "I have to tell the queen."

"Better you than me," Listener said. "I do not want to explain to my parents what I was doing out here."

"I can leave you out of it, if that's what you want," Clearsight said. Her mind was racing ahead. Who to tell first? Her parents would have to go through official channels, but Darkstalker could get her an audience with the queen tomorrow.

Tomorrow was better. There were several possible nights ahead when the invasion might be launched, but the sooner they figured out how to stop it, the better.

Listener started tracing shapes in the sand with one claw, staring out at the ocean. "Clearsight," she said hesitantly. "Listen, I — I know I told you I don't want to know the future. But if — if I ever have to evacuate my family — I mean, if it's a question of saving their lives . . . if something really, really bad is about to happen . . . then I guess I do want you to tell me."

"It's not that bad yet," Clearsight said, wrapping one wing around her friend. "But I promise I will, if I'm ever worried."

It won't come to that, she reassured herself. *We'll stop them. I'll save the whole tribe.*

She was sure she could do that. The queen would listen to her, and the IceWing invasion would be taken care of without one more serrated white claw setting foot on their shores.

So why, then, were ominous visions still spinning behind her eyes?

Visions of NightWings flying away in droves, as though the entire tribe were fleeing some horrific danger?

Clearsight wasn't sure . . . but she had a terrible, sinking feeling that tonight, some dark future had become a little bit more real.

CHAPTER 17

FATHOM

Fathom had been given his own suite of rooms in the Night Palace, which he was sure he would appreciate very much if he could ever find them again.

"This hallway looks familiar," he said, hesitating at another intersection.

"Black marble walls and mirrors every three steps?" Indigo said. "You're right. Because that's what *every hallway in this castle* looks like."

"The mirror thing is weird, isn't it?" he whispered. "I'm not the only one who thinks so?"

"NightWings are very pretty and very special," she informed him. "They deserve to be reminded of that all the time, everywhere they go."

He laughed. They were lucky there weren't any NightWings around to hear them. "Pearl would probably love it, too."

"Well, she can decorate the Summer Palace with as many mirrors as she wants," Indigo said. She started down the new hallway and he hurried to catch up with her.

"The Summer Palace?" he echoed. "I thought she wanted nothing to do with that place."

"She's changed her mind — you didn't hear?" Indigo glanced over, then down at her claws as though she'd just remembered that no one talked to him. "Everyone thinks the Island Palace is haunted. She can't keep any servants there, and most of the dragons who were at the — the party never want to go there again. So she's moving all surface palace business to the Summer Palace and abandoning the Island Palace."

"Oh." Fathom blinked. It made sense. He himself had trouble walking through the Island Palace without remembering bloody talonprints everywhere. The smell of jasmine sometimes made him sick to his stomach, and he never wanted to see a red hibiscus again as long as he lived.

But still — that had been the SeaWings' above-water palace for generations. Was it gone forever now?

A black dragon carrying a tray came out of a door a few steps ahead of them.

"Excuse me," Indigo called. "We're looking for the guest suites."

"I can take you there," he said with a bow. "This way."

As they followed him, Fathom watched Indigo out of the corner of his eye. He wasn't imagining it — she changed completely when there were other dragons around. She squared her shoulders and stood up taller; her voice went deeper and more commanding. The spear in her talons was suddenly a weapon rather than a prop. She really looked like she was ready to kill someone to protect him. Like a true bodyguard.

That should make it easier for him to keep her at a distance, if he could remember to think of her that way. *Just a guard. Not the most important dragon in my life.*

"Here you are," said the NightWing servant, gesturing with his tail at a large black door that looked very much like all the other doors they'd passed. "The guest suite for visiting SeaWings."

"Thank you," Fathom said. "Um. When is breakfast?"

The black dragon snorted a laugh. "Around midday," he said. "NightWings never wake up before then, unless the queen rises early and commands our attendance. Usually we stay awake all night and go to sleep at sunrise."

"Oh," Fathom said, shivering at the strangeness of this kingdom.

The NightWing paused for a moment, looking Fathom up and down as though he were expecting to see something magic happen. Evidently disappointed, he bowed again and whisked away.

"This tribe is weird," Indigo observed, shaking her head.

The door opened into a dark antechamber, where droning snores announced that Wharf and Lionfish were fast asleep. Indigo frowned and stepped toward them, but Fathom stopped her with an outstretched wing.

"Let them sleep," he whispered. "It was a long flight here."

"They're supposed to wake up when someone comes

through here," she whispered back. "Like for instance someone planning to attack you. That's kind of their whole job."

"And they already hate it," he observed, heading toward the inner chamber. "We don't need to make it worse by waking them up to yell at them on their first night here."

They slipped through into the next room and closed the door on the snoring. In here, where Fathom was supposed to sleep, the only sounds were the splash of a fountain in the corner and the rush of wind outside on the balcony. Several small candles were set around the room, flickering their orange light against the darkness.

He realized that this was the first time he'd been alone with Indigo since . . . since the massacre.

"I'll have to yell at them tomorrow, though," Indigo said, looking unexcited about that prospect. "I wonder if they even bothered to search this room." She shook out her wings and snapped into bodyguard mode again, poking her spear into all the corners and lifting all the rugs.

"You don't have to do that," Fathom said quietly. "I know I'm the real danger here." He caught one of the billowing curtains and tied it down, avoiding her eyes.

"Is that what you think?" she said. She stopped, only a few steps away from him. "Do you think I'm here to save other dragons from *you*?"

"You should be," he said. He held out his front talons, watching the candlelight glow through the webs between his claws. "These are dangerous."

"Not to me." Indigo suddenly gathered his talons between hers and stepped closer, holding them near her heart. "Fathom, not to me."

The curtains rippled in the breeze, reaching for them with long soft tendrils. He was close enough to feel her breath on his scales. He wanted to dive into her eyes and catch the tiny flames reflected there. He wanted to tell her how much he had missed her.

"*Especially* to you," he said. "You shouldn't have come here with me." He tore himself out of her grasp and turned away, blinking back tears.

"I thought . . . I thought it was Pearl who was keeping us apart," Indigo said. "She said it was your idea, but I didn't *believe* her."

"She's right, though," Fathom said. "You make me more dangerous. No matter how many oaths I swear, there's always you — the one dragon who could make me use my power again. Don't you understand that?"

There was a long pause. Finally he rubbed his eyes and turned to look at her.

Indigo had her wings folded back and was studying him seriously. He'd seen this thoughtful face on her before, whenever they'd been asked to debate two sides of an issue in history class. *The way she listens. The way she really thinks.* Two more things about her he'd forgotten he missed so much.

"You're not Albatross," she said.

"But I might be," he said.

"I'm not leaving you," she said. "Do you want me to leave you?"

Say yes. Say yes immediately so she'll believe you and she'll have to go.

But nothing came out. The words were caught in his throat, swallowed by the dark room and the nearness of her, after missing her for so long.

A moment passed, and she stepped toward him again, reaching to brush one of his wings with hers. He forgot to breathe.

"I trust you not to use your power," she said softly. "I'm not afraid of you. I believe we're safer together, and I think I can protect you from Darkstalker. So I'm not leaving."

Fathom fought with himself, knowing what he *should* say, knowing he should push her away and send her home. That normal, happy life was waiting for her back there.

"I should go to sleep," he said finally instead.

"Yes," she said, making her "bodyguard face" again. "I'm going to sleep here, at the balcony door, to make sure no one tries to come in this way."

"All right," Fathom said. He was torn between relief — he didn't want to sleep in this big unfamiliar room alone — and anger at himself. *Why are you letting her stay? Don't you care about her?*

Indigo lay down in the open archway that led to the balcony and coiled her tail around her talons. In the moonlight, she was a solemn silhouette, quiet as the depths of the ocean.

Fathom dragged a pile of blue-green pillows over to a spot near the fountain and punched them around for a long time before finally settling down on top of them.

"Well done," Indigo called sleepily. "Those pillows will never question your authority again."

He smothered his laugh. He didn't want her to think that everything was fine, that they could be friends again the way they were before. If she had to stay, the only way this would work was if he kept her at a distance.

I mustn't let the NightWings know she's important to me, he realized. *That could put her in danger, too.*

Worries tumbled around in his head as he drifted into sleep. *Is it safe to like Darkstalker? What does Queen Vigilance expect from me? Are Wharf and Lionfish spying on me and Indigo and reporting back to Pearl?*

What's going to happen to us now?

CHAPTER 18

DARKSTALKER

The night was starting to fade toward morning when Darkstalker got home from the palace. He'd swooped by Clearsight's on the way, to see if he could find her, but her parents said she was out with Listener, which left him feeling sort of disgruntled and abandoned.

Arctic and Foeslayer were already asleep, or at least quiet behind the door of their room, having left the party much earlier than he had. Darkstalker stepped softly past his sister's room and unlocked his door.

He didn't like this time of day. When the birds started chirping and the sky began fading to purplish gray, that meant it was almost time to sleep. He wished he never had to sleep. He had so much to do, so much he wanted to get done. Not only did sleeping feel like a waste of time, but it also gave him an itching restless feeling of missing things — like something important might happen without him there to affect it.

Carefully he tucked his earring into his jewelry box and unclasped the tail band. For a moment he stood holding it, tracing the embossed silver scales. Tonight, this had been his only protection against a possible killer. If Indigo had moved faster — if she hadn't stopped to discuss her plan with Fathom — could she have killed him?

He wouldn't even have been able to use his power to heal himself. It was all here, hidden inside his scroll. He could have bled to death, completely helpless — he, Darkstalker, the most powerful dragon in the world!

He took a deep breath. Indigo's attack must have rattled him more than he realized. *So do something about it,* he told himself. He was good at solving problems. Here was a problem: how could he use his magic to defend himself if he didn't have his scroll with him?

Darkstalker extended his talons and studied them, then ran his claws lightly over his throat. Another piece of jewelry? But jewelry could be removed, or fly off during a fight, and wouldn't it be suspicious if he wore the same thing every day anyway?

Perhaps he could embed a jewel into his body somewhere. He'd seen dragons with small diamonds buried between their scales. Or something in his teeth — there had been a SandWing envoy at the palace once with two gold teeth.

He touched his neck again. No, nothing removable. He needed something that could always be a part of him. Indigo was a smart dragon; she already suspected him of enchanting his jewels. She might be able to spot anything else he added and figure out what it did.

What if . . .

Could he enchant his actual scales?

Why not?

He swept his claws down his side, suddenly feeling hyper-aware of all the ways he could be stabbed or sliced or burned or frozen. The more dragons knew about his power, the more danger he would be in. And he didn't want to leave the world before accomplishing everything he could see in his shining future.

Darkstalker hurried to the wall and the painting that was enchanted to hide and protect his scroll. He took the scroll out carefully, rolled it to the next blank spot . . . and then paused.

Clearsight.

She always read the new spells in his scroll. She liked to discuss them with him and come up with new ideas. Usually she said the right admiring things.

But what would she think of this?

A quiet warning was starting to chime at the back of his mind. He could sense an argument in their close future — the kind where she got judgmental and anxious and made him question all his decisions. The kind of argument he hated.

And perhaps he could avoid it. Wouldn't that make them both happier?

He rolled the scroll backward, scanning the spells he'd already cast.

Here, near the beginning — there was space for him to write a new spell between the lines of the others. With luck

Clearsight wouldn't go back and reread these; maybe she'd never notice it. And if she never noticed it, she couldn't question him about it.

It was a makeshift solution, but it would do for now. He'd come up with a better way to hide his secret spells later.

He dipped his claw in the green ink and wrote:

Enchant Darkstalker's scales to be invulnerable to harm of any sort, to heal instantly if injured, and to shield him inde-structibly from any threat of death.

That was a little dramatic, but he liked the sound of it. Maybe he should go a step further and cast a spell that would make him immortal. That was something to think about. Imagine everything he could do for Pyrrhia if he could live forever!

First, though, he should test this spell, since it was pretty unusual. He went to his trunk and dug under the extra blankets until he found one of his daggers — long, wickedly curved, with a gleaming sharp edge.

Deep breath. Nothing to be afraid of. (Ever again, if this worked.)

He set the blade against the skin of his shoulder and slid it firmly toward his neck.

It was like trying to cut diamonds. His scales repelled the knife smoothly, beautifully, with no fuss at all.

Darkstalker tried stabbing himself in a few other spots, his excitement mounting. The dagger bounced right off him, unable to draw blood.

He'd done it. He'd made himself invincible.

Don't get too cocky yet. Make sure you think of what else someone could do to you, and find ways to protect yourself from everything. Poison, for instance. Poison didn't seem like Indigo's style, but someone else might try it one day.

For now, though, he could take a moment to be proud of himself. *I wonder if any other animus has ever thought of enchanting their own scales.*

I suspect I'm the only one who's ever come up with something like my scroll. See, I was obviously given these powers for a reason. I can use them more wisely than any other dragon before me. I just have to be careful and smart, that's all.

And now that his safety was taken care of, he could focus on a more fun project.

What could he use to make a soul reader?

As he began prowling his room, looking for inspiration, another thought occurred to him.

If I can enchant my entire body like that . . . what could I do to other dragons?

CHAPTER 19

CLEARSIGHT

Darkstalker had an odd twinkle in his eye when he came to pick her up the afternoon after Clearsight's vision at North Beach. But he didn't explain why, and he didn't have the nervous energy that usually meant he wanted to tell her something, so she ignored it. She had more important things on her mind, such as saving the entire tribe from invading IceWings.

"Do you really think the queen will listen to me?" she asked him again, fidgeting with her tail. They were waiting outside Queen Vigilance's throne room. It felt early to her, the sun high in the sky, but Darkstalker assured her that the queen was awake at all hours and especially loved conducting business whenever it might seem peculiar to other dragons.

"Of course," he said. He reached over and adjusted the length of the necklace he had given her to wear, which was sweet, but made her feel even more self-conscious. She did know how to wear a necklace, for moons' sake.

"I should have enchanted this to make you feel as confident and beautiful as you look," he whispered in her ear.

She wrinkled her nose at him. "No, thank you. You wouldn't really do that, would you? Change my feelings with magic? You know that would be completely not OK with me, right?"

The doors to the throne room swung open before he could answer. Two guards ushered them inside, and Clearsight saw to her dismay that there were several members of the NightWing court present — including her seer-training teacher, Allknowing.

Allknowing glittered with poise and diamonds, standing on the dais beside the queen's throne. Her face was composed, but her nostrils flared slightly when she caught sight of her student waiting to see the queen.

"Whoa," Darkstalker said, wincing. "There is a dragon in here who already doesn't like you very much."

"That's the teacher I told you about," Clearsight whispered. "The queen's top seer."

"Approach," Queen Vigilance called out.

Uh-oh. Her head was starting to pound: visions were coming. *Keep it together. Don't collapse.*

Darkstalker sitting on that very throne, wearing the twisted crown.

Darkstalker standing over the body of the queen, blood staining his claws.

She clenched her talons. Those were the dark paths, the violent paths. They didn't have to happen. They *weren't* going to happen; she wouldn't let them.

Follow the bright visions instead, the way Darkstalker always tells me to. Like this one of me and Darkstalker presenting our six little dragonets to the queen. The queen's grandson chasing Eclipse in circles, the two of them giggling, Vigilance cracking a rare smile.

Slowly Clearsight's heart calmed down and the visions faded, but her wings were still shaking as she stepped toward the queen. She'd never had so many important dragons looking at her. She'd also never revealed the extent of her power to anyone before, except Darkstalker. But now she had no choice.

"Your Majesty," she said with a bow.

"This is?" Queen Vigilance said to Darkstalker.

"Clearsight, Your Majesty," he answered. "She is a very gifted seer."

"Ah," said the queen with a sigh, as Allknowing's eyes narrowed. "Seers. Always so illuminating. You may speak."

"I come with a warning," said Clearsight, launching into the speech she'd rehearsed all night long. "The IceWings are planning an invasion by sea at the North Beach. I believe they intend to attack very soon — most likely the next time two moons are new at once, when they can slip by under cover of darkness."

She paused, realizing the queen was leaning forward with glinting eyes.

"What is this?" Queen Vigilance said avidly. "Don't you have a prophecy for me?"

Clearsight hesitated again. She thought of the lessons she'd had with Allknowing, where they all had to take their visions and contort them into enigmatic rhyming couplets. Should she have done that with this warning for the queen? But there was nothing cryptic about it. The IceWings were coming, and Clearsight knew exactly how and where, along with a few intelligent guesses as to when. Why make that cryptic and confusing? The queen needed to know precisely what Clearsight had seen, in order to protect the tribe.

"I saw a pair of IceWings scouting the North Beach last night," Clearsight said. "That triggered a vision of hundreds of IceWings swimming in to invade our territory. They're coming soon and I knew I had to come tell you."

"My, my," said the queen, shooting a sideways look of suspicion at Allknowing. "How straightforward."

"I'm sorry it doesn't sound fancier." Clearsight spread her wings. "But I'm sure it's true. The only futures I can see where they don't attack are the ones where you find a way to stop them."

A curious murmur scurried around the throne room. The queen wasn't the only one staring at Clearsight like an undiscovered type of gemstone.

Queen Vigilance tipped her head slowly to regard her own seer. "Allknowing. What have you seen of this?"

Allknowing bared her teeth. "If you recall my last prophecy, Your Majesty, there were references to *waves of ice dragons* and a *midnight menace*."

"Yes," Vigilance said with chilly stillness. "Very poetic. But I don't recall anything about an underwater attack focused on North Beach in the next month."

"That — that —" Allknowing sputtered. "The nature of visions — specific details are not — that's not how it works."

"Maybe not for you," said Vigilance. "Dragonet."

It took a moment for Clearsight to realize she was being addressed. "Yes, Your Majesty?"

"You work for me now. Move into the palace tonight."

"Oh," Clearsight said, startled. That had been an option in one or two timelines, but she hadn't taken it seriously. She was supposed to be sent home with a pile of gold, followed by a celebratory dinner with her parents. What had she said to land herself here instead? Or had someone else accidentally tipped the future in this direction? Maybe Allknowing, by annoying the queen somehow? "But — my parents —"

"Will be amply rewarded." The queen stood up and spoke to the general on her left. "Call a war council meeting." She swept down the steps, pausing for a moment beside Clearsight. "I want everything you know about this attack written out by morning."

A moment later she was gone, with nearly everyone else in the throne room following in her wake.

Darkstalker bounded over and threw his wings around Clearsight. "Aren't you clever?" he crowed. "You were right, that was a genius way to introduce yourself to the queen. Totally worth the wait."

Allknowing stalked down from the dais, glowering so fiercely that sparks shot out of her nose. "I knew you were trouble," she snarled. "But I didn't realize you were planning to betray me."

"Huh," Darkstalker said thoughtfully. "Sounds like you're not a very good seer, then."

"I'm *not* betraying you," Clearsight protested, elbowing him in the ribs. *Ow. Why does it feel like he's wearing armor?* "It's a serious threat, so I had to warn the queen, didn't I?"

"Well, enjoy her attention now that you've got it," Allknowing growled. "You'll soon see what happens to dragons who show off around here." Casting a withering look at Darkstalker, she slithered out of the throne room, hissing to herself.

"Oh dear," Clearsight said, pressing her talons together.

"Don't worry about her." Darkstalker nudged her happily. "I think maybe now *you're* the queen's top seer."

"That wasn't the plan!" Clearsight closed her eyes and tried to study the futures. Was she really going to live at the palace now? And share all her visions with the queen?

Not all of them. No way. Not if I want to keep Darkstalker alive.

She opened her eyes again as they stepped out of the throne room into the central courtyard. Darkstalker had told her this was the heart of the palace: a series of grand ballrooms, gardens, and atriums with tall glass ceilings, where the party had taken place the night before. A few sleepy-looking NightWing servants were climbing around, taking down the decorations and polishing the floors.

And across the way, four blue and green dragons were gathered around one of the pools, staring down at the darting shapes of the bright gold-and-white koi.

With her mind more than half in the future, Clearsight saw a familiar SeaWing face and reacted instinctively.

"Fathom!" she called, bounding over with her wings spread wide to embrace him. "You're here!"

One of the other SeaWings leaped forward, fast as a bolt of lightning, flinging herself in front of Fathom. "Stop right there!" she cried. "Don't touch him!" Her spear came up and nearly caught Clearsight in the throat.

"Hey!" Darkstalker roared. "Unnecessary!"

Clearsight yelped, skidded to a stop, and covered her face with her front talons. "Oh no! I'm so sorry!" *Galaxies and geckos, what is wrong with me?* "Aaargh, I've never done that before."

"Who are you?" the bodyguard demanded.

"I'm Clearsight." She spread her wings, trying to look nonthreatening.

"She's with me," Darkstalker said, frowning.

Oh, am I? Clearsight thought. *I thought I was the queen's new top seer.* "I — I see the future, and I've seen Fathom in my visions — but I forgot we hadn't actually met yet. I'm sorry," she said directly to Fathom.

"Me?" said the nervous green dragon. "You've seen *me* in your visions?"

"Lots of times," she reassured him. "We're going to be friends, I promise."

The SeaWing brings death. The SeaWing brings salvation. Don't let him come. He must come, or all is lost.

She hesitated as the old line from her scrolls chased through her mind. *Nice and cryptic. Allknowing would be pleased.*

But she wasn't going to worry about that now, in her first meeting with Fathom, at long last.

"Oh!" she said, turning to the bodyguard. "And you must be Indigo." She'd seen this SeaWing face, too — sometimes fierce and snarling, sometimes crying, sometimes covered in blood. Maybe she shouldn't look too carefully at those time-lines right now. She was already scaring the new dragons enough with all her talk of visions.

"It's all right, Indigo," said Fathom. "Wharf, Lionfish, you may go hunt. We'll be fine." He gave Clearsight a tenta-tive smile as the other two SeaWings shrugged and flew away. Oh, she felt like she knew him so well — how shy he was, how uncertain of what to say next. How all the guilt and worry weighed down his wings.

"Guess what?" she said to him. "I'm moving into the pal-ace, too! We'll basically be neighbors. You've already met Darkstalker, right?"

"Last night." Darkstalker leaned over as though he was going to nudge Fathom's wing with his own, but then he glanced sideways at Indigo and pulled back. "He gave me a great idea, actually. Can I show you guys?"

"All right," Fathom said. The way he looked at Darkstalker — as though he so badly wanted to trust him. Clearsight sure recognized that feeling. "We're not doing anything right now," the SeaWing went on. "I'm not sure what we're supposed to do. I'm afraid the queen might have forgotten we're here."

"She's having a bit of an emergency today," Darkstalker

explained. "And I'm pretty sure your only real mission is to hang out with me, so you're doing excellent work right now."

Fathom's smile became a little bit more real.

"Well, you're also supposed to be teaching him things. Maybe try looking more stern," Clearsight suggested, grinning at Fathom. "Or a little menacing. Say something wise and insightful now and then."

"Um," Fathom said. "Like, never eat the purple variety of long-legged sea crab?"

Darkstalker started laughing, and Fathom blinked at him with delight.

"Just like that," Darkstalker assured him. "That's the kind of advice I like."

Clearsight tipped her head at him, wondering if that was a dig at her. She knew he didn't always like the things she had to say about his animus experiments. But too bad; she was also quite sure he needed to be with someone who would say those things, instead of someone who smiled and nodded and had no opinions of her own.

"Anyway," Darkstalker said, flipping open his pack. "So I went home and started thinking and ended up not sleeping at all because I was too excited and here's what I came up with." He pulled out an odd little contraption that looked like a telescope with a small golden hourglass mounted on the side. "Watch this." He pointed it at Clearsight, and the hourglass began to spin. Around and around it went, three times. When it stopped, a mountain of black sand was in the bottom half of the hourglass, and a tiny scattering of white sand was in the top.

"Awww," Darkstalker said. "Look at how good you are."

Clearsight peered closer. None of the sand was moving from one side to the other. Now that it had stopped spinning, the hourglass was perfectly still.

"What in the world?" she said. "What does it mean?"

"This is a soul reader," Darkstalker said proudly. "Point it at anyone, and it'll tell you what the balance of good and evil is inside them. Think of all the sand as your soul, and this will show you how much of it is evil. Black sand for good, like the NightWings, white for bad, like the IceWings. See, you are almost entirely good, with just little bits of bad."

Little bits of bad! Clearsight squinted at the white sand. *How am I bad? What have I done? Why do I have any white sand at all?*

"You really made it," Fathom whispered. Clearsight glanced up at him and saw that the SeaWing looked sick to his stomach. "But didn't you hear me? I warned you — you have to stop using your magic. Every time you do, it gets worse. You can't . . . you can't just . . ." He shuddered from head to tail.

Darkstalker hasn't told him about the scroll yet, Clearsight realized. She could understand why . . . but poor Fathom.

"It's all right," Darkstalker said. "Here, look. Clearsight, point it at me." He handed the telescope to her. She lifted it up and sighted through the eyehole, finding Darkstalker at the end of it.

The hourglass started spinning . . . and spinning . . . and spinning . . .

"You've confused it," Clearsight tried to joke.

"It takes a moment sometimes," he said with a shrug.

Finally the hourglass settled. Black sand lay in drifts around the bottom half. A substantially smaller pile of white sand huddled in the top. More than Clearsight had, but not very much, really, she told herself.

"See?" Darkstalker pointed at the soul reader. "I'm fine. My soul is almost entirely good. Isn't that cool?"

Clearsight thought it was pretty clever, actually. This could be a useful device for keeping an eye on other animus dragons. She swung it around toward Fathom.

"*Don't* point that at him," Indigo objected, blocking the way. The soul reader landed on her, spun, and ended up with a pile of black sand as big as Clearsight's.

"It won't hurt him," Clearsight said. "You saw, we just pointed it at each other."

"But it could be specially enchanted," Indigo said. "To — to do something to him." Behind her back, Darkstalker rolled his eyes at Clearsight.

"Let her do it," Fathom said, touching Indigo's tail with his own. "Please? I want to know."

Indigo gave him a very concerned look, and Clearsight guessed what she might be really worried about: that Fathom would discover he had more evil than good in him. *She's trying to protect him in more ways than one,* Clearsight thought sympathetically.

But the SeaWing stepped back, and Clearsight lined up the telescope so she could see Fathom's anxious face on the other end.

Once again the hourglass spun — and when it came to a stop, the black sand outweighed the white. It looked a lot like Darkstalker's balance, in fact, with about one-quarter white sand and three-quarters black.

Fathom stepped hesitantly over to the telescope and touched the hourglass with one claw. "This is real?" he said to Darkstalker.

"I promise," Darkstalker answered. "We kind of have matching souls, don't we? Doesn't that make you feel better?"

Fathom stared at the hourglass for another minute, then up at Clearsight. "Yes," he admitted. He turned to Darkstalker again. "But please, please stop using your magic. My grandfather — I don't know what it was that tipped him over into madness and evil. It could be anything. One spell might make all the difference."

"Fathom," Darkstalker said gently. "Your power is a gift. You shouldn't be so terrified of it. You just have to figure out how to use it safely and make it work for you." He paused, then shot a surprisingly hostile look at Indigo. "It's not a trick. I just want him to be happy. Don't you?"

Indigo looked him directly in the eye. "I believe he can be happy without any magic."

Clearsight didn't like the energy that suddenly vibrated between them. She especially didn't like the way it spun out into a thread that ended in a world with no Indigo in it.

Not going to happen, she told herself fiercely. *I'll keep an eye on them. I'll fix this.*

"It's a beautiful day for flying," she said, trying to distract them both. She nudged Fathom. "Why don't we show you around the Night Kingdom? There's a great beach not too far from here."

Fathom's face lit up, and Clearsight felt the tension give way a little bit. She would still have to be careful. She didn't see a clear path to a place where Indigo and Darkstalker could trust each other, but maybe if she kept them apart, everything would be all right.

The important thing was that Fathom was finally here — their soon-to-be best friend, the future godfather of their dragonets. This was a happy day.

She lifted off into the sky, steering around the clouds, keeping the sun bright in her eyes.

Don't look down.

Don't chase the storm.

Don't let the dark visions win.

CHAPTER 20

FATHOM

Weeks passed in a blur that got happier and happier each day. After a year of cold silences and unfriendly looks and solitude, Fathom suddenly found himself wrapped in warmth and attention. Darkstalker and Clearsight weren't afraid of him or his magic. More than that, they seemed to actually *like* him. They sought him out every day, taking him flying and hunting, sharing scrolls and secrets about the royal court. They made him laugh. They made him forget, for hours at a time, what he'd been through and what he'd had to do.

He never forgot his mission, though. He still watched Darkstalker constantly for signs that he was using his magic . . . or about to turn evil. One evening he found the soul reader on his desk with a note that said:

By all the shining moons, your brain is driving me crazy. Here, you keep this, use it on me whenever you want, and STOP WORRYING SO MUCH.

"SO suspicious," Indigo said when he showed the note to her. "He's probably enchanted the thing to show you that he's always good, no matter what he does. Or worse, maybe it has a spell on it to make you trust him more every time you touch it."

"Aren't you paranoid and clever," Darkstalker said, sailing in over the balcony. "We're lucky *you're* not an animus, with ideas like that."

Indigo froze, trying to put on her blank bodyguard face, and Fathom stepped between them in a hurry. "Thank you," he said to Darkstalker. "You really don't mind if I keep it?"

"I've used it on my father already," Darkstalker said, folding his wings. "He's almost as bad as I thought, but not all the way evil yet. I might need to borrow it back to show my mother one day, but she's got enough to deal with in the war right now. So you hang on to it for me, if it makes you feel better."

Fathom tipped the telescope toward Darkstalker and checked — the same levels of black and white sand as before.

"See? Totally not evil," Darkstalker said with a grin. "Let's go bother Clearsight!"

Fathom followed him out into the hallway with Indigo behind them. "She said she had to work today, remember?"

"Queen Vigilance wants her to work *every* day," Darkstalker said, rolling his eyes. "She's already quit school to do this full time. It's not good for her. Flying and hunting and swimming with *me* is what's good for her." He narrowed his eyes at Indigo. "Do your other two bodyguards do anything useful? It seems like this one is the only one who's ever on duty."

Fathom flinched. He wasn't doing a very good job of hiding how important Indigo was to him; she really did go with him everywhere. But that was partly because neither of them trusted Wharf or Lionfish and partly because none of the other NightWings ever seemed to notice who Fathom was with, anyway. Of course Darkstalker would, though.

"Um, well . . . Indigo is the strongest," Fathom stammered awkwardly. "The other two haven't exactly, um, adjusted to the sleep cycle around here." That was actually rather true. Wharf and Lionfish were often sleeping during the NightWings' waking hours.

"Well, you're lucky you've got this one," Darkstalker said, with a hint of something like amusement in his voice. "She seems to be very good at her job."

Fathom glanced at Indigo. Her expression was troubled, but she didn't say anything.

They rapped on Clearsight's door and heard a clatter of things falling as talons thumped toward the door. Finally she poked her head out and gave Darkstalker a stern look.

"I knew it was you," she said.

"REALLY?" Darkstalker said with a gasp. "It's like you can PREDICT THE FUTURE!"

"You are not distracting me today!" she cried. "Go away! The queen wants a full report on the next year of IceWing maneuvers by tomorrow morning!"

Darkstalker bundled past her into the room, sweeping Fathom along with him. The floor, as usual, was covered with scrolls, as was every available surface. Fathom could recognize Clearsight's handwriting at a glance now; it seemed as if she'd filled a hundred scrolls with her densely packed notes since she'd moved into the palace.

"Great kingdoms," Indigo said, startled, from the doorway. She looked down at her claws as if she didn't know where she could possibly put them in this erupting volcano of paper.

"You have to tell Vigilance that an entire year of information is impossible," Darkstalker said to Clearsight. "Especially when you're dealing with a whole tribe, an unpredictable queen, and all the little ridiculous things that can go wrong in a war."

"They're not little or ridiculous when hundreds of lives are at stake," Clearsight said, pressing her talons against her eyes. "And Queen Diamond isn't completely unpredictable; she just changes her mind a lot. Besides, this is important — I helped us win the skirmish at sea last week, and I made sure the army avoided that ambush in the cactus mazes. But every time I'm right, Queen Vigilance wants more details. How many dragons in this location exactly; what time of day will they attack precisely —"

"How many grains of sand in the next sandstorm," Darkstalker finished. "You're going to lose your mind, trying to track all of this. Come flying with us," he wheedled. "It'll clear your head."

"I can't clear my head!" Clearsight protested. "I need it full of information! This information! Important information! In three months there might be a dawn attack on one of our supply routes! Quick, pass me that scroll." She reached for an inkwell and nearly spilled it on one of the maps of the Kingdom of Sand.

Darkstalker gave her the scroll she'd pointed to, waded through the paper, and flung open the window. Moonlight poured in, along with the smell of the distant ocean and the sound of dragons singing far below in the Great Diamond.

"You are coming flying with us," he said, "because I have made you a present, and because there's a pack of delicious wolves running through the forests of Borderland Mountain, and because tomorrow is your hatching day, so Queen Vigilance can snort a bucket of worms for all I care."

"Tomorrow's your hatching day?" Fathom said to Clearsight. "How old will you be?"

"Oh," she said, touching her head. The black ink on her claws matched the black of her scales. "I guess it is. Five. Wow, I can't believe I'm only five years old." She blinked at the scrolls, as if she'd lived several more lifetimes through her visions.

"Clearsight's hatching day: the best thing that's ever happened in the history of the world!" Darkstalker cried. He swept Clearsight off her feet and spun her around, scattering scrolls everywhere. "Let's celebrate! Let's fly!" He tossed her out the window and she caught the wind with her wings, laughing breathlessly.

"You loon!" she shouted at him, swooping around in a circle. "What am I supposed to tell the queen?"

"That I love you and she can talk to me if she has any concerns," Darkstalker proclaimed. "Come on, Fathom!"

"Me?" Fathom said. "You really want me to come? Wouldn't you rather —"

"Shh!" Darkstalker knocked on Fathom's head and tugged him toward the window. "Enough with the self-doubt! You're our friend, and the present is partly for you, so let's go, let's go!" He leaped into the sky and barreled into Clearsight, tumbling through the sky with her.

Fathom climbed onto the windowsill and watched them wistfully for a moment. They made it look so easy, being happy and in love. They never seemed to worry about all the reasons to stay apart. They were sure they'd have dragonets one day — Clearsight even thought one of them might be an animus, but she didn't care. Darkstalker wasn't afraid of what he might do with his power for her, and she didn't seem to be afraid for his soul.

Which had to mean something, since she could see the future.

Maybe . . . maybe Darkstalker was right, and Fathom should stop worrying so much, too.

He looked over his shoulder at Indigo. She had her head down, reading one of the scrolls on the floor.

With a sudden rush of horror, Fathom remembered the look on Albatross's face as he strangled Indigo. He remembered the gleaming madness in his grandfather's eyes and the trail of blood that had led from the pavilion back to the scene of the massacre.

No, he thought, his heart pounding. *I'm right to worry.*

Darkstalker should worry more. That's what I'm here to tell him, if I can figure out how to make him listen.

He took off into the air, following his friends. They were racing around the clouds now, blowing puffs of smoke at each other. He could hear Clearsight's laughter echoing through the sky.

He wished he could at least treat Indigo like a friend in front of them . . . but she didn't want him to. She agreed that it was safer if everyone thought she was just his bodyguard, and so that was how she acted, trailing after them silently wherever they went.

Tonight Darkstalker led them into a forest that swept along the lower reaches of the mountain, beyond the palace. He and Clearsight each caught a wolf and then landed beside a lake so Fathom could catch a fish and join them. Darkstalker built a fire and pulled a feast out of the bag slung over his shoulder: giant tomatoes, roasted nuts, something he called "cheese" that Fathom had never had before, bear paws, camel jerky, and several mystery fruits he'd bought from a traveling RainWing peddler at the market.

"I've had this one before," Clearsight said, poking a small fuzzy brown sphere. "It's called a kiwi and it's all tingly in your mouth. Ooo, don't eat that one with the purple spots; it'll make your breath smell like vultures for a week."

"How do you know that?" Fathom asked. "A vision?"

"Experience," she said, pointing significantly at Darkstalker. "I can't believe you bought it again, after last time!"

He laughed, flicking her with his tail. "I forgot what it looked like! Anyway, I seem to remember it was deliciously worth it."

"For you, maybe, but not for me!" she protested. "You can have it if you promise to stay far away from me for the next week. Actually, considering how much work I have to do, sure, go ahead."

Darkstalker picked up the offending fruit and threw it in the lake. "There," he said. "Now some poor unsuspecting fish will probably have a terrible first date because of you."

"Thank you, handsome." Clearsight laughed, poking him gently with her tail.

"Time for presents?" Darkstalker said. "Yay absolutely yes?"

"I don't have anything for you," Fathom said. "I'm sorry."

"It's totally fine," Clearsight said. "Darkstalker's being dramatic. I don't need presents."

"Wait — maybe — hang on." Fathom jumped up and hurried into the trees. Indigo was pacing outside the circle of firelight, peering into the shadows and scanning the sky. She stopped as he went past her and watched him paw the ground.

"Are you all right?" he asked her.

"Sure," she said quietly, glancing back at the two NightWings. "I'm just . . . worrying. I feel like something bad's about to happen."

"You should join us," he said, lowering his voice to match hers. *I wish you could. I wish this could be normal, that we could be like them.*

She shook her head. "I should keep watch."

If anyone attacks us, Darkstalker would probably use his magic to protect us, Fathom thought. *It's bad that I find that a little comforting.*

He found what he'd been looking for: a piece of wood just the right size and shape. He took it over to show Indigo, standing close enough to feel her wings almost brush his.

"Remember the dolphin?" he said.

"The beluga?" she corrected him with a small smile. "I brought it with me."

"And . . . Blob?" he asked. The octopus had vanished from their bungalow along with Indigo and all her things, but he'd never seen it with her, even here. He was sort of afraid Pearl might have done something to it.

"I have Blob, too," she said softly. "I keep him hidden. I didn't want to remind anyone . . . what you can do."

"Right." *Of course,* he thought bitterly. *Because what I can do is so terrible, even when it's just an innocent pet octopus.*

He saw Darkstalker turn to look for him and stepped away from Indigo quickly, hurrying back over to the fire.

"What *are* you doing?" Darkstalker asked, peering at the wood.

"You'll see," Fathom said, starting to slice and carve it with his claws. It was softer than the wood he normally worked with, but he thought it would turn out all right.

"Falling stars," Clearsight said in an awestruck voice. "Look how fast you can do that."

"Lots of practice," he said with a shrug. *Lots of time on my own with nothing else to do.*

Swiftly it started to form a shape between his talons, as if a tiny dragon were trying to hatch right out of the wood. He whittled the tiny claws, smoothed a lashing tail at the end, and dug out sharp spikes all along the dragon's back.

"I've never made a NightWing before," he said apologetically.

"Wow," said Clearsight. "I *love* it." She held out her talons and he gently set the finished dragon in the curve of her claws. "It looks just like my friend Listener, doesn't it, Darkstalker?"

Darkstalker tilted his head at the little carving. "Can you make me one of those?" he asked. "I mean, not right now, whenever you get a chance. I want a SeaWing."

"Yeah, absolutely," Fathom said, feeling warmly pleased. He loved making things, but no one at home wanted anything from him anymore. It was kind of thrilling to have friends he could give his presents to again. He glanced around at Indigo, but she wasn't looking their way.

"Well," Darkstalker said, "it seems a little unfair that I have to follow *that*. But hopefully you guys will think this is amazing anyway. Fathom, don't freak out. It was just a little tiny spell."

Fathom's heart sank as Darkstalker fumbled with his bag. "You used your magic again?"

"Ta-da!" Darkstalker said, opening his talons. Three sapphires glittered in the firelight, shining like captured blue stars. "One for each of us." He passed one to Clearsight.

When Fathom didn't reach for his, Darkstalker tossed it at him so Fathom had to jump to catch it.

The sapphire was cool and heavy and didn't seem to radiate particular menace, but Fathom felt dizzily ill looking at it. How could Darkstalker have done another spell after everything Fathom had told him?

"I said *don't* freak out." Darkstalker batted at Fathom's wing. "You *just* read my soul, remember?" That was true, Fathom realized. And the balance of sand hadn't changed even a tiny bit, as far as he could tell. Didn't every spell tilt an animus a bit closer to evil? Or were some spells safe? Or was Darkstalker's soul reader enchanted to give the wrong results, as Indigo had guessed?

"Shh," Darkstalker said, tapping Fathom's skull again. "Listen. I call these dreamvisitors." He held his own out toward the flames, turning it so they could see all the facets of the gemstone. "You can use it to walk in the dreams of any sleeping dragon you know or have ever seen. This way we can be together even when we're asleep. I can visit either of you in your dreams, or you can visit me. You can even step into the dreams of someone all the way across the continent, if you want to. Although I highly doubt anyone else is having dreams as interesting as ours." He beamed at Clearsight. "Happy hatching day."

"It's beautiful," she said, leaning over to hug him. "Isn't it, Fathom? And now we have something that's just ours, the three of us. Because we're best friends."

Best friends.

Wasn't it a small miracle for him to have best friends, after everything that had happened?

He studied the sapphire again, trying to remember the last time someone had given him a present or included him in a group just because they liked him. Was it two years ago, when Indigo made him a mango shrimp cake for turning five? His sixth hatching day, last year, back in the Kingdom of the Sea, had come and gone without anyone saying anything about it. He was pretty sure no one had even spoken to him that day.

He looked over at Indigo again, and this time she was looking his way. She was staring at the sapphire, her face a mask of worry and fear that mirrored his own.

I wish I could just take this and be happy, he thought with a sigh.

But he should refuse it; he should give it back, along with another lecture about why this was too dangerous and another useless heartfelt plea for Darkstalker to stop using his power.

He leaned forward, but before he could start, Clearsight suddenly grabbed Darkstalker's talons and jumped to her feet. The flames seemed to flare in her eyes, and she stared into the fire, trembling.

"What is it?" Darkstalker shook her talons and pulled her face toward him. "What did you see?"

"It's your mother," she said. "Darkstalker, it's Foeslayer! She's in danger — Queen Diamond — there's a plan — we have to find her." Her words scrambled over one another, throwing themselves frantically out into the night, and her wings whooshed open. "We have to find her and stop her or everything is going to go awful, it's *awful* what happens to her. Oh no, and then to everyone." She was crying now. Fathom had never seen her cry; he'd never seen a vision slam into her so hard before.

"We'll save her," Darkstalker said grimly. "Fathom, can you find your way back to the palace on your own?"

Fathom nodded, and a moment later Darkstalker and Clearsight were aloft, winging their way toward the moons, toward Foeslayer and whatever calamity they had to prevent.

It wasn't until they were gone, swallowed by the darkness, that he realized he was still clutching the dreamvisitor in his claws.

CHAPTER 21

DARKSTALKER

"Where is she now?" Darkstalker called to Clearsight as they arrowed into the sky.

"I don't know," she said. "In my vision, she was in the Kingdom of Sand — she was separated from the rest of her wing, and she was surrounded by IceWings, and Queen Diamond was there. But I don't know when it was. It felt very soon, but I don't know, I'm sorry." Her wingbeats faltered and she shook her head. "Why didn't I see it before? Something must have happened — it came out of nowhere. I'm sorry, Darkstalker."

"Don't be," he barked. "We'll save her."

She didn't answer, which felt like a spear through his heart. There *must* be a timeline where he saved her. What was the *point* of Clearsight's visions if they couldn't even keep safe the dragons they loved?

"Mother was at home this morning," he said. "She's supposed to be home for the next three days. Let's try there first. Maybe she hasn't been sent out yet."

They soared south, diving toward the ravines. It was the middle of the night, and dragons were everywhere, filling the air with wingbeats. Darkstalker wished he could hurl them all out of his way.

His front door was open, light spilling out across the canyon, but he couldn't hear his parents fighting. Some other strange, unrecognizable noise was coming from his house. He landed and tumbled inside in one movement, catching himself just before he knocked over Whiteout.

It was his sister making the noise; she was standing in the middle of their living room, her white wings spread wide, keening a weird kind of distress call at the ceiling. She sounded like a great alien bird, piercing and sad and maddening all at once.

"WHAT IS WRONG WITH HER?" his father bellowed from the other side of the room. "SHE'S BEEN DOING THIS NONSTOP FOR AN HOUR!"

All Darkstalker could get from Whiteout's mind were flashes of silver that stabbed like poisonous needles, over and over again. He couldn't block it out; could barely think in the same room as her.

Clearsight flew to Whiteout's side and wrapped her wings around her, forcing the shrieking dragon to fold and crumple until she was small again, buried in Clearsight's chest, and the sound was muffled by Clearsight's wings.

"Shhh," Clearsight murmured in her ear. "I know, I know, it's awful, I know . . ."

"Where's Mother?" Darkstalker yelled at Arctic.

"How should I know?" his father snapped back. *Picked another stupid fight with me, as usual. Flew off in a huff around sunset,* his mind grumbled.

"Did she go back to the war zone?" Darkstalker demanded.

"Why?" Arctic was suddenly alert from horns to tail, zeroing in on Clearsight. "Did you have a vision?"

"Queen Diamond is going after her," Darkstalker snarled. "We have to find her before your mother does."

"Diamond is miles away!" Arctic shouted after him as Darkstalker ran down the hall to his room. He slammed the door and pulled out his scroll. There wasn't time for elegant, carefully constructed spells right now.

He grabbed the first piece of paper he could find and laid it on top of the scroll, scrawling *Enchant this paper to show me where Foeslayer is right now.*

A map blossomed in ink across the page: the Night Kingdom, the Kingdom of Sand, and the Ice Kingdom, with the positions of the troops marked in different colors: blue for IceWings, black for NightWings. And there, a small red dot, moving across the border into SandWing territory, aiming straight for an encampment of IceWings.

Where is she going? Why is she leaving the Night Kingdom now, when she was supposed to be home for three more days?

He looked around frantically and pounced on one of his silver armbands. *Enchant this armband to protect F —*

He stopped. She already *had* something like this.

Darkstalker rushed back into the living room and grabbed Clearsight's shoulder. She jumped, startled out of the rocking motion she'd been doing with Whiteout. His sister looked up, tears streaming down her face.

"Mother can't be in danger," Darkstalker said to them both. "Diamond can't get to her, because she has the earring Father enchanted for her when they first met. It keeps Mother safe no matter the threat — right?" He turned to Arctic.

And read the truth in the agonized fury on Arctic's face, even before he heard it in his father's mind.

The fight.

Foeslayer accused him of not caring about her or the troops, of being too cowardly to sacrifice anything to save her or her friends.

Arctic had shouted back that she wasn't exactly risking her own scales, since she knew nothing could hurt her as long as she wore the earring he gave her.

I don't wear this for protection, she'd yelled. I wear it because I love you!

You love my power, he'd yelled back. That's all you ever loved. You wanted my magic and you got it. That's why you came to the Ice Kingdom in the first place, isn't it? You were looking for me. This was all a NightWing plan. It wasn't ever about me. You didn't ever love me. You came to steal my power.

How dare you? she'd screamed. I love you more than anything. I wish you weren't an animus. I wish you'd never had a shred of magic. I don't want it; I don't want anything to do with it!

And then she'd taken off the earring
and thrown it at him

and flown away
north
to the Kingdom of Sand
where Diamond was waiting for her.

Darkstalker followed his father's gaze to the corner, where his mother's diamond earring glittered like the last stubborn icicle of winter.

"She took off her earring," he said, disbelieving. "And you let her fly away without it?"

Arctic hissed and flicked his tail. "She was angry. She'll be back for it soon, when she's ready to admit that she needs it."

"No, she won't," Darkstalker shouted. "Do you know who hates Mother more than anyone else in the world? A certain mad queen who's related to you, and who happens to be an animus."

Arctic was already shaking his head. "My mother wouldn't use her magic against Foeslayer. She's already used it once, for her gift to the tribe. The rule is she can never use it again."

"She's making an exception for vengeance," Darkstalker said. He turned to Clearsight. "It's an enchantment, isn't it? A spell that summons my mother to her. She probably put it in place years ago, but it could never work because the earring protected Foeslayer. But then Mother took off the earring — and now there's nothing to protect her. That's what changed so suddenly tonight; that's what you didn't see coming." He glared at his father. "This is *your* fault," he hissed.

"Darkstalker," Clearsight said. "Don't . . . your sister . . ."

Whiteout had buried her face in Clearsight's neck and was starting to make the noise again; whirls of a sick hideous blue color were spiraling around and around in her mind.

"I'll fix it," Darkstalker said. "I can save her."

He ran back to his room, trying to think. What did he have? What could he use?

Could I do the same spell, summoning her back here? He had a feeling Diamond's spell would be ironclad. Once she had her claws on Foeslayer, she was never going to let her go.

Can I enchant the earring to fly to her, to reach her before she gets to the IceWings? No, looking at the map, there was no way it could get to her in time.

Maybe I should just kill Diamond. I could send something to do that right now.

He turned toward his trunk of weapons and found Clearsight standing in the doorway.

"You can't kill Queen Diamond," she said.

"I thought *I* was the mind reader around here," he said. "And yes, I can, and it's a great idea, too." He threw open the trunk and started tossing out knives and daggers. Which one was his sharpest weapon? Which would be guaranteed to work?

"You can't," Clearsight said again, "because her only heir is a niece who is far more ruthless and cunning than Queen Diamond is. Diamond is obsessed with Foeslayer and Arctic and revenge, but at least there's no timeline where she wipes out the whole NightWing tribe."

"The whole tribe?" Darkstalker said. He found a dagger with a satisfyingly wicked curve to it. "I think you're exaggerating."

"No," Clearsight said. "If Queen Diamond dies now, and Snowfox ascends to the throne, there are at least four highly probable futures involving a genocide that wipes out the NightWings. You can't kill her right now, Darkstalker. Please believe me."

"But she's going to kill my *mother*," Darkstalker said. "Are you suggesting I let her get away with it?"

Clearsight bowed her head. After a moment, she said, "Snowfox has a daughter. In seven years that dragonet will be ready to take over the tribe, and then both Diamond and Snowfox can meet an unfortunate end — any kind of horrible thing you want. But until then, the consequences . . . you have to look at the big picture. You have this same power; you must be able to see it, too."

She was right; he did see what she saw, but it was hard to care about a nebulous future vision of the tribe's destruction while he was watching the small red dot, his mother, flying right into the heart of the IceWing camp.

"It's too late," Clearsight whispered.

"It's not," said Darkstalker. "I'll get her back. It might take a while, but I'll figure it out." He just had to find the right spell, the perfect spell.

Whiteout squeezed past Clearsight and came over to Darkstalker, throwing her arms around his chest. He sank to the floor, holding his sister tightly. Their wings folded around them, black over white over black like overlapping leaves.

"The hole is too big," Whiteout whispered. "We're going to fall into it forever."

"Not forever," Darkstalker promised. "We'll see her again."

Whiteout thought about that for a moment, tears sliding down her snout and trickling over Darkstalker's scales. "Only one of us will," she said. "Depending on who loses the future."

Darkstalker shivered. If that was Whiteout's version of a prophecy, he didn't want to walk into the dark corners of it and try to figure it out.

But there was one thing he knew, clearly and surely, here in the present.

Mother was gone.

And it was all Arctic's fault.

CHAPTER 22

CLEARSIGHT

Clearsight was in the palace library when Queen Vigilance hunted her down shortly after sunrise, five days after losing Foeslayer.

"What are you doing?" the queen asked, eyeing the piles of scrolls on the table beside Clearsight.

"I'm looking for clues about how animus power works," Clearsight said wearily. "There's so much we don't know. Can one animus spell override another? Is there anything animus magic can't do? Do different spells affect their souls in different ways, or are they always the same? But all the scrolls are about IceWings, and it sounds like they've always restricted their magic so much that no one's had a chance to find out anything. I mean, of course no one wants to run experiments on animus dragons, even if you had more than one at a time for comparison, to see who goes evil first. So it's all anecdotal, and . . ." She trailed off, realizing that there was a strange glint in the queen's eyes.

"*We* have more than one," the queen said. "We have *three*."

Arctic, Darkstalker, Fathom: an IceWing, a NightWing, and a SeaWing. Was the power any different in different tribes? Clearsight wondered.

"But Fathom won't use his power," she pointed out, "and Arctic shouldn't."

The queen paced slowly over to the window, narrowing her eyes at the pale pink sky and the rising sun. A twittering sparrow hopped from vine to vine outside, coming to rest for a moment, unwisely, on the windowsill. Queen Vigilance snatched it up and crunched it between her jaws in one bite.

"With three animus dragons," she said, turning to Clearsight, "why haven't I won this war yet?" She picked a small brown feather out of her teeth, glowering.

"Oh," Clearsight stammered. "It's — well, it's complicated — there are so many consequences — and spells can go wrong, especially with a war scenario where it's all so chaotic. It's kind of an unspoken rule that tribes don't use animus magic in war, isn't it? Because if we use animus magic, then *they* might retaliate with animus magic, and then it gets . . . well, really bad . . ." *So* bad her brain was already starting to hurt, tracing the possibilities.

Queen Vigilance picked up a scroll and hurled it at the door with a loud thump. Immediately one of her guards poked his head inside.

"Yes, Your Majesty?" he said.

"Bring me Darkstalker," she ordered.

Clearsight twisted her front talons together. "I'm not sure this is a good idea," she said. "I haven't — I didn't calculate animus magic into my predictions for the next year — it'll throw everything off."

The queen selected one of the blank scrolls from the rack behind the librarian's desk. She swept all the history scrolls off the table in front of Clearsight and slapped the blank scroll in front of her.

"Start calculating," she hissed.

"Y-yes, all right," Clearsight said, sitting down. Visions were already crowding in, trying to fill the space of these new ripples, new timelines unrolling. There were too many new futures all of a sudden, ones she'd never even glimpsed before. Some of them wrapped back around to link up with previous visions — Darkstalker in the crown, or them with their dragonets — but some of them spilled out into awful new directions.

Never let the queen find out about Darkstalker's scroll — that was the first, most obvious lesson of her visions. If Vigilance ever discovered it, she'd have Darkstalker killed (if she could . . . it wouldn't be easy, Clearsight could see hints of that) and then she'd use it herself, and like Snowfox, Queen Vigilance also had no problem with wiping out entire tribes. A continent ruled entirely by NightWings would be fine with her.

Wingbeats sounded outside, and Clearsight looked up to see Darkstalker swoop by the window. Her heart jumped — happy to see him, terrified about what might happen next.

A few moments later, he came in through the giant double doors of the library, already smiling at the queen.

That smile — it was new, and Clearsight didn't like it. It was an "everything's fine" smile. It was a "bad things can't happen to me, and so I won't let them happen" smile. And Queen Vigilance might not realize it, but it was a "better not stand in my way while I arrange the world the way I want it" smile.

Clearsight knew that there were only three dragons Darkstalker loved: herself, Whiteout, and his mother, Foeslayer. She thought Fathom might be on the list, too, either now or one day, but she wasn't entirely sure. Sometimes she worried that Darkstalker was friends with him only because Clearsight thought they should be.

But he truly loved Foeslayer, and losing her . . . she knew he must be furious, and devastated, and broken into a thousand pieces on the inside. It scared her that he could hide it so well.

"Darkstalker," said the queen. "Unfortunate about your mother."

"Yes," he agreed. "Very unfortunate."

"That was always Diamond's first demand," Queen Vigilance said, studying him. "She wanted Foeslayer, and Arctic, and you and your sister."

He bowed his head slightly. "Thank you for not giving us to her."

"Well," she said. "I had my reasons." She left a significant pause.

"You were hoping to use our animus magic yourself," Darkstalker filled in pleasantly. "And you feel that you've been very patient. And you think now would be a good time for some return on your investment. What did you have in mind?"

Queen Vigilance held herself very still, as if she had just discovered Darkstalker could read her mind and was trying not to show how surprised she was. *She thought she was better at shielding her thoughts,* Clearsight guessed. *She didn't realize Darkstalker's powers were so strong.*

"Hmm," the queen said slowly. "I'd like to hear *your* ideas."

"Oh, I have a few," Darkstalker said with a jaunty smile. "Clearsight, darling, may I?" He crossed to her table, slid the blank scroll over to his side, and started sketching. "Let's see. Clearsight warned me that killing Queen Diamond at this point could lead to the destruction of the entire NightWing tribe. But what if we get them first? Imagine if I could take a stick, any ordinary stick, and say 'I enchant this stick so that the moment I break it, every IceWing in Pyrrhia will keel over, dead.'" He tapped the scroll, where he'd drawn a thin line snapped in half, a dozen bleeding corpses all around it.

Clearsight stared at him in horror. Vigilance's eyes were shining. "You can *do* that?" the queen whispered greedily. "It's that simple?"

"I'm not sure," Darkstalker said with a shrug. "No one's ever tried to wipe out an entire tribe with one spell before, as far as we know." He shot one of his new unsettling smiles at Clearsight.

"But that spell would kill you," Clearsight said. "You're part IceWing. And your father, and your sister."

"We could include exceptions, I'm sure," he said.

"You can't wipe out an entire tribe," she said, more firmly. "There are hundreds, maybe thousands of innocent IceWings. Think of all the little dragonets who aren't part of this war. You're not a dragonet-killer, Darkstalker." *I didn't think you were an anyone-killer, actually. Not now, not the version of you I thought I knew and could safely love. But maybe I'm wrong . . .* "Not to mention what it would do to your soul."

He gave her an ironic look — a "you know perfectly well it won't affect my soul" look. She felt a twist of fear in her stomach. She'd thought putting his magic in the scroll would protect him — but if he wasn't worried about his soul, did that mean there was nothing to hold him back?

"Those little dragonets *will* grow up to be part of this war," he pointed out, "unless we stop them. And isn't tribal genocide exactly what you foresee them doing to us?"

"No!" she said. "Only if things go very, very wrong, and we won't let that happen!" She turned to the queen. "Killing all the IceWings would turn the other tribes against you. It makes things worse, I know it does." Worse by Clearsight's definitions anyway. She didn't have to tell Vigilance about the futures where an IceWing genocide led to the NightWings ruling the whole continent.

"Well," Darkstalker said with a shrug, "if this is too effective for Clearsight's delicate sensibilities, perhaps we could do something more targeted. I could enchant a pile of rocks — let's say at least a hundred — which, when dropped on an IceWing encampment, or hidden in the sand where they'll pass by, would explode and kill every IceWing in sight. Then we'd only hit soldiers . . . probably. Would that make you feel better, Clearsight?"

She turned away from him. She couldn't bear the look on his face, or the queen's, so pleased with their own wicked ideas.

"I need to study the consequences," she said. "Give me some time to trace the futures before you do anything. Please?"

"You're a seer, too," the queen said to Darkstalker. "Can't you see these 'consequences'?"

"Some of them," he said, studying Clearsight sideways. She lifted her chin. Was he going to take her job? It wouldn't be hard to manipulate Vigilance if he became top seer, if he decided to do that. He'd be able to make the queen do almost anything he wanted.

Darkstalker shifted his wings as if he were shrugging off a blanket. "But Clearsight's visions are clearer than mine," he said. He spread one wing around her, giving her a reassuring hug. "She spends a *lot* more time studying them than I do. Thinking about the future is basically what she does all the time. If she wants to check all the timelines first, I suppose that's probably a good idea."

He's still in there, behind the fake smile and the angry ideas. He'll calm down and come back to me, she thought . . . she hoped.

"What about defense?" the queen asked. "The IceWings

have their cliff that kills anyone who's not an IceWing. Can we have one of those?"

"We don't want to keep out all the other tribes," Clearsight interjected quickly. "The NightWings are famous for our intertribal relations and open trade partnerships. Our scrolls and artwork are sold across the continent. Dragons bring us new ideas and inventions and discoveries from all over. If we close our border, especially with violence, we lose all of that. We lose everything that makes us who we are."

"Pffft," the queen spat.

"So maybe it just kills IceWings," Darkstalker said. He took his wing away from around Clearsight and leaned over the table, sketching again. "An invisible shield around the whole kingdom, perhaps. That would free up your air defense teams to join the attack." His dark eyes met Clearsight's. "Seems reasonably harmless. Even you can't object to defending our kingdom from our enemies, right, Clearsight?"

It was one of the least terrible of all the bad options, and it would appease the queen for a while. Clearsight nodded reluctantly. "As long as there's a way to disable it in the future, when we're at peace with the IceWings again."

"That's never going to happen as long as they have my mother," Darkstalker said coldly.

"Get started," Queen Vigilance said, rapping the table once with her claw. She pointed at Darkstalker. "You, the shield." Her sharp eyes shifted to Clearsight. "You, the futures where we crush our enemies with magic." She smiled a thin, sinister smile. "We're going to make an excellent team."

The queen turned and swept out of the library, leaving scrolls fluttering in her wake.

"Better not tell Fathom about the shield," Darkstalker said to Clearsight. "Or any of these ideas. He's already driving me *crazy* with his high-anxiety brain, wondering how soon I'm going to snap." He rolled his eyes.

"What is happening to you?" Clearsight demanded. She poked Darkstalker in the chest. "You're not a mass murderer. You don't want to spend your magic on making war and killing easier for the queen."

"It's not for the queen," Darkstalker said, catching her talon before she could poke him again. "I want to teach the IceWings a lesson. I want to scare them into giving Mother back."

Clearsight wavered. "Oh, Darkstalker . . ."

"You don't see a future where she comes back," he said grimly.

She shook her head. She didn't know what to say. She'd been searching for days, trying every possible timeline, and she couldn't find Foeslayer anywhere. It was as though Diamond had erased her from the map — and from the future.

"Neither do I," he said. His wings slumped slowly down behind him. "I've done three spells that should have brought her home, but none of them worked. And I tried to reach her with the dreamvisitor. I've been trying around the clock since she left, but nothing. It would only work if she was asleep . . . but she must sleep sometime. Unless . . ."

Unless she's already dead.

"What does your map tell you?" Clearsight asked.

"The dot has moved to the Ice Kingdom, far on the other side of their wall," Darkstalker said. "It's been in the same place for the last two days."

"That doesn't — that doesn't mean —" Clearsight started.

"That she's alive? I know. It could be showing me where they buried her. I suppose I could enchant something to find out for sure." His voice suddenly cracked, and he dropped to all fours, leaning into Clearsight's shoulder. "But I don't want to know that, Clearsight. I don't want anything to tell me that she's dead." He buried his face.

"I'm sorry, my love," Clearsight said. "I know it's the worst thing," she said through her tears. "I know it hurts and you're not all right and you're angry and you want to punish the IceWings, but you have to fight the anger and the darkness. Darkstalker, I'm so, so scared. The things I've seen in the future because of this — the things that happen to *you*, the things that you do and what you become — it's all so dark, I almost can't see the light anymore. I'm afraid we're losing our bright paths . . ."

"Stop," Darkstalker said. He sat back, brushing tears out of his eyes. "Don't give up on me, Clearsight."

"I'm not," she said faintly.

He put his talons on either side of her face, looking into her eyes. "Believe in me. Keep looking at our happy futures and I will, too. If we can just stay focused on those, we'll get there. I promise."

She nodded, because she didn't want to make him feel worse right now.

But with Darkstalker's sketch of dead IceWings on the table right beside them . . . it was hard to believe in any kind of bright future at all.

CHAPTER 23

FATHOM

It was raining, endless and drizzly and gray from horizon to horizon. Fathom rested his chin on his talons, staring out the window.

Indigo and Wharf were in his room, too; Wharf was sharpening weapons and Indigo was writing a letter home to her father. Lionfish was supposed to be out hunting, but Fathom guessed he had taken refuge from the rain in one of the busy restaurants or museums somewhere in the city below.

Fathom glanced across the room at Indigo. He wished they were alone, although it was safer for them not to be. He wished he could go over there and flop into her side and fall asleep with her back rising and falling peacefully below him, the way he used to. He wished he could lean against her shoulder and read a scroll with her and tell her all the things he was worried about.

Although, really, it was just one thing.

Darkstalker. Sad, furious Darkstalker, who'd been in mourning for the past three weeks, but a strange kind of angry mourning where he kept insisting his mother would be home soon. Fathom hadn't even seen his friend at all in the last two days. Clearsight was still around, but she was always in the library or her room with her nose in a scroll, and she looked so anxious all the time that he didn't want to bother her.

Last night she'd come to his room for dinner — well, dinner for him, breakfast for her — and she'd been more talkative than usual about her power. He hadn't realized how complicated it was, or how many different versions of the future she could see. It almost sounded worse than not being able to see the future at all, but of course he hadn't said that to her.

Clearsight had finally buried her head in her talons with a sigh.

"The hardest thing about being a seer," she'd said, "is that the future is always a million possibilities — I can see so many ways my life could possibly go. But the past is only one thing. Once something happens, that's it. I can't change it anymore. I can't do *anything*. All my possibilities narrow into one fixed life, and then we're trapped in that world. I think I can control the future, but the past — it's gone. I can't fix it anymore."

Fathom knew a lot about wishing he could change the past. But he'd never felt any kind of control over his future, either. It was sort of mind-boggling to think about.

As if his thoughts had summoned him, a gleaming wet figure appeared outside, winging his way toward Fathom's balcony. Darkstalker swooped in and shook himself grandly, scattering water everywhere.

"Hey!" Indigo objected, covering her letter to keep it dry.

"Hey," Darkstalker replied offhandedly without looking at her. "Fathom, there's an epic lightning storm coming. Want to fly up to the Royal Tower and watch it with me?"

"Sure!" Fathom said, jumping to his feet.

"Isn't the tallest tower in the castle exactly the wrong place to be in a lightning storm?" Indigo objected. "Not to mention flying while there's lightning doesn't sound like a great idea."

"We'll be fine," Darkstalker said dismissively. "You can stay here."

She gave him a "when the Kingdom of the Sea freezes over" look.

"Oh, Darkstalker," Fathom said, hurrying over to his desk. "I finished the carving for you." He picked up the SeaWing statue he'd made for Darkstalker, turning it over between his talons so he could check the little webbed claws and the graceful curving neck. He liked the intelligent expression on the wooden dragon's face, although he had to admit that it made the miniature dragon look unmistakably like Indigo. Would Darkstalker notice? Would he want a statue that looked so much like a dragon he didn't seem to particularly like?

There was something odd about Darkstalker's expression as he took the carving, a funny combination of triumph and regret, perhaps. He did glance at Indigo, maybe noting the similarity, but when he turned back to Fathom, he was smiling.

"This is so cool," he said. "Thanks, Fathom. I got you something, too." He reached into a pouch around his neck and pulled out a goblet made of shimmering sea-green glass, the same color as Fathom's scales and imprinted with a pattern like ocean waves. "I was in the market and saw this, and it made me think of you."

"Wow," Fathom said, delighted. He took the goblet carefully and cupped it in his talons. It reminded him of home, of swimming through sunbeams after pods of singing whales.

"I found Clearsight a pair of moonstone earrings to match her bracelet, too." Darkstalker touched his pouch thoughtfully. He finally seemed to be in a much better mood than he had been in weeks. His eyes were bright and his wings snapped sharply instead of drooping under the weight of his mother's loss.

"You seem happier," Fathom observed cautiously.

"I am," Darkstalker said. "I'm finally doing something about all my most annoying problems." He tossed his head with a grin. "I mean, I'm Pyrrhia's most powerful dragon, aren't I? I shouldn't *have* any problems."

Fathom wasn't quite sure how to respond to that. Every dragon had problems . . . and how exactly was Darkstalker dealing with his? But he didn't want to push Darkstalker away now that he finally seemed to be coming back. He'd bring it up again later.

He carried the goblet over to the fountain to fill it with water. He wished he were as small as his carved SeaWing so he could dive into the green glass bowl and swim around. He lifted it to his snout to drink.

The blow was sudden, knocking him sideways as the goblet flew across the room. It smashed into the marble wall and shattered into a million tiny green shards.

"Why did you DO THAT?" Darkstalker roared at Indigo. For a moment he looked consumed with rage, fire crackling through his veins as he glared at her.

Fathom stared at Indigo, his ears still ringing. She faced Darkstalker, her chin raised defiantly.

"I saw the way you were watching him!" she said. "There was a spell on that cup! You couldn't wait to see what was about to happen. What was it? What were you trying to do to Fathom?"

Across the room, Wharf looked up, confused.

Darkstalker spread his wings, looking deeply injured. His rage vanished as quickly as it had appeared. "It was *not* animus-touched. I didn't do anything to it at all. I just thought it was beautiful and that Fathom would like it. You have an overly suspicious mind, Violet."

"Indigo," Fathom corrected him automatically, dazed.

"I'm sorry about your present," Darkstalker said to Fathom, sweeping small green pieces into a pile with his tail. "I'm pretty sure it was one of a kind." He narrowed his eyes at Indigo.

"I swear he did something to it," Indigo said to Fathom. "I don't know what — I can only imagine. Something horrible and manipulative, I bet." She glared back at Darkstalker.

"Oh, Indigo," Fathom said. "I'm sure it wasn't enchanted. Darkstalker wouldn't do that to me, right?"

Darkstalker nodded, putting one wing around Fathom's shoulders. "Of course I wouldn't," he said. "I can't believe anyone could even think that."

"She's being a good bodyguard," Fathom said, although honestly, he was pretty upset with her. No one had given him something that could be called treasure in a very long time, and the goblet had been so beautiful. And now it was so gone.

Darkstalker sighed. "Well, let's go to the Royal Tower before we miss the lightning. I'll leave this here so it doesn't get wet." He set the SeaWing carving down on Fathom's desk, tapping its nose gently.

Indigo turned, her shoulders tense, to reach for her wet weather flying gear.

"Actually," Fathom said, "I think maybe Wharf should come with me this time."

The thick-headed guard fumbled his knife and looked up at Fathom, clearly startled. Indigo stood with one hand on her spear, her face a mess of hurt and disbelief.

It's not you, Fathom wanted to say. *It's not because you broke the goblet. It's because of the way Darkstalker is looking at you right now, and the fact that he's looking at you so closely at all, and it's just that I think everything will be easier and safer if you quietly fade into the background for a while. That's all. It's not a punishment. I'm upset with you, yes, but I know why you did what you did. And I want you to stay here so you'll be safe.*

Of course, he couldn't say any of that in front of Darkstalker. He'd have to explain when they got back.

Wharf lumbered to his feet and wrinkled his snout at the pouring rain outside.

"We're, uh . . . we're going out in that?" he asked.

"Yup," said Darkstalker. "You have gills, I think you'll survive. Let's go!" He dragged Fathom to the balcony, with Wharf following sullenly behind them. Cold drops of rain pelted Fathom's snout, and lightning crackled in the distance. He glanced back at Indigo, but she'd returned to her letter and didn't look up.

As they stepped out onto the balcony, Darkstalker opened his pouch again.

"Want to see the earrings I got for Clearsight?" he asked Fathom. "I'm so excited about them. Shoot, my pouch is all dirty from that squirrel I caught yesterday." He shook some dirt and pebbles into his talons, shaking his head, and tossed it all over his shoulder into Fathom's room. "Here they are." He held out the earrings, beautiful milky orbs like translucent moons, and Fathom agreed that they were perfect for her.

They flew off to the Royal Tower, and the whole way there, Fathom kept telling himself he didn't have to worry. He'd be back soon, and then they would talk, and Indigo would understand. He'd convince her to be less paranoid about Darkstalker's intentions and more careful about picking fights with him.

Everything would be fine.

They returned through the winding interior of the palace instead of flying in the storm again. There was enough lightning outside at this point that most sensible dragons were staying safely indoors. Wharf stomped behind Fathom and Darkstalker, dripping on the white carpets, clearly grumpy about being forced to do his actual job.

Fathom had a feeling something was wrong as he approached his room, although he wasn't sure why. Everything seemed normal from the outside. It was very quiet, but that wasn't surprising, with only Indigo inside.

Still, a strange worried sensation was crawling up the back of his throat as he pushed open the inside door and realized that the room was completely dark.

"Indigo?" he called.

"She's not here," Wharf said, although that would have been obvious even without their night vision. The room felt abandoned, like a snail shell with the snail sucked out of it. Beside the balcony, the curtains wafted in and out. Darkstalker stepped inside first and glanced around curiously.

"But . . . where would she go?" Fathom asked.

"Hunting?" Wharf guessed. "Swimming? Out for a walk? Gone to give her letter to the messengers?"

Those were all reasonable guesses, if it hadn't been

pouring outside, but Fathom had a distinctly unreasonable feeling about this.

"Wharf, go check the kitchen and the messenger center," he said. "Um. Please."

"All right," Wharf said with a long, drawn-out sigh.

As the door closed behind the guard, Fathom crossed to the balcony and peered out at the furious downpour. Indigo wouldn't have gone out for *any* reason in this weather, surely.

Behind him, Darkstalker breathed a burst of flame to light the lamps by the door and the two candles over the fireplace. Fathom heard him walk across the room and then pause. A moment later, Darkstalker let out a small murmur of surprise, and Fathom turned around.

Darkstalker had picked up the lamp on the desk and now stood there, looking down at something.

"What is it?" Fathom asked, hurrying over.

His friend pointed at a damp, torn scrap of scroll lying on the desk. On top of it, holding it down, was the wooden SeaWing Fathom had carved, and the handwriting on the paper was clearly Indigo's.

Fathom,
    I'm sorry. You were right. I don't feel safe here. It's not worth the risk. ~~I don't~~
    I'm going home.
    Please don't use your magic to find me.
    Good luck.
    Indigo

The earth dropped out from below Fathom's talons. He was floating over an abyss, all the light suddenly hollowed out of the world.

His eyes were stuck on the crossed-out words. "I don't . . ." what? Love you? Want to be with you? Trust you anymore?

How could she leave like that?

Without saying good-bye?

It didn't feel like something she would do at all.

But maybe it was the smart choice. This was what he'd wanted her to do, wasn't it? Get far away from him, so she could live a normal life?

Still.

He couldn't believe she was *gone*.

"Sorry, Fathom," Darkstalker said sympathetically. "She was a really great bodyguard."

Fathom nodded, too shocked to respond. He picked up the SeaWing carving and traced the curve of her neck. She really looked so much like Indigo.

"Hey, Darkstalker," he said, "would you — would you mind if I keep this, actually?"

It seemed like Darkstalker hesitated for the briefest moment, but Fathom must have imagined it, because almost immediately the NightWing nodded and pulled Fathom into a hug.

"Of course," Darkstalker said. "Of course you can keep it, if that's what you want. Although — things that remind you of her probably aren't going to make you feel better."

"I know," Fathom said, but he set it back on his desk anyway. He needed it there. Maybe it would hurt to look at it, but it would also remind him that Indigo was out in the world, having adventures and a great life, somewhere where she didn't have to worry about animus magic or what Fathom might do.

I'm on my own now, he realized. Well, sort of — at least he still had Darkstalker and Clearsight. They still believed in him.

If Indigo didn't anymore, that was only logical.

He sighed. This was probably for the best.

At least she was safe now, wherever she was. Safe from him . . . and safe from animus magic forever.

Ice Kingdom
Sky Kingdom
Queen Scorpion's Stronghold
Claws of the Clouds Mountains
Kingdom of Sand
Queen Vigilance's Palace
Jade Mountain

PART THREE

— CHAPTER 24 —

CLEARSIGHT

"You can see the whole Great Diamond from up here," Listener said, stretching her long neck to peer out Clearsight's window. "By the Scorching, is the *entire* tribe coming to this festival?"

"No." Clearsight peeked over her shoulder. The enormous piazza below them looked like it was swarming with fireflies. In the lights from the hundreds of lanterns, she could see dragons everywhere. "Don't forget all the soldiers out defending the kingdom." *Testing out Darkstalker's new fire-shooting weapons,* she thought with a wince.

"All right, gloomy snout," Listener said. "I can't believe I'm getting ready for the jubilee in the queen's own palace! I knew it would be a good idea to make you my best friend. This is going to be the greatest night *of all time.*"

"It's just another party," Clearsight said, laughing. "The queen seems to have one every other night. There's a full moon, let's celebrate! A second full moon, celebrate again! Her oldest son's hatching day, time for a party! One of her daughters sneezed, someone alert the chefs we need a cake! It's kind of exhausting."

"Oh, you poor thing," Listener said. "Living in the palace, eating truffles with the queen, burdened with all these beautiful necklaces." She cast a sidelong glance at the tangle of jewelry in the wooden box beside Clearsight's mirror.

"You goose. You can borrow anything you want," Clearsight said.

"Really?" Listener bounded over and started fishing out long sparkling chains. "Oooo, I wonder what Thoughtful would like. Sapphires, do you think? Or moonstones. No, you're wearing moonstones — *again*, I might add. Oh wow, opals!"

Clearsight touched the moonstone earrings Darkstalker had given her about a month ago.

"I thought they'd match your bracelet," he'd said. "Aren't they cool?"

"I love them," she'd answered, cupping them in her talons. "They don't have any spells on them, right?"

"That is SUCH A RUDE QUESTION." He'd given her his most injured expression. "Thank you SO MUCH for your faith in me. You are WELCOME to check the scroll and see, if you really think I would do that."

"No, no," she'd said, clipping them on. "I was just asking, don't get all huffy." They were beautiful earrings. And they made her feel all sparkly and hopeful, but not in a fake magical enchanted way. (Still, she did check the scroll later, when he was out picking up dinner, just to be sure, although she felt extremely guilty about it. And there were no moonstone earring spells, so basically she was a terrible dragon for even suspecting him for a moment. Poor Darkstalker.)

"Wait," she said to Listener. "Who's Thoughtful?"

Listener hesitated, holding a web of opals up to her neck. "I guess you're going to meet him tonight anyway." She scrunched her eyes shut. "He's the dragon I'm going to marry. Fix your face, fix your face!"

"I'm not making a face!" Clearsight objected. "I'm having zero visions at all right now, I promise. But aren't we a bit young for marriage plans?"

"I mean one day, after we graduate and I propose. There are a few steps we haven't gotten to yet, but we will!"

"Steps like . . ." Clearsight prompted her.

"Like . . . doing things together," Listener confessed. "And him realizing he loves me."

"Listener, have you actually ever spoken to this dragon?" Clearsight asked.

"Yes!" Listener drew herself up, looking offended, although the effect was muddled by the sixteen necklaces she was trying to fit over her head at the same time. "*He* said, 'Excuse me, is this the way to the strawberry garden?' and *I* said, 'It certainly is!' and *he* said, 'Thank you' and *I* said, 'Are you going to the jubilee festival tonight?' and *he* said, 'Urgh, I suppose I have to,' and *I* said, 'Cool, see you there!' so, obviously, we are destined to be together forever. Don't you dare tell me otherwise!"

"I wouldn't dream of it," Clearsight said. "I didn't say one word about the last disaster, did I?"

"I didn't even let you meet the last one," Listener said. "You're thinking of the one before that, and no, you never *said* anything, you just *looked* like you'd eaten a bucket full of limes every time you saw him."

Clearsight sighed. "I don't see what would be wrong with letting me nudge you toward a decent dragon once in a while."

"I can find my soulmate on my own, thank you very much," said Listener. "In fact, I have, and his name is Thoughtful, and he's absolutely dashing."

"Wonderful," Clearsight said, resolutely not looking at Listener's timelines. She was getting better at that — at avoiding the things she didn't want to see.

That was easier to do when she spent most of her time studying the war with the IceWings for Queen Vigilance. There were so many small things that could change the course of a battle, or wreck a carefully crafted plan, or spin a formation into panicked chaos. She thought the information she fed the queen was helping, but it was hard to tell, as the queen was not exactly prone to effusive gratitude. But at least she'd managed to do enough so far to delay the most horrible new animus plans.

"All right, I'm ready," Listener said. She grinned at Clearsight, twinkling with gemstones and excitement.

I hope this dragon is worth it this time, Clearsight thought.

Together they hurried to one of the grand balconies and launched themselves into the sky, swooping down toward the plaza below them. Listener found a clear spot to land near the food tents, where the cold air crackled with the smell of roasting meat, sizzling onions, and fried bananas.

The queen's favorite musicians were playing somewhere, but the music was drowned out by all the laughing, chattering dragons. An intricate lacework of wires traced over the whole diamond, hung with paper lanterns that had been painted bright gold and purple and green by the kingdom's dragonets.

But the highlight of the festival was the glasswork competition, in honor of what Queen Vigilance was calling her Glass Jubilee to celebrate forty years of her being on the throne. The entire plaza was dotted with elaborate glass sculptures that glowed in the lamplight. Twisting spirals, weaving tendrils, and delicate beads mingled with glorious bells and vast shipwrecks, towering trees and clusters of captured fireworks. Clearsight wished she could run her talons over every smooth or bubbly surface. She wished she could change her scales to the same shimmering colors as the glass, like a RainWing might.

"Let's go find Fathom," she said. She knew he was here somewhere with Darkstalker. They were supposed to meet near the musicians before midnight, but she wanted to find them sooner.

"Your pet SeaWing?" Listener said. "Do we have to?"

"He's the sweetest dragon, if you'd just give him a chance," Clearsight said. "And he's lonely here." *Especially since Indigo left. He tries to hide it, but he's so, so sad without her. How could she do that to him? I thought she cared about him as more than a bodyguard, but I guess I was wrong.*

"I highly doubt that," said Listener, "considering that you

spend practically every waking moment with him." She tossed her head indignantly, but followed Clearsight through the crowd without further complaint.

They navigated around a group of dancing NightWings and through a forest of tall, copper-colored glass spikes. Clearsight guessed that Fathom would want to be in the quietest corner of the festival — he was better at handling parties now that he'd been to so many of the queen's gatherings, but they still made him a little jittery.

She was right. Fathom, Darkstalker, and Whiteout were inside one of the game pavilions, playing scales-and-squares on a small board near the central fire. Lionfish stood guard beside them, watching the NightWings around him with a wary expression. Long white curtains hung around the outside of the pavilion, muffling the noise from the rest of the festival and sheltering the fire and the games from the wind.

Listener wrinkled her snout when she saw them. "Playing board games at a festival?" she snorted. "How lame can you THERE HE IS!" She clutched Clearsight's arm frantically.

"What?" Clearsight said, startled.

"That's Thoughtful," Listener whispered, hiding behind Clearsight's wing. "The one with the scroll tower."

Clearsight glanced around the pavilion and finally spotted the dragon Listener was talking about. He was playing a game by himself that involved stacking small marble scrolls into increasingly complex towers according to a set of patterns. As far as lame solitary party games went, it was kind of at the top, frankly.

He was handsome — of course, since he had caught Listener's eye — but he had a sort of kindness and worry in his expression that made him different from her usual choices. Silver wires wound around his horns and down his forehead, suspending a circle of glass in front of each of his eyes. He looked tired and very focused on what he was doing.

"Isn't he wonderful?" Listener said dreamily.

Oh dear, Clearsight thought, looking at the dragon and feeling the undertow of visions pulling her away. *Oh no . . .*

Two clear futures lay before this NightWing.

One was easy and unremarkable — a pleasant-enough life with someone who loved him more than he loved her, where both of them felt vaguely unsatisfied all the time, but at least nobody died.

The second was harder and darker, but in it waited great love, and on it depended futures too far distant for even Clearsight to understand.

Listener was not that great love.

Unlike her previous crushes, this dragon could actually be hers, if nobody intervened. But he shouldn't be. He was meant for someone else.

Clearsight slammed a blank expression on her face. *Don't react. Don't let her see what you're thinking.*

What am I going to do?

Do I let Listener have this kind, worried dragon, or do I interfere and disrupt both of their timelines . . . in ways probably neither of them would thank me for?

"Are you going to say hello?" she asked her friend, in what she thought was a commendably calm voice.

Listener shot her a suspicious glance anyway. "Not yet," she said. "I'll give him a chance to notice me and come over first. Let's go say hi to your weirdo friends."

Darkstalker looked up as they approached, his whole face alight with joy.

"You look like you're winning," Clearsight said, sprawling on the cushion beside him.

"I'm winning at *life*," he said exuberantly, twining his tail around hers. He hadn't looked this happy since Foeslayer was captured, although he'd been gradually coming back to normal every day. She touched his face and wondered if something had happened. Had he enchanted something to make himself feel happier — to help him move on from mourning Foeslayer? If he did, would that be wrong?

"In this turn of the hourglass, yes," said Whiteout, moving one of her green scale tokens to capture a black square of Fathom's. "But when I crush you with my heart piece, then everything flips."

"Don't you even know what you're playing?" Listener asked her. "This game doesn't have a heart piece."

"Did you see the *Sunrise Ferns*?" Fathom asked Clearsight. "Those were my favorite."

"I haven't really looked around yet," she said. "Maybe when you guys are done with this game we can all go check out the sculptures."

"And get something to eat," Darkstalker suggested. "I wouldn't mind, like, six goats on sticks right now."

"We don't have to go anywhere YET, though," Listener said, poking Clearsight meaningfully.

"Just go talk to him," Clearsight whispered.

"He's already looked at us twice," Listener hissed back. "He'll come over any moment now."

"Aha!" Fathom chortled, seizing one of Darkstalker's white squares. "I have totally figured out your mystifying game. I am the new scales-and-squares champion!"

"Ooooh, sorry, friend," Darkstalker said. He hopped a blue scale over three of Fathom's squares and swept them off the board. "Too slow, so sad."

Listener suddenly dug her claws into Clearsight's shoulder.

"OW," Clearsight protested.

"Act normal!" Listener barked. "Not weird! Totally completely normal!"

"You mean like you are?" Clearsight observed, rubbing her shoulder.

"Hey," said a deep voice behind her.

Clearsight and Darkstalker both turned around, and Fathom looked up. Listener's wings fluttered unconsciously and she whacked Clearsight's tail with her own about eighty times in rapid succession.

"Hey," Darkstalker said, sounding guarded. "I know you from . . . music class? You're Thoughtful, right?"

"Yeah." Thoughtful's gaze bounced off Listener and

skidded around the others. "I just, uh — I just wondered if anyone wanted to try a scroll tower challenge with me."

Listener looked as though she had lightning darting along her wings. "Maybe," she said coyly, starting to stand up.

Argh, Clearsight thought. *I have to do it. I have to. Listener's going to kill me, but it's too important. And it'll only get harder if I don't do it right now.*

"I'm Clearsight," she said, smiling at Thoughtful. "Our SeaWing friend is Fathom, and" — she took a deep breath — "and have you, um . . . have you met Whiteout?"

"WINNER!" Whiteout shouted, nearly overturning the board as she hopped one of her scales around it. "Empress of all scales and queen of all squares! Weep for your tokens, adversaries!" She sat up, clapping her talons gleefully, and finally spotted Thoughtful, who was looking at her in a vaguely rapt way.

"Oh," she said with wonder. "Look how shiny you are."

"Shiny?" Listener said, snorting a fake laugh. "Whiteout, what are you ever talking about?"

"*You* made the *Cascade of Dreams,*" Whiteout said, ignoring Listener. She reached out, took one of Thoughtful's talons, and squinted at his palm. "Words and glass, spun flutes and verse. Waterfalls of language in fire-blown claws."

"What?" Listener said uneasily.

"You noticed?" Thoughtful said, tilting his head at Whiteout. "No one — you really saw the pieces of scroll inside the waves?"

"Tangerine," Whiteout said. "Probability. Spelunking."

"OK, now you're literally just saying random words," Listener said.

"I can't believe you saw them!" Thoughtful said. "Nobody's ever understood one of my pieces before."

"I think you should teach me glassblowing," Whiteout said, "and I should teach you clarity."

"WHAT. Is she being ironic?" Listener asked Clearsight.

Thoughtful ducked his head, glanced down at the board, and shot a shy smile at Whiteout. "How is the empress of scales at scroll tower?"

"Amazing," said Whiteout. "You're going to die of awe." She rose, shook out her strange white wings, and led the way back to the other side of the tent with Thoughtful close beside her, beaming.

Clearsight couldn't believe how well that had worked, with such a small nudge from her. They really were destined for each other. Hiding a smile, she turned away from her friends and noticed movement behind one of the curtains. It was Darkstalker's father, Arctic, watching them all with a grim look on his face.

"Um, what just happened?" Listener demanded. "Can anyone explain that to me?"

Don't figure it out, Clearsight prayed. *Don't blame me.*

But before Listener could turn accusing eyes on Clearsight; before anyone could answer her question; before Clearsight could come up with a distraction, a dragon tore through the curtains, vaulted into the pavilion, and drove a spear into Darkstalker's heart.

CHAPTER 25

FATHOM

What Fathom saw was a bolt of steel flashing past; he heard curtains rip and Listener screaming and ivory pieces cascading across the wood floor.

No. Not again. Not again.

He saw Darkstalker stagger back, looking stricken.

I can't lose anyone else.

He saw Lionfish tackle the assassin, who roared and slashed at his face with iron-tipped claws. He leaped forward to help, but by the time he reached Lionfish's side, the attacker was dead. The unfamiliar NightWing lay at his feet, his neck twisted in a horrible unnatural way.

"Darkstalker?" Clearsight was still standing, frozen, reaching one talon toward her soulmate. "What — how — ?"

Fathom took a step back from Lionfish and the dead dragon, and he saw the spear lying on the floor, and he saw that the polished wood was clean, and there was no blood, and then, finally, after all that, he saw that Darkstalker's scales were smooth and unblemished, and his friend was completely unhurt.

"That's impossible!" Listener shrieked, nearly in hysterics. "He killed you! I saw it! He killed you!"

Darkstalker spread his wings, revealing the glimmer of the ice scales underneath. "I guess he missed."

"He didn't miss!" Listener backed away, pointing at Clearsight. "You saw it, too. Didn't you? Didn't you? That spear should have gone right into his heart."

"I —" Clearsight glanced at the gathering crowd, then at Darkstalker again. "I don't know what I saw."

Listener roared with frustration, darted out of the pavilion, and shoved her way through the gathering crowd until it swallowed her up.

"It's nothing," Darkstalker said. "Really," he added to all the watching dragons. "This pathetic lizard tried to kill me and failed. Nothing to panic about." He stepped over to examine the corpse at Lionfish's feet. "I would like to know who this is, though."

"And *why* he tried to kill you," Clearsight added.

Darkstalker's eyes slanted sideways at Lionfish for a moment. "Too bad he's dead and can't answer any questions."

Lionfish shrugged. "Sorry," he said without a shred of actual repentance. He looked rather pleased that he'd finally had a chance to do some actual bodyguarding.

"I don't know him," Clearsight said, edging away from the dead dragon. She looked at the far corner of the pavilion and frowned slightly, as if she'd expected to see someone there.

Darkstalker turned to Whiteout and Thoughtful, who had rushed back over. "Do either of you know him?"

"I do," Thoughtful said. "By reputation, anyway. His name is Quickdeath and he was — well, you can guess."

"A killer for hire?" Clearsight said. "Are you saying somebody *sent* him to kill Darkstalker?"

Darkstalker put one wing around her. "But he failed. See, I'm so fine. Don't be scared."

"Don't be — what if that somebody tries again?" Clearsight demanded. She touched her head. "I can't see exactly . . . I feel like there are very bad things branching from here, but they're all blurry. I don't know how they fit together, or what comes from what."

"We'll figure out who hired Quickdeath," said Darkstalker. "That's easy. And then we stop them from trying again." His eyes went cold and hard, like onyx beads. "Trust me, that'll be even easier."

Fathom had never seen his friend look so much like his grandfather. He shivered and sank onto one of the cushions, realizing that his wings were shaking. He had to keep it together, especially in front of all these NightWings. It seemed as though hundreds of them were emerging from the dark, pressing toward the edge of the pavilion to see what the commotion was. Everyone stared at Darkstalker, whispering to one another.

How had he survived? What had stopped the spear?

Lionfish poked Fathom. "We should get you back to the castle," he said. "In case there's a second attack."

"He wasn't after me," Fathom pointed out.

"Maybe not this time," he said, "but let's get somewhere safe, just in case."

"Yes," Darkstalker interjected. "I'd like to get out of here as well." He nudged Quickdeath's body with one talon, frowning as though he were wondering whether he could do something useful with it. "Thoughtful, can you stay here and watch the body until we send someone from the queen's guard to investigate?"

"Sure," said Thoughtful.

"I'll stay with him," said Whiteout. "Protect him from angry spirits."

Thoughtful cast an uneasy glance at the ceiling, as if Quickdeath's ghost might be hovering there with its claws outstretched.

Half in a daze, Fathom followed Darkstalker and Clearsight out of the pavilion. The crowd of dragons fell back before them, most of them averting their eyes, others staring openly. A pair of small dragonets took one look at Darkstalker and fled with little shrieks of alarm.

"What was that for?" Darkstalker muttered grumpily. "I'm the one that got attacked!"

But Fathom understood; he, too, felt a layer of fear spreading underneath his worry for his friend. The more he thought about it, the more he couldn't make the pieces fit. He was *sure* that spear had been aimed straight and true at Darkstalker's heart. How could Quickdeath have missed so completely? And then why was the spear lying in front of

Darkstalker, as if it had bounced off, instead of somewhere beyond him?

A horrible suspicion was growing inside him. Darkstalker had used his magic again, somehow, even though Fathom had begged him not to.

He eyed the pieces of jewelry the NightWing was wearing. Something that would protect you from any attack . . . he saw the appeal, of course. He had often wished he could make something like that for Indigo, before she left. But was it worth protecting someone on the outside, if doing so made yourself more dangerous on the inside?

They flew back to Fathom's room in the palace, where Lionfish went inside first to make sure it was safe. Wharf was somewhere down in the festival, probably blissfully unaware that he might have been useful tonight.

"All clear," Lionfish said, holding the door open.

"You can go," Darkstalker said to him brusquely. "Back to the festival or wherever."

Lionfish shook his head, his expression vaguely surprised. "I'm not supposed to leave Fathom alone," he said. "Indigo's orders."

"He won't be alone," said Darkstalker impatiently. "He'll be with me. And if Indigo was so worried, she wouldn't have flown off and left him, right?"

Fathom winced.

"Yeah," Lionfish said slowly, as though he hadn't thought of that before. "Good point."

"It's all right, Lionfish," Fathom said. "I'll be safe with them."

Lionfish shrugged and left without any further argument.

As soon as they were safely behind closed doors, Clearsight whirled on Darkstalker. "What did you do?" she demanded.

"Um, survived a deadly assassination attempt?" Darkstalker said. "Hooray for me?"

"Listener was right," she said. "That spear hit you exactly in the heart. There's no way you should have survived it."

"You sound awfully disappointed," Darkstalker snapped back. "Is that why you didn't warn me that was going to happen? Because you were hoping it would succeed?"

Her face twisted in outrage. "You *jerk*," she cried. "I don't know everything, all right? Minor timelines sometimes become reality before I know it, especially if other — if someone is trying to surprise me. And I'm glad you're not dead, but I want to know *when* you made yourself invulnerable and *why* you didn't tell me about it!"

Fathom crossed the room and started digging in his trunk as they argued. There was something he had to know.

"Isn't the more important question *who tried to kill me*?" Darkstalker shouted. "Shouldn't we all be like, wow, great idea, Darkstalker, we're so glad you're alive, now let's get on with hunting down the actual bad dragon in this situation?"

He turned toward Fathom with his wings spread wide, as if looking for reassurance, and found Fathom pointing the soul reader at him.

"SERIOUSLY?" Darkstalker shouted. "I'm the good guy here! What is wrong with you?"

"You shouldn't have used your magic," Fathom said, scrunching his eyes to fight back his tears. "That's a huge spell, invulnerability. It could have tipped you over all by itself." The hourglass was spinning slowly, slowly, white and black grains mingling and diverging. *Please be good,* Fathom prayed. *Please please please don't lose your soul.*

"Well, it didn't," Darkstalker snapped. "It so happens I enchanted my scales before I made the soul reader, so you'll find that your little hourglass will give you the exact same result as last time. But thank you all so much for your faith in me."

The hourglass stopped. Fathom realized that Clearsight was studying it as intently as he was.

If Darkstalker hadn't used his magic since the last reading, it should show the same balance of white and black sand.

Did it? Fathom blinked. He wasn't sure. Was it just his imagination, or were there more white grains of sand this time than last time? Did the hourglass tilt a little more than before? Had the balance shifted slightly toward evil?

Maybe he was being paranoid. It wasn't a big difference, certainly. The black sand still outweighed the white sand.

So why did Clearsight look troubled as well?

"There," Darkstalker said. "See? Now can we get on with tracking down my killer?"

"Not with magic," Fathom said quickly. "I know that's what you're thinking. Please, Darkstalker, we can find another way. You don't need to spend your magic on this."

"It's a tiny little spell," Darkstalker said dismissively. "And then we'll know for sure. Are you picturing us as stalwart detectives, following leads and interrogating suspects? I don't have time for that, if we're going to figure this out before he tries again."

"You think you already know who it was," Clearsight said. She was pacing in front of the fireplace, her wings shaking.

"Isn't it obvious?" Darkstalker asked. "He's wanted me dead since the moment I hatched."

Clearsight hesitated. Darkstalker's expression, watching her, seemed to be waiting for something.

"He was there," she said finally. "I saw him."

"Who?" Fathom asked.

"My father," Darkstalker said. "I know, I heard his brain muttering."

"But — if he was there, why didn't he come over to make sure you were all right?" Fathom said, feeling as if he was missing something. "Why didn't he jump in to stop Quickdeath?" He felt a deep stab of the grief he usually kept buried. *That's what my father would have done.*

"Because he *hired* Quickdeath," Darkstalker said. "You're really slowing this conversation down, Fathom."

"Did you hear him think that?" Clearsight asked. "When you heard his thoughts — was there anything about the assassin or wanting you dead?"

Darkstalker thought for a moment. "No more than usual. What I caught mostly had to do with my sister. Father hated the way she was looking at Thoughtful. He's probably the one who needs to watch out for assassins next."

"So maybe it wasn't Arctic," Clearsight said. "Wouldn't he be thinking about it, if he knew it was about to happen?"

"Not necessarily." Darkstalker plucked a stalk of bamboo from one of Fathom's tall vases and started methodically shredding it. "Besides, I stopped listening to him after the first few grumbles." He flung a piece of bamboo into the corner. "*I'm* sure it was him, but we can all be sure if I do a spell to find out."

"No!" Fathom cried. "Please don't. Think about your soul. Clearsight, you agree with me, don't you?"

Clearsight looked between them for a moment, rubbing her forehead. "You should tell him about the scroll," she said to Darkstalker.

"Really?" He looked surprised. "You think that's a good idea?"

"I think it's safe," she said. "As far as I can tell, you show it to him in all of the good timelines."

"And the bad," he pointed out.

"He's not the one who turns them bad," she said quietly.

Darkstalker scowled at her. "Your faith in me is so heartwarming."

While they argued, Fathom went to tuck the soul reader back in his trunk, and as he did, he saw a flicker of movement under his blankets.

A small white tentacle lifted one corner, and small dark eyes peeked out at him.

Blob!

Fathom covered the little octopus quickly, although he wasn't entirely sure why he was hiding him from his friends.

Why is Blob still here?

He knew that Indigo had flown away without most of her stuff — he'd guessed she was in a hurry to leave before he got back. But he'd always thought she'd taken Blob with her. If she hadn't . . . what did that mean?

Did she leave him as a message to me? To make sure I know she wants nothing more to do with me?

That didn't seem like something she would do. She loved Blob, didn't she?

"Fathom?" Darkstalker said behind him. "I'm trying to tell you something totally momentous over here. It'll change your life, trust me."

Fathom turned to his friend with a smile, but his heart was starting to whisper anxiously.

Why did Indigo decide to leave without Blob?

Was there something else going on?

Is there something I'm missing . . . and how can I find out what it is?

CHAPTER 26

DARKSTALKER

The sun was sliding cold yellow claws over the eastern horizon as Darkstalker flew home from the palace. Below him, the detritus of the festival was being swept away by a busy flurry of worker dragons. Soon only the paper lanterns and the gleaming shapes of the glass sculptures would remain. He spotted one dragon industriously scrubbing out the game pavilion, even though Quickdeath had died bloodlessly and his body had been removed.

Darkstalker beat his wings to rise higher, as close to the sun as he could manage.

His talk with Fathom had not gone exactly as he'd imagined.

He'd expected a little more excitement — a little more *gratitude*. He'd expected that Fathom would be thrilled to find a way to use his powers without damaging the soul he worried so much about. He'd rather expected Fathom to make his very own animus scroll right then and there.

But instead his friend had remained stubbornly unconvinced. "It could still be affecting you," he argued.

Darkstalker could see the images piling up in Fathom's mind: Albatross stabbing the queen, the dead bodies of his parents, the blood everywhere. Every time Fathom thought about animus powers, that was straight where his mind went — massacres and devastation and the loss of nearly your entire family.

Not only that, but tonight his mind was suddenly occupied with the mystery of some kind of octopus. Fathom's thoughts were all *Indigo, Indigo, Indigo* again, just when they'd been starting to get interesting. He spent more of their conversation thinking about *her* than focusing on the wonderful news Darkstalker was telling him. And as he often did, he forgot to even worry about Darkstalker reading his mind.

Finally Fathom had rubbed his eyes, shaking his head fiercely. "Nobody knows exactly how animus magic works. The only safe option is to avoid using it at all."

"Why would we *have* this power if we're *never* supposed to use it?" Darkstalker had shouted in frustration, which was when Clearsight had decided it was time for everyone to go home and get some sleep.

Whatever. If Fathom doesn't want to listen to reason, that's his problem.

My *problem is that someone tried to* kill *me tonight.*

He set his jaw grimly. There were plenty of future time-lines where Arctic tried to kill him — but not many where he succeeded.

Still, there were a few, even with Darkstalker's invulnerability. Now that Arctic surely knew about that, he'd have to plan his next attack on Darkstalker more carefully . . . maybe even use his own magic. Arctic, in fact, might be the only dragon in the kingdom who could actually kill Darkstalker.

He should have used his power to do it right the first time. So why didn't he?

Because he didn't want anyone to know it was him who killed me. Right?

Darkstalker soared down toward his front door, which was just starting to turn from gray to red as the light of the sun reached it. All the flowers in their miniature hanging gardens were dead. No one had gone anywhere near them since losing Mother.

He pushed open the door and found Whiteout lying on the couch, staring at the ceiling with her wings flopped out to either side of her. She was wearing one of the trinkets from the festival, a black rope necklace with a golden glass seashell pendant, turning it between her claws. He wondered if Thoughtful had bought it for her.

"Good morning," he said, nudging his sister's tail affectionately. "Dreaming of your new admirer?"

"Thoughtful," she said, a statement rather than a question. "Yes and no. I do like him."

"Do you want me to try to foresee what will happen with you two?" Darkstalker asked. He still wasn't as good at this as Clearsight — he tended to see the most probable outcomes, and everything else was usually muddled by random events and small deviations. Perhaps if he had a lot of time to devote to studying all the futures, the way she did, he'd be able to follow them more clearly. But who had that kind of time, or that kind of focus? He'd have to be trapped underground for months with nothing else to do.

"No, thank you," said Whiteout, which was such an ordinary response that Darkstalker peered at her curiously.

"Are you all right?" he asked, touching her neck. It didn't feel warmer than it should.

"I feel funny," she said. "All my words are coming out wrong."

Actually it seemed as if they were coming out right for once, which was worrying. Darkstalker wished that he could read her mind and see what was going on in there.

"Maybe you just need some sleep," he said. A small clatter from one of the back rooms distracted him. "Is Father here?"

She nodded.

Darkstalker stepped quietly down the hall until he was standing in the doorway to his father's room. Foeslayer's side of it still looked exactly the same, everything untouched except perhaps her blankets, which looked as though someone had been lying on them. But it was freezing cold in the room, with actual icicles hanging around Arctic's sleeping spot. He must have been using his frostbreath to make the room a bit more to his own liking.

Arctic had his back to Darkstalker, fiddling with something at his desk. Fragments of ice were scattered around his feet and a piece of parchment that looked like a map stuck out from under his tail.

Can't wait much longer, his brain muttered. *Not sure this will be enough, though.*

"I'm alive," Darkstalker announced. "In case you were worried."

Arctic stiffened, then cast an evil glance over his shoulder at his son. "Can't say that I was."

"I know you were there," Darkstalker said. "At the pavilion. Watching."

"Indeed," said Arctic, turning back to his work. "Care to explain how that spear bounced off your scales?" *This one gets more dangerous all the time,* he thought. *Maybe I should do what Mother wants.*

"Did you know the dragon who attacked me?" Darkstalker asked instead of answering.

His father shrugged. "I've seen him around court, but never spoken to him. I'm not interested in knowing every common NightWing in the tribe."

Darkstalker paused, waiting for Quickdeath's name to appear in Arctic's thoughts. But it didn't. Arctic had a brief memory of passing Quickdeath in the halls of the palace, and that was it.

Could Darkstalker be wrong? Or had Arctic finally developed the strength to shield some of his thoughts?

"Why do you think he tried to kill me?" he tried.

Arctic snorted. "Because you're an arrogant fool. Because you flaunt your magic and don't care who you offend. Because you insulted his mother, or stole his prey, or cheated off his test, or read his mind when he told you not to. I can think of a million possible reasons, but what does it matter? He's dead now, isn't he?"

That idiot, Arctic thought, flicking his tail. *He should have known it wouldn't be that easy to kill an animus dragon. Couldn't have gotten* me *that way, either, not if I was wearing my shielding earring.*

Darkstalker tipped his head. He hadn't known that his father had a "shielding earring." He wondered which one it was: the light blue diamond in his left ear, or the silver narwhal in his right.

More important, these didn't sound like the thoughts of a dragon who'd just tried to have him killed. Arctic seemed more . . . disinterested than anything else.

"You're probably right," Darkstalker said, backing out of the doorway and heading to his own room.

Behind him, he heard Arctic swivel around again, thinking, *Now* that *was suspicious. What does he mean, I'm probably right? What's that dragon hiding?* And then, a few moments later, as Darkstalker was unlocking his door, Arctic thought, *Better act soon, before anyone can stop me.*

Darkstalker paused, listening, but Arctic's thoughts didn't elaborate further. *Maybe he wasn't the one who hired Quickdeath,* Darkstalker thought, *but it certainly sounds like he's still planning to kill me eventually.*

Darkstalker locked the door behind him and started pacing up and down in his room. He wished Clearsight were here, to help him figure out what to do next. What would she see Arctic doing, if she looked ahead in his timeline?

Although he had to admit his faith in her powers was shaken by the attack tonight. Why hadn't she seen it coming? Who could have known enough to trick her foresight that way — and his, for that matter?

He'd have to find out later what evil scheme was circling around Arctic's head. Right now all that interested him was finding his would-be killer.

Who besides Arctic might want Darkstalker dead?

He paused next to his desk, thinking of the last dragon who had dared to threaten his life.

He remembered the cold prick of steel at his throat. The tension that hummed through her wings whenever he walked into the room. Her dark blue eyes, always watching him, as though *he* was the one who posed a danger to Fathom.

Dragons who try to kill me don't fare too well, do they, SeaWing?

He swept the clutter off his desk. *Sorry, Clearsight*. He had promised her he'd wait before doing any spell — that she could be there if he decided to do it. But he didn't want to wait. He hated the idea that someone was out there wishing for his death, planning to kill him . . . planning to derail all his glorious futures and blink all his dragonets out of existence. How *dare* they. He needed to find out who they were and *punish them*.

Whoever it was had to know immediately that they couldn't do this to him and get away with it. They had to suffer the consequences as soon as possible. He was the most powerful dragon in Pyrrhia. He should act like it.

He took his scroll and his secret inkwell out of their hiding place, rolled it to the newest blank spread, and weighted down the corners with little statues. Next he pulled out a scrap of parchment and set it on top of the scroll. He dipped one claw in the red ink and wrote, *Enchant this parchment to reveal the name of the dragon who hired Quickdeath to kill me tonight.*

As he carefully wiped the ink off his claw, jagged red letters began to appear on the parchment, slowly scrawling a name across the stark white page.

Darkstalker froze as he realized what it said.

Oh, yes. There are definitely going to be consequences.

Now I know who has to pay.

CHAPTER 27

CLEARSIGHT

Clearsight slept very poorly that morning, troubled by nightmares of horrible futures — betrayals and murders and war without end. It seemed as though all her worst possible visions were crowding through her head at once.

She woke up with massive pain in her temples and jaw, as though she'd been clenching her teeth all night. The sun stabbed sharply through a gap in the thick curtains, pouncing on her eyeballs and setting them ablaze. She covered her head with a pillow and tried to find a timeline with an instant miracle cure for headaches in it.

Drinking water would help. So would breakfast. Hiding under the covers for the rest of the day would not.

She got up, taking deep breaths, and adjusted her moonstone earrings, which had slipped half off in the night. She had to remember: sometimes dreams were just dreams, not visions of the future. Even if it felt like the end of the world, the argument last night didn't have to be the beginning of a horrible spiral into darkness.

And if it was, she could stop it. She wouldn't *let* the darkness come for her and her friends. As long as Darkstalker listened to her — and he would, in almost every timeline she could see now — everything would be all right.

Clearsight stumbled to the window that looked over the inner courtyards of the palace. She twitched the curtains aside and peered out at the garden below. It was after midday, and not many dragons were down there, but she spotted a line of royal guards blocking off one section — and beyond them, a pair of NightWings, walking and talking close together.

One was obviously the queen. The other . . . Clearsight recognized the long neck and sharp-edged bones from afar.

That was Allknowing — Queen Vigilance's fired seer.

What was she doing here?

Clearsight rubbed her eyes and splashed water on her face, then hurried down to the garden, taking the stairs instead of flying, so it wouldn't look as if she was swooping in on the queen's private conversation.

The guards saw her coming and one of them called to the queen. "Your other seer is here, Your Majesty."

Queen Vigilance poked her head around a rosebush and eyed Clearsight. "I see," she said. "Any new visions?"

"Not about the war, Your Majesty," Clearsight said with a bow. "Not in the last day. My previous predictions still stand."

"*Really*," said the queen. She beckoned Clearsight forward until the three of them — Vigilance, Clearsight, and Allknowing — were ensconced inside the rose bower.

Allknowing smirked down at Clearsight. Her flicking tail caught a few yellow roses and ripped them loose, scattering petals like drops of gold everywhere.

"So," the queen hissed to Clearsight. "A question for you. Have you ever had any visions about your truly beloved?"

"About — you mean about Darkstalker?" Clearsight blinked with surprise. Of course she'd had hundreds, thousands of visions about Darkstalker . . . including several the queen would surely quite like to know about. But those were the ones that weren't going to happen.

She could still tell part of the truth, though. "Most of my visions about Darkstalker have to do with our future together," she hedged. "I've had visions of our dragonets, of our future home near the palace, of the ways in which we both keep using our powers to serve you."

"And have you seen how I die?" the queen demanded.

Chills slid along Clearsight's neck and spread through her scales. What had Allknowing told her?

"I've seen a few possibilities," she said carefully.

"Oh, yes?" said the queen. "Not worth mentioning, were they?"

"They're all so far into the future," Clearsight protested. "It'll be another ten years before one of your daughters has the courage to challenge you, and the probability of her winning is very low."

"Hmm," said Queen Vigilance. Her suspicious look encompassed both of her seers now. "And of all my death scenes, which comes the soonest?"

Clearsight tried. She closed her eyes and concentrated as hard as she could, looking for the darkest paths, which made her realize she hadn't had any visions of Darkstalker in his twisted crown for at least a month. She'd assumed . . . she'd *hoped* that meant it had fallen out of the realm of possibility. That maybe Darkstalker's recent contentment was real, and everyone was going to be safe.

Now, searching for it as intently as she could, flashes began appearing behind her eyes: Darkstalker, the crown, the dead queen — but she couldn't keep them there. They flashed away as soon as she tried to look at them or piece them into the web of the future.

"Don't hurt yourself," Allknowing sneered. Clearsight opened her eyes and looked at her former teacher. How could Allknowing have a vision of Darkstalker doing something terrible when Clearsight couldn't see it?

"Share your mumbo jumbo," Queen Vigilance ordered her former seer, flicking Allknowing in the face with her tail.

Allknowing cleared her throat and fluffed her wings importantly.

"Hatched of ice and hatched of night
Cursed with moons all shining bright
Longs for power not his own
Comes to steal your very throne."

Queen Vigilance snorted. "Remarkably clear. For the first time ever." Her pitch-black eyes narrowed at Clearsight. "Any of that ring a bell?"

"She's making it up!" Clearsight protested. "Darkstalker wouldn't do that!"

"Why should I believe you?" the queen demanded, furious now. "You're so enchanted by him that you wouldn't tell me even if he was a threat, would you?"

"I don't have to!" Clearsight cried. "He's really n —" She broke off suddenly.

Enchanted by him.

Am I?

Her talons went slowly to her earrings. *But I checked the scroll.*

And yet . . . I didn't notice an invulnerability spell in there, either.

If he can keep one spell a secret from me, he could have done another.

But how? It would have *to be in the scroll. Wouldn't it?*

The chills had become a cold gusting wind of terror. Had he been lying to her all along? Did he really keep some of his animus power in his own claws? But surely she would have seen it in some future, if that were true.

She fumbled to unclip the earrings, dropping them with small plinks on the ground.

And visions rushed in, visions upon visions upon visions, all the darkness she'd ever seen but worse and worse and worse and worse: Darkstalker murdering the queen and stealing the throne; NightWings fleeing by the thousands; the city burning, the ground shaking; Darkstalker in his crown laughing and killing with ease.

These weren't visions of the distant future, either. These were about to happen *now*. The tipping point was trembling on a knife's edge. If Clearsight could do anything to stop it, she didn't have a moment to lose.

"It was you," she said to the queen, bewildered. "*You* sent the assassin after Darkstalker."

"After I heard her prophecy," the queen said, tipping her head at Allknowing, "how could I not?"

"You *fool*," Clearsight cried. "You're the one making it happen! He wouldn't have — he might not — but now, but now . . ." She took a step backward. He was coming, it was all coming, all the bad things rushing their way. "I have to go."

"No," said the queen sharply. "I won't let you conspire with him anymore. Guards! Lock her up!" she shouted.

Burly NightWing guards pounced from behind the rosebushes, as if they'd been lying in wait for this moment, but Clearsight saw them coming. All at once the future was spread clearly over the present, as it hadn't been since she put the earrings on, and she saw where the guards would be to grab her and she saw how to twist away and her escape path into the sky, and she took it, winging free in one wild heartbeat.

"I'm the only one who can stop him," she shouted to the queen's furious upturned face. "And I will. I promise I will!"

She evaded the talons that reached for her and the wings that blocked her way, diving and dodging until she was over the palace wall and soaring down toward the Great Diamond.

A moment later, new wingbeats came up alongside her

and she nearly lashed out, before she realized with a surge of relief that it was Fathom, glowing emerald green in the sunlight.

"What happened?" he called. "I heard shouting — I saw you and the queen out my window — are you all right?"

"We have to stop Darkstalker," she cried. "He's on his way here to kill the queen."

"What?" Fathom's wings faltered. "Now? Why — oh." His features shifted as he figured it out. "She's the one who sent the assassin."

"Darkstalker *really* doesn't like it when dragons try to kill him," Clearsight said.

"Maybe we can reason with him. He forgave Indigo, remember?" Fathom pointed out as they swooped past the library.

Clearsight's heart stopped again. *Did he?*

What if she didn't really leave? What if he did something to her with one of his secret spells?

WHERE IS SHE?

"I see him!" Fathom cried, adjusting his flight path.

Darkstalker was beating his way toward the palace, menace radiating from every scale. Not many NightWings were out now, in the middle of the day, but those that were swerved wildly to get out of his way, then gathered to whisper together as he passed.

I knew the whole tribe would know who we were one day, Clearsight thought, *but I wanted us to be their saviors — not for everyone to be scared of him.*

"Darkstalker!" she yelled.

He paused and hovered in place, looking around as she and Fathom swooped up to him. She saw his gaze move to her ears, and she saw him realize that she'd taken off the earrings. He knew that she knew what he'd done. His face set into lines of defiance.

She pointed to the roof of the library, and the three of them soared down to land on an open flat spot between the graceful spires.

"I'm not going to let you kill the queen," she said as their talons touched down.

"She started it," Darkstalker said, his mouth quirking unbelievably into a little smile.

"She's an idiot," Clearsight said, "but we can stop her from trying again. We can go back to the way things were."

"Yes, please, Darkstalker," Fathom said, pressing his front talons together.

"Can you really see that?" Darkstalker asked Clearsight. "She'll never trust either of us. You'll always be in danger, and therefore so will I, because I care about you, and Vigilance will use that against me." He paused, looking her over. "Unless I enchant *your* scales, too." His talons reached for a bag slung around his neck and Clearsight realized with a jolt that he must have his scroll with him. *So he can use his magic on the queen.*

"No," she said, so sharply that Darkstalker and Fathom both winced. "I don't want any more spells on me, Darkstalker. I can't *believe* you betrayed me like that."

"Like what?" he said innocently.

"The earrings!" she cried. "You put a secret spell on me! You messed with *my power*, Darkstalker. Don't you see how wrong that is?"

Fathom took a step back, his face crumpling into shock and sorrow.

"Oh," Darkstalker said, flipping his tail dismissively. "That was such a little spell. I just wanted to keep you focused on the happy futures, like we talked about. I knew you couldn't do it on your own, no matter how much you promised me you would. So the earrings faded back all the dark paths, that's all. I was only trying to make you *happier*, Clearsight." He tipped his head, looking for a moment as though he really meant it, as if he cared about her more than anything and had been trying to help.

He might actually believe that — but the truth is, he was just making his life easier. He didn't want me standing in his way as he went down those dark paths.

"That's why I didn't see Quickdeath coming," Clearsight said. "Between the earrings and Allknowing trying to trick me — that's how I was taken by surprise. What if all my predictions about the war have been wrong, too, Darkstalker? While I'm handing out all these rose-colored prophecies, dragons could die in the real future."

"I was double-checking your work," he said, smiling. "Don't worry."

"You arrogant porcupine!" she shouted.

"This has been delightful," he said. His wings flared open. "But I have a queen to kill."

"Stop!" Clearsight leaped at him, tumbling him backward on the roof until she had him pinned down. "I'm not going to let you do that!"

Darkstalker looked up at her, and she saw with a shiver of fear that he was genuinely puzzled.

"Why not?" he asked. "I'll be a great king. Can't you see that? We'll be the strongest tribe in Pyrrhia. Our kingdom could stretch from shore to shore. You and me, side by side, bringing harmony to the whole continent, with our dragonets inheriting the throne after we're gone."

"After we're gone?" she said bitterly. "You won't ever let that happen. It's a short step from invulnerability to an immortality spell. Have you done it already?"

His silence answered that question. Darkstalker was immortal now — which was one of the most important things Clearsight was supposed to prevent to protect the future.

Was there any hope left?

A vision trembled through her mind, rumbling up from below and gathering strength like a volcano.

There was only one way to stop Darkstalker from killing the queen right now — and it might not save Vigilance in the future, and it definitely led to more bloodshed, but it would give them at least a moment to think, if she took this path.

If she told him what was happening at this moment, while his back was turned.

Then she saw that she didn't have to; the vision was sweeping over him as well. He sat up abruptly, knocking her away.

"Whiteout," he said in a strangled voice.

"Your father has her," Clearsight said, touching her forehead. "He's taken her and they're flying . . ."

"North," Darkstalker finished. Murder glinted in his eyes. "He's taking her to the Ice Kingdom."

CHAPTER 28

FATHOM

They were flying before Fathom quite realized what was happening. He only knew his friends were going north as fast as their wings could take them and he was going, too.

At one point he felt something like a shock sizzle through the air, just as they flew out of the mountains. It startled him into glancing down, and he nearly tumbled out of the sky, his stomach heaving. The land below was littered with IceWing corpses, charred and ripped apart into tangles of white-blue limbs.

"What happened here?" he yelled to Clearsight.

She glanced at Darkstalker, flying furiously ahead of them. "He put up a border shield," she called back. "It kills any IceWings who try to enter the kingdom."

Fathom should have guessed. *His magic did this.*

He closed his eyes tight, beat his wings faster, and flew on.

Soon he saw sand below him, a vast expanse of desert that rippled like a pale ocean. Down there was the Kingdom of Sand, ruled by Queen Scorpion. All he knew about her was that she allowed the NightWings and IceWings to battle across her territory in exchange for large piles of treasure from each of them; rumor had it she played both sides and didn't care who won. The desert kingdom was big and empty enough for the battles to play out without much collateral SandWing damage, as long as the warring dragons stayed away from her oasis towns.

The sun had passed the high point of the sky and was sliding down into late afternoon, but it was blisteringly hot on Fathom's scales. He wished he could dive into an ocean to cool them off. He wondered if they had made a grave mistake, flying into the Kingdom of Sand without water. But he followed his friends; he would follow them anywhere.

He couldn't believe their fight. He could barely understand it. From the outside, he'd thought their relationship was perfect. The way they'd suddenly exploded — the idea that Darkstalker had cast a spell on Clearsight — the fact that he'd been on his way to kill his own queen! Fathom wondered if he really knew his friend at all.

So why are you following him into a strange kingdom? whispered the worries at the back of his mind. *Without either of your guards?*

"Darkstalker," Clearsight called. She swept one wing around at the endless desert. "They could be anywhere."

He checked himself in the air, frowning at her, and then soared quickly down to the ground. When Fathom landed beside him, Darkstalker was unrolling a scroll on the shifting sands.

That's the *scroll,* Fathom thought with a start. *Where he keeps all his power.*

Darkstalker reached into his bag again and pulled out a dagger. Its jagged edge caught the sun, flashing into Fathom's eyes and blinding him for a moment.

"What are you going to do with that?" Clearsight asked, resting her wing against one of Darkstalker's.

He shook her off. "Not what you think." He placed the dagger on the scroll, weighing down the flapping paper, uncapped an inkwell, and scrawled *Enchant this dagger to lead us to Arctic and Whiteout, then stab Arctic once in the foot, injuring him enough that he has to stop, but not so badly that he bleeds to death. Above all else, stop him from crossing the Great Ice Cliff.*

Darkstalker wrote with unhesitating confidence, ignoring the shiny green beetle that popped out of the sand, scurried over his claws, and buried itself again. The wind lifted his wings and the sun burnished his scales to gleaming ebony. He looked heroic and sure. He didn't even have to pause and think. He knew exactly what he wanted to write, his carefully crafted spell.

He has no doubts, Fathom thought. He wished he could have just a moment of feeling that way, of that kind of belief in himself.

But it was better that he didn't. The world might not survive it if he let himself stop being afraid, even for a moment.

Darkstalker shot him an irritated glare. He'd finished the

spell, but the dagger wasn't moving. "Why isn't it working?" he growled.

"Maybe he's protecting himself with his own magic," Clearsight suggested. "Maybe instead of attacking him, we should —"

Darkstalker flicked his tail, cutting her off. "Yes! His shielding earring!" He stabbed his talons into the sand and dragged out the green beetle, who squirmed frantically in his claws. It had tiny black pincers that snapped at the air.

Enchant this beetle to find Prince Arctic as fast as possible and take off his shielding earring, Darkstalker wrote.

The beetle flickered into the air like a puff of smoke and a few moments later, the dagger rose up and spun like a compass needle. Suddenly it shot away, heading northwest.

"Let's go!" Darkstalker cried. He threw the scroll back in his bag and hurled himself into the sky. He flew as if his wings were possessed and Fathom had to strain every muscle to keep up. Next to him in the air, Clearsight flew with the same determination. Her eyes had a distant measuring look, as though she was climbing down into a dark abyss, trying to see the bottom.

The dagger flashed and danced ahead of them as they flew and flew. Finally, as the sky was just starting to fade to darker blue, the dagger put on a burst of speed, and a moment later there was an agonized shriek from somewhere up ahead.

Fathom caught up to Darkstalker in time to see a silvery white shape fall out of the sky and crash-land on a dune below them. Another figure, black-and-white, drifted down after him.

"We found them!" Darkstalker cried exultantly.

They landed in a semicircle around Arctic, with Clearsight and Fathom on either side of Darkstalker. Whiteout crouched beside her father, examining one of his back feet, where the dagger was buried to the hilt and blue blood poured out over the sticky dark sand. Another thin trickle of blood slid down his neck from one ear, where an earring had once been.

Arctic glared up at Darkstalker, his face twisted with pain and fury. "Just let us go," the IceWing hissed. "I let you live. Do me the same courtesy. We never have to see each other again."

Darkstalker calmly slid his scroll out of his bag. "Where do you think you're taking my sister?" he asked.

"She wants to go with me," Arctic snarled. "Tell him, Whiteout."

"I want to go with Father," she said. Even Fathom could see that there was something wrong with her voice, with her eyes. Clearsight reached for her and Whiteout jerked away, keeping her talons on her father.

"She's going to marry an IceWing prince," Arctic said, his breath coming in short gasps. "Not some lowborn NightWing."

"That's right," Whiteout said. "I'll be an IceWing princess. And have lots of baby IceWings. And live there forever. Where it is very, very cold."

"You are not taking her to the Ice Kingdom," Darkstalker said. "She would be miserable there, even worse than you were." He unrolled the scroll to a blank section and carefully set a rock at each corner to hold it down.

"I'm doing this for your mother," Arctic spat. He tried to sit up, setting off another gush of blood from the dagger wound, and fell back again. Whiteout blinked anxiously and pressed her talons to his foot. "Queen Diamond will let Foeslayer go if she has me instead."

"Mother is dead," said Darkstalker. Fathom shivered at the eerie blankness with which he said those words.

Darkstalker uncapped the inkwell and placed it gently on the edge of the scroll. "You are doing this for yourself, Father. You have no reason to stay in the Night Kingdom anymore, now that Mother is gone. So you're taking your chance to go home, like you've always wanted." He dipped one claw in the ink. "You're planning to tell Diamond all the secrets you know about NightWings to help her defeat us. You may even use your power again, to launch an attack on us."

Fathom glanced over at Clearsight and saw from her unhappy face that it was true.

"I might, but only to protect Whiteout," Arctic said. "If that's the only deal Diamond will accept to keep her alive." He reached down and yanked out the dagger, hissing furiously as blood spurted out. "You'll be fine with your invincible scales, don't worry. Now say good-bye to your sister and let us go before Diamond's army finds you."

"I *want* to go to the Ice Kingdom," Whiteout said. "I want

to be with Father. You go home," she said, pointing at Darkstalker. "I don't even like you."

Darkstalker paused, meeting her cool blue eyes, then turned back to Arctic. "But you made one odd mistake," he said. His claw was poised above the scroll, ink gleaming on the tip. "You should have killed me before you left, like Diamond wanted you to." He tilted his head at his father. "I'm not sure why you didn't."

"I wasn't going to kill my own son," Arctic snarled. "Whatever you think of my soul, it's not so far gone that I would actually do that." He started to laugh, a cracking, bitter sound like icicles snapping off a roof. "I know I should, though. One more spell, and I'll probably be there, won't I? I mean, what are you going to do to stop me?" He spread his wings, staggering upright. "Our magic is equal, you and I. Our souls are equally doomed. What are you writing, you little monster?"

"Darkstalker, please, please don't," Clearsight pleaded. Fathom took a step toward him, but he didn't know what to do. He could rip the scroll out of his talons — but then what would happen? Would Arctic attack? Of these two dragons, if one was about to use magic, wouldn't it be better if it was Darkstalker?

It was too late anyway. Darkstalker's claw was sliding smoothly across the paper, words falling into place, spelling out the beginning of the end of the world.

"Now," Darkstalker said to his father. "Stop talking."

Arctic opened his mouth.

And nothing came out.

"Never use your magic again," Darkstalker said pleasantly. "Never attack me or my friends ever again. Don't try to escape."

Arctic clutched his throat. His tail was lashing like a snake on fire.

"What did you do?" Fathom whispered. On the other side of Darkstalker, Clearsight had her face buried in her talons. He couldn't tell whether she was crying or planning or spinning herself into the futures to get as far away from now as possible.

"Release Whiteout from the spell you put on her," Darkstalker went on, ignoring Fathom.

Arctic's claws reached toward his daughter, although he was clearly trying to fight them. He seized the golden glass shell necklace around her neck, pulled it off, and smashed it.

Whiteout let out a gasp. She shook her head, blinking like mad, then looked around, taking in the scene as if she'd just woken up.

"Oh no," she cried. "It's too late. The sand is falling."

"You're all right, Whiteout," Darkstalker said, reaching to take her front talons in his. "I saved you." She touched his snout gently with hers for a moment, then stepped back.

"I'm grateful to be unfrozen," she said. "But I'm sorry for winning."

"Don't be," he said. "We both win. We're going to have the greatest future I can give us. All of us." He swung his head to include Fathom and Clearsight, then rolled his eyes at the expressions on their faces. "Calm *down*. I saved the day. It was amazing, didn't you notice?"

"Let me see," Clearsight said, holding out her talons.

Darkstalker shrugged and slid his scroll toward her. Fathom stepped around him and read the spell over her shoulder.

He'd known what it would say. It was clear from what he'd seen in front of him.

But still, seeing the words in black and white . . .

Enchant Arctic the IceWing to obey my every command.

"No," Clearsight breathed.

Fathom was dizzy, falling, the world and everything he knew rushing past him.

If it was possible to enchant living dragons this way — to treat them like objects, to use them however you wanted . . .

He looked at Clearsight. It could start as simply as a pair of enchanted earrings. A small shifting of the world, rearranging other dragons to make your life a bit easier, telling yourself it was harmless, for the best, even.

But once you took a step down that path, once you let yourself think manipulating someone else was all right . . . when every new turn seemed right to you, seemed justified, no matter how far you went . . .

Where would it ever stop?

CHAPTER 29

DARKSTALKER

All things considered, Darkstalker thought he was doing a remarkably admirable job of keeping his temper.

His queen had tried to kill him, after everything he'd done for her.

His father had bewitched his sister and tried to betray the entire tribe.

Clearsight was acting as if his gift of the earrings was some enormous life-altering horrible treachery, instead of a perfectly sweet, kindhearted gesture he'd made to make her feel better.

And now Fathom was flooding Darkstalker's mind with panicked screaming mobs of DOOM DOOM THE SKY IS FALLING MY FRIEND IS EVIL THE WORLD IS ENDING blah blah overreacting melodramatic nonsense.

Darkstalker was doing exactly what he needed to do. He had to stop his father. He had to save his sister. He had to protect his friends. He was clearly the good guy here.

If Clearsight and Fathom couldn't see that, what kinds of

friends were they? Trusting him and supporting him . . . as his best friends, wasn't that their ONE JOB?

He clenched his claws, stamping his rage down to a simmer below the surface. His work was not done. He needed to make himself and his friends safe permanently, forever. He needed everyone to know that you *never* came after Darkstalker.

"Follow us back to the Night Kingdom," he ordered Arctic. "Keep up. Don't try anything. Don't even think about anything except flying, one wingbeat after another, until I tell you you can land."

His father was beautifully, magically silent. He could do nothing except stare at Darkstalker with seething hatred. Arctic was finally, finally no longer a threat to anyone.

And now he's going to pay for what happened to Mother, for what he did to Whiteout, and for what he nearly did to the tribe.

"Maybe we should rest first," Clearsight said hurriedly. "Whiteout looks tired, right, Fathom? We could all sleep for a while, maybe find something to eat. Maybe talk about . . . everything."

"I have things to do," Darkstalker said, packing up his scroll and putting it back in his bag. He knew her so well. He knew that she was trying to delay the inevitable. She was hoping to wrestle them onto a new timeline. She thought that if she had a little more time now, tonight, she'd be able to change the future.

But she couldn't. He was weaving the path now; no more tweaks and tugs from her. Even if he had to drag her along it kicking and screaming. Once they got there, to his beautiful future, she'd admit it was the best one and he'd been right all along. He spread his wings. "We're going now."

"Darkstalker," Clearsight said. "*Please* don't do what you're about to do. Please stop and look at the timelines with me — we can still find one that's safe and peaceful for all of us."

"I know we can," he said. "We're on it. Accept your destiny, my love. We're the ones who bring the peace, once the throne is ours. And who's safer than the king and queen?"

He took off, relishing the sound of all their wingbeats hurrying after him. These were his dragons, Clearsight and Fathom and Whiteout. They might fuss and worry at him, but they'd follow him to the edge of the sky. They'd be right beside him as he took his throne, and they'd love him no matter what.

He didn't stop once, the whole way back to the Night Kingdom. The sun buried itself below the horizon and darkness spread cold wings over the desert. A few times as he flew, he saw the flicker of campfires or the shadows of moving dragons, preparing for yet another battle.

That will be my army soon, he thought. *We'll crush the IceWings easily once I'm king. I'll punish Diamond for what she did to my mother.*

Rage surged through him again. He'd delayed his vengeance for months, listening to Clearsight's worries, following Queen Vigilance's strategy instead of using his own. He'd made her a stronger queen; he'd given the tribe a shield and strengthened her army, and then what did she do? Send an assassin after him!

She'd brought this upon herself.

The mountainous border of the Night Kingdom loomed up ahead. Darkstalker had enchanted his shield to allow himself, Whiteout, and Arctic to pass through safely. He wondered what would have happened if he'd left Arctic out of that equation. Would he have died on his way out of the kingdom?

It didn't matter. This path was going to be much more satisfying.

Fathom's anxiety intensified to a shrieking fever pitch as they swooped closer to the palace. *Oh no, we shouldn't enchant other dragons! Dragons aren't objects! You can't use them like puppets! Is my friend completely evil? There's nothing we can do!*

He really needed to calm down. Darkstalker would put that priority high up on his list, once he was king. Something that would shift Fathom's brain into a much quieter state; something that would take all that freaking out and stuff it away where Darkstalker didn't have to listen to it all the time. He knew he could make Fathom a happier dragon. Honestly, he'd thought he could do that by getting rid of Indigo, but apparently that wasn't enough. The self-loathing was too entrenched.

No matter. It could be done, and it would be, soon.

He looked over his shoulder for Clearsight, hoping to catch her eye and maybe find her smiling. Maybe a night of flying had given her enough time to think about why he'd done everything he was doing. Maybe she was a little closer to understanding him.

But she flew with her head down, looking just as doubtful as ever.

He flexed his talons irritably. Had anyone even noticed what he saved Whiteout from? What Arctic did to her was basically exactly what Darkstalker had done to him. It wasn't quite as impressive — Arctic had enchanted the necklace, because like every other narrow-minded animus dragon, it had never occurred to him that he could enchant a living being. But he'd forced Whiteout to go with him; he'd erased her love for Darkstalker and her interest in Thoughtful; and worst of all, he'd used his magic to try to make her *normal*. Arctic had never loved Whiteout's strange way of speaking. It made sense that when he tried to control her, he would start by taking that away.

Darkstalker snarled angrily.

This was what Arctic deserved.

His friends would understand that eventually. They'd see that Darkstalker was right.

The Great Diamond was below them, bustling with dragons shopping, dragons on their way to work, dragons going to the library or the museum or school. Dragons who didn't have any idea what or who was important, or how the world was about to change.

He twisted in the air to meet his father's eyes. "You will land beside me and stand there quietly until I tell you what to do next."

Arctic's eyes were blank, trapped. There was nothing he could do but obey.

Darkstalker landed on the stage set up in the center of the plaza, where there were supposed to be concerts for the next few weeks, celebrating a series of upcoming hatching days in the royal family.

The moons shone palely overhead, two of them almost full, one a needle-sharp sliver on a carpet of stars.

Talons hit the stage behind him, *thump thump thump*. Fathom, Whiteout, Clearsight, with their beloved, frustrating, worried faces. And right beside him, Arctic, exactly as Darkstalker had always wanted him.

Down below him, dragons turned to look up, their faces curious and wondering.

"My friends," Darkstalker called in a booming voice. *My subjects,* he thought. "You're about to see something no dragons have ever seen before. Gather your families; everyone come watch! This is the most important day of your lives!"

He sat down and waited as the square filled with dragons, murmurs passing from one to another, everyone wondering what he was going to do. Everyone's eyes on him. Everyone finally about to see him for the dragon he really was: his power, his heroism, his intelligence and strength.

After tonight, no one would ever insult him or underestimate him again.

And no one would *dare* attack him, or hurt the dragons he loved.

"Darkstalker," Clearsight said from beside him, her wings brushing softly against his.

"One last try, my love?" he said, smiling at her. He put one wing around her and she leaned into his side, twining her tail around his. She was warm and beautiful in the moonlight. She was the future he wanted, right there on the throne next to his.

"Where's Fathom?" he asked, noticing that the SeaWing's worried thoughts weren't weighing down his mind anymore. The rush of thoughts from the crowd below was swarming in, taking up all the space instead.

"I told him to go back to the palace," Clearsight said. "He's seen enough violence in his life from dragons he trusted. He doesn't need to see any more."

Darkstalker rolled his eyes. Clearsight was brilliant and empathetic, but sometimes she laid it on a little thick.

"I think he'll survive," he said. "Hang on, wait, actually; I know he does. You can see it, too. I'm going to find him a nice NightWing to marry in a few years."

"I don't like her," Clearsight said. "Her laugh makes me itch."

"Well, there aren't a lot of choices willing to both marry a SeaWing and never have dragonets," Darkstalker pointed out. "If we change his mind about that last part, we have a few more options."

She shook her head, probably dwelling on some boring

objections to what Darkstalker might mean by "change his mind."

"How can we be looking at the same futures," she asked, "and see them so differently?"

"I think I know," he said. "You're focused on the ones where I'm a terrible king who kills dragons for fun. I know those are there, but I'm not worried about them. That's not me. *I'm* looking at the ones where we spread peace across the continents, unite the tribes under our rule, and raise the sweetest, funniest dragonets. You should focus on those, too."

"Eclipse," she said sadly. "Shadowhunter."

"And Fierceclaws," he said, hoping she would laugh. "Still pretty sure I'm going to win that fight. It's a great name, you'll see."

She didn't respond. He reached down and lifted her chin so he could look into her eyes.

"Trust me," he said. "We have a wonderful future ahead of us. Just stay in the moment with me and you'll see."

"What kind of wonderful future starts with bloodshed and queen-killing?" she asked. "Can't we please —"

"Enough," he said, putting two claws over her mouth. "Stop doubting me. Watch and see: it'll all be fine."

He turned back to the gathering crowd, which was now hundreds of dragons deep. He felt Clearsight step away from him and wrap her wings around herself, shaking. He'd fix that later. He knew they'd be happy together again, one day not too long from now, even if it required a little magic.

"Thank you for coming!" he called to the crowd. "What a beautiful night! A perfect night to punish a traitor!" He swept one wing toward Arctic and a shocked whisper hissed through the audience. "First, let's consider the evidence. Arctic, tell our listeners. Tell them what you were about to do, before I stopped you."

"I was going *home*," Arctic roared, his voice set free again. "I'm not a traitor!"

Darkstalker took a step closer to his father. He could hear the hubbub of curiosity boiling below. Why wasn't the IceWing chained up? Why didn't he fly away? Why was he just standing there, confessing?

"Tell the truth," Darkstalker said. "Tell them *exactly* what you were planning."

Arctic lashed his tail. "I was taking my daughter to Queen Diamond," he growled. "I was going to offer her talons in marriage to whomever Diamond chose, so she could hatch some heirs for the throne who might have animus blood. I was going to live in an ice palace again, sleeping at night like a normal dragon. I was going to find out if Foeslayer is still alive. I was going to offer the IceWings a detailed map of the Night Kingdom and a way to get inside to destroy you all, in exchange for her life."

The NightWings stared at him, shocked into utter silence. From the stillness behind him on the stage, Darkstalker guessed that even Whiteout and Clearsight were stunned by the extent of Arctic's villainy.

Darkstalker shook his head regretfully. "You see," he said

to the crowd. "He admits it all. He would have wiped out our entire tribe without a shred of remorse. He is the worst dragon who has ever lived, and he deserves to die. Don't you agree?"

He raised his chin, listening to the hurricane of reactions in the minds below. Of course there were some wishy-washy responses, some dragons who thought this might be a trick, others who wondered where the queen was, and wasn't punishing traitors up to her? (She was in the palace, he was sure, watching from one of the balconies.) But most of them agreed with him. This IceWing who looked like the enemies they'd been fighting for years — he'd been planning to kill them, just like his brethren had killed NightWing brothers and sisters, mothers and fathers. They'd given him shelter, fought a war to protect him, and he had betrayed them!

He DID have to die!

"Kneel," Darkstalker said to his father.

Arctic knelt, and the crowd whispered again. How did Darkstalker make him do that? Without any guards or weapons standing by?

"Admit that I am the greatest animus of all time," Darkstalker hissed.

"You are the greatest animus of all time," Arctic choked out.

Darkstalker spread his wings toward the audience. "Tell them there is no more powerful dragon than me."

"There is no more powerful dragon than you."

"Now say you wish you had been a better father."

Arctic let out an incredulous, startled laugh. "I *do* wish I'd been a better father," he said. "If I were, I would have strangled you the moment you hatched."

"Cut out your tongue," Darkstalker said coldly.

Arctic's eyes became round holes of horror as he reached up to his mouth, pulled out his long blue forked tongue, and sliced it off with his own claws.

Darkstalker could feel the waves of terror rolling off the watching NightWings, making him stronger and stronger. *Yes. Fear me. Respect me. See me.*

"Now." Darkstalker leaned toward Arctic, his claws gouging into the wood of the stage. "Take your talons, rip open your stomach, and show us all what you're really like on the inside. Pour out your life on this stage."

It took a long time, and it was messy, and at the end of it, when Arctic was definitely dead, Darkstalker did not feel nearly as happy as he'd expected.

But he'd done what he needed to do, and the crowd reaction was exactly what he was hoping for. Now he would go kill the queen — quickly this time, get it over with, no need for more theatrics. And then he'd be king, the first king in the history of Pyrrhia, and there would be peace and prosperity and happiness, because now he and everyone he loved was safe forever.

He turned around wearily. He needed the warmth of Clearsight's wings right now.

Whiteout was standing alone on the stage behind him. Her eyes were closed, and tears were running down her face, leaving little puddles on the stage. Her white wings lay askew at her sides like broken leaves. He felt a stab of guilt — but he shouldn't; he had saved her from a terrible fate.

"Where is Clearsight?" he asked. "When did she leave?"

Was she trying to make a point, missing his moment of triumph?

Or . . . a vision flashed in his head, a warning, and he scrabbled for the bag slung across his chest. It couldn't be true. She wouldn't —

His scroll was missing.

She must have taken it when she was hugging him, whispering to him about their dragonets.

How DARE SHE.

"Clearsight has your scroll," Whiteout whispered without opening her eyes. Behind her, Darkstalker saw Thoughtful pushing through the crowd, coming toward her with worried eyes. Good, yes; Thoughtful could take care of Whiteout while Darkstalker dealt with Clearsight. "She said to tell you she'll meet you at Agate Mountain."

Darkstalker growled under his breath. He couldn't kill the queen without his scroll — well, perhaps he could. Vigilance certainly couldn't kill him. But he wanted to do it quickly, with magic. And he didn't trust what Clearsight might do, now that she had *his* power in her talons.

I can't trust her.

The realization was swift and startling. Of all the dragons in the world, he thought he'd been sure of her, at least.

He threw himself into the air, fuming.

Maybe the future was going to be a little different than he'd planned after all.

Maybe there would be no queen on the throne beside him.

CHAPTER 30

CLEARSIGHT

Clearsight's heart thudded with terror as she crept off the stage into the crowd, leaving Darkstalker's grand scene in the middle of Arctic's confession. The black leather case crumpled around the scroll as she clutched it under her wings.

She couldn't save Arctic. The next few minutes were inevitable, and terrible, and far too horribly clear in her mind already. *Blue IceWing blood everywhere.* No, he was lost . . . and now she had to save Fathom, and Indigo, and maybe the queen, and the whole rest of Pyrrhia, if she could.

It was a slim chance, and it only might work because she could thread the possibilities and read the ripples better than Darkstalker could. He was distracted by his vengeance and his horror show, and she'd spent the entire flight home untangling the one frail thread of hope until she knew what she had to do.

As she ducked through the crowd, avoiding all the looks and whispers, she ran directly into a set of familiar talons.

"Clearsight!" Listener whispered, grabbing her shoulders. "What. Is. HAPPENING."

Clearsight shook her head. "I can't . . . I can't explain."

"I can!" Listener said. "Your boyfriend is a psycho, just like I always thought!" She finally noticed the tracks of tears on Clearsight's snout and leaned in to wipe them away. "Oh, moonbeam, you'll be all right."

"No," Clearsight said. She seized one of her friend's talons in hers. "Listener, this is important. Remember when you told me that you did want to know the future if it meant saving your family's lives? If something really, really bad was about to happen?"

Listener fell back, a look of dawning fear on her face. "What's going to happen, Clearsight?"

"I don't know, exactly," Clearsight said. But if her plan failed, and Darkstalker returned, even stronger and more furious than before, without her to hold him back anymore . . . it was all destruction and death and nothing but darkness from there. "But it's really bad. Please, Listener, if you've ever believed anything I've said, do this for me. Find my parents, gather your family, and leave the Night Kingdom. Fly as far and as fast as you can. Take them somewhere safe where . . . where no one will ever find them."

She was suddenly aware that other dragons were listening, that she had the attention of several frightened faces.

"And the queen?" Listener asked.

"If you can get to her," Clearsight said, "tell her to escape, too. I'll give you all as much time as I can, but I don't know if my plan will work." *Will he come after me? Will he kill the queen first? Will I survive what I'm about to do?*

"Clearsight —" Listener started, reaching for her.

Clearsight threw her wings around her friend, hugging her fiercely. "Thank you for being you," she whispered in her ear. "I hope your life is everything it should be."

Then she pulled herself away and shoved through the crowd, ducking under long necks and wings until she was far enough from the stage to take flight for the palace.

Fathom was waiting in his room, where she'd told him to go, pacing back and forth and twisting his talons together.

"Did he suspect anything?" he asked as she swooped in over the balcony.

"Not yet," she said. "We have to keep you away from him until it's done, or he'll hear something in your thoughts." She pulled out the scroll. "Here."

"I don't want to touch that," he said, backing away.

"We have to. We have to use it to make something that will stop him," she said. She brushed a tear out of her eye. There was no time for crying, *none*.

"Not with his scroll," Fathom said, shaking his head. "It could be enchanted to signal him whenever someone else uses it. Or it might kill anyone else who tries to write in it. Or he might know, somehow, every spell that's written in it. We can't use that."

"I don't think he was that devious when he first made this," Clearsight said with a stab of sorrow for that dragon Darkstalker had been, that day when everything had looked so bright up ahead. "But you're right, he might have added it later. We have to risk it, though."

Fathom put one talon over hers, stopping her. "I'll do it. I'll use my own power."

"Your oath," Clearsight said. "You can't —"

"I *have* to," he said. "It's the only way. This is just like my grandfather . . . I'm the only one who can."

The timeline thread trembled in Clearsight's mind and she steadied herself on it, focusing as hard as she could. "Quickly, then. Remember, he's invulnerable and immortal now."

"I know," he said. "I think I know what to do, but I need something to enchant. You can't take anything with you." Fathom's voice dropped to a whisper. "Or else he'll know . . . he'll guess . . . if he suspects . . ."

"I know," Clearsight whispered back. Her breath caught on a sob. "He might kill me." That future was horribly clear, real behind her eyes even as her mind refused to believe it. She wrestled the bracelet off her arm. Moonstones and copper wire, his gift to protect her — the one she'd known would be important one day. "Use this. But make sure it keeps the enchantment it already has, too."

Fathom turned the bracelet over in his claws, tears brimming in his eyes. "Are we really doing this?" he asked. "Shouldn't we use the soul reader on him first, to make sure he's as far gone as we think?"

"We don't have time, and he's left us no choice," she said. "It only gets worse from here, Fathom. There are some futures that aren't completely terrible, but there are many more that are too frightening to risk. This could be the last moment we have where we're both free and thinking for ourselves. It's our *only* chance to stop him."

"All right." He held the bracelet between his talons and closed his eyes, concentrating fiercely. Finally he handed it back to her. It looked and felt exactly the same.

"It's done," he whispered.

"You're sure this will work?" she said.

"You'd know better than I would," he said.

That was true. She could see that the spell was strong; it would work — if she could get the bracelet on Darkstalker's arm. If he didn't figure out what she was doing. If she was fast enough . . . if, if, if . . .

"Thank you," she said. "If this works, you've saved the world, you know."

He shifted his wings, looking down at his talons as if they might accidentally set something on fire. "It'll be more you than me," he said. "Be careful."

She hugged him and thrust the scroll into his claws. "One more thing," she said. "I — I'm afraid he did something to Indigo." He looked up, his eyes wide. "Search through here and find it. I don't know how he hid it from me, but it must be in there somewhere. Maybe you can bring her back, or . . . well, whatever it is, you should know the truth."

He nodded, barely breathing.

"Then hide that scroll and get as far away from the Night Kingdom as you can. Whatever you do, *don't destroy the scroll,* or else he'll get all his power back." Clearsight rubbed her eyes, stepping toward the window. She knew she would never see him again. "Good-bye, Fathom."

"Good-bye, Clearsight. Good luck."

She was out in the sky a moment later, flying on aching wings toward Agate Mountain, far to the east. She didn't look back, but she knew Fathom was standing in the window, watching her go.

The timelines were all narrowing to one moment now.

She flew toward her last chance to save the future.

CHAPTER 31

FATHOM

He did something to Indigo.

Fathom turned away from the window and the dark sky that had swallowed Clearsight. He was still shaken from what he'd done — betraying his friend. Breaking his oath. Using his magic.

But all he could really think was *Indigo*.

What had Darkstalker done?

Is she . . . could he have . . .

No. *No.* She had to be alive. With all his power, Darkstalker could have done anything to get rid of her — he didn't have to kill her. Maybe he'd enchanted a necklace that made her want to leave Fathom. Or an earring that made her forget he even existed. Something that made her stop loving him.

She did love me. His heart was pounding. *If Darkstalker got rid of her — that means she didn't leave me.*

But she would never have accepted a gift from Darkstalker; she always suspected everything he touched of being cursed in some way.

So what could he have done to her?

He knelt on the floor and spread the scroll out so he could see the entire thing.

There were so many spells! He hadn't realized how much Darkstalker had been doing, quietly, without Fathom noticing. All these small enchantments. A plate that kept prey warm for his mother when she was late for dinner; a blanket that made sure she slept peacefully when she was out in the desert with the army. A set of paints for Whiteout that never went dry and never ran out. And here, near the end, a bell that would ring to let Darkstalker know whenever Fathom was feeling sad or lonely.

Guilt rippled through Fathom. That was how Darkstalker had always known when to show up, always lifted Fathom out of the worst loneliness. Darkstalker did care about him. Look at all these spells that showed his kindness.

Were they making a mistake?

Was Darkstalker's good side strong enough to outweigh his potential for evil?

But then there were the big spells — the shield that killed any IceWing who approached the Night Kingdom. A weapon that shot fire ten times as far as any dragon could normally breathe it.

And the last one: *Enchant Arctic the IceWing to obey my every command.*

Not to mention whatever he did to Indigo, if Clearsight was right.

Could he have enchanted her the same way he did Arctic?

And all the blank space still left at the end, where Darkstalker could write spell after spell to control the world, to kill anyone he pleased, to have everything his way.

Fathom bent his head and started reading. He read the entire scroll from beginning to end, pausing over each spell to try to imagine if it could be used to make a dragon disappear.

But there was nothing — nothing about Indigo, nothing that hinted at where she might have gone.

He sat back, frustrated. It *must* be in here. Unless Clearsight was wrong, and Indigo really had left because she wanted to.

The scroll lay quietly in front of him, beckoning as though it were full of dark secrets.

Darkstalker's handwriting was messy and sometimes hard to read, a tight jagged line of sharp points and hard strokes. It seemed to get angrier in the later enchantments, the marks pressing harder into the paper.

But there was something else that changed.

The earliest spells were written fairly close together, one right after another, in an orderly row down the page. Clearsight's bracelet that prevented mind reading; a scroll that would read out loud to them.

But the later spells were spread out, with a lot more space between them.

Why had Darkstalker left so many gaps? Didn't he want to conserve every inch of space carefully?

Fathom's eyes were starting to hurt, and he realized he'd been reading with his night vision. The closest candles had gone out, and only one was still flickering, over by the balcony. He got up and brought it over, hoping the extra light would help give him a clue.

As he set it down and picked up the scroll to move it closer, a shadow seemed to flicker across the page, drawn by the flame.

What . . .

Cautiously he lifted the scroll so the candlelight shone through it.

And in the blank spaces, words began to appear.

Fathom caught his breath. *He's been writing spells in invisible ink.*

To keep them hidden from Clearsight, he realized a moment later. *Oh, Darkstalker.*

Here was his immortality spell. Here was the spell on Clearsight's moonstone earrings — an enchantment that kept the dragon who wore them focused only on the brightest, happiest futures, hiding anything truly bad that might happen up ahead.

He found a spell enchanting the scroll to send Darkstalker a mental twinge whenever someone else used it — so Fathom was right about that, and they were lucky not to have written in here.

And then — oh no.

Enchant this goblet so that the first time Fathom drinks from it, he will stop loving Indigo, forget about his oath, and decide to freely use his animus magic again.

He was horrified. The glass goblet *had* been enchanted,

and just as terribly as Indigo had suspected. He still remembered the sound of it shattering against the wall. Indigo was right after all, right about everything. She'd saved him from it — saved him from Darkstalker's manipulation — and he hadn't even believed her.

Another spell appeared. *Enchant this dagger to fly into the Kingdom of Sand and kill one IceWing every full moon, in secret, under cover of darkness — and keep doing so for one year, or until I summon it back. Enchant it to leave messages carved near the body, warning that the Darkstalker is coming for all of them and soon they will all be dead.*

Fathom wondered if the queen knew about that dagger, or if that was Darkstalker's own personal secret revenge for the loss of Foeslayer. *The IceWings must be terrified,* he thought. *It must feel like he's haunting them. I wonder how many it has killed so far.*

As the enchantments appeared, dark words curling across the paper, Fathom felt as though he was uncovering Darkstalker's most hidden thoughts and plans. No wonder he hadn't wanted Clearsight to see this side of him. There were spells to torment classmates he hated in small, creative ways. A spell that sent nightmares to haunt Queen Diamond with all the ways he planned to kill her.

And then — Fathom sat forward so quickly he nearly set the scroll on fire.

Enchant this pebble so that when it rolls into the same room as Indigo the SeaWing, she shall be instantly trapped inside the small wooden carving of a dragon made for me by Fathom.

Right below it:

Enchant this piece of paper to look like a note written in Indigo's handwriting, with a short, believable message saying she's leaving Fathom and not coming back.

Fathom let out a cry of despair. He dropped the scroll and ran to his desk, where the little dragon carving had been sitting for months, quietly reminding him of his lost love.

He picked it up and cradled it in his claws. "Indigo?" he whispered to her. "Indigo, I'm sorry — I'm sorry." He started to cry. "I should have listened to you. I should have realized how dangerous he was. I didn't know what he would do. I'm so sorry."

I can still save her. If it will work. Albatross said I couldn't bring dragons back from the dead — but she's not dead — right? She's still in here, somewhere.

This was it, the choice he'd feared would come again — the choice to save Indigo for the price of his soul.

It was no choice at all.

"Bring her back," he whispered fiercely to the carving. "Turn back into Indigo, my friend, exactly the way she was before Darkstalker did this to her."

The carving twitched in his claws, suddenly warm to the touch. A soft glow surrounded the little dragon, and as he set it down on the floor it started to grow, and shift, and change.

And then she was there, alive and right in front of him, herself again.

Indigo stretched her wings as wide as they would go and pressed her talons down into the floor.

"Yowch," she said. "Did I fall asleep? Great starfish, I'm hungry. Oh no, Fathom, why are you crying?"

Her wings went around him and he held her close, sobbing with relief. "You're alive," he said shakily. "You didn't leave me."

"Of course I didn't leave you," she said crossly, straightening up to face him. "I said I never would and I never will. Get that through your thick skull."

"I love you," he said.

The sun came out across her face, lighting up the world.

"I *thought* you did," she said. "But you were being such a *weirdo* about it."

"I'm still dangerous when I'm with you," he said. "But I never want to be without you again."

"Sounds like my kind of plan," she said. "Exactly my plan, actually." She twined her tail around his.

"We have to get out of here," he said. "A lot's happened — I have to tell you everything. But first . . ." He pulled away and hurried over to his trunk. "I need to know how bad it is." He held out the soul reader to her. "Indigo, I did something terrible. I used my magic."

She took the soul reader out of his talons and threw it into the fountain.

"Hey!" he protested, starting forward, but she stood in his way and flared her wings.

"That thing doesn't know your soul," she said. "*I* know your soul. Tell me what you did."

"I enchanted a bracelet to stop Darkstalker," he said.

"And I brought you back from — you were — he did this spell — I brought you back."

"Oh," she said. She glanced down at her scales, as if wondering whether they were real. "Wow. I guess I did miss something."

"So I'm probably evil now," he said, his voice shaking. "Two spells like that — my soul could be almost gone. You need to know so you can get away from me."

"ROARGH," Indigo cried. "Using your magic doesn't make you evil, Fathom! Doing evil things makes you evil! Have you done anything evil lately?"

"Well," he said, faltering. "I betrayed my friend . . ."

"The supervillain," she put in.

"He's not —" Fathom hesitated. "Yeah, he sort of is."

"Let me guess," she said. "You did something to stop him from killing loooooots and lots of innocent dragons."

"Um," he said. "Yes. How did you know?"

"Because I've met him," she said, "and I could see where that was going. So, sorry, no, doesn't count. Not evil."

"I broke my oath to Pearl —"

"To save dragons," she said.

"To save you," he said.

She shook her head. "Not evil."

"Indigo —"

"Shush. Fathom, listen. Our choices are what make us good or evil — what we do, how we help or hurt the world. You make the world a better place by being in it. With or without your magic, that's always been true."

"Not really," he said. "Without my magic, I'm no one special."

"How can you say that?" she said. "You're an artist. You're my friend. You're kind and funny. I'd call that special."

"You're biased," he said, touching his snout to hers. He felt illuminated from the inside, as though he had luminescent scales lit up all the way through him.

"I'm right," she said with a grin. They stood like that for a moment, smiling at each other.

"Besides," she said, "you've stopped *two* actually evil animus dragons from destroying the world. That's pretty impressive."

"Um," he said. "Well, maybe."

"Maybe?" She tipped her head to the side.

"I'm not sure yet if the enchantment on Darkstalker has worked. Clearsight just flew off with the bracelet and he's meeting her and hopefully she can use it on him, but it's possible she won't be able to, and then he'll be *really* mad, and then he might come back and . . . you know, destroy the world after all."

"WHAT?" she said. "That's happening now? Right now?"

"Right now," he admitted. "That's why we have to get out of here."

"You didn't want to *lead* with that?" she cried. "You don't think maybe that's *priority number one*?" She whacked him with her tail. "I'm ready! Let's go! Escape first, save the sappy pep talk for later!"

He ducked away, wondering how he could feel like laughing at a time like this. Quickly he rolled up the scroll and stowed it in its black leather case. Then he lifted up the top of his desk and reached his front talons inside.

The little octopus clambered joyfully up his arm and waved all his tentacles at Indigo.

"Blob!" she cried happily. She scooped him up and settled him on top of her head. "Hang on tight, little guy. We're going to be flying really fast."

Blob seized her horns and scrunched down as if he was ready to steer.

Indigo and Fathom brushed their wings together, ran onto the balcony, and leaped into the air.

Below them, dragons were spilling out of the palace, out of the school, out of the ravines and canyons of the Night Kingdom. The NightWings were fleeing, their terror of Darkstalker driving them out of their homes to some unknown, faraway place where they might be safe, where he might never find them.

Even if Clearsight's plan works, Fathom realized, *that dagger he enchanted is going to make everyone think he's still alive for a long time — that he's out there hunting them.*

They might never come back here.

I know I'll *never come back here.*

"Farewell, Night Kingdom," he said softly.

And then he turned and flew away forever, with Indigo right beside him.

CHAPTER 32

DARKSTALKER

He found her near the peak of Agate Mountain, the tallest mountain in the Claws of the Clouds range. She was sitting in the mouth of a small cave, looking east to where the sun was rising over the twin peaks of Jade Mountain, casting dark green shadows over the valleys below.

Darkstalker landed beside her, folding in his wings. It didn't look as though she'd brought anything with her. Where was his scroll? Had she used his magic? He hadn't felt any twinges from his spell on the scroll, so it seemed like she hadn't. But then why steal it?

"Did you know," Clearsight said thoughtfully, "that this won't be the tallest mountain in Pyrrhia for much longer? There's going to be an earthquake soon and this whole side will collapse. Then Jade Mountain will be the tallest."

"Is that supposed to be a metaphor?" Darkstalker said, flicking his tail back and forth. "Something about the most powerful dragon falling and someone else taking his place? Because it's a bit muddled. Not your best work."

She actually laughed, just a little bit. "No," she said. "Not a metaphor. I just thought it was interesting. A piece of the future that is definitely true."

"Anything about the future can be changed," he said. "Even that. I could enchant the mountain to stay up if I wanted to. We can make the future turn out however we like."

"Not if we want different things," she said, pulling a small yellow wildflower out of the dirt. She started shredding it between her claws. "Not if we can't even agree on what is right and what is wrong."

He took a step toward her. "If you don't want to be with me, just say so." He wanted to know . . . but he wasn't going to let her go. He loved her too much.

"Nothing I did *worked*," she said. "I thought I was so careful, and we still ended up here. All that studying, all the timeline scrolls. Now it's all happened, and I can't change any of it, and I still don't know where it all went so wrong."

"Because it didn't," he said, taking another step closer. "It's not wrong. We're on the right path, Clearsight. We're so close to our happy future. The bad part's almost over. Almost all my enemies are dead."

"Including Indigo?" she asked. Her eyes lifted to meet his, and he froze for a moment. *Does she know? Did she find the hidden spells? No . . . she's just guessing.*

"What do you mean?" he said. "Indigo left. That was nothing to do with me."

"Maybe it started the first time you lied to me," she said, turning to the sunrise again. "Or maybe it was losing Foeslayer and not being able to do anything about it. Maybe it was all the small moments where you felt threatened or powerless or out of control, and all the things you did to fight those feelings."

I've never been powerless, he thought. *Nobody threatens me.* "Everything I did was for a good reason," he said. "To protect you, or Whiteout, or our future dragonets. Why can't you trust me?"

She took a deep breath and looked back into his eyes. "Or maybe it's just part of you, something you hatched with. Maybe that's what you really got from your father, along with your magic. Maybe you were always going to turn out this way, no matter how I tried to save you."

He lunged toward her, fury flooding through his veins, and seized her wrist, twisting it painfully. "I'm nothing like my father," he snarled. "I don't need saving. I can choose my own future, and I like the one I see, and you're going to learn to like it, too. *Where is my scroll?*"

Something slid coolly along his scales and he glanced down. Clearsight had slipped the moonstone bracelet off her own arm and onto his.

For a brief flash of a moment her mind was open to him again, unguarded for the first time in years, and he saw with perfect clarity how she loved him, how she feared him, how many terrible futures lay before them, and how she was betraying him to save everyone else.

Good-bye, my dearest love, her thoughts whispered.

And then . . . blackness rushed up toward him, enfolding him in its wings, and he was gone.

CHAPTER 33

CLEARSIGHT

Clearsight would never forget the look on Darkstalker's face as he realized what she'd done. It was only there for a moment — the utter shock, the disbelief, the bewilderment and betrayal — and then his eyes closed and he collapsed to the ground with a heavy thud.

She knelt beside him, resting her talons lightly on his neck. His chest rose and fell steadily. He was still alive, still breathing, but he would never wake up again, not as long as the bracelet was on him.

Darkstalker had made himself immortal and invulnerable to any kind of attack, but a simple sleeping spell had taken him down. Fathom had done his part well.

Clearsight dragged Darkstalker far back into the cave, letting her tears fall but not stopping to give in to her grief. The cave ended in a small chamber, solid granite on all sides. She rolled him against the back wall and checked the bracelet to make sure it was securely fastened around Darkstalker's arm.

Then she filled in the cave with boulders from the hillside, piling them up to hide the sleeping dragon inside. He could never be found, never be set free, or else Pyrrhia would be in danger all over again.

When that was done, she found another mountain where she could watch and wait for the earthquake to come. Once Agate Mountain had collapsed, burying Darkstalker deep in the earth, she'd know it was safe to leave him there.

The sun spread across her wings as she sat on the ridge, breathing in the light of the new dawn.

It worked.

I did this.

All those futures I saw, all the plans I made to take us along the right paths . . . that's all gone now. We never got married. We never took the throne or stopped the war. We never had our dragonets.

She closed her eyes, trying not to think about that. How could she mourn dragons who'd never existed in the first place? They were no more real than anything else about the timelines she'd shattered.

But she could still see their faces in her mind, and she knew she would always miss them.

What am I going to do now?

She took a deep breath and let the new futures roll out before her.

There was nothing for her back in the tribe. The other NightWings would never trust her again after seeing her on that stage with Darkstalker, even if she told them what she'd done to him — and she couldn't tell anyone that. No one could ever know where he was or how easy it would be to wake him up.

Rejoining the tribe led to some more dangerous paths, too — the ones where she felt so alone, and missed him so much, that the temptation to return and release him became too great. Even knowing the Very Bad Things that would follow, she could see how she might fall.

I could stay with him. I could lie down in the path of the avalanche and wait to die.

Right now she was sad enough to think for a moment that maybe that was the best choice.

But she was also a seer. She could feel her overpowering grief right now, and at the same time she could look into the future and see a time when she would not be this sad.

There were futures where she was happy.

There were futures where she didn't have to be afraid all the time about everything going horribly wrong.

As hard as it was for her to believe right now, there were even futures with another love and other dragonets.

She raised her wings and lifted her head to the blue-and-gold-streaked sky.

She was sad and alone . . . but she was also free. Her life had been tangled up with Darkstalker's for so long — forever, from the moment she had her first vision of him — that she'd never before seen any glimpse of what it might look like without him.

Clearsight remembered a long-ago dream that came from a

scroll she used to love to read. It told stories of the lost continent and the secret tribes of dragons that lived there.

In that dream, she was an explorer. She went out and found new worlds, places no NightWing had ever been or even imagined.

Now she could see it — that dream could be *real*. Visions of a strange land were already unrolling behind her eyes, of unusual trees and odd animals and unfamiliar dragons that didn't match any tribes she knew. She knew where to go. She knew how to get there.

The future was in her talons now, and she could do anything she wanted to do.

EPILOGUE

Five Years Later . . .

INDIGO

Sun showers sprinkled the beach with little bursts of rain, sparkling in the cheerful sunlight. A coconut thumped softly onto the sand and rolled toward Indigo's talons. She picked it up, remembering the day of the animus test. She'd been so relieved to find she was normal, that she didn't have some kind of spooky magic lurking in her claws. And that was before she knew anything about animus power.

It was nothing, though, compared to the relief she felt once they were sure none of their dragonets had it.

"AAAAAAAAAAAAAAAAAAAAAAAHH," Clearpool screamed. The little green dragonet stomped her feet furiously in the waves. "I can't GET IT! I'LL NEVER GET IT! ALL THE FISHES ARE STUPID!"

"Remember the song about being patient?" Indigo said, patting her gently on the head. "You have to wait and wait and wait and *then* pounce."

"I DIIIIIIIIIIIIIIIIIIIIIIIIIIIIIIIIIIIIIIIID!" she yelled. "I waited and waited and THEN POUNCEDED and it GOT AWAAAAAAY."

"Ah, well, there's your mistake," said Indigo. "You forgot one of the waits."

Clearpool's wails cut off abruptly. The dragonet tipped her head, thinking. "Oh," she said. "Yeah, I did. OK, fish! I'ma get you now!"

She splashed away, leaping over crabs and kicking sand in the hole her brothers were digging.

"Roar!" Cowrie yelled at her. "Get your big galumphing talons out of here!"

"I was NOT galumphing!" Clearpool yelled back. "THIS is GALUMPHING!" She slammed her feet into the sand like a woozy elephant and the whole side of Cowrie's hole collapsed.

Over the ensuing shrieks of fury, Indigo felt Fathom come wading up behind her. She spread her wings and they leaned into each other, and she felt, like she always did, that she could grow roots right here and be happy entwined with him forever.

"I *think*," she said, "that we may have named the wrong dragonet after Clearsight."

"AAAAAAAAAAAAAAAAAAAAAAAAAAAAAAAAAA AAH!" Clearpool howled again, flinging herself into the shallow water and rolling around in a fit of temper. "THIS BROTHER IS A KELP-FACE!" Indigo buried her face in Fathom's neck, hiding her giggles.

"Maybe she'll grow into her quiet wisdom," Fathom said. "Like you did."

"I *beg* your pardon?" Indigo said. "ME? I have ALWAYS been quiet and wise."

"I seem to recall just a *few* shrieking fits when you were that age," he said, starting to laugh. "Remember the time I ate the last salmon at breakfast?"

"You didn't just eat it!" she cried. "You were *smug* about it! You totally deserved to be dumped in the koi pond!"

Cowrie and Clearpool were wrestling now, getting absolutely covered in wet sand. Next to them, Ripple popped his head out of his own hole, realized that someone else was getting more attention than he was, and promptly scrambled over to flop on top of his brother and sister.

"WHAT ARE YOU DOING?" Clearpool shouted at him. "GET OFF!"

"I loooooooooooooove youuuuuuu," Ripple said, poking his snout in their faces. Blob clambered out of the hole behind him and lolloped over to join the pile.

"Arrgh! Yuck!" Cowrie flailed his wings as he tried to get free. "Ripple! You're squashing me! DAAAAD! MOOOOOOOOOOOOOOOOOOOOOOOM!"

"Everyone stop squashing one another," Fathom called without moving.

"RIPPLE IS THE SQUASHER!" Clearpool bellowed.

"Quit mashing one another into the sand and I'll tell you a story," Indigo said.

The three dragonets instantly jumped away from one

another and came scampering over, plunking themselves into an attentive semicircle around their parents' talons, with Blob perched happily on Ripple's head.

"Tell us about the Kingdom of the Sea again!" Clearpool demanded. "And all the palaces!"

"It looks a lot like this," Fathom said, flicking his tail at the island around them. "Maybe we'll take you there one day, when you're all grown up."

When there's a new queen, who doesn't know about Fathom's promise to Pearl, Indigo thought. Their island was off the southern coast of Pyrrhia, within sight of the rainforest, and they kept up with tribe news by visiting and trading with RainWings every couple of months or so. That's how they knew that the NightWings had vanished, and nobody knew where they'd gone. There had been stories of Darkstalker sightings everywhere for a while, and then gradually fewer and fewer until they dwindled away. Clearsight must have succeeded, but Indigo wished sometimes that she knew exactly what had happened, and where Clearsight was now.

As for their own tribe, surely Wharf and Lionfish must have returned home after they lost Fathom, still believing Indigo had left him. Queen Pearl probably thought Fathom and Indigo were both dead, or that Fathom had fled with the NightWings. She never needed to find out that they were alive, and together, and happy.

It had taken Indigo such a long time to convince Fathom that it was all right for him to be happy. That he wasn't a secret monster waiting to be unleashed. That he wasn't the one who did all those terrible things, and they weren't his fault, and he didn't have to punish himself forever.

"*I* want to hear about you and Mommy," Ripple said. Blob snuggled around his neck, flipping his tentacles contentedly. "About stuff you did when you were little like us."

"Oh, we were very good," Fathom said solemnly. "We were never, ever naughty."

"FIBS!" Clearpool cried, splashing him with her tail. "You were, too!"

"Well," Fathom said, "all right, I suppose Mommy was, sometimes." Indigo whacked him with her tail and he grinned at her.

"Mommy," said Cowrie, "do you know any stories about bad guys?"

Indigo and Fathom exchanged a glance and Indigo felt a weird shiver, like someone was swimming over her grave.

"What do you want to know about bad guys?" Fathom asked.

"Like, how do they get that way," Cowrie said, poking a piece of driftwood. "And why do they do bad stuff."

"Well," Fathom said slowly, "there are lots of ways, and lots of reasons. Sometimes it's because they're sad or angry. Some dragons become bad when they have too much power."

"And some don't," Indigo said, twining her tail around Fathom's. If there was one thing she believed with her entire soul, it was that Fathom had too much goodness in him to ever turn out like Albatross or Darkstalker. He was kind and good all the way through.

"Sometimes . . . sometimes they don't *know* they're bad guys," Fathom went on. "They think what they're doing is the right thing."

"Oh," said Cowrie. "So who decides if it's the right thing or not?"

Fathom hesitated, looking lost.

"ME!" Clearpool suggested.

"How would I know if I was a bad guy?" Cowrie added with a worried wrinkle between his eyes.

"I would tell you," Indigo said, "and then you'd go back to being good."

"Or me! I'd tell you and whack you and smush you!" Clearpool offered with great enthusiasm.

"You do that even when I'm being *super good*," Cowrie pointed out.

"You know, there's really no such thing as bad guys," Fathom said unexpectedly, and Indigo gave him a quizzical look. They had plenty of evidence that *that* wasn't true.

"There isn't?" Ripple echoed.

"I mean . . . there are dragons who do bad things," Fathom said. "But maybe that doesn't make them all bad. Maybe they can also do good things. Maybe some of those bad things are just mistakes."

"No," Indigo said firmly. "Some dragons are definitely bad and have to be stopped."

"I don't know," Fathom said. "I don't think any dragons are *all* bad."

"Then you have a selective memory, my love," said Indigo. "We knew a bad guy once," she said to the dragonets.

They all gasped with delighted horror.

"A dragon who did bad things," Fathom amended. "But also some good things, and he cared a lot about his friends." He saw the look on Indigo's face and added quickly, "Mostly bad things, though. Anyway, he's gone now."

"That's right," Indigo agreed. "He's gone, and he's never coming back."

"Will you tell us about him?" Cowrie asked, his blue eyes round and dazzled.

"And how you WHACKED him and SMUSHED him?" Clearpool cried.

"Maybe when you're older," Indigo said. *Maybe when Fathom has stopped having nightmares about him.* She smiled down at her squirming, beautiful, hilarious dragonets. "Race you to the seal rocks!"

They pelted off down the beach, shrieking with laughter, and Indigo nudged Fathom with her wing.

"It's true. He's really never coming back," she said. "You did the right thing, Fathom. You saved Pyrrhia from him forever. It's safe to be happy."

"I know," he said. He unfurled his wings, shaking off the memories, and gave her the smile she'd fallen in love with back when they were tiny dragonets. "I am."

— POST-EPILOGUE —

Two Thousand Years Later . . .

Centuries later, as the dragon planet spun through space, a comet passed by, close enough to shine like a fourth moon in Pyrrhia's sky.

Close enough to change the tides and shake the continents.

As earthquakes rumbled through the ground, long-buried rocks shifted that had been in place for thousands of years.

Deep underground, in the darkness, copper wires snapped.

And a dragon awoke . . .